Critical Acclaim for

The Return of the Goddess

This is an extraordinary book to share with all those you love — family, friend or lover. A good story told with wit, compassion and sexiness, it's about the most important things in our lives. And it has the power to build bridges across a gap of silence.

Robin Larsen

author with Stephen Larsen of *A Fire in the Mind: The Life of Joseph Campbell*

A magical tale of spiritual renewal .... Brings together themes of interest to women such as earth-centered life, the need for feminine rituals, and the link between spirituality and sexuality.

Values & Visions

This is how we long to meet the Immortals — in the flesh! In *The Return of the Goddess* the double entendre of *passion* drives the plot. The Church of our Fathers and the Mother's sacred ground collide and explode into sparks. The pace is perfect, her images linger. She's packed a terrific story into a full deck of divinatory cards, playing with everyone's current marital and spiritual discord. Such a pleasure to read — so sweet and sexy and politic — laced with mother wit and ultimately satisfying.

Nor Hall

author of *The Moon and the Virgin* and *Those Women*

Cunningham's characters are lovingly realized, her chapters tightly spun about evocative themes, her prose is lean and empathic, and her politics correct.

Yoga Journal

One of the best novels I've read in some time .... This story is the type that wraps you in a cocoon of warm delight, engulfing you in the living, breathing fires of its characters.

Friends Review

An entertaining novel written with grace, humor and perceptiveness ....
A delightful rarity.

Convergence

This compelling novel tells many stories on different levels. The legendary, the mystical and the poetic weave in and out of the characters' lives. The novel is about truth and fighting against evil, about the earth and its riches, about the goddess's fight against the Father Church, and about women's struggles to create themselves.

The Christian Century

Cunningham knows her landscape and characters in a very rare and deep fashion.

New England Review of Books

A wonderful book .... A love song to the land.

Gazette Advertiser

This contemporary treatment of the popular goddess theme is virtually unique in present-day fiction.

Wisconsin Bookwatch

A tremendously entertaining novel of of self-discovery.

Taconic Week

A highly sexual, highly sensual spiritual realm .... Passionate and unified at the same time.

Woodstock Times

Readers will be fascinated and caught up in the fanciful spirit.

West Coast Review of Books

The **Return** *of the* **Goddess**

A · DIVINE · COMEDY

Elizabeth Cunningham

STATION HILL PRESS

Published by Station Hill Literary Editions, under the Institute for Publishing Arts, Inc., Barrytown, New York 12507. Station Hill Literary Editions is supported in part by grants from the National Endowment for the Arts, a Federal Agency in Washington D.C., and by the New York State Council on the Arts.

Distributed by the Talman Company, 131 Spring Street, Suite 201E-N, New York, New York 10012.

Cover design by George Quasha and Susan Quasha.
Front cover photo by George Quasha.
Photos at beginning and end of the text and back cover photo by Douglas C. Smyth.

Four lines from the poem, "Who goes with Fergus?," used as an epigraph, are reprinted with permission of The Macmillan Publishing Company from *The Poems of W.B. Yeats: A New Edition*, edited by Richard J. Finneran (New York: Macmillan, 1983).

Library of Congress Cataloging-in-Publication Data

Cunningham, Elizabeth, 1953—
    The return of the goddess: a divine comedy/ by Elizabeth Cunningham.
        p.   cm.
ISBN 0-88268-115-X: $22.50 (cloth) — ISBN 0-88268-157-5: $12.95 (paper)
PS3553.U473R47   1992
813'.54--dc20   92-10395
                                                  CIP
Manufactured in the United States of America.

*Midway in our life's journey, I went astray
from the straight road and awoke to find myself
alone in a dark wood.*

—Dante

CONTENTS

INVOCATION

I am she who has no name
and a thousand names.
I am the Virgin, and the unicorn
sleeps in my lap; the crescent moon
bends to my bowstring.
This is my grove, my sacred grove,
my maiden bower.
Here I hunt the deathless quarry,
Here I run the restless race,
Here you may glimpse my foot
and dance with my shadow.
Here you may dream.

> I am she who has no face
> and a thousand faces.
> I am the Mother, and my belly
> is big with the moon, live
> with the fishes of the sea.
> This is my grove, my sacred grove,
> my birthing bed.
> Here I ride the stag into dawn,
> Here I blossom to the bee,
> Here you may drench yourself in my dew
> and bathe in a fountain of milk.
> Here you may drink.

I am she who has no secret
and a thousand secrets.
I am the Crone, and the snake
coils round my arm; the sickle moon
lies ready to hand.
This is my grove, my sacred grove,
my burial chamber.
Here I gather my harvest,
Here I draw down the darkness,
Here you may seek me or seek to escape
and still find my gates.
Here you may die.

BOOK ONE

HALLOWE'EN

HER BELLY IS THE WORLD 1

SHE liked to make things: cookies, pie crust, Hallowe'en costumes, bread. Today Esther Peters and her sons had made playdough. They sat outside with it now on the back steps of the rectory where the birds could eat the inevitable doughy little turds instead of her having to sweep them up. It was Hallowe'en, or would be soon, the brief afternoon almost spent.

The days draw in, her grandmother had always intoned at this time of year, the days draw in. Esther, as a child, would picture day gathering in bright folds in the back room, just as her mother drew in laundry from the moving clothesline, leaving only darkness behind. Now that she was the mother she knew what night meant, what winter meant. Warmth and light migrated to her kitchen, which became cluttered with loud, hungry boys.

While she could, she kept them outdoors. Each warm day might be the last. Earlier in the afternoon, she had taken the boys to the playground. Overcharged with Hallowe'en parties at nursery school and kindergarten, wild with anticipation of trick-or-treating that night, they'd run and run, unleashed, like the puppies they were. Since Jonathan, the younger one, had turned three a month ago, they had both scorned to nap. Still they needed time to be quiet; or she needed it. And they had quieted, soothed by the pliant lumps of dough they worked in their hands.

Now and then a breath of wind sifted the leaves she and the boys had raked into haphazard piles in the backyard. Or the leaves themselves breathed, exhaling the dying heat of day, their yielding to earth and air making a perfume of decay. Esther glanced at her sons, both content, intent, the energy that had scattered all over the playground concentrated now, directed through those small fingers, taking shape in dough. This lull would pass any moment into the customary chatter, like that of squirrels, that formed the background of her day. Sometimes she listened, sometimes she didn't, though she felt guilty when she caught herself not hearing them. Silence with two children was so rare. She rested in it now, this fleeting Sabbath, and let herself feel that it was good.

What "it" was precisely had never been clear to her. There was nothing she could finally hold in her hands—as she now held the playdough or as God, metaphorically or otherwise, held the universe—and say, "Here, look what I made." Not that she dealt in intangibles. There were the pumpkins that she had carved with the children, grinning jaggedly on the front porch. In another week they would rot. There were the Hallowe'en costumes, also transitory, constructed of boxes left over from the move and of grocery bags. Always there was the daily bringing forth of dinner.

Esther thought with some pride of the pizza, even now in the oven, ready to bake: the homemade crust, which had inspired the playdough, made with whole wheat flour from the food co-op she'd joined; the sauce, also her own, made with tomatoes and herbs she had grown in her first garden. In Syracuse, where Alan had been curate—or associate, as they called it these days—they'd lived in a cramped apartment without a yard, let alone a garden. They had arrived at St. Paul's, White Hart, in June, too late for lettuce and peas but not too late for zucchini, basil, or September tomatoes. Here the children had room to grow, too, in a large rectory with expansive lawns, and, if that weren't enough, an overgrown estate next door owned by an ancient parishioner. Everything would be all right, was all right, now that Alan had his own parish, now that she had her own garden.

Alan should be home soon; he had promised. It must be close to five. She had planned to feed them early, so that Alan could take the boys trick-or-treating and have them back in time to unwind for bed. She would have liked to take them out herself, but someone had to be at the rectory to answer the door to other trick-or-treaters, and it was important for Alan to do things with his sons. This evening, with all the preparations made, even the table set, dinner would proceed smoothly, pleasantly. She and Alan might even have a chance to talk to each other while the children's mouths were crammed with pizza. Even if Alan did not fully comprehend what it was she did all day, at some level—perhaps the unconscious—he would be forced to marvel at the work of her hands.

The sound of wheels on gravel rent Esther's revery. Someone had turned in at the lower end of the church driveway. Alan? St. Paul's property, a turn-of-the-century extravaganza, occupied almost a whole block. Esther peered through the shrubs that veiled the back yard—"the Rector's Privacy," a parishioner had explained—to see if she knew the car or driver. The motor didn't sound like Alan's. There was a possibility that someone might be coming to see her, some other mother she'd met at the co-op or the nursery school car-pool, but the odds were against it. So many more people wanted her husband, though some would settle for her and the refreshment she felt obliged to offer as consolation. They seemed to feel that his job description was to be on the grounds when they called—busy doing something, of course, whatever it was rectors did—but ready to set it aside for the more important task of spiritual counsel.

The white car—she didn't know makes, though David had been trying to teach her for years—came into view, and Esther made out the handsome profile of Alisha Adams. Our-Lady-of-the-Perpetual-Tan, Esther's outrageous friend Gale had dubbed Alisha, during Gale's less-than-successful visit, which had coincided with the annual St. Paul's Rummage Sale. Alisha ran the Rummage Sale and anyone who had volunteered, or had been commandeered, to help. She was also the president, more or less for life, of the WOSPs (Women of St. Paul's). Alisha could have been described as a well-preserved matron, with her teenaged son and daughter tucked away in Episcopal boarding schools and her husband a successful trader on Wall Street, while she presided over house and stables and any volunteer organization within a twenty mile radius. But Esther had to admit that Alisha had more verve and spark than the word matron implied.

Alisha was a borderline case in that she might be looking for either Alan or Esther. She had directed the re-decoration of the rectory, which everyone had assumed obligatory when Esther and Alan moved in—what else were funds from the Portion Supper for?—and she had spent hours with Esther consulting about wallpaper and tiles. Yet Alisha also found it necessary to have luncheon—that's what Alisha called it—with Alan at least twice a month.

Alisha's car slowed for a moment at the curve in the driveway where the parish house loomed, no doubt taking in the fact that Alan's car was not parked there. Nor was Nancy Jones' car, the church secretary. Nancy always left in time to meet the schoolbus, an arrangement which irritated Alan. Esther's car, the one they owned, was being repaired again. There was nothing to indicate that anyone was at home. Esther hoped—aware that her feelings were uncharitable, not to mention inhospitable, a serious failing in a clergy wife—that Alisha would just keep on going out the other end of the driveway. It looked as though she might. Alisha neglected to turn her head towards the back steps, which the shrubbery did not obscure, as she drove past.

"Whose car is that, Mama?" Jonathan asked, not taking in the driver.

Cars were terribly important to him, too, more so than their owners, but it was something he had to know about them: any car, anywhere. He could never accept, as they walked past parked cars downtown, that there were limits to her knowledge. He suspected her of withholding information from him for cruel and inscrutable reasons of her own.

"It's Mrs. Adams," David answered. "Volvo station wagon."

Neither boy made a move towards getting up. There were some parishioners they raced to greet; why, Esther could not always fathom. They particularly liked some of the elderly ones, a yearning for grandparents, perhaps. She and Alan were both mother-less, which gave them that in common. The children had only grandfathers, equally remote, one in Florida, one in Arizona. Mrs. Adams held no interest for them. She had no young children for them to play with. She also had a tendency to fuss over them noisily when she encountered them and to kiss them, leaving lipstick marks. After that she would completely block out their presence while demanding one, the other, or both their parents' total attention.

Esther heard the motor die and a car door slam. Sighing, she resigned herself to being pleasant and welcoming.

"She wants Daddy," Jonathan predicted.

"Where is Dad?" asked David.

"I don't know." Esther registered the fact that she hadn't a clue. Unless she lied, she would have to admit her ignorance to Alisha Adams.

The doorbell sounded in the house, a phrase from a Bach chorale prelude, "Come thou now to save mankind," a device installed by a predecessor with a musical sense of humor.

"I'll get it! I'll get it!" shouted both boys.

They might be indifferent to Mrs. Adams, but charging to open the heavy front door was a competitive sport.

"Neither of you is going." Esther set down her dough and grasped an arm each. "You're both covered with playdough. Stay here. I'll be back in a minute."

"But, Mom, your hands are all doughy, too," David pointed out.

"Why, so they are." She paused and considered them, crusted with dough of the peculiar color that had resulted from her attempt to create purple—a shade between mud and blood.

The doorbell rang again. Esther continued to gaze at her hands, not registering that she could simply walk around the house and greet Alisha on the front porch. Then came the bang of footsteps as Alisha retreated. Esther listened. Not heels, no. Exercise sandals, she thought, the kind that were supposed to mold your calves, all while you clunked around on your daily errands. The car door opened and slammed again. Angrily? Or was that just Esther's guilty imagination? The motor started, and Esther pictured gravel spraying in all directions as Alisha tore out of the driveway.

"She's gone," announced David unnecessarily.

Esther picked up her dough and sat down again, guilt giving way to childish glee at having gotten away with something—or from someone. The dough in her hands felt warm, alive, in contrast to the chill beginning to settle over the earth, giving the air a menace, a bite befitting Hallowe'en.

In a little while, they would have to go inside. She would send the children to wash their hands and hope that the bathroom would not be flooded before they were through—hand washing had a way of turning into water play. She would bake the pizza, make salad dressing with fresh crushed garlic and the rosemary, thyme, and oregano she had potted and brought inside the kitchen. But not yet, not just yet. Inside was the clock, and she didn't want to watch it. Her uptightness, as Alan referred to it, about time had become an issue in their marriage. "There are no time-cards in the Church," he would insist. "Irregular hours"—(twenty-four of them?)—"come with the territory." It probably wasn't as late as she thought. She just wasn't used to the short days yet.

"Look, Mom, look at my dinosaur," said David. "It's a Tyrannosaurus Rex."

"Is it very fierce?" she asked absently, smoothing the dough in her own hands, caressing, shaping.

"Yes, very fierce."

"Mine is, too," put in Jonathan. "Mine eats people."

"There were no people in dinosaur times," David corrected his brother. "Daddy told me."

"But mine likes to eat people."

"Yours is a brontosaurus," pronounced David, appraising Jonathan's lump of dough. "They were vegetarians."

"Yes, mine is a brontosaurus." Jonathan was agreeable. "It eats people."

"I told you!" said David in the exasperated grown-up voice that both amused and shamed her, because it was a direct imitation. "There were no people then."

"But if there were," Esther mused, her fingers squeezing here, rounding there, "they might have eaten people. Or people might have eaten them. What do you think? Would you like to have brontosaurus burgers for dinner?"

"Yuck," said David.

"Yum," countered Jonathan.

"Tyrannosaurus T-bone? Stegosaurus stew?"

"Yuck!"

"Yum!"

"Yuck!"

"Yum!"

They were giggling now, forgetting the source of their dispute in the pleasure of contradicting each other at the top of their lungs. Inside, she would have insisted that they lower their voices. Now their shouts rose skyward, mingling with the commotion of starlings, a huge flock, winging downward in spiral flight to shelter in the branches of Blackwood, next door to the church. A sudden breeze tore through the yard, raising the dry leaves. Esther thought of the breath of God raising the army of dry bones. She could almost feel the earth spinning, whirling into night. Into Hallowe'en. She imagined the Dead, stirring in their dreams, reaching for their dancing shoes.

"What are you making, Mama?" David asked when the shouting match wore out.

"I don't know," said Esther.

Curious herself, Esther cupped the dough in her hands and held it out.

"Let me see! Let me see!" Jonathan demanded.

Her sons flanked her. In the waning light, the three of them gazed at what her lump of dough had become, apparently of its own volition. Esther had no awareness of having chosen the form that now confronted her.

The shape was profoundly female: global breasts resting on thighs drawn up in a squat. Her feet were strong, broad, like the hands spread over her round belly. Her face merely suggested features, a pinch here, a hollow there. Her hair stood out from her head. Without knowing it, Esther must have rolled many small pieces into curls that could be snakes. Who was this figure? Where had she come from? Small and crude as the form was, there was something powerful about it. Primitive. Frightening, really. All at once, Esther felt uneasy about holding it in her hands, displaying it to her sons, with its vulva peeking out from beneath the belly. Esther did not understand. How had her homemade playdough—(made with whole wheat flour from the food co-op)—and her own fingers conspired to bring this figure into being?

"It's the Lady," Jonathan stated.

"The lady?" Esther repeated.

"And look," pointed David. "Her belly is the world."

Sudden, silent tears astonished Esther. They ran in hot streams on her cold cheeks. She put out her tongue and tasted them.

MY FLESH IS FOOD INDEED 2

MARY Spencer Blackwood Crowe set aside what she called "the everlasting sock"—she'd been knitting one after another more or less continuously since World War I—and reclined among the pillows in the four-poster three-quarter bed of her maidenhood. She liked to watch the night come: houses in the village lighting up from inside like jack-o-lanterns, the branches of the maple tree in the rectory yard next door spread against a sky stained with afterglow. A wind had risen as the sun set; it circled the turret room of the Gatehouse. Until her confinement, Spencer had been too busy to take much notice of the vagaries of the weather. Now she knew that dusk was often a time of stillness. Perhaps tonight Hallowe'en was stirring the air.

"There's things abroad that usually sleep," Moira Hanrahan, once Blackwood's housekeeper and Spencer's own wetnurse, might have said. Now, if indeed the Dead did walk, Moira might be among them. Would she visit her son? Spencer herself hadn't seen Fergus, except from a distance, in more than a decade. It had been longer than that since they'd spoken, though he lived in Blackwood. Haunted it. As if she were a child, Spencer felt a prickle of pleasurable fear in the fine hair at the back of her neck. Something, the wind, the night, seemed to want her attention.—Really, how fanciful she was becoming!—The branches of the Rowan tree in the tiny walled yard tapped insistently at the North windows. It was Moira who had planted that tree, Spencer remembered. The tree with eyes, she called it. A watch tree.

"Come in," Spencer longed to invite whatever it was. "Come in."

She would not turn on her bedside lamp until darkness was complete. Perhaps not then. By lamplight, the six windows reflected her tiny room, crammed with cherished possessions—what the antique dealers who had taken over White Hart called "priceless heirlooms"—and the shrunkenness of her world bore in upon her.

She had been bedridden since the Feast of the Assumption, otherwise known as the St. Paul's Portion Supper, when she had broken her hip playing softball with the children. It had all been the fault of her skirt—

too narrow. She should have ignored the other WOSPs and hiked it up. Her legs, even now, if revealed, could inspire envy. She had always been active, making it a point never to drive when she could walk. Until last Summer, walking distance had meant anything under three miles.

It was tedious to be stuck in bed, and so out of character. All her life she had been the one to call upon the sick—the "shut-in" as they were referred to by the WOSPs—or women who had to care for aging parents or ailing husbands, young mothers with newborns. She would bring nosegays from her garden and gossip. That was what she did. That was simply who she was. The Lady of Blackwood.

And she was Lady of Blackwood still. Never mind that the changes in this century that had grown old with her had made it necessary to let go the large staff of servants and gardeners and to move from the Big House, as everyone called it, to the Gatehouse. Those were mere alterations, practical measures. But she did find it trying not to be able to make her rounds. It was more difficult to keep track of everything and everyone, to make all the necessary connections between people. Under the circumstances, living in the Gatehouse had advantages. It was at the edge of the village and right next door to the rectory. People who stopped there eventually found their way to her. Though she was shut in, she was by no means shut out of church and village affairs. The bread she had cast upon the waters returned to her now, a bit soggy and tasteless at times, but nourishing.

Tonight, no doubt, there would be hordes of little ghosts and goblins. Children were fascinated by the Gatehouse, as she had been as a child. It was child-sized, really, an overgrown dollhouse, a mouse house. A witch house made of frosted gingerbread. Now the Gatehouse to Blackwood boasted a real Crone. She would have Sabine, her companion and housekeeper, send the children up the stairs to see her as an extra Hallowe'en treat, in addition to the fudge Sabine had made. All children loved the spiral staircase to the turret room.

Suddenly curious about how she would appear to the children, Spencer switched on her bedside lamp and reached for the silver-backed hand mirror she kept close by. Well, there was no point in false modesty: she was beautiful. Always. She'd simply been born to beauty as she'd been born to Blackwood. And she had lost neither. Any girl can be pretty, her father used to say. Beauty is bred in the bone.

There were her eyes, still the color of summer sky, deceptively tranquil. Her hair, all gray for three decades—she need not dress it up by calling it silver—massed around her face and shoulders, clouds of it, abundant, stormy. She had never had it cut or crinkled into an old lady permanent wave or tinted with whatever it was that turned so many older women's hair that unbecoming shade of puce. Since she had taken to her bed, she often left it loose. It amused her to brush it, play with it, as she had as a young girl when it was a rich hue just beyond red. The free hair did lend a witchy effect. And, she had to admit, her nose and chin, though hairless and wartless, were a trifle long and sharp, subtly exaggerated by the falling away of youthful flesh. But it was not displeasing to play the old woman, the witch. Queen of the Night, in her silver satin bedjacket. It was the season. Due season. Her own Hallowe'en.

The wind lulled. Spencer laid aside the mirror, which suddenly felt too heavy to hold. Why did she feel so tired when she'd done nothing all day but take her ease? She'd almost dozed off earlier, but then Alisha Adams had barged in unannounced. How had Sabine let that happen? Oh, yes, Sabine had been outside with the stepladder mounting the jack o'lanterns on the gate pillars. Alisha Adams always grated on Spencer's nerves, with her presumption of intimacy between them, her condescending deference. Alisha's attempts at casting Spencer in the role of dowager Queen Bee and herself as regnant were pathetically obvious and, finally, beside the point. Spencer had no interest in running the Rummage Sale or presiding over business meetings of the WOSPs. She merely wanted to know everything. She suffered Alisha Adams as a source of information.

Perhaps she'd just have a little catnap before Sabine brought up her supper tray. They were eating early because of Hallowe'en. The aroma from the kitchen—you could smell everything in this house—was promising: garlic, onion, some pungent herb, rosemary maybe. She closed her eyes, only to open them again at the sound of a car door slamming; footsteps followed, then the doorchime. Early trick-or-treaters? Surely the clock hadn't yet struck six. When this group had gone, she'd better have Sabine help her to the commode—decorously concealed, of course, behind a Chinese screen and heavily scented with lavender water. The tea she had taken with Alisha Adams half an hour ago was ready for drainage. When one had nothing to do all day, one became more aware of one's plumbing, of the endless busyness of the body. It was quite tiring to contemplate it.

"Madame?"

Sabine was French, and she preferred Madame as a form of address to Mrs. Crowe. So did Spencer, though she had invited Sabine to call her by her Christian name when Sabine moved into the Gatehouse last Summer.

"It's Father Peters. Are you receiving?"

"But I thought I heard a car, Sabine. Why ever would he drive from next door?"

"He has been making calls, I believe, Madame. He brings the Elements."

Spencer entertained a fleeting image of Father Peters crossing her miniature threshold attended by winds and torrents, hail, lightning.

"Well, I suppose, Sabine. If it doesn't interfere with your plans for supper?" she added, hoping.

"The omelette is made in moments, Madame. I have completed the
sauté. I will mull cider and finish preparing the treats for the children
while you Communicate, Madame."

Sabine herself was a Roman Catholic, though Spencer often felt her Ca-
tholicism was a veneer over something, well, more primitive. Sabine reminded Spencer of Moira. The two women had never met, Moira
Hanrahan having died shortly after the First War and Sabine arriving in
the wake of World War II, a war bride without a word of English. Imagine, marrying without a common language; for Sabine's late husband had
never learned to speak French. So romantic. Spencer's fancy had been
quite taken. Sabine spoke some dialect, too, or was it another language.
Provençal?

Sabine had a reverence that bordered on superstition, in Spencer's opinion, for the Sacraments, though what she thought of Father Peters personally, Spencer never could divine. Sabine, like Moira, was maddeningly
reserved. Spencer herself was not altogether sure what she thought of the
new young Rector. He did have a way of offering Home Communion in
the vicinity of half past five when one felt obliged to invite him to stay
for sherry afterwards.

"Very well, Sabine. Send him up."

"Sabine!" she called a moment later, suddenly remembering the demands
of her flesh. It was too late. An exchange of pleasantries between Sabine
and Father Peters obscured her plea. Then she heard Father Peters' step on
the stair.

"Dear Father Peters," she greeted him before he reached the door in
order to avoid the awkwardness of his knocking on an open door or,
worse, his failing to. "How very faithful you are."

Indeed, rather tiresomely so, she felt. He brought her Communion almost every week. Though she did not think it tactful to say so, she was
not mad for the Eucharist the way all the young people seemed to be
these days. Morning Prayer three Sundays out of four used to suit everyone very nicely.

"Spencer." He called her by her given name, as apparently he did everyone. "You are the faithful one."

He put the Elements on the moveable standing bed tray—like the ones
in hospitals—where her supper would later be served. Then he pulled up
a chair beside her bed and took her right hand in both of his.

"What would St. Paul's be without you? It is so important to us all that you share in our Communion."

Spencer briefly returned his gaze, taking in his baby blue eyes where she sometimes feared she saw dreams of a Diocesan Conference Center in Blackwood, just as in her nephew-by-marriage Geoffrey's eyes images of condominiums lurked. Father Peters, unlike Geoffrey, who was lean and hungry looking, had sandy hair, tousled, and a clean-shaven face, almost as round as his darling younger son's. He had a certain boyish appeal, she supposed, and the overeagerness of a puppy, which could be both sweet and exhausting. Really, she was tired.

Spencer withdrew her hand and brushed a vagrant wisp of hair from her face with an air of studied weariness. Thus far, Father Peters had used the full Eucharistic Rite One when administering home Communion to her, no doubt thinking to please her with the archaic language preserved from the 1928 Prayer Book. Someone had probably tipped him off about her opposition to the revisions. Of course, she was now resigned to the new Prayer Book. Its deep red cover was attractive at least, especially after one had suffered through all those hideous green paperback trial versions. She had never made a study of the new Book of Common Prayer, as the former Rector, an enthusiast, had urged them to do. But surely there was some shortened rite? What was the use of the book if there were not? How to hint that she would welcome brevity?

"You know, Father Peters," she leaned towards him, "I've never had any use for the sort of old person who does nothing but try other people's patience with endless descriptions of ill-health." She paused.

Father Peters smiled. "Your cheerfulness has been an inspiration to us all."

"But I think perhaps I can confide in you that I am not feeling quite up to snuff today." She lowered her voice, as if Father Peters alone could be privy to this confession of fleshly frailty. "Perhaps instead of the full rite...." She hesitated delicately.

"Communion under Special Circumstances?"

Spencer's relief was so great, she almost relinquished control of her bladder.

"Certainly, if that's what you want. I would have offered it before, but you're so full of vitality, it's hard to think of you as an invalid."

Was he hurt? Was there a barb concealed in that compliment? Really, she was past caring, so long as he hurried.

"Luckily, I brought along some reserved Sacrament for my hospital calls."

How fortunate. Of course, she did not even know what reserved Sacrament meant. The long succession of priests, high and low, that she had seen come and go at St. Paul's would be shocked if they guessed her ignorance of and indifference to most liturgical matters, so long as they let her dip her own wafer. Extinction, was it called? No, that couldn't be right.

Spencer leaned back again as Father Peters prepared the altar, which he would stand behind, facing her. Then he began to arrange his priest's stole over his black shirt and dog collar. That struck Spencer as a bit affected, as stoles were clearly designed to go with robes. He set great store by this stole. Apparently, it had been hand-embroidered, with garish flowers and butterflies, by some women at his former parish. So Alisha Adams had told her, displaying some jealousy.

Women sewing for the clergy was nothing new. In her girlhood, Spencer had done her stint on the needle guild, hand-stitching, with the other maidens and matrons, the sumptuous altar hangings that were used at St. Paul's to this day. All for the love of darling Father Hearon. Alisha Adams was too young and, if the truth were told, too new to the One True Church to remember this form of female devotion.

Of course, Alisha Adams "adored" Father Peters. She claimed he was doing wonders with what she called "outreach." Spencer wouldn't recognize half the congregation, Alisha repeatedly assured her, oblivious to her irritation. Former rectors had largely left outreach to Spencer, though she never would have used such a vulgar made-up word to describe what she did as a natural expression of her character.

Spencer felt her eyes closing, and she could not summon the effort to lift them again. Perhaps, if she just nodded off for a few moments.... Dozing, after all, was one of the privileges of old age. But she had a terror of her mouth dropping open, of snoring, or worse, drooling. And in front of a man! Spencer forced her eyes open and focused briefly on Father Peters, vested in his ostentatious stole, frowning as he leafed through the whisper thin pages of the Prayer Book.

Didn't anyone commit anything to memory any more? She knew the exact page for everything in the old Prayer Book, not that she had needed to look up anything. She had known all the services by heart. She'd never had to read, never even had to listen, and didn't want to understand. That wasn't the point. It was the sound that mattered, so soothing, like birdsong or water running over rock. Words that simply carried you along, as if you had no particular weight of your own.

Spencer floated now, not quite awake, not quite asleep. Her full bladder swelled like ocean waves. She bobbed up and down, in and out of consciousness. Man or no man, and, really, priests weren't quite one or the other, with their flowing robes, their feeding of the flock. Then why had so many, herself chief among them, objected so violently to women priests? Because their sex made you think of sex? God has no sex, the liberals assured them. Then how had He begotten His only Son?

> *Jesus said, "I am the living bread which came down from heaven; if anyone eats of this bread, he will live forever."*

Because the shortened rite was unfamiliar, Spencer heard the words as she usually did not. No, she saw them. They dove in and out of the waves. They skimmed them, a flock of seabirds lighting on a swell.

> *"...For my flesh is food indeed, and my blood is drink indeed. Whosoever eats my flesh and drinks my blood abides in me, and I in him."*

Really, she had not known there was all that about food. How carnal! Or did she mean carnivorous?

> *"Abide in me, as I in you...I am the vine, you are the branches."*

A dark wave rose, and she went under, deep, deep. To surface again, she had to swim through water, through wine, the warm salty stickiness of blood, until she stood astride the beginning of the world. Her breasts hung in heavy clusters, fruit of the vine that grew from the crux, twining her body like snakes. Her thighs were warm and gave off the scent of fresh bread....

"Let us join together in the Confession of Sin," Father Peters hinted loudly.

Her dream dissolved in primal waters. And Mary Spencer Blackwood Crowe wet the bed.

BETWEEN THE WORLDS 3

For Fergus rules the brazen cars,
And rules the shadows of the wood,
And the white breast of the dim sea
And all disheveled wandering stars.

WANDERING, disheveled, Fergus Hanrahan murmured the lines of the Yeats poem his mother used to croon. The words reminded him of who he was, which gave him some certainty, since he did not know where he was—or when. He ran the risk of losing himself altogether whenever he stepped beyond the bounds of Blackwood.

Blackwood. Fergus halted his hesitant progress and leaned on his carved staff. With his eyes closed he could call up Blackwood in minute detail: each tree by name and where it stood rooted in relation to all the others, the ripples of power spreading out from the holy ring of trees in the heart of Blackwood; the exact spot in the pond where the spring welled up. He could stand in the apple orchard and know through the soles of his feet the underground maze of woodchuck burrows, mole tunnels, rabbit warrens. He knew which branches and vines sheltered nests and where the deer made their beds, leaving the imprint of their bodies in thick sweet grass.

In Blackwood he knew where he was. When did not much matter. Only round time existed in Blackwood. He, Fergus, was the keeper of the wheel. As long as he turned with it, he did not get dizzy. It was straight time that confounded him, for the end and the beginning did not meet.

Fergus opened his eyes again. He was standing in a flood of light. When he looked up, the fierce fluorescence of the street lamp obscured the stars, which mapped the heavens and might have given him some direction. Venus, the wishing star, would be in the West just now. If he could find her, then he would know East, where Blackwood lay in relation to White Hart.

Surely he was in White Hart, though what he saw around him did not match his memory of the place. He had come for matches, he believed, matches being chief among his necessities. Unaccountably, he had run out before the woman—in Blackwood he knew her name; now he could only recall her face—replenished his supply of staples, as she did generally at the new moon. Tonight the moon, Lady of round time, was on the wane, almost dark, as befitted the feast of Hekate, Queen of the Night. She would not rise until the coldest hour. If he had to, he would wait, then follow her home.

Meanwhile, there was his pipe. He had secured those matches, had he not? He reached beneath his tattered cloak and felt in a small satchel that he carried slung over his shoulder. His fingers encountered several boxes of good, wooden matches. Strike anywhere. He got a clay pipe out of his pocket. When he had filled it, he raised his staff and stilled the air. Then he struck a match against the night and watched it instantly ignite. He drew on his pipe, taking pleasure in this modest power he seemed to retain even in the wide world. And many a drink and many a meal and many a warm bed he had won with this childish display during the roaming years.

Of course, it was possible to spark fire without a match at all, but this feat required great concentration and so depleted a magician's reserves of energy it was not worth the effort for the lighting of a pipe or a stove when a match would do. Young man's magic, his mother had dismissed it when he'd first mastered the technique. Fool's play.

And, indeed, he had played the fool, fancying himself the master of fire, when the fire of his own youth had overmastered him, reducing his dreams to ash. Yet surely there were coals, live coals, concealed but still burning, just waiting the right moment to burst into renewed flame. This time he would be ready. This time....

But how much time was left? Fergus puffed on his pipe, then studied the hand that held it. An old man's hand, spotted with age, knuckles gnarled and grotesque. How could he be old? How could she?

Fergus was diverted by the motor of some sort of wheeled conveyance, as the vehicle pulled into a lot across the street. The engine died, and two men hauled themselves out of the shiny, low-slung contraption. They slammed doors heartily, as if they were slapping backs, and started across the street.

Fergus thought he recognized one of them. At least the set of the jaw and the line of the brow were familiar. But how had the old under-gardener—Tony Giardina, the name came to him—grown so young? Bewildered, Fergus turned towards the approaching pair, considering whether to call out some greeting. The other man glanced in his direction for an instant but kept right on talking. Tony—if it was Tony—did not look his way at all. In a moment, both men mounted some steps and disappeared into an establishment named, in glowing letters, Vinny's Bar and Grill. He supposed he could follow this former fellow laborer into what must be a tavern of sorts—perhaps they brewed the elixir here?—but a strange misgiving had come over him.

Could it be that he was not apparent to others? Had he outlived his form and crossed the border into that other country without knowing it? Tonight of all nights the veil between the worlds was thin. Had it parted for him? But he was not ready yet! He had unfinished business. And that, he could almost hear his mother saying, is the very definition of a ghost.

For comfort, Fergus drew deeply on his pipe and exhaled a series of smoke rings. He defied a ghost to do that, though, if his mother were to be believed, ghosts were capable of far more dramatic material manifestations. The smoke rings floated across the street, holding their shape despite the wind that had risen once more, and they wreathed the cars, the brazen cars not ruled by him. They were altogether alien and incomprehensible. He could not name a year or a make or connect them with anyone he knew, quick or dead.

Then, all at once, as he scanned the far reaches of the lot, his eyes connected with something unchanged: a building with a steep sloping roof and a large overhang with ornate white trim, the walls composed of vertical planks and gothic windows. Beyond the building, he could just make out the gleam of tracks. Across the tracks rose a dark breast of hill that was still planted every year in corn or hay, as it had been in his youth when trains powered by coal and steam pulled into White Hart. He let out a long smoky sigh of relief. The station was due West of Blackwood.

Closing his eyes once more, Fergus sank roots through the cement of the sidewalk, deep into the earth. Then he sent branches through the top of his head soaring skyward. East, South, West, North, he called the directions, and, extending his stick, he slowly pivoted and traced the sacred circle round himself. Fully located, he turned to face the East. He pointed his staff in that direction until he could feel the pull of Blackwood through it. He had carved the stick himself the first Summer of his return, from an old boundary oak that had been struck by lightning. The rod remembered its roots. Wood answered wood. With his inner compass restored, the stick would keep him on course.

It led him now a hundred yards South, then round a corner and East again up the back streets of White Hart. These were not so garishly lighted as Front Street or Main. The darkness was soothing. Most of the houses were his age or older and had not changed place or face, a disconcerting tendency he had remarked in store fronts and other places of business.

Usually the side streets of White Hart were deserted after dark, but just ahead Fergus descried a strange company of small beings, some bearing lights that bobbed up and down on theiir erratic course. As he drew nearer, he saw that their faces were obscured: masked, painted or otherwise distorted. It was their noise that betrayed their nature: shrill, excited, a cacophony of squeals, shouts, and giggles. Children.

When his path was about to cross theirs, one of the children pointed at him and shrieked. Then the rest scattered, like a flock of startled birds, screaming in an ecstasy of fear. At any rate, his form, whether ghostly or mortal, was visible. He looked back and watched as the little hobgoblins regrouped and rushed to the porch of the nearest house where twin jack o'lanterns leered in welcome. Then he turned and went on.

He had his own All Hallow's Eve rite to observe in Blackwood in the ring of trees. His mother had always held that Samhain, as she called it, the Feast of the Dead, marked the New Year. "For just as the child is conceived in the womb and there takes shape," his mother would intone, "so time begins in darkness, when the last leaf gives up the ghost and the seed dreams in the ground and each night is longer than the last. All beginnings are dark. The world was without form and void and darkness brooded over the face of the deep," she would conclude. "So mote it be." Then she would kneel and unbind her long black hair, loosing her powers, as she bent over the scrying bowl to search the water for the shape of things to come.

As her only son, Fergus attended her, his awe changing over the years to resentment as he perceived that his mother's strangeness and reserve, her occult pursuits, set both of them apart from their fellows. His mother revelled in mystery. She veiled herself with it—even from him. One All Hallow's Eve, when he was just shy of sixteen—the last Samhain's rite they would hold together, though he did not know it then—she had invoked a great vision. As was their custom, they had come to the ring of trees, he bearing a lantern, she the bowl and a jug of water. If he had been just a little older, he might have rebelled outright and refused to come. As it was, he punished her with sullenness, a display of boredom calculated to undermine her high seriousness, to make her appear ridiculous to herself; failing that, to provoke her wrath. She was not distracted by him in the least.

He glowered ineffectually, concentrating on his irritation with his mother in a vain attempt to ignore the strains of a waltz wafting from the Masquerade Ball at the Big House where She danced at the heart of a world sealed against him. How he hated that music, leaking out into his night, insinuating itself down through the terraced gardens, floating across the pond into the heart of the wood, his heart. He could feel rage coursing through his limbs. He longed to raise his arms and call the winds, whip up a storm to drown out that sound. But he knew very well, if he played that game, used the elements to serve his mood, his mother's powers were such that she could strip him of his fledgling strength and reduce him to idiocy.

Now the wind was rising of its own accord; or else in answer to his mother's whispered invocation. In spite of himself, his determined indifference gave way to uneasy alertness as his mother began to sway, chanting wordlessly. At first Fergus barely noticed the shift from sheer sound to sense.

"This is my grove, my sacred grove, my maiden bower."

Her swaying, the repetition, his long training all had their effect.

"This is my grove, my sacred grove, my birthing bed."

His mind emptied and opened.

"This is my grove, my sacred grove, my burial chamber. This is my grove, my sacred grove."

When her chanting ceased, the silence felt heavy, charged, like the air before a storm. Then she began to moan; or rather she gave her body as an instrument to some mute power. The voice rose to a wail, and the hair on Fergus' spine rose with it.

Pictures began to flood his mind, as if the scrying water had turned tidal wave. Trees, huge trees, toppled, many of them trees Fergus knew intimately. Trees of Blackwood, the trees of the holy ring. Somehow, in the seeing, Fergus knew: as each tree fell, its fall echoed the fall of other trees, in other times and other places. Trees felled—or burned—not out of need alone, or even greed, but out of fear and vengeance, because they were Hers.

"This is my grove, my sacred grove."

For an instant he saw. Beneath the earth the roots of the holy trees twined as above their branches spread out against the sky, tracing the patterns of the stars. A silent link. Then, once more, the trees of Blackwood were falling, each one singing a death song, as it rent the air and tore the fabric of creation.

"This is my grove, my sacred grove." The voice spoke again. "Save it. Save it."

Fergus did not know if he asked aloud or only in his mind: How? But an answer came.

"The Great Rite. It must be enacted, the Sacred Marriage, to restore the balance of the wheel. The Sacred Marriage. In this grove. Before all memory of the Great Rite vanishes and the Earth is barren. The Sacred Marriage must be enacted. In this grove."

When Fergus came to himself again, his mother was slumped, unconscious, before the overturned bowl, her vision spilled out with the water. She could never remember that seeing, and it maddened her. She suspected its importance. For weeks thereafter, she questioned him minutely. He told her very little. He didn't know, exactly, what prompted him to withhold. Partly, it was the pleasure in having the power to do so, partly the fear of what use she might make of the knowledge if she possessed it. He did not wish to be instructed in her understanding of the Sacred Marriage. Besides, perhaps the vision was really his, to fulfill as he saw fit. His. So he persuaded himself when he was a young man and foolish.

The carved stick led the old man around a corner for several strides, then East once more, not on a street this time, but up a gravel driveway. A gradual incline he would never have noticed in his youth now caused him some shortness of breath and more awareness than he welcomed of those bits of bone and gristle that passed for legs. He was almost home. Beyond the floodlit church yard swayed the trees of Blackwood, black against hazy stars.

He had failed to force prophecy to fulfill itself properly. Yet he was still the keeper of Blackwood, holding it in enchantment, even as it held him. For his lifetime; at least for his lifetime. And hers. And hers. Perhaps tonight the scrying water would give him some sign, show him what remained to be accomplished while there was still time. Time. If only he weren't so weary. It had been a mistake to come out today. It had cost him too much strength. Strength he needed for seeing.

Inadvertently, he paused by the steps to the parish house, within a hundred yards of the gap in the wall that led to the carriage road of Blackwood. Just as he was about to go on, a loud report rang through the wind, and Fergus froze, all his senses and extra senses on the alert. An instant later, someone ran from the porch of the rectory into the middle of the driveway where she—for it appeared to be a woman—stood confronting the church.

The wife, no doubt. Fergus didn't know this one's name; he rarely knew their names, the priest-wives. They often reminded him of female fowl, all gray and brown, discreet in their plumage. Their soul lights, which his mother had taught him to discern at will, were weak, guttering like candle flame about to drown in wax.

The woman standing in the driveway, with her back to him, seemed no different, a darkness in the glare of floodlight. But something had made her rush out of the house, and his unintended witness linked him to her in this moment. He felt his own hands clenching and unclenching, as he sensed hers must be, in an effort to control whatever it was, to keep it from rising. Her shoulders, too, were tensed, and her jaw.

Then, without warning, she let go and loosed a cry that would put a banshee to shame. Her lights, so dim before that he'd hardly seen them, flared a phosphorescent purple, dulling the floodlight, glowing, shimmering. Sparks flew from her head as she raised her arms, fists still clenched. Then, slowly, her fingers uncurled, and her hands opened, palms up.

She stood in the ancient stance of a moon priestess. Did she know? Could she possibly know what she was doing?

The moment passed. The woman turned back towards her house, briefly facing in Fergus' direction. She did not appear to notice him, but he took note of her. In those hands that she had held outstretched, Fergus saw the gifts: a golden snake in her left hand, and in her right a spindle trailing a thread the color of moonlight. She was unaware, he sensed, not fully awakened. But in the depths of his being, Fergus knew: She was the one; on that gossamer thread hung the fate of Blackwood.

It was a seeing. It was a sign.

HEAD
OVER HEELS 4

MARVIN Greene, riding the last train from Grand
Central to White Hart, pressed his forehead against the dirty
window and looked past the reflective glare to see the sign at
this station. He had failed to comprehend the conductor's bored bellow,
not that he was afraid of missing his stop; White Hart was the end of the
line. He only wanted a rough idea of how much more time he had to do
in this dingy, unventilated smoking car. Briardale, he read. He ran through
what he could remember of the names of towns his cousin Raina had recited for him. Then he copped a look at the Rolex the dude across the
aisle had on display. 9:46. If the train was on time, White Hart should be
next.

The train jerked and groaned, and the lights of Briardale Station slipped
into the night. As the wheels balanced, Marvin restacked his playing cards,
not bothering to complete his winning game of solitaire. Locking the table
back into the seat in front of him, he stood and retrieved his luggage from
the overhead rack, if you could apply the word "luggage" to an old suitcase left behind by Raina's ex-husband and embossed with his initials: RSJ.
Marvin could never remember what the letters stood for. He had missed
that part of Raina's life, her brief marriage to a white man.

Lawyer that she was, Raina had legally reclaimed her own name, Washington, and bestowed it on her daughter. Tana was thirteen, and, Marvin
guessed, one of the reasons Raina was happy to lend him—no, give him—
a suitcase and wave him off on a train. He didn't hold it against Raina
that she considered him an unwholesome influence. She had more than
done her duty by him as a family member, visiting him whenever she
could all those years.

Marvin opened the brown leather suitcase, almost as small as a briefcase, and nestled his playing cards next to his tarot deck, which he kept
wrapped in black silk, like Selena, his onetime gypsy lover, had taught
him to do. She had also warned him not to mess with the cards in public
unprotected places like commuter trains. The cards did not have much
company: a toothbrush and paste, a few reefers, cigarettes, a razor, tweez-

ers and a mirror, shaving cream and his scents, two complete changes of clothes—one State issue—a few extra shirts, socks, underwear. Nothing to strain his weightlifter's biceps.

He closed the suitcase, with the same mixed feelings he always had lately, and laid it on the seat beside him. When you had all you owned in a suitcase that small and one bankroll between you and next week, you were free. Free as any fool God ever made. Free as that twelve-year-old kid he'd been, running down a red dirt road between cotton fields, looking for Highway 61 like he'd heard about in an old blues song. As free and as close to the edge.

But he wasn't a kid anymore. He was thirty years old. That was old in the Street. It blew his mind to think how five years ago, he'd been a Prince. He'd held a whole lot of power and riches in his hands and seen it all run through his fingers to nothing. Now here he was, with his borrowed suitcase and a couple of hundred dollars. Some of that money he'd won in illegal card games with the C.O.s; the rest had been invested in his future by female volunteers in the programs he'd attended mostly so he'd have a good in-house record when he went to the Board. It was nothing he couldn't blow in a week—or a day—if he wasn't careful. And to top it all, he was on a train to some hick town with no idea why.

White Hart had been no part of his plan—either his plans for himself or those he had fabricated for the Board, getting carried away with a vision of his reformed self, soaring with his theme like a jazz horn or a preacher getting hot. Testifying. That was why he had ended up taking such a late train; his parole officer had rolled out all the red tape to "facilitate" this temporary change of address. What Marvin had hoped would be a routine matter had taken two weeks. All the hassle had motivated him. Damned if he couldn't go to White Hart if he wanted to. He could always leave again if he didn't like it. That's what being Outside was all about: you could come, and you could go.

Marvin felt for his cigarettes. He had about half a pack left in his pocket and another pack in his suitcase. They might have to last him awhile. No bartering with the guy in the next cell, no running out to the corner store. Marvin lit up. He was in for some clean living, as Raina put it with that evil laugh of hers.

"Maria will make you go out back behind the woodshed to smoke," she'd warned.

Maria was Raina's mother. The "i" in her name rhymed with eye, and when Raina was in a nasty temper she sometimes referred to her mother as the Black Maria, like the police wagon of the same name. Everyone called her Maria, including Raina. It was a title, like Majesty. There had been so many stray kids in and out while Raina, Maria's only born child, was coming up, Raina had lost the knack of saying "mama."

A stray kid. Was that how Maria would see him? Of course Raina put it the other way around.

"Go on up and stay with my mother for awhile. Maria could use some looking after."

Raina didn't have time, what with her job as director of legal services for the Bronx and with running Tana around every weekend to this lesson and that activity. The suggestion that he might visit Maria and "check out opportunities in White Hart" was put to him in the light of being a favor to Raina. There was no doubt that he owed her. Why he'd agreed was the mystery. A sense of obligation was not his strong suit; he'd inherited the lack from his mother. He'd left his own grandmother who raised him without a backward glance. When she got sick, well, he'd been on the Inside then. As for her funeral, the State wasn't about to give him compassionate leave and an escort all the way to Georgia.

Marvin took a deep drag on his Lucky Strike and turned his attention to the smoke as it curled from his nostrils, then the corners of his mouth. He watched it do its snakey dance up towards the ceiling of the car where it thickened the blue cloud that already hung there.

It didn't do to think about things too much. Could be that was his trouble: too much thinking on the Inside. He hadn't reckoned on its effect; that everything would look different, feel different when he got out. He thought he'd been hip to the changing times. He'd watched television, read the headlines. He'd kept a sharp eye on the styles civilian women wore and the way female C.O.s did their hair—the only part of them that looked any different from the men. He sounded out any ladies he encountered about their attitudes and opinions on anything from abortion clinic bombings to Princess Di's maternity wardrobe. He considered it keeping up with his profession.

He had kept a close watch on himself, too. He was his own capital. He'd scrutinized his face in the mirror each day, trimming his hair and beard to an immeasurable length—more a shadow than a growth of hair—that emphasized the perfect shape of his head and his features: arched brows over almond-shaped eyes, prominent cheekbones, come down to him from the Cherokee branch of the family tree, a nose just slightly beaked, giving a predatory look to a face that would otherwise have been merely beautiful. He had full lips and adequate teeth, which had received more professional attention in prison than in his entire life before, and very smooth, very dark skin lit with a hint of red. He was in good physical condition. He had played basketball, and he'd worked out with weights—a matter of survival for someone with a slim build like his. He was only 5' 8", weighing one hundred and fifty pounds, but he looked bad, dangerous, worthy of his Street name, The Marvelous.

With all those precautions, all that attention to the fine details, Marvin had thought to take up his life, the Life, with scarcely a missed beat. But apparently there was something he had overlooked, something elusive. Even now, a month and a half on the Outside, he couldn't put his finger on where the change was. In himself? In the Street?

There was the crack factor and AIDS, new on the scene since he'd been Inside, and almost six years of Reaganomics, as well as a whole lot of punk kids that had come up and claimed what used to be his turf. And the girls in the bus stations and coming out of shelters—the SROs had almost all closed down—that he might have put the moves on, all looked like they were twelve years old and in need of a meal, a bath, sometimes a hospital bed. There were more people on the Street these days that didn't have any kind of game at all, not just bugs dumped from the institutions, but men his age begging change, women with kids. Fact was, the Street didn't look too much different from the Inside, except it was dirtier, there were no regular meals, and people had even less idea what they were doing there.

Marvin let out a drag with a long loud sigh that ended in a muttered, "Shit." The white man across the aisle glanced up, shifted uneasily in his seat, then bent closer to his newspaper, *Wall Street Journal*, no doubt. A long ash that had built up on the man's cigarette—one of those brands that advertized you were practically improving your health, it was so low in tar and nicotine—dropped onto the man's suit. Halstead, estimated cost four hundred and fifty dollars. He brushed it away irritably, probably blaming that arrogant Black stud for making him nervous.

He did make the man nervous, Marvin knew. His antennae were finely tuned, a survival adaptation as necessary in prison as in the Life. He and Mister Charley here and an older white woman were the only passengers left in the smoking car. Despite Raina's quoting statistics to the effect that about one fourth of White Hart's population was Black, color, except for Marvin, had gotten off the train three stops back.

Marvin studied the man, whose fear was almost palpable, causing little electric storms in the air between them. Of course, everybody knew all Black males were dope-dealing and dope-crazed, carried a piece and would as soon blow your head off as give you the time of day. Except nowadays, especially since Bernard Goetz, Whitey was just as likely as anyone to have some "justifiable self-defense" in his pocket.

Goetz was a cracker. Marvin doubted this dude ever condescended to ride the subway. He reeked of money: an apartment on the East Side, a small estate in White Hart, where he kept his wife and kids and a few horses to keep his Old Lady busy while he snuck around town looking for "girls" and "parties"—a classic John. That he could intimidate this ofay by exhaling audibly gave Marvin a measure of satisfaction that faded quickly when he considered the likely difference between their bank accounts. To think that he had once pulled in a couple of thousand on a daily basis.

So what was wrong with him now? Why hadn't he been able to make a move? Jump in. Sink or swim. Maybe having Raina to fall back on was messing him up. When he'd first arrived in the Big Apple at age eighteen, he hadn't connected with her yet. Nothing like the sheer drive to survive to sharpen your instincts. Lately, he'd been waking up in a nightmare sweat to the fear that he'd lost it, that unnameable something that made him an ace Player. More than instinct, akin to art, the power that hummed in your fingers, telling you the exact moment to throw the dice so they'd roll your way; had he lost it when he was busted? Had there been some split second when he'd hesitated and lost the beat, lost his nerve, lost the game? Had Lady Luck turned him loose—or did she just have other plans for him?

Last night he had read the cards. He'd gotten good at reading on the In- side and didn't need Selena to explain the cards anymore. Not that she was around. Five years was a long time in the Street. People got burned out, locked up, moved on. Most of his business associates were now guests of the State. He had seen some of his former ladies, but naturally they had found other protectors and could not afford to know him. He understood how it was, though he had always held in contempt those of his competitors who had to resort to violence to keep their girls in line. Marvin hadn't had to keep his ladies in line; they'd lined up themselves for what he had to give. Time was.

Now late night often found him alone with the cards. He'd asked five or six different times, five or six different ways about his future, and every time, in one position or another, he'd turned up the Fool. In his deck—a rare one of Spanish-Moorish origin, a love gift from Selena—a Black Fool in outrageous threads was in the act of doing a hand-spring. There was such magic in the card—or in his mind; he never knew which, and Selena said it didn't matter—that if he stared at it long enough, he could feel the motion, see the dizzying vision of the world turning upside down, hear the jingling bells of the Fool's cap. Tied to his back was his "bundle of tricks," as Selena called it, containing the Elements: Earth, Air, Fire, and Water that became the tarot suits. Springing up from the ground on hind legs, as if greeting the Fool, was a small black dog. Behind the pair, a red sun rose—Selena assured him it was rising—in a golden sky. In the upper left hand corner, a purple butterfly spread its wings.

Marvin knew enough to receive the card as a compliment from the cosmos: the Fool, first and last of the Greater Trumps, the beginning in the end, the zero, the great nothing that contained it all. Surely Lady Luck had plans for him. But to find out, he'd have to go with the Fool. Act on impulse. Whistle in the dark. Jump off a cliff and wait for the wings to sprout. That's how he read it anyway. White Hart seemed as blind a lead as any he'd ever followed.

The train began to slow with a series of jerks. Marvin and his aislemate both stubbed out their smokes on the floor; the ashtrays were too full. Opening a briefcase almost as large as Marvin's suitcase, the man stuffed his newspaper inside. Then, when the train stopped, he just sat there, despite the conductor's call of "last stop," until Marvin, assured that this was White Hart, moved into the aisle. In a moment, Marvin heard the man behind him; then he understood: Mr. Rolex hadn't wanted to have Marvin at his unprotected back. Annoyed, Marvin briefly considered menacing the man in the parking lot, just following him to his car before he walked on. Exiting the train after the dumpy little white woman, he dismissed the idea. That kind of a fool, he was not. Not while he was still on parole.

Marvin remained on the lighted platform while a half a dozen or so others headed for the parking lot. Envy gnawed at him as he watched his fellow traveler unlock a BMW and tear into the night. Shit! He'd paid five years of his life for a Jaguar he'd never even gotten to drive. Shaking his head, he reached into his pocket for Raina's directions, wondering what the hell he was doing in White Fucking Hart at 10:00 P.M. on a Friday night with a mile's walk to Old Lady Maria's house.

"Cross where the State road curves and becomes Main Street," he read. "Bear left on Water Street, past a graveyard, past the Town water works, cross a bridge where a dam makes a waterfall that used to turn the mill wheel. Keep on that road," he wasn't reading now but remembering her voice as she explained the written directions, "down into the deep, damp part of town, the lowland, the flood level, the heart of Old White Hart that is now the outskirts. The road will wind, following the stream. After the third curve, on the left you'll see Maria's house, just perched on a bank and like to slide into the stream."

Marvin pocketed the directions, looked around for the State road, then made for the crossing. Water Street, unmarked as Raina had predicted, seemed to be in the right place at the elbow of the curve. To the left of the State road were the locked gates of a public park or garden. Two beat-up cars were parked there, along with a gang of some strange kind of small-town hoodlums perched on the hoods. Keeping the street between himself and them as he crossed, Marvin estimated about ten young bodies, high on reefer and beer to judge from the fumes wafting his way. When they spied him there were catcalls and hoots. Marvin risked a glance. White Hart must be weirder than Raina remembered. These kids had their faces painted so you couldn't tell if they were black or white, male, female. Some of them were wearing what looked like sheets—Shit!—and one of them, Marvin swore, had on an ape suit. Damn, Marvin suddenly realized, it must be Hallowe'en.

Walking down Water Street, the raucous laughter of the juveniles receding, Marvin tried to fight off a menacing loneliness. Hallowe'en used to be one helluva night on the Street. He'd blow the girls to a big party before they went out to work. All the ladies would be wearing costumes, painting their faces to look like cats or Egyptian princesses. Some of them even made up their nipples like eyes, rouged the cheeks of their ass. There'd be Johns walking around dressed up like Count Dracula or Tarzan. Everybody'd be out on the Street looking for action, looking for a party, looking to get high, get freakish. And he'd pull in almost twice as much hard cash as he did on any other night of the year.

Now look at him, walking down a deserted street that was fast turning into a country road. After two blocks the sidewalks and the street lights ceased. Darkness gaped between houses that stood farther and farther apart. The pavement was patchy, uneven, a pothole here, a frost heave there. The fuzzy-looking stars overhead didn't do much to relieve the situation; their point seemed to be to show up the sheer black of everything else. There was no moon in sight. He sensed, more than saw, the graveyard when he passed it, an unquiet silence, alive with eyes and ears. This was the Dead's night to party. Against his will, he remembered the tales of that crazy old lady, Tante Lisette, about body snatchers and zombies. He quickened his step, then let out the breath he'd unconsciously held.

Marvin had forgotten the meaning of night. All those years in the Life, night had been his working day, time to do business, to see people, to pursue pleasure. In the cell-block, human noise never stilled, night or day. Darkness meant danger, so it was kept at bay, burned away with harsh, fluorescent lighting.

With relief, Marvin approached the brightly lit, industrial looking convocation of water towers and works on the other side of the road from the dam. Once he crossed the bridge and left behind municipal property, he was in the dark again, real animal dark, thickened now by deep woods on both sides of the road. The hair on the back of his neck prickled; his senses went on the alert. He could hear the stream on his left as it slid over and around rocks, carrying stray sticks and leaves on its current. He could smell the dampness and the rich odor of fresh rot. He shivered in his synthetic clothes.

After years of breathing over-heated, over-used air, what he breathed now seemed wild, deregulated, alive in itself, seeking out his every unprotected pore. Hardest of all to handle was the ground under his feet: it would not lie flat. In the city, in prison, he had grown accustomed to straight lines, to boxes. Here the world was unruled, unruly. It rose and fell around him in solid waves. He had to hesitate with every step and hold out his hands like a baby learning to walk.

Just as he was beginning to get the hang of it, to regain a degree of confidence, a drainage pipe, exposed where the road had eroded around it, reared without warning, not only a different level and angle but a smoother surface. Marvin's right foot slipped. Thrown off balance, he landed with his left in a ditch, a foot lower than the pipe. His struggle for recovery sent him pitching headfirst over the guardrail, down, down the steep stream bank, his borrowed suitcase leading the way.

After what seemed like a long time, Marvin found himself, more or less in one piece, lying on his back with his feet downhill and his head up, having turned at least one complete somersault. Above him bare branches, bristling with stars, clattered and creaked. Marvin lay still, waiting to see what hurt and if he dared make a move. To his surprise, beneath the surface chill, the earth felt warm, as though it still hugged the heat of day. The warmth seemed to reach for him. His breathing slowed and deepened, and all the leaves, the fresh fallen and the old dry ones, breathed, too. The bruised places in his body began to name themselves; still the ground beneath him felt, not soft exactly, but welcoming, knowing, like he was just another leaf that would crumble in time, turn to earth.

Suddenly afraid that he would pass out, Marvin raised himself on his elbows, then rolled over. Something in that very motion, the muscles it involved, recalled the act of turning towards a lover, covering the body of a woman with his own.

All that time in prison, no matter what else he was doing—working, sleeping, shooting the shit with the other guys in the cell-block, playing cards, drinking wine—the image of female flesh was always there: sometimes particular, sometimes anonymous, sometimes black, sometimes white, sometimes the only thought in his mind, sometimes the ground beneath all other thoughts. But always there, so intense at times, he didn't just see the image; he could feel it, smell it, bury himself in it. He had always figured that as soon as he got out, the very first thing he'd do would be to find a woman. But it hadn't worked out that way. Not that any woman had refused him; he hadn't even made the move.

Now, for an instant, pressing the length of his body against the earth, inhaling the moist richness of living decay, his sex rising in response, Marvin knew: the earth was alive; it knew him. And the earth was female, more fiercely and deeply female than any woman he had ever known.

BOOK TWO

ALL SAINTS

FUCKING 5 MOSES

ALAN rolled off Esther.

It is accomplished. The words wandered through Esther's mind, and, for lack of other thoughts, she tracked them to their source in the Gospel, the Crucifixion, no less. She squirmed at the blasphemous associations of which her stream of consciousness seemed capable. She would much rather have laughed with Alan about it. There were times when he relished irreverence, ecclesiastical in-jokes, one of the privileges of the priesthood that occasionally extended to the immediate family.

"God can afford a joke at His own expense," Alan would say in response to the rare complaints of his jocular preaching style. God wasn't the problem; it was sex. Alan was touchy about that in a way that still confused her, even after seven years of marriage, still threw her off-balance. She had learned to be careful, to walk on tiptoe around his masculinity. But because she didn't understand, she frequently made missteps.

Right now, for instance, she could not be sure that it would be all right for her to turn on her side to look at him as he lay, back on his own side of the bed now, recovering—that was the word that came to mind.

"You're so lucky!" one effusive female parishioner had gushed to her. "Alan is such a teddy bear. So cuddly."

Almost all women, all ages adored Alan. She should be used to it by now. His effect on women had been evident to her since seminary, where they'd met and where Alan had been a general favorite, except with the most "militant-feminist-types," as Alan called them. She had never completely comprehended how he had come to choose her from among all those exciting, even brilliant women, most of whom had a much clearer idea of what they were doing there than she had. Everyone told her how fortunate she was when she and Alan became engaged.

Women had never ceased congratulating her on her marriage, some openly envying her, which had the unhappy effect of making close friendships with other women in the parish difficult, both at Trinity, where they'd first lived, and now at St. Paul's. It struck Esther that her marriage, in their minds, did not exist in the mundane. It had to be exalted, mystical, like Christ's with the Church. In fact, Esther sometimes felt that women confused Alan, their priest, so sensitive, so understanding—unlike their husbands—with Jesus himself.

Not that Alan bore much resemblance, physically, to the traditional depictions of Christ, who could hardly be described as a teddy bear. Nor was it clear, at least from her reading of the Gospels, that Jesus was cuddly. Alan certainly appeared to be. Esther had observed him, with some bewilderment, at the innumerable gatherings they attended. He touched both men and women frequently: a pat on the back here, an arm around the shoulder there. Hearty, warm. He routinely pricked the little bubbles of private space that most people, Episcopalians in particular, preferred to keep intact.

Yet here, now, on this rainy Saturday morning, which could have been cozy, alone with him in their king-size bed, Esther did not dare to reach for him or to ask him to hold her. He would tense, even if he complied. She would feel his restlessness, his wanting his body to himself again, after contact with her body and its damp clinginess.

Sometimes, in the midst of the act, Alan could become frenzied, bucking, straining, seeming to gallop towards a release that would obliterate them both. But then, so often, when it was over, in the way he held his body, the careful control of the muscles of his face, she sensed revulsion, such as someone might feel on opening a container in the refrigerator that had been left too long and gone to mold. So lately she hadn't reached. She did not know how to convey that her yearning for closeness was not a further demand.

"Didn't you come?" he had sighed wearily, angrily the last time she had tried to touch him afterwards, pressing her front to his back, placing her hand over his heart. "I thought you came."

She had, of course. He had seen to that. He had some technical expertise. She did not like to think of where he had acquired it, but she had seen the manuals in a discreet corner of his study, among more general books on pastoral counseling. She knew, too, that Bob, the rector of Trinity, Alan's former boss, had referred couples with marital—sex—troubles to Alan. Alan considered himself something of an expert on "sexuality" and had led more than one adult education series that explored the theme. His sermons were famous for sexual innuendo that either delighted or appalled but never failed to titillate congregants.

Certainly he was not one of those boors who had never heard of female orgasm, let alone the name and location of the clitoris. He knew all about "the clitoris." It was a point of pride with him: his sensitivity, his skill, his determined lack of inhibition. Yet somehow his approach made her think of a good child screwing up his courage to eat spinach or liver to please his mother, because she had told him it was good for him and would make him big and strong.

Her own response, especially when a long time had elapsed between episodes, shamed her. She would feel that he was right, that there was something monstrous about her, that she was all mouth, insatiable, devouring. So she tried to be careful, to keep herself within bounds. She lay quietly now, not even spilling over into talk.

They had not talked last night—or rather she had not—about what he referred to as his lateness, what she thought of as his indifference. He would not admit that he had forgotten about early dinner and trick-or-treating. In fact, when she had returned home from their rounds, having finally taken the boys herself, Alan had reproached her for not waiting, not trusting. He had castigated her for being rigid, overly-scheduled. Then, resting his case, he had insisted on taking complete charge of bedtime procedures.

Esther had returned to the uncompleted task of sorting and folding the laundry she'd left piled on the master-bed, her fury mounting as she listened to the children wheedling and Alan conceding: just one more candy, just one more. Finally she had been able to contain her rage no longer. She had rushed out of the house, childishly banging the screen door, then stood in the driveway screaming at the top of her lungs, for perhaps the first time in her life. Even now she could hardly believe she had done it. She had never been given to tantrums as a child; she'd been too busy being good.

Luckily, no one had seen her, and if anyone had heard her, well, there were always high jinks on Hallowe'en; no one would suspect the rector's wife. As for Alan, he and the children had been completely unaware that she had left the house at all. She had returned to find them in the advanced stages of a chasing and tickling game. Alan knew no other method of getting pajamas on children. Of course, it had taken an extra half hour to calm them enough to sleep. That had been her job, the lullabies, the reassurance. No, there are no monsters in the house, no ghosts, no witches. No wolves under the bed, no snakes....

When she had come downstairs again, she'd found Alan sitting on a stool at the kitchen counter, eating the candies she'd set out in a bowl for the trick-or-treaters and reading the local paper. Had his presence in the kitchen, when he could have been in his study or spread out on the living room couch, been a form of penance? Or had he been there to make sure she noticed that he'd washed his own supper dishes—yea, even emptied the dishwasher—a preventive measure, perhaps, so that she could not punish him with the loud silence of cleaning up after him.

Esther had felt thwarted; she'd had no recourse. What was more, she'd understood that she was supposed to feel guilty for her unreasonable rage towards him—and she did. After all, he'd been visiting an elderly, infirm—not to mention rich—parishioner who had pleaded with him to stay for drinks. Lonely old soul. And Esther had deprived Alan of the pleasure of trick-or-treating with his sons by rushing off in a huff.

Esther had stood for a moment, watching Alan carefully unsheathe the tiny bite-sized assorted chocolate bars, one after another. He had eaten quite a few, because there was a little mountain of foil balls on his right and, on his left, several stacks of intact paper wrappers. Cute, his game with the wrappers, like something the boys might have done. There had been maybe half a dozen candies left. He would stop before they were all gone, because it wasn't Christian to eat the last one of anything. She could have joined him, if she'd wanted to. Perhaps that was what he'd been inviting with his adorable arrangement of refuse, that they should be reconciled, eat chocolate together.

But she hadn't wanted to eat two or three candies to make Alan feel better. She'd wanted a whole bagful to herself, the delicious self-destruction of excess, enough to make her as sick and miserable as she'd felt. As it was, she'd refused to eat even one. Without a word, she'd left the kitchen and gone to bed.

Alan had joined her some twenty minutes later, fumes of winter-fresh-gel obliterating the chocolate. He'd made the concession of reaching for her, lifting her nightgown and placing a tentative hand between her legs. Reluctantly aroused and suddenly relieved that he was not angry with her any more, Esther had gone to the bathroom to put in her diaphragm. When she'd returned, she'd found him unconscious—with Alan it always seemed more like passing out than falling asleep—knocked out by a sugar low. Conscientiously, Alan had finished the job in the morning.

Now Alan sat up, felt for his pajama bottoms under the covers, swung his legs over the side of the bed, and pulled the pants back on. From down the hall came a series of thuds and screeches, the thundering of a small herd of feet. It sounded as though a ball were being ricocheted off the hall walls.

Alan and she agreed about not having a TV for the children, though Alan had a small one in his office for football games and the occasional late night movie. So there were no Saturday morning cartoons to put the children out of commission. That was Esther's main reason for not having one: not just the content—the violence, the mindlessness and the mindset-ting of consumer indoctrination—but because she knew the temptation to turn the TV on and the children off would be too powerful to resist.

"Sounds like the natives are getting restless," Alan quipped, as he did almost every Saturday morning.

He stood up, demanding plaintively of the cosmos, which Esther, of course, represented, where in the universe his slippers could possibly be.

"The bathroom," Esther answered on creation's behalf; she had stumbled over them in the middle of the night.

A crash from the direction of the stairwell shook the bedside lamp.

"I guess I'll have to wait until after breakfast to shower," Alan sighed, coming out of the master bathroom with his slippers on.

He crossed to the door and smiled at her before he opened it; then he closed it behind him with ostentatious care and quiet. His air of cheerful martyrdom was intended to remind her of how wonderful it was that he took care of the children faithfully every Saturday morning—that is, when he was not away at a weekend conference—allowing her the luxury of lying in bed while he and the children made breakfast.

This hour or so, she understood, was his quality time with the children. All Alan's time with them was quality time, as opposed to hers, which was merely quantity. Also, Esther had noted, Saturday morning quality time frequently provided Alan with amusing anecdotes for Sunday morning sermons. Today being All Saints Day, Alan was holding a noon-day Eucharist, so his getting breakfast as usual was especially righteous, though she believed he did not intend to preach. People could hardly expect—or desire—sermons on two consecutive days.

Now let us praise famous men and our fathers who begat us, was the Old Testament text. The Gospel for the day was the Beatitudes. She did not blame Alan for wanting to get that over without comment. How inadequate, how superfluous and presumptuous anyone, even Alan, must feel preaching a sermon on the Sermon on the Mount.

Blessed are the meek, Esther mused as she lolled obediently, considering the possibility of going back to sleep—the kitchen was far enough away in this oversized house that the pandemonium there would take on an impersonal quality, like the roaring of surf. Or should she read? All she had on her bedside table was a magazine on parenting—too distressing; whatever she read led her to believe that she was doing everything all wrong— and a novel by Barbara Pym, pressed on her by the local librarian, who was a parishioner. It depressed Esther to think of her own possible resemblance to Pym's dowdy, mildly eccentric women who surrounded the inevitable clergyman, whether as wife, spinster, or sister.

Of course women in Barbara Pym novels generally did not have children, at least not small obstreperous boys; there was the odd almost-grown daughter. Perhaps that saved her from too close a likeness to a Pym heroine. Also, if they ever lay sticky with the Vicar's sperm, Barbara Pym did not say so. Really, that settled it. She would take a bath. With her period due any minute now—(could yesterday's behavior be put down to PMS?)—she was not in the fertile part of her cycle and could afford to ignore the usual restrictions about bathing with a diaphragm. She hardly needed Barbara Pym to tell her that clergy wives did not walk around reeking of sex.

Funny, Esther reflected, as she ran the water and cleared the tub of toy boats and moldering sponge-shapes, she had not understood about that at first, the necessity of washing afterwards. During her first full sexual experience—a matter of three or four weekends with someone she'd met on a blind date and to whom she'd succumbed mainly because her twentieth birthday had been approaching and she hadn't wanted to enter her third decade a virgin—she had enjoyed the feeling of semen trickling down her legs. She'd let it dry there, forming a musky film that she wore beneath her clothes, hidden evidence of her new knowledge. The affair hadn't lasted long enough for her to learn sexual etiquette.

Alan had been the one to teach her. For a long time, he had insisted that she douche, until a doctor suggested that her recurring infections might be due to the practice, as "douching kills the natural flora and fauna necessary to a healthy vaginal environment." She had explained to Alan about the flora and fauna, carefully quoting the doctor—she had considered asking the doctor for a written excuse. Though Alan had blanched—no doubt at the thought of those necessary little organisms inhabiting her vagina—he had accepted the doctor's authority and dropped the matter.

Esther stepped into the tub now, relishing the intensity of the water's warmth in contrast to the chilly air—they kept the thermostat at sixty degrees. Her nipples puckered with goosebumps, making her breasts look momentarily fuller, a semblance of their former selves. After a total of three years of nursing, her breasts had pretty much had it. Though they were the same moderate size they'd always been, they'd lost their bounce. They drooped, like the breasts of tribal women in the National Geographic magazines she'd gazed at as a child with fear and fascination.

In childhood, she had never seen any other bared breasts, least of all her mother's, who, like most women of her generation, had chosen bottle-feeding. When Esther heard the recent finding that nursing reduced a woman's chance of developing breast cancer, she had wept. Her mother had died of breast cancer.

Esther eased the rest of her body into the tub, until she was fully reclining. Good. The water covered her stomach entirely, a little island of flesh rising from the deep. That meant she was doing all right with her weight, not that she had a particular problem, but vigilance was in order after thirty. The water line in relation to her stomach was one measure, along with a certain pair of jeans and, of course, the scales.

Esther leaned her head back and closed her eyes. Leave well enough alone. Weight she might control to some extent. There was no point in pinching loose skin, irrevocably stretched by two pregnancies. And why scrutinize stretch marks, which under water appeared raised, like jagged mountain ranges on a three dimensional map. Just let it be, poor old body, Esther thought, feeling a sudden tenderness towards her flesh. Just let it be.

Cradled by the warm water, Esther's whole being uncoiled, unclenched, eased open. There was wisdom, ancient wisdom, in what was called the LeBoyer bath, named after the doctor who had most recently made the connection between warm water and the amniotic paradise from which we are expelled at birth. Esther remembered both her babies, outraged at the sudden exposure to an alien element, rigid and screaming, going limp in the bath and beginning to look around with immense new eyes.

Esther opened her own eyes again and gazed at the bathroom, so cozily cluttered with evidence of her family's existence. The front bathroom, at the top of the stairs, with its Victorian dragon-footed tub, was larger, but as it was the one that visitors used, she felt it must be pristine, impersonal. If some eccentric parishioner were seized by an impulse to bathe, he would find no ring around the tub, no rubber ducks, no pubic hairs. A guest could wash his hands at the sink, even pry into the medicine cabinet and discover nothing of the rector's or his family's personal habits: what brand of deodorant or toothpaste they used, whether they favored aspirin or acetamenophin. The intimacy of their lives was secret, secured in the back bathroom. No one would ever see Alan's shaving cream or razor, her desiccated lipsticks—she rarely wore make-up—or her diaphragm case. All this was theirs alone!

Esther lay and relished this exclusive realm. Last night's anger ebbed and seemed petty as it receded. Really, everything was all right. She was lucky. They were lucky, she and Alan, with their two beautiful, healthy children—and maybe someday a third, though she hadn't yet broached the subject with Alan. Their marriage might not be perfect, but whose was? Alan was happy and successful in his work. Maybe successful wasn't the right word to describe a sacred calling. But the parish rolls were growing, many new young families drawn by the force of Alan's personality. He wasn't at all like the priests in Barbara Pym's novels; he was so much more dynamic.

As for herself, well, she would go back to work eventually. She had been a Head Start teacher, so there wasn't much difference between her pre- and postpartum vocations. Alan wanted her to resume her career, not that they needed the money right now with housing, utilities, telephone and Alan's car provided by the church. There was the boys' education to consider and, as Alan put it, "the importance of her development as a person."

It behooved her not to be boring, she supposed, though she did not think she was bored. What could be more astonishing to witness than the growth of her own children from infant enigmas to their complex and definite yet ever-changing selves? She smiled to think of them: David, Jonathan. Soon one, the other or both would come bursting through the bathroom door proclaiming that breakfast was almost ready and "It's pancakes, Mama!" or "It's a surprise!"

Esther sat up, reaching for the soap, seashell-shaped to encourage the boys to use it. When she had washed her armpits, she raised herself to a kneeling position so that she could soap her thighs and crotch. Just as she had her hands between her legs to work up a lather, the door opened, and Alan, unaccompanied by children, stood looking down at her.

"Just what is this?"

He thrust towards her face the playdough figure, holding it gingerly between thumb and forefinger, as if he could hardly bear to touch it. Hands curved protectively over her pubic bone, Esther confronted her creation, eyeball to vulva.

"I found it in the pantry." Alan made the location sound like an accusation.

"Next to the whole wheat flour," she added unnecessarily.

"What was it doing there?"

"Well, that's where I put it."

"Obviously." His sarcastic tone was a warning. "But what is it?"

"It's playdough, actually."

"I can see that."

Esther knew she was making him angrier, although she didn't think she meant to.

"What I want to know is why an obscene figurine, made of playdough, found its way into our pantry where anyone—anyone!—including our two young children, might find it? I take it you are not denying responsibility for its existence or its location?"

"Well, yes and no." Esther felt confused. Obscene? Responsible? Responsible for obscenity? "Let me try to explain."

"I'm all ears."

"I was outside with the boys yesterday, and we were all playing with the dough we'd made. The boys were making dinosaurs, and I, well, she just happened without my knowing it."

"She?"

"The Lady."

"You call that a lady!"

"Well, that's what Jonathan called her, and it seemed—"

"You let the children see this!"

"Well, they wanted to see what I was making, and—"

"Good God, Esther, this is really the limit. What's happened to your judgement? I mean, you sit around all the time reading books on child development and psychology, and then you have no more sense than to expose your children—your sons!—to an image like this!"

"I don't see what's so awfully wrong—"

"You don't see! You don't see!" He was shouting at her now, menacing her with the figure. "Well, look at it, damn it! And just why were you hiding it in the pantry?"

Hiding it! A moment ago he was talking as if she had it on display.

"You say you didn't realize you were making it. Even supposing it was unintentional, which I find hard to believe, keeping it was deliberate. What I want to know is why? Why didn't you just roll it back into a ball as soon as you saw what it was?"

Esther struggled against tears. His anger always threw her. He was such a thundering of righteousness. She couldn't think. She couldn't hear herself.

"I just didn't want to unmake her. I—"

"Her!" Alan cut her off again. "Her! This is not a "her." This is an "it." A graven image! An idol!"

And who are you, Fucking Moses? A voice inside her snarled. It was not her voice; it was more like her friend Gale's. How she wished she could open her throat and let it out.

"I didn't think it was so terrible," she mustered a protest. "Good grief, Alan. It's just a naked woman. Why are you so upset? You're not one of those New Right Fundamentalists!" That was a sly maneuver, she told herself. "You've always been so liberal. In your sermons, you—"

"Look, Esther, this has nothing to do with politics. It has to do with plain common sense and decency. You don't go showing this sort of gross female genitalia to small boys. It's simply—"

The ear-shattering screech of the smoke alarm slashed Alan's speech. Wails from the children rose to compete.

"Goddamned waffle iron!" Alan swore.

He turned, graven image in hand, to deal with the crisis. Then Esther, impelled by some power, rose from her knees.

"Give me that!" she demanded.

Alan did not hear her, but because he was holding the figure with such distaste, she was able to snatch it away without damaging it. Startled, Alan whirled around to face her once more.

"I'm warning you, Esther!" he screamed to make himself heard over the smoke alarm. "Get rid of it! I will not have it in this house!"

Still soapy, Esther stepped out of the tub and closed the door tightly after Alan. Then she set the Lady on the sink, next to Alan's shaving equipment, and got back into the tub to rinse herself off. At last the smoke alarm ceased. Esther let out the water and gazed at the figure as she reached for a towel.

Alan's wrath confirmed it: some power was here, power that had pulsed through her fingers into form. Not taking her eyes from the figure, Esther dried herself. Her belly is the world, David had said. All at once, she could see it: across the Lady's belly swam continents on seas that heaved and rippled. Her hair was alive, a nest of vipers, a garden of sea fronds that rose and fell with invisible swells. And her vulva, breathing with the same sea rhythms: coming, birthing, pushing out, drawing in....

A little frightened, Esther shook herself and stuffed the towel into the rack. There wasn't much time. She would have to think fast. Not think, act, while Alan and the boys still coped with culinary disaster.

In the bedroom, Esther yanked open bureau drawers, grabbing the first underwear, socks, sweater, jeans that came to hand. Dressed, she returned for the Lady, then sneaked down the stairs and past the kitchen, where Alan was still cursing and both children were shouting at once, trying to get his attention. In the front hall, she searched the closet, donned a poncho, and thrust her feet into boots. Opening and closing the front door soundlessly, an art known to mothers of sleeping babies, she tiptoed off the porch and out into the slanting rain. She cradled the Lady, sheltered and dry, against her womb.

S PENCER Crowe sat in her wheelchair, her walker to one side, a tray with the remains of her breakfast in front of her. Yesterday's mild air had blown away, and now rain slashed down, spearing the few last leaves, hurling them earthwards. Spencer could feel a draft seeping through the cracks of the window. No doubt it was bad for her to sit exposed to the damp. No doubt next week Sabine would see to it that the window seams were sealed with putty for the Winter. For the moment, Spencer enjoyed even this minimal contact with the elements. She loved storms: being out in them, looking out at them. Of course today there was no question of her going outdoors, but the rain did enhance her enforced confinement.

Sabine had lit a fire in the fireplace to encourage the bed to dry out, and the room glowed with the light of the flames, all the colors enriched in dramatic contrast to the stark, gray world outside. Only the Rowan berries, still clinging to the tree, remained undimmed, so bright they might have been clusters of sparks escaped from the hearth.

With weather this wet and windy, she probably wouldn't have many visitors today. Saturdays tended to be a bit slack. People felt obliged to spend time with their own families, she supposed. Or they had chores to do, preparations to make, so that they could go out in the evening or entertain guests. Then, too, so many people visited her on Sunday before and after church, troops of them. Really, the refreshment committee might as well set up coffee hour in the Gatehouse.

Poor Father Peters. She would be surprised if more than two or three showed up for the noon day All Saints Celebration. There was really no good time for church on a Saturday. She should have invited Father Peters to hold the service over here. She rather liked that passage "Now let us praise famous men and our fathers who begat us." It made her think of her own father: so handsome, so, well, virile. Yes, that was the word. But then he hadn't begotten any sons—so far as anyone knew for certain!— only herself, Mary Spencer. It was she who had chosen, of her two given names, to be known by the one that was his.

She could use a quiet day, Spencer supposed. Her lawyers were coming on Monday, and she hadn't even skimmed the formidable stack of papers they had sent her. These men were not as sympathetic as their predecessors, she felt. Of course gentlemen of the old school were an extinct breed. At her age, she could not expect to have advisors who were old enough to be her father. Still, it was a bit disconcerting to receive counsel from men young enough to be her grandsons.

Ah, if only she had grandsons, sons, daughters, nieces, second cousins twice removed: anything to mitigate Geoffrey, who was not even a blood relation. She wished she could be fonder of her nephew-by-marriage. As a rule, she got on well with the younger generations, but there had never been much warmth between Geoffrey and herself, even when he was a child, or perhaps especially when he was a child. He had despised the condition of childhood and had spent his youth waiting, with ill-concealed boredom, to be forty-five. This pinnacle he had now achieved, and he seemed, at least on the surface, the more genial for it. Still, Spencer found a lifetime habit of dislike hard to break.

Geoffrey had been the one to engage Grigson and Bates when her old retainers retired. He had insisted that the distinguished old law firm of Smith, Smyth, Smyth, and Smith—used by her father because one of the Smyths was a remote relation—was fusty and out-of-date. She had been accustomed all her life to letting men make such decisions for her. Not, of course, that she wasn't capable of making them herself; she merely refused to understand anything so boring as all that legal folderol. The same went for arranging financial matters. That was what men were there for. It gave them something to do, something to talk about at their clubs.

Yet she had to admit that over the course of the last several years, she had felt increasingly ill-at-ease with Grigson and Bates and their various minions. There was no doubt that they represented Geoffrey's interests. Fifteen years ago she had taken neither Geoffrey, then a priggish thirty-year-old bachelor, nor his interests seriously. She hadn't even wondered what they might be. Since she had been bedridden, his interests had become alarmingly obvious to her.

Spencer had never before given much thought to her own mortality; she'd been much too busy. While there was no need to rush things—a broken hip wasn't fatal for heaven's sake!—it was perhaps time to meditate on her inevitable end, whenever it might occur. Clearly, Geoffrey had already taken her pending demise into his consideration.

She must make sure to use the commode before Grigson and Bates arrived. She did not want Geoffrey or that bloodless wife of his, Jessica, gloating over reports of incontinence. They would be looking for signs of senility next. Her lapse in front of Father Peters had been humiliating enough. To cover her embarrassment, she had shooed him into the tiny upstairs parlour for sherry almost before he finished pronouncing the Benediction. When Sabine had set her to rights, Spencer had joined Father Peters in her wheel chair, explaining that she liked to observe the formalities and change before drinks, especially when she had company. So important for the morale not to let one's standards slip.

Indeed, there would be no more slips, Spencer resolved. Or Sabine might insist on getting a plastic cover for her mattress. So uncomfortable. The mattress was quite old, she believed. To replace it, she'd have to have one custom-made. There were no modern beds like this one: wider than a twin, narrower than a double, and several inches shorter than was currently standard. When the bed was crafted—by hand, of course, Queen Anne style, some wistful antique dealer had told her—human beings did not routinely grow to be six feet tall.

Spencer was quite attached to the bed, though it was not the most comfortable one she'd ever slept in. It had come down through several generations of her mother's family, at one point crossing the Atlantic. Her parents had moved it into her room the day she turned thirteen. When she had married and left her maiden bower behind, she had intended to present the bed to her own oldest daughter on her thirteenth birthday. She had wanted to have lots of children; six at least.

But there had been no daughter, and by the time Spencer might have had a child of thirteen, she had been sleeping in that bed again herself, leaving her husband, Gerald, to occupy the master bed alone on the increasingly rare occasions that he stayed in Blackwood at all. Gerald had much preferred what he called his "digs" in town.

Odd, in memory her marriage did not seem quite real to her, not in the way her childhood did. Perhaps it had never been real to her, even when it was happening. Admittedly, her marriage had not been an unqualified success, though the arrangement she and Gerald had come to was not uncommon in those days, and certainly a great deal more decorous than a divorce. Divorce was so public—how had Emily Dickinson put it?—like a frog. One knew what she meant. Well, it was all over and done with, these twenty-five years now. Widowhood suited her well enough.

Yet she could still remember, so vividly, sleeping with a morsel of her dear friend Charlotte's wedding cake under her pillow, so that she might dream of her future bridegroom. And dream she had! She'd never told anyone about that dream. She would not have known how. The thought of it still brought a blush to her cheeks. Gerald had not figured in her dream at all. No, not at all.

Spencer poured herself another cup of tea and glanced at the bed stripped of its clothes. It had good bones, so to speak, just as she did. The tips of the four posters gleamed, flame-shaped, beneath them exquisite carvings, which Sabine carefully dusted, of flowers, leaves. The headboard rose like a hill or a dark sun. Set in that regal frame, the naked mattress looked so vulnerable—mortal, absurd....

Really, how maudlin! Spencer looked away from the bed. She must keep a grip on herself. All this time alone in her room was beginning to take its toll. And what a peculiar dream she'd had yesterday! Ordinarily, she did not pay much attention to dreams, though in her charitable rounds she'd listened often enough to other people maundering on about their dreams. She would have to guard against that; she didn't want to become an old bore.

Directing her attention out the window again, Spencer was rewarded by the sight of a human figure—at least she assumed it was human. Hooded and cloaked as it was, it might have been a haunt that had lingered too long and gotten caught by daylight. There was something furtive about the way it scurried up the last bit of town sidewalk on the other side of the Gatehouse yard's wall, like a squirrel going to secrete a prize nut. Where could whoever-it-was be going? When the sidewalk ended, there was only state road curving away into the countryside.

Of course it might be going to turn towards her gate to visit her or to enter Blackwood. She was not at all punitive about trespassing, despite what it said on the posted signs. Her property had long been an unofficial town park. Vandalism had never been a problem, no doubt because of all the tall tales about the old man in the wood, his strange rites, rites that might involve the skewering and roasting of children, particularly boys with a tendency towards frog torture.

Yes, it was going to turn! Spencer leaned forward to keep the apparition in sight for as long as possible. Just then it looked back over its shoulder, presumably to make sure it was not being followed. Spencer glimpsed the face before the figure rounded the corner of the Gatehouse. A woman.

Now surely she recognized her, Spencer told herself. She knew every-one, and she knew she knew that woman. But who was she? The identity evaded her maddeningly for a moment. The difficulty was that there were so many others like her: plain and pleasant but indistinct, their edges blurred with obligations to others, husbands, children. Thank goodness that had never happened to her; at least she could be grateful to Gerald for that! But who was this woman? Well, any minute the doorbell would ring. Why would anyone stroll in Blackwood in this weather?

Spencer strained her ears for the sound of footsteps on the porch. As she listened it came to her: Mrs. Peters, the rector's wife; that's who she was. No wonder it had taken Spencer time to remember. With two notable exceptions—and Spencer hadn't gotten along with either of those women; they hadn't understood their place—all the rectors' wives resembled each other more than they did themselves. But how curious to have a call so early on a Saturday morning. One could hardly be expected to have completed one's toilet at such an hour.

Spencer smoothed her hair and was about to call Sabine to tell her to make another pot of tea when she realized: the bell should have rung by now. It hadn't. Mrs. Peters wasn't stopping. How very odd. What could the woman be up to? And if what she really craved was a lonely walk in Blackwood in the midst of a nasty storm, why hadn't she taken the short cut by the Parish House? That was the way rectors and their families always entered Blackwood unless they were going to the Gatehouse. And what about that surreptitious glance over her shoulder? One might almost say she had an air of guiltiness. Could she possibly be meeting a lover? Such trysts were not unknown in Blackwood. But Mrs. Peters? And in November? Surely in these rather tasteless times there were motels for that sort of thing. In any event, Spencer had to know.

"Sabine!" she cried. Satisfaction of her curiosity required immediate action. "Sabine!"

"What is wrong, Madame!" Sabine puffed into the room, clearly alarmed by the urgency of the summons.

"Quick, Sabine! Get your umbrella and follow Mrs. Peters at once. She just passed by. She came in through the gate, and she's heading into Blackwood. I must know why!"

Sabine, the most loyal of companions, the most discreet and unquestioning of servants, balked.

"Hurry, Sabine! Or you won't be able to catch her up!"

Sabine remained silent, hands on ample hips, regarding Spencer as she would an adorable but badly spoiled child.

"Sabine," Spencer began to wheedle. "You know I have to know. Well, aren't you even the least little bit curious? Here she is, the rector's wife, sneaking into Blackwood for all the world like a, well, like an escaped convict!"

Sabine sighed pointedly and picked up the breakfast tray.

"Oh, well, it's too late now." Spencer sulked. "Really, Sabine, it's too bad of you to spoil my fun. I'm horribly at the mercy of your morals, stuck up here in this wheelchair."

Sabine began to cross the room. Spencer addressed her upright back.

"You think I'm a snoop, don't you, Sabine. Everyone does, I know. But what else is there? I ask you! And what's wrong with it anyway, taking a charitable interest in your neighbor?

"I'm warning you, Sabine," Spencer added as Sabine approached the doorway, "if you continue to thwart me, I'm going to get a stairlift, have a ramp made, and put a motor in this contraption. Then I'll do whatever I please and go wherever I want."

Sabine paused on the threshold, her shoulders shaking so that the silver tea service and the breakfast dishes rattled. For one moment, Spencer feared that she had offended Sabine to the point of tears.

Then Sabine turned towards her, clearly trying to smother laughter.

"Chère Madame, you don't need a wheelchair. You need a broomstick."

Spencer watched as Sabine disappeared through the doorway. Well, only a person as impeccable in her character and as secure in her position as Sabine Desjardins Weaver could carry off such impertinence. Unless Spencer was very much mistaken, Sabine had just called her a witch.

THE VIEW FROM
THE APPLE BARN

FERGUS sat in his mother's horsehair rocking chair by the south-facing windows and watched the wind and the rain chase and tussle. Mild weather out-of-season often had a storm on its heels. This one was entertaining, playful as a tiger kitten, the wind dodging in and out among the trees in the old orchard, holding its breath for a moment as if engaging in a game of hide-and-seek, then whipping suddenly into whirlwind frenzy. The sky had a strange cast, at times almost yellow-green, like a tiger's eyes, dangerous, the sort of sky that boded ill: sudden flash floods, trees crashing down on power lines.

It was the Dead, Fergus thought, the wake of their revels; their restless feet had stirred the elements, raised the powers. Fergus was ready, ready and waiting for the next sign. Maybe the storm would bring it.

Fergus filled his pipe and poured another cup of scalding tea, kept just shy of boiling on the wood stove. She did not know it, but he never used the electric baseboard heat or the electric lights that she had commanded in her regal way when she had discovered that he was "camping out" in the apple barn. Finding that she could not roust him and house him more suitably, she had had the loft insulated and furnished and had even installed a kitchenette and a full bathroom. Over time he had succumbed to indoor plumbing, but he persisted in using gas lamps and wood heat. He had a perhaps unreasonable conviction that electric heat and light would deaden the scent of apples, which had become as necessary to him as the air they imbued with their fragrance.

The barn below the loft boasted a working cider press and what remained of the year's harvest. The very floor boards beneath Fergus' feet, the walls around him had aged with the sweetness of apples. Their smell contained and informed all others: woodsmoke, Revelation tobacco, Red & White tea, the dirt and sweat of his labor in the wood that went deeper than water and soap could penetrate. He breathed this blend as a baby imbibes his mother's scent with her milk, its potency diluted only by the draft seeping through the cracks of the floor-to-ceiling windows.

These windows, installed where the upper barn doors had once been and opening outward in the same way, might have been a serious source of heat loss if they had faced any direction but South. As it was, on bright Winter days he could sun himself in a flood of light. In Summer's heat, he could lower bamboo shades if he chose. More often then not, he flung wide the windows, opening the loft to the breeze from the orchard. In blossom time, he moved his bed next to the open space and woke to the sound of bees.

The windows, high enough above the orchard trees that they gave an unobscured view of the carriage road and the pond, also made the apple barn a watch tower for Fergus. The pond was a midpoint, a watery boundary between the ancient, untouched wood and the formal gardens, now grown wild, spreading out from the empty mansion further up the hill. Exercising the ancient magnetic power of water, the pond eventually drew any wanderer in Blackwood into the range of his vision.

His sight was still incredibly sharp, although sometimes Fergus was not sure if it was his actual eyesight that was so keen or the ways he had learned to extend it. What difference would it have made to him if the distance was, in fact, a blur? He knew every variety of grass that grew in the orchard and on the banks of the pond, how each flowered and went to seed. He knew all the leaves, what colors they turned in the Fall and when they fell. He knew them emerging sticky and glowing in the Spring. He knew all their changes, how the wind lifted them before a thunder storm, revealing their secret undersides that always looked moonlit. He knew how the pond reflected their greenness and how the dead leaves lined the bottom of the pond. He knew all secret passageways through the tangled undergrowth and every subtle dip or rise of earth. Here was the ground of his being, the body of his Beloved.

Now, in his last days, Fergus could sit in the loft and be anywhere in Blackwood. One technique in particular his mother had made him practice ceaselessly as a child, the way another mother might have stood over the piano and kept her son at finger exercises. Thus, when he spied the figure at the edge of the pond, its cloak flapping and billowing, making it look like a wounded bat, he was able to follow his vision out over the orchard to the tip of a branch on the Crone Tree: an ancient apple that stood apart from the rest of the orchard, beside the stone bridge at the edge of the pond. Fergus chose a stubborn apple, still clinging to the bough, and entered it so that he might see from its perspective. He saw her.

The woman, she was the one he had witnessed last night, the one who held the snake and spindle in her hands. He was almost certain. It was not that he knew her face; he had only seen her from a distance, and this extension of sight did not so much afford him fine detail as it allowed him to receive a stronger impression. He brought to bear upon her all his powers of concentration.

As if she were glass or water, her face gave back the sky: its color, its mood. It was her presence he recognized, that sense of tension coiled in her, the possibility of power rising, breaking through, as when her lights had flared in the night sky. The cape hid her body, but he sensed, as much as saw, that she was holding something beneath the cape, protecting it with her arms, a gesture that made her appear to be with child.

She had been looking about her, slowly turning in a circle. Now she faced the pond again and gazed straight across it. All at once she became perfectly still, the shifting uneasiness of being at a loss gathered into a single focus. She remained poised for a moment while whatever idea had come to her—Fergus could not see that—took shape in her mind. Then she turned purposefully, crossed the bridge and disappeared down an overgrown trail on the other side, one that would lead her around the pond. Fergus knew the path, of course. He had deliberately allowed it to turn into a tangled maze in order to discourage people from crossing the dam. In a moment, if she kept to the pond trail—and she had little choice—she would come into view again. Then he would speed his vision across the water and take up another watch.

Ah, there she was, crossing the dam with no perceptible slowing of pace, her head bent to the onslaught of wind and rain. Now she was among the trees on the other side of the pond; he could just discern her motion. She was approaching the old icehouse. Fergus gathered his vision, aimed for a pine bough that might well brush her cheek, and hurled his sight with all his mind's might into the sharp green coolness of pine needles fanning out at the end of a twig.

His judgement had been accurate. She was walking towards his bough, her hands still occupied beneath her cloak. Though she ducked, his needles brushed her hood, which fell back, exposing a tangle of uncombed curls. Suddenly everything blurred and swayed as a gust of wind tossed his branch. When a lull came, she was nowhere in sight. How could she have disappeared so quickly?

Then Fergus saw that the door to the empty icehouse was open. A moment later she emerged from its depths, hoisting herself to the ground, first onto her stomach, then her knees, with her hands, which were now free. So! Whatever she'd concealed beneath her cloak, she had left behind in the musty darkness of the icehouse, beyond his present range of vision.

She stood for a moment; then she began to gather small rocks. When she had as many as she could hold, she leaped down into the icehouse again. After a time, she scrambled once more and went in search of pinecones, which she also carried with her into that void. Yet again she surfaced from the sunken floor. Fergus watched her eyes lighting on some Bittersweet growing nearby. She plucked a couple of branches. Then, turning directly towards the source of his sight, she advanced, hand extended.

Fergus felt the snap in his own spine. For an instant he was utterly unmade, suspended between forms, flailing, limbless, in terror. And then, there was his hand, curving around his mug of tea that was still warm. A wisp of smoke curled from his pipe. With ordinary sight, he looked out the window, across orchard and pond to the trees on the other side, where he could no longer see if she was still there, engaged in her mysterious rite.

Calm returned to Fergus, laced with excitement. He set down his mug and tamped out his pipe. Then, donning his oilskin and hip boots, preserved from his days as a sailor, he went forth to seek the second sign.

CHECKING OUT THE COMPETITION 8

MARVIN Greene followed Maria Washington and the usher—a large, white male whose arm had been offered to Maria and accepted—up the aisle of St. Paul's Episcopal Church. Even to Marvin, who was unfamiliar with the routine, it was clear that there was no question about where Maria would sit. The escort was a matter of style, part of the dignity of Maria's entrance. The second pew from the front on the right hand side simply belonged to Maria, as surely as if her name had been engraved on the brass plaque that was fixed to the arm in memory of someone dead and gone.

Marvin could have wished it otherwise. Sitting in the front of the church—it appeared that no one sat in the very first pew; that would have been too brash—made it difficult for Marvin to check out members of the congregation discreetly. That was the main reason Marvin had agreed to accompany Maria to church: to see what prospects there were for any sort of enterprise he might wish to consider.

Maria, as Raina described her and as Marvin himself had observed with admiration in the less than forty-eight hours he had spent with her, was a hustler. She was a fine, upright, righteous woman—generous, too, forever taking in kids, all races; forever bearing down on the sick, all races, with platters of fried chicken and cakes so thickly frosted your stomach turned just looking at them—but a hustler. Members of the Black community in White Hart always helped each other out, Raina said, regardless of feuds and factions, but Maria had a string of white people, too, who, for one reason or another, considered themselves under obligation to her.

Raina now sent money to Maria on a regular basis and generally looked after her interests, financial and legal. When Raina had been a child, if a landlord raised their rent unduly, refused to make repairs, or tried to evict them on some false pretext, supposing he was dealing with an unprotected Black widow—(Never mess with a Black Widow, was one of Raina's sayings)—he would somehow find himself having a sudden change of heart. Although Maria steadfastly refused to explain how it was done, all Raina's college expenses, over and above the full scholarship she'd won herself, had been paid.

Maria had begun attending St. Paul's in the early nineteen sixties, when Raina was just entering her teens. The minister at that time had been a Civil Rights activist and was hell-bent, as Raina put it, on integrating the church. Though three or four other Black families had joined since, Maria and Raina and such children as she had in her care at the time, had been the first, causing all the white liberals to be eternally grateful to them. That's how Raina had explained the situation to him when she'd briefed him for this visit to White Hart.

That Sunday morning Maria, whose car had given out two years ago along with her night vision, had arranged to ride to church with Mrs. Potter, a woman Marvin guessed to be in her sixties. Claire Potter, Maria had told him, lived in an enormous house all by herself, way out on a dirt road. Her children had long since grown, and her husband only put in a guest appearance now and then. Mrs. Potter kept horses and had a lot of pasture land, and she might well, Maria hinted, need some work done around the place. The man she'd had for years, also Black, was crippled up with arthritis. Maria didn't seem to feel that Marvin's total lack of acquaintance with horses should present any problem.

Marvin had been charming but noncommittal in response to the heartiness of the small, plain white woman who had picked them up in her 4WD Subaru. The car was a recent make, Marvin had noted, but crusted with accumulated mud and dust on the outside, and the seats, especially in the back where Marvin had been sitting, were coated with dog hair, of which the car also smelled quite strongly. Now why, Marvin had wondered, if you were rich enough to own a horse farm, would you keep your car looking and smelling like that?

And the woman herself: she wore no make-up, had gray hair bluntly cut without style. Her clothes, plain but expensive, jacket and skirt 100% virgin wool and lined with silk, he'd wager, were also covered with dog hair. There was some hay sticking to the back of her jacket. Clearly she'd been out in the stable seeing to the horses herself that morning.

Mrs. Potter was quality, Maria had assured him. The crème de la crème, by which Maria meant not just money but manners. He could do worse than to get on her good side. Marvin had answered what seemed like genuinely friendly questions with his characteristic skill and grace, so that the lack of information imparted was all but imperceptible.

He had not had much time to develop his rap. Maria had informed him only at breakfast that at no time in his life—for as long as he remained in White Hart—had he ever seen the inside of a correctional facility. And he did not and had not ever lived in New York City, either. Black and New York, in the minds of people in White Hart, equaled drugs and crime. No, she decided, he was visiting from Georgia. That had a nice quaint ring to it, bringing to mind *Gone With The Wind* and the Civil War. Whites up here believed they were in the clear on that score. It kept it all at a remove.

Marvin wasn't sure he could go for it. The deception didn't bother him. It was a matter of bringing it off. He'd left the South almost fifteen years ago, and it wasn't any South anyone had ever seen at the movies. In any case, if he had to invent a new life story, he was going to be the author of it, not Maria. They'd have to get that straight. For now he'd oblige her by keeping it cool.

Not that Maria was taking any chances. As soon as she could, she had jumped into the conversation. She and Mrs. Potter had gotten going on how was this one's gall bladder operation and that one's cataracts and had Mrs. Potter looked in on old Mrs. So-and-so with her broken hip this week. It seemed like between the two of them, they knew everyone in the County who was sick, ever had been sick, or even thought of being sick. Marvin, out of his element, had started to lean back, then thought better of it. He had on a dark suit, and he'd wanted to keep the dog hair at a minimum.

Now, since he couldn't very well crane his neck to watch as the church filled up behind him, Marvin settled into the pew, only to be nearly blasted from it by an eruption of sound that turned out to be music. He did feel justified in turning around to look for its source, which he located in the back of the church. A tremendous wooden structure, which took up the whole wall, enclosed what he guessed to be organ pipes. A skinny white woman was at the keyboard, set a few feet back from the pipes, throwing her body around, playing the instrument with her arms and her legs. Marvin had never seen or heard an organ like that. In the church back home that his grandmother used to take him to, they only had a piano. At the Protestant Center in prison there was a small, portable, electric organ. This was something else; you didn't just hear this music; you could feel the vibrations right through the pew.

"That organ hand-built by some folks come all the way from Germany," Maria relayed the impressive facts. "Back about ten years ago."

You didn't have to know music to know money when you saw it. Lots of it. Solid.

The music stopped, and all over the church, pages rustled and conversation subsided. Maria thrust a thick book at Marvin and pointed to a number on the program, indicating that he was to find the opening hymn.

Marvin obliged, and the organ blasted off again, raising the congregation to its feet.

The Church's one foundation
Is Jesus Christ her Lord;
She is his new creation
By water and by word...

The people belted it out—Maria, too. Obviously this song was some old favorite. Marvin didn't know it and decided he didn't need to fake it. Nobody could tell by looking at the back of his head whether or not he was singing.

A side door to the right of the front pew opened, and a Cross-bearer entered—white, male, middle-aged, what was left of his thinning colorless hair slicked back with water or grease. He was followed by a flock of women wearing loose, white, flappy-looking tops over black robes. There was only one Sister, middle-aged (Marvin was beginning to wonder was there anyone under the age of forty-five in White Hart?), the rest of the women were white. A few men, wearing the same get-up as the women and looking, Marvin thought, a little embarrassed, straggled after the women. Last came one man walking alone, all in white, a thin white rope tied around his waist. Draped over his neck, hanging down on both sides, the man wore some sort of scarf decorated with butterflies and flowers. Whatever turns you on, Marvin thought to himself, concentrating on keeping his face expressionless.

The choir—that's who Marvin figured they must be—turned left at the corner of the pew and headed down the aisle towards the organ. The dude with the butterflies turned right and up one step to stand, facing the congregation, in the gap of a wooden railing that separated the raised area behind him from the rest of the church. The set-up was similar to a court room, only instead of a judge's bench there was an altar; in place of a witness stand, a pulpit.

"Father Peters, the Priest-in-Charge," Maria whispered to Marvin as the hymn ended, emphasizing the title of the robed man who stood not more than ten feet from their pew.

There was no doubt about in charge; he had the stage to himself, except for a woman in the background—white, middle-aged—who had lit the candles before and now stood aside by one of the heavy, carved wooden chairs. With the altar behind him and his head aligned with a suspended wooden Cross, the Priest-in-Charge stood, a book in one arm, the other arm extended, palm up, just like Jesus in the raised velvet painting of the Last Supper that Maria had in her dining room. Jesus just as blonde and blue-eyed as you please, same as the Priest-in-Charge. Marvin guessed that's what the P.I.C. was supposed to be: a stand-in for the real thing.

Maria jabbed Marvin with a book again.

"Blessed be God: Father, Son, and Holy Spirit," began the P.I.C.; his voice was kind of high for the role, Marvin considered. "And blessed be his kingdom, now and forever. Amen." the people answered.

"Almighty God, to you all hearts are open, all desires known, and from you no secrets are hid...," the P.I.C. continued.

Marvin caught on. This book he was holding for himself and Maria had the script all written out. Marvin's estimation of the P.I.C., about sea level to begin with, took a dive. Shit, any fool could read lines. Marvin had never been one for religion, but he had to admit that some of the preachers down-home or on the Street could put on a fine show. They didn't need any book. If they quoted Scripture, they had it off by heart.

The whole point of their performance was to get the people moving: shouting, singing, dancing, fainting. Everybody got into the act, so the preacher had to have skill, working people up till they lost control and at the same time making sure he was the one in control. If someone got the Spirit and started jabbering in tongues or fell down on the floor twitching and foaming at the mouth, the preacher had to be fast on his feet, work it into his act, praise the Lord for a miracle, cast out a devil, whatever was called for, whatever would please the crowd.

> Lord have mercy upon us.
> Christ have mercy upon us.
> Lord have mercy upon us.

The congregation was singing the next prayer, slow and draggy, like they were at their own funeral. Definitely, nobody was going to be falling down on the floor, unless someone fell asleep during one of these long printed-out prayers. Must be they used the same ones every week.

Now everyone sat down again, including the P.I.C., who settled himself in one of the big wooden chairs in the altar yard. Then Marvin heard a sound, familiar but so out of context that for a second he couldn't place it. Ah...spike heels, clicking on the brick floor. He was not the nostalgic type. No, emotions belonged to other people and were there for the purpose of being played upon. But he couldn't help it; the sound moved him, calling up images of another world, one he had once dominated.

Marvin turned his head, just enough to see a woman walking up the aisle: white, middle-aged, yes, but not giving in to it. The clicking heels Marvin estimated to be about three inches high, giving shape to her legs. Her dress, a deep red clinging knit that ended just above the knee, revealed her figure to be ample in the right places. When she walked past him, he observed the sway of her hips, exaggerated because of the heels. Just before the step up to the altar, she turned to face the congregation. Marvin rated her make-up: a bit heavy-handed but skillfully, applied. Her hair looked a little like a battle helmet, sculpted and frosted but you could tell time and money had been put into the style. Her eyes were a hot blue, which could have been the result of colored contact lenses, but natural or not, their effect was heightened by the deep permanent tan that many well-to-do white women maintained year round, either by using sun lamps or taking regular vacations in the Bahamas. Marvin preferred to assume the latter. This was more like it!

The woman opened a heavy book to a place marked with a ribbon, and Marvin caught a flash of rings on her fingers, no doubt among them a wedding band. But that didn't matter; all the better; essential, really, for the game plan beginning to form in his mind. Her fingernail polish, he noted with approval, matched her dress. He liked women to pay attention to the details of their appearance.

"A reading from Isaiah," the woman began in a surprising—with that body—little-girl voice.

> Hear the word of Yahweh, you rulers of Sodom; listen to the command of our God, you people of Gomorrah.

Her reading was sing-song, as if she didn't much understand or care what the words meant. Marvin didn't either. He had caught the words Sodom and Gomorrah, which he knew were synonymous with sex, particularly freakish sex. He had long ago decided that given a choice between sin and salvation, there was no contest. What got on his nerves was that some preachers, who were so hot in the pulpit, were also hot other places and could put down some of the fiercest competition he'd ever had to contend with. As far as he was concerned, there wasn't that much difference between a preacher and a player—except that a player was generally more upfront about the nature of his game.

> New moon, sabbaths, assemblies; I cannot endure festival and solemnity.
> Your new moons and your pilgrimages, I hate with all my soul.

The Lord God sure got himself worked up. He was a jealous God. That's what the preachers always said. Marvin had never gone in much for jealousy himself. Jealousy was all about losing control of yourself while you tried to control someone else. A waste of time. Stupid, too.

> *If you are willing to obey, you shall eat the good things of the earth. But if you persist in rebellion, the sword shall eat you instead.*
>
> *The mouth of Yahweh has spoken.*

"The word of the Lord," concluded the woman, lifting the book and casting a foxy eye over the assembled; Marvin believed her gaze rested on him for a moment with more than a flicker of interest.

"Thanks be to God," responded the people.

"A-men!" Marvin agreed, ignoring Maria's elbow slamming into his ribs. He carefully did not look at the lady as she sashayed by, but he caught a whiff of her scent: "Joy," if he were not mistaken. Expensive.

Now the choir was singing something while the congregation sat and listened. Not bad, but no back beat. Marvin studied the program, trying to figure out how much more there was to go. That woman must have given the Old Testament reading. There was her name listed beside it: Alisha Adams. He made a mental note and resolved to keep the leaflet. This music must be the Gradual, by William Byrd. Shit, there was still New Testament, Gospel, Sermon, Communion, plus about three more hymns. He really needed a smoke.

Marvin didn't pay much attention to the New Testament lesson—some letter from St. Paul saying everybody better accept Jesus Christ, or else—except to observe the reader: white, male, middle-aged with a paunch hanging over his belt, broken blood vessels drawing attention to a lumpy nose, and watery blue eyes behind frame glasses. All Marvin's observations that morning pointed to an obvious conclusion: there might well be a market in White Hart for the services of the Marvelous. Of course, his advertising would have to be discreet. He didn't need Maria to tell him to leave his belt buckle—made up of the letters of his Street title and worn slung low over the parts it described—in the closet for today.

Marvin focused again as the P.I.C. stepped down through the railing to stand before the congregation.

"The Holy Gospel of the Lord, according to St. Luke," he said, lifting the book.

"Glory to you, Lord Christ."

> *He entered Jericho and was going through the town when a man whose name was Zaccheus made his appearance; he was a senior tax collector and a wealthy man. He was anxious to see what kind of man Jesus was, but he was too short and could not see him for the crowd, so he ran ahead and climbed a sycamore tree to catch a glimpse of Jesus who was to pass that way.*

Despite himself, Marvin listened. The P.I.C. was a better reader than the other two, but it wasn't just that. It was the details of the story; they made you see pictures: this little short dude clambering up a tree, a sycamore tree.

> *When Jesus reached the spot he spoke to him: Zaccheus, come down. Hurry, because I must stay at your house today. And he hurried down and welcomed him joyfully. They all complained when they saw what was happening. He has gone to stay at a sinner's house, they said. But Zaccheus stood his ground and said to the Lord, Look, Sir, I am going to give half of my property to the poor, and if I have cheated anybody, I will pay him back four times the amount. And Jesus said to him, Today salvation has come to this house, because this man, too, is a son of Abraham, for the Son of Man has come to seek out and save what is lost.*

"The Gospel of the Lord."

"Praise to you, Lord Christ."

"All right," Marvin murmured, softly enough so that Maria didn't hear. You had to hand it to this man Jesus: he did what he wanted to do, didn't matter what anyone else said.

"Please be seated," said the P.I.C. closing his Bible.

All the pews creaked together as they received the weight of so many broad middle-aged behinds. When all those cheeks were settled and all the leaflets had stopped rustling, the P.I.C. remained standing, silent, like he was waiting for the Lord to give him his cue.

Since the sermon was next on the menu, Marvin felt at liberty to look at the P.I.C., take his measure. Marvin judged the man to be taller than himself by two or three inches, which meant the P.I.C.'s height was average. His build put you in mind of football rather than basketball, though it was hard to tell with the robe. Marvin estimated his age to be not more than thirty-five years. He looked younger, but that could be the effect of his clean shaven baby-face.

He supposed the man could be considered good-looking, if you liked the type, and some women did. Some men, too. He would feel sorry for this dude's ass if it ever got locked up in prison. His eyes were his most noticeable feature, very round and blue. Right now they were making a survey of his congregation, pausing every now and then to connect, Marvin had no doubt, with the females of his flock. Marvin didn't need eyes in the back of his head to tell him that the ladies were sitting up and taking notice.

"Do you know," the P.I.C. began, "what is the loudest sound in the whole world?"

He paused; people waited.

"It is the sound of someone sitting next to you in the Cathedral of St. John the Divine trying to unwrap a cough drop." He paused for the laughter. "Quietly." More laughter. "I'm here to tell you it can't be done. Might as well be World War III. Louder than my kids on a Saturday morning."

Marvin laughed along with the rest of the congregation. That was a general rule: Don't step out from the crowd unless you're ready to sell tickets; particularly if you are the only adult Black male present, and you are sitting in the second pew. But he was not impressed. This guy's act seemed more like a second rate comedy routine than a sermon. What was next, mother-in-law jokes?

"Seriously, folks, yesterday was All Saints day. Now I know from the vast turn-out"—nervous laughter—"for the noon-day Eucharist that most of you forgot about it, or didn't feel the need to observe the feast, or were too hung-over from, uh," deliberate pause, "trick-or-treating." Laugh track. "Of course, I realize there was nasty weather: slippery leaves, a fallen branch or two. Nevertheless, with a few of the faithful, I drove down to the All Saints Evensong Celebration at the Cathedral simply because I wanted to remind myself of crowds. Throngs. Of Saints.

"Unlike those who dabble in the Eastern religions that are so fashionable these days, when you are a Christian, you don't go off and meditate in an empty room, seeking individual enlightenment, you don't go off into the woods and worship trees like a pantheist. No. When you are a Christian, you join the crowd, the Church, the Communion of Saints living and dead. Because a saint is not some old guy running around in a hair shirt. A saint is you. A saint is me. A saint is simply any sinner who has received the Grace of Our Lord Jesus Christ."

Now he was getting into it. Despite herself, Maria let a "Yes Lord!" escape her lips. Marvin could tell that she didn't approve of jokiness in a priest. She wanted to hear the Word of God preached.

"Take Zaccheus in today's Gospel. A sinner, the people called him. Now a lot of people like to go on about how Jesus loved sinners, the poor and the outcast. Some people even go so far as to imply that Jesus preferred the sinful to the upright, that his favorite people were prostitutes"—titter, titter—"although in fact the Gospel mentions nothing about prostitution specifically."

Then why are you? Marvin felt like interrupting. What do you know about prostitutes? About as much as Marvin knew about the Bible, he'd bet, which wasn't much. But Marvin had gotten the impression that Jesus went over well with the ladies, who all seemed to be named Mary and spent a lot of time weeping over various parts of his body. "Oh, Mary, don't you weep, don't you mourn," a fragment of a song his grandmother used to sing rose from memory.

"But it was never the sin Jesus loved; it was the sinner. And we are all sinners, ever since Eve took that fatal bite. What this Gospel is telling us is that Jesus came to save not just the Jews but the Gentiles, not just the poor but also the rich. Take Zaccheus, a wealthy tax collector. Now to the average person of Jesus' time, his singling out and favoring this man would be similar to his coming back today and saying, Hey, Ed Meese, come down out of that tree!"

The P.I.C. paused again for the laugh track, which came with a slight but perceptible delay. Marvin sensed there was some difference of opinion in the congregation about Ed Meese's need of salvation—or his right to it. As the laughter subsided, Marvin stole a quick glance around the church: the red brick walls; the stained-glass windows picturing long-haired white men in red and blue robes that made him think of the old-time hippies you used to see on the Street. The people, quiet again, were sitting still, their faces turned towards this guy, whether they liked his jokes or not, just like school kids, or like the civilians that packed the courts to watch a hot shot trial lawyer put on a show.

"But again," the P.I.C. resumed, ignoring the opening and closing of the door at the back of the church, admitting some latecomer. "You have to re-member, the whole point...."

The P.I.C.'s voice trailed off. Behind Marvin pews creaked as one person after another turned around. Marvin turned, too, following the P.I.C.'s per-turbed gaze down the aisle to the sight that had drawn all eyes. Not just some latecomer tiptoeing shame-faced into the nearest pew. No.

This man was standing at the end of the aisle, opposite the P.I.C. but staring all around him, like he'd never been on this planet before, like some UFO just dropped him here without instructions. Matter of fact, he resembled something out of a sci-fi flick, Star Wars, maybe. He was old, with long white hair flying back from his face, as if a wind nobody else could feel was blowing through it. He had a long, white beard to match his hair, and he leaned on a thick, carved wooden stick. Yeah, Ob-iwankanobe. Anyhow, some kind of bug. The P.I.C. didn't have a script for this.

Then the old guy started to talk, too quietly at first for Marvin to catch the words. Just muttering like some of the Street people in the city who walked around out of their heads or rode the subway all day when the weather was bad. He was saying something over and over, and it seemed like everyone, from the P.I.C. on down, was hypnotized. Nobody made a move.

"Where is she?" His voice got louder and clearer. "Where is she? Where is she?"

"Just who are you looking for?" The P.I.C. finally came to.

For the first time the old man focused on the P.I.C.. He stared at him, frowning.

"You know," he said at last. "You know where she is. The lady!"

"No, I'm afraid I don't. And may I suggest that you—"

"Where is she? The lady!" The man started in again; his confusion was turning him ornery. "I saw her. Before. The lady. Where is she?"

At a sign from the P.I.C., the ushers started moving in from behind. They each took hold of one of the man's arms, those big beefy men. Marvin got the impression that the old guy was as light as the wind that seemed to surround him, dry as a grasshopper husk. He was too out-of-it to offer much resistance.

"The lady," he kept repeating. "The lady. Where is she?"

The congregation craned its neck like one animal until everyone heard the click of the closing door.

"Whew!" the P.I.C. made a gesture as if mopping sweat from his brow. "Who do you think he was looking for? Don't we have any ladies here?" Uneasy laughter. "Hey, that's no lady, that's my wife!" The people laughed louder, all except for Marvin. "Now, that's the punchline. I can't remember the joke. But I think we've just had it."

The P.I.C. rolled his eyes and nodded his head in the direction of the door, leaving no one in any doubt about who was the joke and who was the joker. In the P.I.C's opinion anyway.

"Now where were we before we were so—uh—interrupted."

Marvin tuned out. He'd had just about enough. More than enough. It wasn't that he had any personal concern for this space case. He had never been one to put himself out for anyone. But it was generally understood where he came from that if a man had lost his capacity, so to speak, you didn't ridicule him. You knew: next time it could be you. One day you'd be riding high, on a roll. But like the tarot card called Wheel of Fortune showed, the wheel kept turning, and another day you could find yourself on your ass: busted, strung-out, broke, or just crazy. It was all a game with Life dealing the hands. Only some folks didn't know it. They thought their luck was their due, so they got all smug and righteous.

While he was hanging around in White Hart with nothing better to do, Marvin considered, he might amuse himself by checking out the P.I.C.'s own personal game, see could he maybe move in on it. After all, like he'd

noted before, they were natural competitors: the player and the preacher—
excuse me, the priest—in the game, for the game. These Episcopal ones
were not like Catholic priests; they could get married, and the P.I.C. had
mentioned his kids. It could be of interest to find out who was the man's
wife. And if the woman were not a total snag, he might just want to see
about her.

WHERE IS SHE? 9

HEY! Look at that!" Bob Whitely, one of the twelve-year-olds in Esther's Sunday School class, pointed out the second story window, then stood up to get a better view. Within seconds the other six students leapt from their seats, some of them vaulting over the table.

Esther sighed, painfully aware of her inadequacies as a disciplinarian. Glancing at her watch, she saw that there were only a few minutes left until it was time to go up to church for Communion. An attempt to restore order to her class would not be worth the effort. Besides, she was only a substitute teacher. Having absolved herself of further responsibility, she got up and joined her charges, who were still glued to the window. When she saw what had drawn their attention, she had to admit it was far more absorbing than today's lesson.

Arthur Billings, the church treasurer, and Karl Lyle, another Vestry member, appeared to be escorting—or strong-arming—the white-haired old man whom Esther had seen from time to time crossing the driveway and the lower lawn to the unofficial entrance of Blackwood. She and the children called him the Mother Goose Man.

"Look, Mama!" Jonathan had shouted the first time they'd glimpsed him. "It's the Man-in-the-Moon-come-down-too-soon!"

"No!" David, equally excited, disagreed. "It's the Man-in-the-Wilderness-asked-of-me-how-many-strawberries-grow-in-the-sea!"

Though her sons disagreed on which rhyme the old man embodied, they were right: he did look as though he had stepped directly from the pages of the Classic Volland Edition of Mother Goose, with his flowing white hair and beard, his ragged cloak, and a truly impressive walking stick. Esther had always wanted to get a closer look at the carving on it.

Right now the Mother Goose Man appeared to be in silent but definite opposition to the wishes of his companions as they grimly propelled him towards the Parish House—or attempted to. Art Billings and Karl Lyle were becoming increasingly distracted from their purpose by the mourning doves swooping down on them, flapping about their heads, creating enough turbulence in the air to disturb Arthur Billing's careful arrangement of his remaining hair over his bald spot.

While the two Vestrymen ducked and shooed the birds, the Mother Goose Man, in contrast, became still and composed. Then, without warning, confounding the impression he gave of slightness and frailty, the Mother Goose Man gave a mighty shake and loosed himself from the hold of his guards, knocking them off-balance. Before they could recover themselves, he turned his stick horizontal to his body, and backed away from the two men, as if they were dangerous and unpredictable. The doves accompanied the Mother Goose Man, making wider, slower circles. When he had put about half the lawn between himself and his former escort, he raised his staff, holding aloft his free arm as well. The birds broke formation, dispersing upwards. The Mother Goose Man turned, with remarkable agility, and made for Blackwood.

"Wow!" said Josh Hollingsworth, as they all remained gazing after him. "It's like the Incredible Hulk!"

"Who is he?" asked Esther. "Do any of you know him?"

"He's some crazy old guy," said Bob Whitely.

"You do not know that!" objected Angelica Jenkins, who resembled her first name, being as plump and fair as any cherub flying around on a Renaissance ceiling.

"That's what my Dad says," countered Bob, as if that settled it.

"Once my friends and me were up to Blackwood pond, fooling around with some frogs—" began Josh.

"Maiming, killing," interjected Angelica.

"What do you know, Angelica," sneered Bob. "You weren't there."

"Anyway," Josh resumed, "the old man, he snuck up on us and scared the sh—"

"The living daylights?" Esther suggested.

"Yeah, and we got out of there so fast, man—"

"He's nuts," Bob reiterated. "My father says he should be put away. In State Hospital."

"He's not crazy, he's magic," asserted Angelica. "You saw those birds."

"Time to go up to church."

The group at the window turned towards Arthur Billings, who must have entered the Parish House while they were staring after the Mother Goose Man. The church treasurer was still visibly flustered and kept pulling at errant wisps of hair in an attempt to restore modesty to his exposed dome.

"What was going on down there, Art?" asked Esther, sweeping her teaching supplies into a shopping bag.

"There was a small incident during the sermon," he murmured in discreet tones, "which, by the way, should be over now." He checked his watch, then turned towards the door.

The kids, accurately interpreting these gestures to mean that they would get no more information from this grown-up, bounded past Art Billings and down the stairs. He waited for Esther.

"Who was that man?" Esther asked Art, their conversation made confidential by the roar of the smaller children erupting from the basement classrooms. "I've never seen him in church."

"He's not a parishioner of St. Paul's, so far as I know," said Art. "He's supposedly caretaker of Blackwood. What that means, I suppose, is that Spencer Crowe can't or won't get rid of him. He's eighty if he's a day. She really hasn't managed the estate very well since her husband died. Naturally she has no business sense, but she won't take advice either. As for the old man, well, you can see he's not quite right upstairs. I think he ought to be put away where he can't do any harm, a nursing home, if nothing else. School property also borders Blackwood. I'm on the school board, and I've said for years that, frankly, he's a menace."

"But what happened today?" Esther pressed him as they neared the bottom of the stairs; any moment her kids would assail her.

"He walked into church in the middle of the sermon, obviously very confused, you might even say highly disturbed. He kept saying: Where is she? Where is she? We don't know who he was looking for. All we could get out of him was the lady."

The Lady! The hair on the back of Esther's neck prickled.

"Who knows?" Art was concluding. "Could have been anyone or no one."

Really, Esther told herself, it was ridiculous to suppose that yesterday's flight into Blackwood with her own Lady had anything to do with the random ravings of an old man. She had seen no one, and no one had seen her. It was just her guilty imagination that made her attach significance to a mere coincidence.

"Excuse me, Esther," said Art, leaving her side. "Karl," he hailed his fellow vestryman as he emerged from the basement surrounded by children. "There's a vestry meeting this Tuesday, you know. Listen, I've been trying to get some action taken on those pigeons for a long time. Now if you'll back me—"

"Mama! Mama!" David and Jonathan, oblivious to the episode with the Mother Goose Man, as their classrooms were on the other side of the building, ran for her, seizing a hand each.

The three of them walked up the driveway, through the bright, chilly, storm-cleansed air, to partake of Holy Eucharist as a family. This practice had been instituted at St. Paul's by Alan. Formerly, children had stayed for the first part of the service and had left just before the sermon.

"Our children," Alan had preached during a sermon on the subject, "must never remember a time when they were not welcome at the Lord's table." Alan had even coined a phrase, which he then had made into a bumper-sticker: The family that receives together believes together.

But it was different for her, Esther felt, standing in line in the aisle, her hands resting on her sons' shoulders. Other wives knelt beside their husbands; she knelt before hers, who was suddenly not just her husband, but her priest.

And what was a priest? Neither her own abortive studies at Seminary, nor her family heritage—her beloved Grandfather had been a priest—nor Alan himself had ever succeeded in making the role clear to her. The priesthood sounded so mystical when Alan described it: the apostolic succession, authority handed down—from Christ himself?—through the ages, through the church, which was both Christ's body and his bride. It was all very confusing, especially if you were married to one of Christ's earthly representatives.

Their turn came, and Esther and the boys approached the rail, knelt and raised cupped hands to receive the antiseptic little wafers—manufactured by Anglican nuns—that had less body than Wonder Bread, let alone Christ's flesh. Also they had a tendency to stick to the roof of your mouth. Esther almost never looked at Alan when he pressed the Host into her palm, murmuring in confidential tones, "the Body of Christ, the Bread of Heaven," although she knew, with a twinge of jealousy, that some women made a point of meeting his eyes. Instead she would study her own hands: the left, with its wedding band, on top, the right hand beneath the left—as she had been taught in Confirmation class so long ago—to guide the wafer to her mouth.

Or she would gaze past Alan's cassocked middle to the wooden Cross where Jesus stood rather than hung, St. Paul's being an Episcopal church and depictions of torture considered in poor taste. There was a platform for his feet, which were bare, a contrast to his Bishop's robes and the jagged crown of his Kingship. His arms stretched out with the arms of the Cross, not as if nailed but as if he were embracing the church. The wood, maple perhaps, was blonde, and Jesus had the traditional shoulder length hair and a neatly trimmed beard. Shadows showed gaunt cheeks and deep-set eyes that appeared to have no iris or pupil. Unseeing or all-seeing, Jesus looked out across the church over the heads of the congregants, his eyes at a level with the organ pipes. Did he know about the bat droppings smearing them?

As if in rebuke to her irreverent musings, the pupilless eyes seemed, all at once, to focus on Esther. Maybe that was why the artist had carved the eyes that way: for just that effect. If you stared long enough at their blankness, the eyes stared back, singling you out.

Uneasy, Esther lifted her gaze to a blaze of Archangels in stained-glass, their Southern exposure allowing the full force of near-noon light. Michael, Gabriel, and Raphael, she read their names, gaudy with their different colored wings and haloes, white-robed and clean shaven, in contrast to the human Saints and Apostles, who generally wore beards. St. Martin, who had a window on the West side, was an exception.

"Where's that one's beard!" Jonathan had all but shouted one Sunday, disrupting the Prayer of Thanksgiving.

"He doesn't have one," she had whispered. "He's a soldier."

Like St. Michael, she observed now, noticing for the first time the Archangel's purple sword and shield. Gabriel held a flowering sceptre and Raphael, a staff, though not nearly as handsome a one as the Mother Goose Man's.

The Mother Goose Man. Esther pictured him standing in the midst of the church, bewildered. She tried to imagine what he would see: the austere lines of the figure on the Cross, the bright, militant Archangels, assorted Saints and Apostles scattered about the rest of the church.

Where is she?

Were there any stained-glass images of women filtering the light? Surely through the ages women had been martyred and sainted by the score. A woman had given birth to Christ, for God's sake. Was she here?

The Lady. Where is she?

Esther didn't know; she had never looked for her.

"The Blood of Christ, the Cup of Salvation."

Nancy Jones, the church secretary, who was also a licensed lay reader, bent to hold the Chalice to Esther's lips, her female form muffled in robes. At least now women could administer the Sacrament and be ordained as priests, even bishops, theoretically. The General Convention had finally ruled in favor of women's ordination in 1976, when she and Alan had been in Seminary, just before they'd gotten engaged. Soon after that, Esther had dropped out.

Esther rose with the boys and turned from the rail, wincing as her high-heeled boot crashed down on the metal heating grate. Why couldn't she ever remember it was there and avoid it? A hand on the back of each son, she sheparded them to the first pew, which was, as usual, empty, and gave the children a good view of Daddy.

Just as she was entering the pew herself, some subliminal awareness, spreading out from her center in ripples of heat, arrested her. She glanced to her right and found herself looking directly into the eyes of a man seated in the second pew next to a kneeling Maria Washington. He did not seem in the least embarrassed to be caught in the act of scrutiny. In fact, having secured her attention, he held it at will—only for an instant. But in that moment Esther lost herself on the plains of his face: a night desert, moon-flooded; eyes, twin oases, brilliant, bottomless.

The prince of darkness.

The words sounded inside her, and she received an impression of horns rising, curving from his perfect head.

Then, without so much as a nod, without a hint of a smile, she was released, dismissed.

Clumsily, she turned to seat herself—or attempted to, only her buttocks met not with the cushioned pew, but with a haphazard arrangement of prayerbooks and hymnals that Jonathan had pulled from the rack and piled beside him. When she half rose to clear the books away, her lumpy woolen skirt brushed the pile and sent it toppling to the floor.

"Ouch!" cried Jonathan as they bumped heads when they bent to retrieve the books.

What blood was not already rioting in her cheeks rushed to join the rest. Finally settled, she stood, knelt, or sat at the appropriate times, joining in the prayers and responses without thinking.

What was wrong with her, she wondered furiously. It was horribly racist to picture a Black man as the devil, her internalized Gale-voice informed her in no uncertain terms. And why should she be so absurdly flustered by a casual glance from an attractive man? She, a middle-aged clergy-wife and mother of two. As an object of even passing sexual interest she was almost by definition a joke. Still, she could not help wishing that she had worn something a little less in character.

Esther was scarcely aware of Alan's Benediction or of the waiting silence during which Nancy Jones extinguished the altar candles. A liberating burst of Bach sent her sons scrambling rudely over her legs. Out of habit, she grabbed their arms.

"We'll be down at the coffee hour, Mom," David informed her impatiently.

All the children raced there in a decidedly unChristian determination to be first at the table where cookies and juice awaited them. "The first shall be last and the last shall be first" was a lesson that had not penetrated any part of their being. Esther turned and watched them ooze down the aisle around adult obstructions: little sparkling streams of energy rushing past boulders. They could have just slipped out the side door at the front of the church, gaining a head start, but the boys, unlike Esther, delighted in shaking hands with the minister outside the door, just like all the other parishioners.

As Esther stood up, she felt a hand clasp hers, and she turned to Maria Washington, whose other hand grasped the sleeve of her young companion's dark suit.

"Mrs. Peters, I want you to meet my cousin Roseann's grandson. She passed away some time ago. This is her daughter July's boy, Marvin. Marvin Greene." She added his surname as an afterthought.

Esther looked up at the man this time, as he was standing, though he was only two or three inches taller than she was. He inclined towards her ever so slightly and extended his hand. When she took it, he held her hand rather than shook it. His grasp was firm, and his hand pleasantly warm.

"How do you do?" he greeted her, emphasizing the first rather than the second "do," which had the effect of making the question seem more than a formality.

Fortunately, since Esther could think of no sensible reply, Maria continued to speak as Marvin released her hand.

"Mrs. Peters is the Rector's wife," Maria informed Marvin, "and those two adorable little boys be hers."

"Little devils," Esther added, smiling. You could always joke with another mother, of whatever age, about your children. Then she blushed as she recalled her dizzying vision of the horns.

"Now, now," Maria chuckled, knowingly, "all little boys be devils. That's just the way they's made. And speaking of the devil," she took hold of her young cousin's arm again, "Marvin here is up visiting from Georgia. He plan to stay for a spell, if he can find him a job. So if you and the Rector hear of anything he might could do, y'all keep Marvin in mind and let me know."

"What sort of work are you looking for?" Esther asked Marvin, remembering that Maria's daughter was a lawyer.

Marvin opened his mouth.

"Oh, Marvin ain't particular," Maria answered for him. "So long as it's honest work. Yes, just so long as it's honest."

Esther stole a glance at Marvin, wondering if he felt annoyed at having this older female relation speak for him, but he seemed more amused than anything else.

"Well, it was nice to meet you, Mr. Greene," said Esther, as they all moved into the aisle.

"My pleasure, Mrs. Peters." Marvin Greene nodded, raising his hand as if tipping a non-existent hat, and turned to escort Maria down the aisle.

"Mrs. Washington," Esther called after her; they both turned. "I just remembered. Alan told me that with the rise in membership there's going to be a sexton's salary available."

"Well, that's fine," said Maria. "And I know there's Vestry meeting this week, too. Well, well. That's just fine. Thanks for letting me know, Honey."

Marvin Greene said nothing for a moment, but one thick, smooth eyebrow, that followed so elegantly the curve of bone, arched slowly, a facial question mark.

"Sexton?" he repeated. "What kind of work a sexton do?"

Before Esther could answer, Maria, caught up in greeting other people, took Marvin's arm, and they moved on.

WHO IS SHE? 10

ESTHER, too self-conscious to trail down the aisle after Maria Washington and her second cousin—not second, her first, once, no, twice removed; that was it—turned towards the side door only to be accosted by a breathless Elsa Endsley. Mrs. Endsley was one of a number of seemingly indestructible widows, without whom the church would surely crash to ruin in short order.

"Oh, Mrs. Peters, what do you suppose? I don't know how we could have—well, you know, my dear, Spencer Crowe and I were both signed up for November Altar Guild, don't you see? We always do November. And I just didn't think—well, I managed by myself yesterday and this morning, but I can't stay now. I have a driver waiting. I'm supposed to be at the airport at two. My sister's flying in. Do you think you possibly could—I know it's an imposition, and I'll have to find someone—"

"I'll take care of it," Esther broke in, having gotten the gist three or four gasps before. "And listen, why don't I just plan to do the rest of the month with you."

"You're an absolute angel!" Mrs. Endsley puffed. Kissing her hand to Esther she breezed out the door, aflutter with silk scarves.

Esther turned towards the sacristy, pleased that she had a legitimate excuse to skip coffee hour. She felt a longing to be alone for a little while. Washing up and putting things away could easily take half an hour without a partner. Then, too, she had not actually served at St. Paul's before, though she'd attended several meetings of the Altar Guild. It would take extra time to figure out where everything went. She'd served on enough different guilds to know that there was usually a detailed instruction manual stowed in some obvious place. Still, a first run in an unfamiliar sacristy was like finding your way around another woman's kitchen.

A kitchen, yes. That was what a sacristy was, after all: a sacred kitchen, Esther mused as she stood in St. Paul's sacristy, the light strong but thickened by the plain, stained-glass, lead-fitted windows over the sink—the piscina, if you were high church. The walls, an ancient, graying yellow, did what they could to reflect the filtered light in a gallant effort to create an atmosphere intended to be cheery.

Esther did feel cheered by the sheer familiarity of this unfamiliar sacristy: the smell of candles, the huge chest for the fair linens, the high counter for flower arranging, the wooden corner cupboard neatly storing glass cruets and vases, bottles of Communion wine, the cleanliness and orderliness of it all.

Sacristies had held a fascination for Esther since she was a little girl visiting her grandfather's church. When it was her grandmother's turn to prepare the altar, Esther would go along to watch. Her grandmother did not explain what she was doing as she worked; rather she declaimed the names of the holy objects she touched, as if she were reciting poetry: the ciborium, the chalice, the purificator, the pall, the veil, the burse, the paten. Esther would trail after her grandmother, as she walked to and fro between the sacristy and the sanctuary, listening to the swish of her grandmother's skirts, the whisper of her silk stockings, her heels on the brick floor, beating out the authoritative rhythms of what her grandmother called "the stately dance." The Divine Service that followed these preparations, her grandfather's role as priest seemed prosaic to the child Esther compared to the mysteries of the sacristy that only women knew.

Esther began a closer inspection of St. Paul's sacristy with an eye to finding the manual. She paused by a bulletin board. A fine pen and ink drawing on yellowed paper, which Esther guessed to be about thirty years old, illustrated step by step the correct procedure for vesting the chalice. Next to the drawing, and of the same vintage, was a page clipped from some devotional pamphlet: *A Privilege* was the title of the essay. Esther read:

> Being a member of the altar guild is a privileged discipline, a service of love, an offering of time, when perhaps the children have dental appointments, ball games, and you yourself have people coming to dinner.
>
> It is preparing the altar for a saints' day, all alone in the sanctuary with the quiet, the peace, the beauty of it all—a special closeness to God; polishing brass and silver, knowing you are doing something beautiful for God, though definitely lousy for your hands—dirty nails and broken cuticles....

Yes, Esther thought, only women could be so privileged. She read no further, but glanced down and saw a more recent posting—a card with black bold-face type:

Requisites for Altar Guild Members

Attend church at least every Sunday.
Make a weekly pledge of support for your church.
Always attend Services when on duty.
Attend altar guild meetings; they are held for your benefit.
Handle Holy Things with reverence and care.
Do not let social activities interfere with your altar guild
work.
Altar guild work is not a job to be done—it is a privilege
given to you to serve Our Lord.

Well, she'd better get on with it. After opening and closing a couple of drawers, Esther found a loose-leaf manual and turned to the instructions entitled *After the Late Service on Sunday,* each step numbered and described in detail.

1. Take vested chalice into sacristy and put it on preparation
towel.

Esther looked around to locate the towel before she fetched the chalice. Any vessel, basin, plate, or the contents thereof, which the priest had consecrated for the altar, must never come into contact with anything so base and worldly as a linoleum counter. The preparation towel was, in fact, pure linen. Unconsumed wafers that had been consecrated were to be tucked into an ornate aumbry and secreted in a little carved wooden wall cupboard next to the side altar. Those that had not been consecrated could be taken from the silver "bread box" and stored unceremoniously in a de-humidifying cracker tin.

Likewise, unconsecrated wine could go back in the bottle. The consecrated remains in the chalice would have been downed by the priest, who would have then wiped out the last drops with the purificator. It was because of those few drops absorbed by the cloth, which would later be rinsed out, that the sink emptied directly onto bare earth. It was considered improper for a consecrated element to pass through a drainage system.

Such were the mysteries.

Esther read each instruction singly and carefully, then tried to execute it with grace and reverence. But she felt that something impeded her, something more than unfamiliarity with St. Paul's particular procedures. She nodded, rather curtly she feared, to the figure on the Cross, whose blank eyes followed her as she fetched and carried the silver and the brass. Since she did not have the prescribed white gloves, she would have to take care to wipe away all her fingerprints before she stored the Holy Objects and the alms basins in their tarnish-resistant Pacific cloths.

When she had retrieved everything from the sanctuary, Esther took the altar flowers from their vases and put them in some buckets she found under the sink. Alan could deal with them later. He would doubtless make hospital calls today, since yesterday he had dashed off to the cathedral. Or perhaps she would take some of the flowers herself to old Mrs. Crowe next door. If the Mother Goose Man was indeed under Spencer Crowe's protection in some way, then she ought to be told what had happened in church that morning and what some prominent citizens, such as Art Billings, were saying about the old man.

Now Esther was ready for washing up. She found a dishdrainer where it was permissible to let vases rest till she got around to drying them. Each Holy Thing must be dealt with singly, not treated as a common dish. She drew a basin of water, using only the hot. "Scalding" was an adjective that appeared several times at this stage of the instructions. Searching in vain for a pair of rubber gloves, she resigned herself and plunged in her bare hands, trying to remember that she was engaged in "a privileged discipline, a service of love."

The whole procedure, painstaking in ritual detail, was taking even longer than she had expected. She began to worry that the boys wouldn't know where she was, or worse, wouldn't care; her absence meant no restriction on cookie intake or on the exuberance of their activities. Alan never seemed to notice their public behavior; or perhaps he merely assumed that she would—or should—be responsible for it. As she scrubbed a vase, Esther looked around for a clock and spied one to the right of the sink, a shiny, new, white clock, incongruous with its stolid surroundings. In the next moment she forgot all about noting the time.

Several inches above the clock, in a cheap wooden frame, hung a picture of the Lady. Esther had not noticed her before. She was well above eye level, the dark frame blending with the wooden ceiling of the sacristy. Putting the vase in the drainer, Esther stepped back to get a better view. The painting seemed muted, suspended in a perpetual dusk. Only the golden flesh of the mother and her child gleamed. Esther crossed to the door and found the light switch.

Now the painting revealed the subtle richness of color that marked it as Renaissance. Of course it was only a paper print. Esther could see the creases where it had once been folded. Someone, some woman or some long ago rector, had unearthed it from a drawer and had it framed and hung in the sacristy to encourage the women, hand-maidens and matrons, in their devotion.

Esther stood gazing at the image. For all that it was a worn print, hideously framed, crookedly hung in a dusky corner of the sacristy—or perhaps because it was—the picture moved her. Mary wore a mantle that could be called neither blue nor green; it was a darkness that held both, a heaviness. Her dress was red, earth red. What you could see of her hair beneath her mantle was a gold that had nothing to do with blonde. Her lids were half-lowered over dark brown eyes. Her skin tones, that glowed even in dim light, conjured images of Mediterranean sun, olive trees, figs, dates, vineyards. So did her son's. Jesus, a deliciously fat, naked baby, about nine months old, was flexing and wriggling his toes. One dimpled arm reached across his mother's breast towards the black lace border of her dress. The other arm, obscured from view by his head, presumably rested on her shoulder. His fat baby fingers curled on the bare skin at the back of his mother's neck.

Esther drew in her breath. The picture was so sensual. She could almost feel the damp stickiness of a baby's touch and the soft roundness of the bottom Mary held cupped in one hand, her other hand just beneath his armpit, close to his heart. Esther studied Baby Jesus' face. There was no doubt in her mind—or apparently in the artist's—whose son Jesus was. He had his mother's gold-brown coloring, her long wide-bridged nose and full lower lip. His cheeks were chubbier as befitted a nursing babe, but he was his mother's son. Absolutely.

Esther raised her eyes to Mary's face again: the smooth, almost perfect oval, the merest whisper of rose in her cheeks, given fuller expression in her lips. Was it the veiled eyes; was it the generous mouth, not pursed exactly, but somehow restrained; was it the artist's intention or her own imagination that made the sweetness of the moment depicted almost unbearably sad?

Both Esther and the painter knew: Jesus would remain behind at the temple, without telling his mother, at the age of twelve. Later he would go off into the desert and into his ministry where she could only trail him with the crowd, if she dared. "Who is my mother?" he would answer when she asked to see him. Repudiated or not, she would watch him die, cradle his dead body as she had cradled him newborn, swaddle him for the grave as she had swaddled him in the manger. She and the other Marys. And what of the Resurrection? There was no account, as far as Esther knew, of a mother and son reunion.

The image swam. Esther touched her cheeks and found that they were wet. Why was she weeping? The inherent pathos of the story? Because she knew her sons would leave her, too? Or was there bitterness in her tears. Even anger. Because being a woman meant tending the body, so that others could ignore it, sacrifice it, transcend it. Wiping the tears and the shit, washing the diapers or the swaddling bands. Rinsing the purificator, cleansing it of lipstick stains and sacred wine. Polishing the brass, breaking your cuticles for God. Quietly, invisibly. Without making claims.

Who is my mother?

Esther switched off the light and returned to the sink where she emptied the basin of water, lukewarm now, watching it form a whirlpool. Gazing into that spiral motion, Esther saw once more the image of the Lady that had formed in her hands: her snake hair, her unabashed sex opening like a flower, like a third eye. What relation did she bear to Mary of the veiled lids and the cloaked head?

The Lady, who is she?

With a roar, the last of the water drained. Esther could hear it pattering onto the earth below. She turned off the taps as tightly as she could, dried and put away the vases, thus completing to the letter the last of the thirteen instructions. Locking the door to the sacristy, she returned the key to its hiding place behind a false-backed row of hymnals in the choir room. Just as she was about to slip out the choir room door, she changed her mind and went back inside the church. She wanted to make a tour of the church windows.

Being sure of the Archangels in the South and St. Martin and Jesus the Shepherd in the West, she headed East to the row of half-size pews that faced the side altar. There was Jesus in the fishermen's boat stilling the waves and then Jesus again dressed as a priest holding aloft the ciborium and the wafer. "Do this in remembrance of me," he commanded in black script below his image. This window made it clear: the priest was the star of the sacred drama; he got to say Christ's lines. "A woman cannot impersonate Christ," was one of the arguments against ordination of women that still persisted.

Esther walked on past St. Francis preaching to the animals, St. Luke writing his gospel, then Jesus again, suffering the little children—all male, Esther noted. Last came Abraham Lincoln, arms outstretched, palms open in a Christ-like manner. In the lower left was a caption that read: "My ancient faith: all men are created equal." Beneath the words was a depiction of a slave auction—with a woman on the block.

Esther found only one other image of a woman: St. Cecelia in a West window of the choir loft, cradling organ pipes in her arms as if they were a baby. Clustered around her skirts were miniature men: St. Ambrose and his choir. In the companion window was a full-size St. Gregory with a tiny Johann Sebastian Bach at his feet—he was gorgeously shod in purple shoes. Esther smiled at JSB, remembering Andy Beaven, who had dropped out of seminary after the first term to attend a conservatory and study organ. Whenever he had to state his religion on a form, he would write "Bach."

Esther turned East again and crossed the choir loft, concluding her tour with a window displaying a beardless and rather sullen looking young Jesus. With one arm, he balanced a long wooden beam; in his right hand he held a hammer. At his feet were a diminutive Noah, holding a miniature ark, and Solomon with the ark of the covenant in his arms. What commanded Esther's attention was the title of the window:

THE CARPENTER, SON OF MARY

Mary's son, Esther reflected, all at once remembering how Maria Washington had introduced her young relation through his matrilineage: her cousin's daughter's boy. Mary's boy. Yet Jesus called himself the Son of Man and spent much of his time talking to or about his Father in Heaven. Abba. The disciples called him the Christ, the anointed one. The Church Fathers, who composed the Nicene Creed, fixed his identity as the "only Son of God, eternally begotten of the Father...by the power of the Holy Spirit he became incarnate from the Virgin Mary...." And yet in the Gospels it was Joseph's lineage that was traced all the way back to David and, in one account, to Adam.

Son of Mary. No one called him that, except at Christmas. Then for a brief, rather pagan, season—which some Protestant sects still refused to observe—people were allowed to adore the mother and child, who so closely resembled each other in the portrait hidden away in the Sacristy.

The Lady, who is she?

A young virgin, ravished by the Holy Spirit and then forgotten? The ground, the background. The eternal silence from which springs the eternal word. Well, not entirely silent. There was the Magnificat, intoned by Anglicans at Evensong. Then, of course, the Roman Catholics had exalted her to the point where she was almost a goddess.

A goddess?

That was part of what the Protestants were protesting, wasn't it? She was an idol, and the Papists were idolators, pagans in Christians' clothing. Idolatry had never been all right with the Lord God. It was against the first of the Ten Commandments. The people's predilection for Idolatry had all the prophets foaming at the mouth. Whoring after other gods, it was called. Whoring. The Whore of Babylon.

The Lady, who is she?

The Catholics called her the Blessed Virgin Mary, the Queen of Heaven. Yet she was revered for her obedience, her unquestioning submission to the will of God. "Be it unto me according to your will." Of course, like many mothers, she was also a mediator. Officially that was her son's role, but the laity had always instinctively looked to her to shield them from God's wrath and punishment—Father's and Son's. She walked that edge that so many women walked, deferring to male authority, never openly challenging it, and at the same time protecting the children from it, softening it.

What would happen, Esther wondered, if Mary ripped off her mantle to reveal, say, dreadlocks? What if she decided one night to dance naked under the moon? What if she took a lover? Or flew into a rage? Even given her eternal maternity, what if the paintings and the statues showed what giving birth was really like: the pain and the blood, the power of it, the fierceness?

They would be afraid, Esther suddenly understood. Labor rivaled crucifixion as a form of suffering. What else was the Resurrection from the tomb but a simulation of birth?

What did she mean "they?" She was afraid. Right now, this minute. Something that had held the lid on, that had sealed off certain passageways, that "something" was floating like so much wreckage on a storm-swollen sea. Yes, the sea, for something else, vast and watery and out of control, was rising inside her.

Would she go under? For a moment, standing alone in the church, she felt panicky. Then a voice came to her from memory. Gale's voice—Gale, who had changed the spelling of her name from Gail to Gale, because of her affinity for storms—Gale teaching her how to swim in the ocean. They had gone on vacation together the summer after freshman year. Esther's family had been lake people, and she had never seen surf before.

"Don't fight the waves. Dive under, bob up, or catch the curl and ride the wave. The ocean is stronger than you; you might as well be a matchstick in comparison. But if you yield to the waves, they carry you, their power becomes yours."

Yes, she would yield. Then maybe this Lady would reveal who she was and what she wanted of Esther. With a jaunty step, almost a dance step, Esther turned from the Son of Mary and made her way out of the church.

BOOK THREE

THE LOAF GIVER

DRIVING HER
INTO THE DREAM 11

THEY were closing in on her. That's what it felt like. With as much violence as she could muster, Spencer Crowe swept her bed clean of the legal documents Grigson and Bates had heaped upon her—in an attempt to bury her alive, no doubt. The various folders did not make the satisfying crash onto the floor that a pile of books would have made. Even that pleasure was denied her in this age of cheap photographic copies. She refused even to attempt to remember that word with all the X's in it that some people actually employed as a verb. So vulgar! How much longer would she have the strength to fend them off: carrion crows hovering around this old carrion, Crowe? Ha! Not a very pleasant pun. Yet it was true. It was her flesh they wanted. Blackwood was her blood, her body. How could she bequeath it to anyone? Yield control of it. She had never done so in life; why should she in death?

Of course she had, for convenience and form's sake, left everything to her late husband, Gerald Crowe. As might have been expected, given that he was fifteen years her senior, Gerald had predeceased her, as the lawyers put it, rendering her will obsolete these twenty-five years. She had named no contingent heir. Until now she had successfully resisted updating her will, finding one excuse or another to put it off.

They had her cornered now, treed, as it were, in her turret room. Grigson and Bates had spent the morning haranguing her—yes, that was the word for it—on Geoffrey's behalf. The phrases "only living relation" and "the late Mr. Crowe's contingent heir" were chanted over and over like the chorus to an interminable ballad. "Time to think it over," had been her refrain, which sounded lame even to her. She'd had a quarter of a century already, as Bates rudely had pointed out. She should have asked—no, told—them to leave. The great thing about a butler of the old school was that he could and, on request, would bodily evict any visitor who committed an unforgivable breach of decorum, who was not, in a word, a gentleman. She could hardly ask Sabine to hurl Grigson and Bates down the spiral stair.

Besides, some intuition told her that stalling, however feeble a tactic, would serve her better than an open display of contempt. As long as they persuaded themselves that they could hope to secure her consent and her signature, they might bide their time. Meanwhile she must not show her hand. She used to be a pretty good poker player. It had amused Papa to teach her. She would bluff them. They would learn nothing of her real intentions. Never mind that she knew nothing of them herself.

For example, she would not tell Grigson or Bates that the only way she would ever have left anything to Geoffrey would have been in trust to his nonexistent children. On the whole, she felt those children were better off in that condition than they would have been with their parents. She did not want to provide Geoffrey with any motive for an eleventh hour reconsideration of his decision; for in fact, Geoffrey and Jessica, both in their forties now, were childless by choice.

They had actually talked about it at one of the Thanksgivings or Christmases they had invited themselves to, not wanting dear old Aunt Spencer—poor thing—to be alone. Spencer, admittedly more out of curiosity than sympathy, had scattered some hints, made a few remarks about the wonders of modern medicine that had not been available, alas, in her day. Jessica, finally gathering what Spencer was talking about, had made it indelicately clear that there were no problems of that sort. She and Geoffrey simply did not want anything to interfere with their "adult lifestyles." Lifestyles! Another of those horrid, modern, made-up words.

What these lifestyles consisted of, as far as Spencer was able to understand, were their careers—not jobs, mind you. Jessica did something terribly important in banking. International banking, Jessica would correct her whenever Spencer tried to remember how to describe Jessica's work in the course of an introduction. One used to introduce people by their family origins. Of course, one knew nothing about Jessica's. As far as Spencer could tell, Jessica had been conceived, born, and brought up in the Bank. She and Geoffrey had actually held their wedding reception there. Spencer had found herself indisposed that day, so she had never seen this famous site. Although she knew Jessica was nothing so common or poorly paid as a teller, she could not rid herself of the image of Jessica in her wedding gown, standing behind the bars of a teller's window, counting out crisp green bills for all her guests.

As for Geoffrey, his late Uncle Gerald had bequeathed him a seat on the New York Stock Exchange. He had settled his hindquarters into it at the age of twenty-five, having drawn a shockingly large income from leasing it in the interim. Her late sister-in-law had insisted on going into sordid detail about it, gloating, as it were, over what she called "dear Gerald's generosity and family feeling."

It was clear, even to someone like herself who did not understand the mysteries of finance, taxes and whatnot, that Geoffrey and Jessica could afford to keep Blackwood as a country estate, even to hire a staff and restore it to its former grandeur. But somehow, though Geoffrey had never been quite stupid enough to spell out his plans, she knew he would not. He had never cared about Blackwood. He would see only its "development potential."

"You're sitting on a goldmine, Aunt Spencer," he had once been indiscreet enough to say.

When she had pretended not to understand what he meant—rose quartz, perhaps, but gold?—he patiently explained to her about the new housing "trend" created by wealthy young New Yorkers looking for a second home in the country.

"Condominium communities," he rhapsodized, "with security, maintenance, and recreation all part of the package."

A look from Jessica had shut him up. While she apparently had no existence beyond the confines of the Bank—well, it was an international bank—Jessica was more astute than Geoffrey and knew the precise value of silence.

But why, Spencer asked herself as her fit of pique subsided, did she find the idea of condominiums in Blackwood so impossible to countenance? Apart from her personal dislike of Geoffrey, of course. As Grigson and Bates had pointed out, anyone who inherited Blackwood was bound to make changes. The property must be made profitable, it seemed. It must earn its keep, so to speak, as if it had no right to exist in its own right. Really, that was what she wanted: Blackwood to go on being Blackwood. Condominiums—adult only, no doubt—heated swimming pools, golf courses and tennis courts, however harmless or even desirable in themselves, struck her, on Blackwood's soil, as an outrage, a violation of, well, the polite word for it in her day was maidenhood. She could not bear it: that Blackwood should be forced to yield, should have no power to resist....

Grigson and Bates were right. She would have to will something. That was how she should think of it: not as relinquishing control but as retaining it from beyond the grave. Not a very Christian attitude, she feared. Lay not up treasures upon this earth where moth and rust doth corrupt, and all that. The whole idea of Heaven was that one was beyond earthly care and strife, which did, unfortunately, make Heaven sound very dull indeed. Well, she needn't go yet.

Meanwhile, she must consider her will, even as she sat helpless on her bed, a princess in her own tower. Escape seemed unlikely. No prince climbing her tresses, kissing her awake. Until now she'd managed to avoid introspection, woolgathering, it was called in her day. Who had time for it?

In her youth all of life was a splendid entertainment: horse-back riding, skating, parties, outings, excursions to the City, trips abroad. Until the age of twelve or so there had always been Fergus and the games they had invented together. She'd had remarkably few restrictions placed on her activities in her girlhood, and she had early formed the habit of doing as she pleased. Her father had called it "giving her a free rein." Both her parents took positive pride in spoiling her. Strong-willed, people had always called her, or willful, if they were feeling cross with her. She had accepted the general assessment of her character without much thought.

Really, all she had ever wanted was for life to go on in the delightful way it had begun. It hadn't, of course. One's childhood came to an end. One's childhood companion became moody and demanding. One went away to finishing school and became a young lady. One's parents grew older. One made an appropriate marriage. One's parents died. Life went on. Times changed and passed one by—as Grigson and Bates had not so subtly hinted. One grew old oneself. Whether one willed it so or not.

If she was willful, perhaps her willfulness lay in being, at the core, untouched. Only at the core. She was not mad, as perhaps Fergus was; she'd never been sure about him since his return. She had made adjustments, made the best of her marriage, such as it was; cared for and buried her parents; made provisions for all her people, as she called the former servants and laborers in Blackwood.

Yet, at heart, she knew she was sixteen. Something had stopped then, as surely as if she had pricked her finger on the fateful spindle and sunk into the hundred year sleep with Blackwood growing wild around her. What she willed, however impossible, was to wake and find she was sixteen again with a lifetime ahead of her in which to be Lady of Blackwood. Only this time, it would be different; it would be real. Not a game, as Fergus had so bitterly accused all those years ago. This time she would show him, show him what she really meant by the word Lady.

"Do you know the derivation of the word lady?"

Spencer could still hear Father Hearon holding forth at tea with herself and Mama. Spencer was thirteen that year, and she was in Father Hearon's Confirmation class. It was also the first year that she could take tea downstairs, if she chose, instead of in the nursery. And so she did choose, when Father Hearon was there.

Along with all the other female members of St. Pauls's, she had worshipped Father Hearon and had joined the needle guild for his sake. He was young and fair-haired and unmarried—the last unmarried priest St. Paul's had ever engaged; it had caused such bitterness among a number of prominent families when he married Fanny Thornehill and not the other contending daughters. Shortly after his marriage, he had moved away, eventually becoming a Bishop, at least in part on the strength of his almost English accent. Though he was an American, he had read at Oxford in Classics and also in Old and Middle English.

"Lady comes from the Old English hlaefdige, kneader of bread. Dheigh is Germanic in origin and refers to kneading clay. Now some people insist that the derivation is from Middle English lafdi, the di, derived from Latin, meaning to give loaves. In either event, there is agreement in associating the word with bread, the staff of life. The Lady of the Manor, then, was the source of the bread, the one who made it and distributed it. The loaf giver, which is almost to say, the life giver."

"Then there are no ladies any more," Fergus had snarled, when Spencer had quoted Father Hearon to him later.

Talk of Father Hearon had always infuriated Fergus. Spencer hadn't understood why; after all, Father Hearon had been tutoring Fergus in Latin and Greek, an arrangement made by Moira and paid for by Papa with his usual generosity. Perversely, Spencer realized now, she had taken every opportunity to introduce the rector's name into their conversations. In fact, conversation was hardly the word to describe their savage exchanges that year they were both thirteen, just before she went away to school.

"But why do you hate him so much!" Spencer had demanded during one of their quarrels. "He doesn't hate you! He says you have a promising mind."

Fergus, Spencer remembered, had actually spat, and she had flown at him with her nails, managing to gouge his cheek before Fergus had seized her wrists and twisted her around, holding her arms behind her back with one of his hands.

"You're no gentleman!" she had shouted, trying her best to kick his shins. "It just goes to show!"

"And what do you know about kneading bread?" He'd released her contemptuously. "You and all your kind."

And he'd started to quote to her from those wretched books and pamphlets he was always reading, the Fabian Socialists or some such nonsense. It was Toby MacAllister's fault, really; he was one of the gardeners and general handymen and an old sourpuss. Fergus hadn't liked Toby either, when he and Spencer were children. They both used to hide from him and play tricks on him, just to see the top of his bald head turn red. But when Fergus had turned twelve, he had started to work under old Toby, who had apparently found in Fergus someone willing to listen to his crazy talk. And to mouth it.

"You just play at being Lords and Ladies, landed gentry, with your fox hunts and your hunt balls and your quaint little church out of Grey's Elegy."

Grey's Elegy, Spencer vaguely knew, was a poem and not a Socialist tract. Fergus had always been more of a one for books than she had. That's why Moira had wanted him to study with Father Hearon. Why couldn't he just be grateful? Why did he have to make everything seem so disagreeable?

"You don't get your living from your land," he had sneered. "Your servants are hirelings, not serfs, thank God. Your family got rich from steel and railroads, from the sweat of workers they never even laid eyes on, let alone gave loaves to. It's not real, I tell you. It's just a pretty little game you play to avoid knowing the truth."

Yet Blackwood was real to Fergus. Why else had he come back to it after all those years? Blackwood had been real long before her grandfather, the one who made the fortune, purchased it. Blackwood had named her family rather than the other way around. They had been Smyths, at least for a generation or two, and before that Smiths. Perhaps it was an affectation, aping the English gentry, whose land and identity were one and the same, but Spencer had always loved the story of her grandfather deciding to name the family for the ancient wood at the heart of the estate.

Blackwood had been called that for as long as anyone could remember. When the rest of the land around White Hart was cleared by the early Dutch settlers, and later the English, the trees of Blackwood remained unfelled. For a long time no one owned Blackwood, though many people went there for kindling and firewood, taking care to clear only the dead trees or the diseased ones or trees that grew too thickly, crowding each other out. In part, to leave a healthy, mature stand of trees was only practical; in part the practice persisted out of superstition. Blackwood was believed to be haunted by the ghosts of Algonquin Indians, whose spirits still hunted the mythical white deer for whom White Hart had been named. To this day, though very rarely, people still caught glimpses of a white deer in the heart of Blackwood. As children, Spencer and Fergus had seen the white hart more than once. The deer had once allowed them to come almost close enough to touch it.

When Spencer's grandfather, John Blackwood, né Smyth, had constructed his gentleman's estate, with the labor of imported Italian stone masons, he had left the essence of the ancient wood untouched, being impressed by the tradition and the tales surrounding it. He had disturbed the wood only to the extent of clearing a bridle path through it and building a stone bridge over the stream that ran through the wood like an artery. The gardens, the orchards, the mansion, the stables rose on abandoned pasture land in a crescent around the heart of Blackwood. To John Blackwood's delight, the Italian laborers confirmed his instincts towards preservation: they avoided it, especially after sundown.

Later, in Spencer's father's time, a young pregnant Moira Hanrahan had appeared in Blackwood one May Eve, mysteriously. Like a vision of the Virgin, said a few sympathetic souls. Like a fairy woman, said others. Strega, said the Italians. Witch.

There in deepest Blackwood, amidst oak and birch, maple and beech, hemlock, spruce, and pine, larch and ash, black walnut and hickory, the children Spencer and Fergus had played together, measuring the girth of the trees with their arms that could seldom meet around the great trunks. It was such an old wood and the leafy roof so thick that there was not much undergrowth. Even where there was no path, Spencer and Fergus could run about freely; playing games of hide and seek, climbing, swinging from tree to tree on an intricate series of ropes they had rigged. They played endless games of pretend, often inspired by books Fergus had read. *Swiss Family Robinson* had enjoyed a long run, *Robinson Crusoe, Treasure Island.* Fergus had loved sea stories, and many a tree had doubled as a stout sailing vessel. Spencer would often play mermaid to Fergus' sailor, using her wiles to lure the unwitting swabby to a watery death. In Summer, the light was so thick and green, it was easy to imagine that they were living full fathom five at the bottom of the sea.

However intertwined the branches overhead, each tree in Blackwood was distinct, and Spencer and Fergus knew each one singly, as if by face or name. When they were old enough to wonder, Fergus and Spencer pondered the tale of his mother's unexplained appearance in the wood. They evolved rival theories: one that she was a tree woman, wedded to a mortal man, who had cruelly abandoned her, Spencer decided, leaving her with a baby and therefore with no choice but to remain in human form. The other possibility was that Fergus' mother was the mortal, wedded to a tree man, under magical circumstances that could never be recreated. When they inclined to this version, they would argue over which tree embodied the magical spirit of Fergus' sire.

It was in Blackwood, at the Ring of Trees, under a circle of dawn sky, the first of May when she was just sixteen, that time had stopped. Or perhaps she meant that time had begun then, ordinary time. Instead eternity had ceased: she had been cast out of it, out of her own paradise. It was outrageous. She had been too young to know what was happening, what it meant or would come to mean. How dare those angels stand there with their flaming swords barring her way back!

That was what she wanted; she willed it: to go back. For what had her life been since then? In her heart, she was as virgin as Mary, her own first name, but her womb had borne no miraculous fruit, no fruit.

And yet Blackwood remained. She had achieved that much. There was still Blackwood, and she was still its Lady, though admittedly on the verge of extinction, like, what was it, the carrier pigeons, the dodo birds? Very well, a dodo bird, and Blackwood the egg she had sat upon, brooded over, jealously guarded all of her life. And for what? Had she been incubating condominiums all this time? Never! As the young were fond of saying, No Way!

"Sabine!" she called, hearing her step on the stair. "What am I to do?"

"Eat your lunch," answered Sabine, stepping daintily over the spilled legal papers and setting the tray on the bed-table. Ah, onion soup with large garlic and herb croutons and a thick layer of cheese.

"I won't be able to kiss anyone this afternoon." Spencer inhaled the steam happily.

"Did Madame have someone in mind?"

"Well, you never know. I feel as though I've been waiting at least one hundred years. It's high time a charming prince put in an appearance. He'd better hurry while I've still got my youthful looks."

Spencer preened briefly, then got down to business with her soup.

"Sabine," she said between mouthfuls, "stop fussing with that flower arrangement and get your own lunch. I want you to eat with me. We've got business to discuss. I'm leaving you my entire estate."

"Madame would not be so cruel."

"Couldn't you turn the big house into an inn or something? Run it with your children?"

"I am planning to retire, that is, of course, after Madame does."

"Such a delicate way you have of putting things. But Sabine, retire? You're still a young girl!"

"Of sixty-three."

"Well, go get your lunch. You must help me think."

While Sabine was out of the room, Spencer registered the flowers. Chrysanthemums, the kind often left over from altar arrangements. Odd, she couldn't remember anyone stopping by with flowers yesterday. And hadn't Sabine only just now brought them in with the lunch tray? Could someone have stopped by this morning while she was closeted with Grigson and Bates?

"Sabine," said Spencer when she returned. "I do hope I am not becoming forgetful, but I cannot think who brought those flowers. Or did someone bring them just now?"

Sabine started in an uncharacteristic manner and miscarried a spoonful of soup. A few drops landed on her silk scarf.

"If I didn't know you better, Sabine, I would say that you were harboring a guilty secret. Come on. 'Fess up."

"Well, Madame, she came yesterday afternoon—"

"Who?"

"Mrs. Peters."

"Mrs. Peters!"

"She brought the flowers from the church service. You had said, Madame, that you did not wish to be disturbed, that you must finish reading the documents, because the lawyers were coming first thing in the morning. Still, I thought you might wish to see Mrs. Peters. I came to announce her, but you had fallen asleep over those papers, so of course I did not wake you."

"Of course. And I suppose you did not even make a discreet attempt to find out what she was doing in Blackwood on All Saints Day?"

"No, Madame. I did not consider it my place. But Mrs. Peters did wish me to give you a message. I thought it best to wait until after you had seen the lawyers, so you would not be—what is the word?—distracted from the documents."

"I know you have my interests at heart, Sabine, but I beg you not to baby me. Well, go on, what is the message?"

"She felt you ought to know. Fergus,"—Sabine called him by his first name; together they tended the kitchen gardens by the Big House—"made an appearance at church yesterday."

"Fergus? An appearance? Do you mean he actually attended church?"

"Not exactly. He came in during the sermon. He said he was looking for the lady."

"For me?" Her heartbeat quickened for a moment.

"No one knows, Madame. People said he seemed confused. Mrs. Peters was concerned, because she heard some people talking of how he is a menace. They mentioned State Hospital."

"Over my dead body!" Spencer declared heatedly.

Then with a chill she realized that whoever wished to clamber over her corpse, be it Geoffrey or some meddling fool from St. Paul's—Art Billings, she'd lay odds—might not have so very long to wait.

And what if Fergus outlived her? She had never before considered the possibility. For so long she had taken for granted—what would one call it?—the state of suspension in which she, Fergus, and Blackwood held their own.

"Sabine, you see Fergus fairly often." Spencer herself had not seen him, not to speak to, in thirty years, not since he had returned and they had made their agreement. "Would you say he is, well, confused? Dangerously so?"

Sabine took her time to answer. "Not when I see him in Blackwood, no. But sometimes I have met him in the village and then, yes, he often does not know where he is or who I am. He spoke to me once as if I were, I believe, his mother."

So Fergus saw the resemblance, too.

"I do not believe he is dangerous, not to other people. But I wish he would stay home, for his own safety. I will speak to him, Madame."

"Oh, Sabine, whatever would I do without you? But what is to be done? Please tell me, Sabine! When I try to understand those papers, when Grigson and Bates are here, pressing in on me, fairly measuring me for my coffin, I panic. I can't think, I simply can't think!"

"Right at this moment, Madame," said Sabine, moving the bed-table out of the way, then plumping the pillows and smoothing the bedclothes, "you must rest. This morning has tired you. You will rest now."

As if Sabine were a hypnotist, Spencer obediently grew drowsy.

"Will you arrange to have Mrs. Peters to tea?" Spencer struggled to speak through yawns. "And the children, too. Find my old book of Mother Goose rhymes and the other toys I've saved in the Chinese chest."

"Yes, Madame. Rest now. Sleep. Your dreams may tell you what you need to know. Sleep now. Dream."

"Dreams. Silly," Spencer mumbled. "Don't mean a thing."

But already she was slipping into the green light and greener shadow of an ancient wood. Facing her was a beautiful, angry boy, with black hair and blacker eyes.

DARK MOON 12

THE dark of the moon is the time to scry. There the old moon dissolves and the new moon is but a dream. There in the darkness of making and unmaking, spill your sight into a cup, into a pool, and wait...."

Fergus Hanrahan sat cross-legged at the edge of the pond in Blackwood, his mother's voice silent once more. Blackwood was silent, too; that's what the deep frost did: silenced the earth. Frogs dreamed in the mud; unborn insects lay coiled in eggs, their ancestors' husks ready to crumble to powder at a touch. The air seemed frozen, too. The trees held their breath, waiting.

Fergus waited, trying to subdue the impatience which all his life had impelled him, swelling at the slightest cause like over-eager buds in a January thaw. Would Spring never come? Would it never come again? Here it was another November, another dark moon and his mother telling him to watch, wait. No doubt, wherever and whatever she was, she knew that he had not scryed on Samhain at the Ring of Trees. He had been too excited by his vision of the woman in the church yard. That had been sight enough for one night, and he had been so sure that everything would fall into place, everything be revealed to him at last.

Then the very next day the woman had come to Blackwood with the figure of the Lady. The Lady was still there in the depths of the icehouse, but the woman had disappeared. He had searched for her fruitlessly in Blackwood. He had even ventured to seek her in the church; the only result of his efforts had been an outrageous assault upon his person by two dark-suited thugs.

Since retreating to Blackwood, he had eased his impatience by braiding a rope of dried sage, rosemary, sweet grass and lavender. Earlier this evening he had gone to the icehouse and burned the herbs to sweeten the dank air and to hallow the cavernous space where the woman had built a makeshift shrine to the Lady.

Now there was nothing to do but wait. Wait and see.

Fergus gazed into the pond, its water still free from Winter's constraint.

The smooth surface gave back the spidery arms of the Crone tree, glittering with reflected stars: Winter blossom, Winter fruit. Fergus breathed the cold air and let it fan the flames of an inner fire. He focused on the image of flame licking, leaping from his center, and soon the warmth spread to his limbs and extremities. Ah, his mastery of these small creaturely magicks had not deserted him.

Mastery had never been difficult for him in any form of learning, whether it was the Latin and Greek he'd studied long ago with that foppish Father Hearon or the knot tying, ship caulking and carpentry he'd learned as a merchant marine. During the long, wandering years he had practiced many trades. He'd been a soldier in the Lincoln Brigade, a short-order cook, an itinerant tinker, an extra in a Shakespearean troupe. During World War II he had stumbled upon an encampment and become part of the Gypsy Underground. Always after interludes on land, he had returned to the sea, until his roots, preserved so long in brine, began to hunger for earth, for Blackwood. These last thirty years he had practiced the green arts of gardening and enchantment. Only the art of patience eluded him; he could not master it with quickness. Still, he had acquired enough craft in his life to know the meaning of mastery. And mastery meant nothing unless it made you ready for what could not be mastered: a storm at sea, a great vision.

Warmed through, Fergus waited for pictures that might or might not come. At last his concentration caused a ripple. Shapes began to form out of the random interplay of light and dark. Or they rose from some muddy deep of pond or sky, sluggish fish, swimming to the surface to snap at stars. Gradually the images stilled, as if someone had been stirring a stew and then withdrawn the spoon.

Fergus saw an old man, with unkempt hair and tattered clothes, standing in some assembly place, surrounded by a sea of unknown faces, and looking crazed. Curiously, the man carried a carved staff that looked exactly like Fergus' own. Now what could that mean?

Then, all at once, with a sickening jolt in the pit of his stomach, Fergus knew: it was himself, himself as he had appeared in the church to all those strangers. He could scarcely credit it. For he did not look at all like that from the inside, his hair being black and he a young man. Before he could fully absorb the shock of this revelation, the image dissolved.

But its meaning remained plain: the vision had come to him as a warning. Or as a reminder, since he already knew or should have known: it was dangerous for him to leave Blackwood. Outside its bounds his power paled, a candle flame at noon. Even if he had found the woman in the church, he would never have been able to make her understand what he still did not understand himself. Fergus felt disgusted. No fool like an old fool. Had only his appearance changed since that May morning when he had tried to seize Fate and shape it to his liking? His life had been a long, long teaching, and he, it seemed, an intractable pupil.

Well, perhaps it was not too late, not too late to wait, to await instruction. If he was not to go ferret out this woman and demand that she play her destined role, whatever it might be, perhaps the water would show him what his own part was. He turned his attention to the water again, casting his thoughts into the pond like so many pebbles, letting them sink into oblivion. Visions had no patience with impatience. A bud could not be pried into flower.

Fergus waited. Light and darkness played games with each other, teasing him, now forming circles, now flaming spears, now the oval of an almost face, a tangle of hair, a jumble of anonymous limbs, now stillness again and the exact reflection of branches and stars. Perhaps it was over.

Then the pond went black. Before he saw anything, he heard her voice, crying his name over and over again as she had that morning when it was too late. Was it too late? Come back, she called to his back. Fergus, come back.

Now he turned and saw her in her white nightgown, dark red hair bleeding down her back and shoulders from the wound her face had become; her eyes with their color snatched from the sky or plucked from the bed of periwinkle at her feet.

Fergus, Fergus.

He opened his mouth to speak, but no sound came out. He tried to take a step towards her, but his legs could not move. Then she was gone, and he found himself sitting at the edge of the pond, trembling and drenched in sweat. There was a taste of salt on his tongue, and he realized he was weeping. It happened like that sometimes: that a seeing would take you right inside. It was like being caught in an ocean breaker and boiled. When you finally washed up on shore, ravished, exhausted, you were too weak even to try to understand the meaning.

All Fergus wanted now was to crawl into his bed in the apple barn and sink into sleep, dreamless sleep. But still he waited, though the fire he breathed into his veins had burned to ash, and the frost crept over his boots. Visions, his mother had instructed him, often come in threes. Like breakers, thought Fergus the sailor. He waited. The next seeing might make it all come clear.

Fergus had almost succumbed to ordinary sleep when the reflections in the water once more shifted into shape. A whole scene formed before his

eyes. This one contained no seed of memory. He did not recognize the figure before him at all or the setting.

Fergus studied the man, a young man, an Ethiope by his complexion
and the cast of his features, with a hint of something else, some sheen of
copper or bronze. He sat on the floor of a slope-eaved room lit by candles
stuck in old wine jugs. In the flickering light, Fergus could just make out
roses on the ancient wallpaper that was peeling in some places and
stained in others from a leak in the roof. The carpet bloomed with roses,
too, and the bed had a ruffled spread, probably pink. There was a dresser
with a lace scarf and a standing mirror. All the other available space in
the room was taken up with bookshelves.

The man sitting cross-legged on the floor seemed indifferent to his surroundings, neither owned by them nor owning them. To his left a gabled
window was propped open by a stick. Smoke from the cigarette dangling
from his lips meandered towards the open window with the same lei-
surely grace that marked the Ethiope's movements. He was unwrapping
an object swaddled in black cloth—the material looked like silk. Then,
holding whatever it was in one hand, with the other hand he spread out
the fabric. Just in time, he took the cigarette from his lips, deftly flicked
the long ash, then stubbed it out in what looked like a tea saucer. His
hand, sporting a pinky ring, looked well cared-for, nails filed to perfect
ovals. Free of the cigarette, his right hand joined his left in shuffling what
Fergus now recognized as a deck of cards.

The vision was so vivid that Fergus could hear the cards as they shifted
the air and pattered against each other, slipping back into a changed
unity. The Ethiope shuffled for a long time, sometimes making the cards
arc in a bridge, sometimes drawing them out, defying gravity, into the air.
Just when it seemed they must fall and scatter to the four corners, he'd
catch them and make them dance up and down, in and out of each other.
The motion of his hands looked so effortless that the cards appeared to
move themselves, while his hands just hovered there providing a boundary, the way a stage frames a play. Most of the time he kept his eyes
closed, eyes so large that Fergus could see their curve beneath the lower
lid.

At last he laid the deck face down on the cloth. He waited for a moment. Then, eyes still closed, he cut the deck three times with his left
hand. By now Fergus felt certain that these were not playing cards but a
Tarot deck. Neither he nor his mother had used cards as a medium, but
he was familiar with Tarot, particularly the Greater Trumps, from his so-
journ with the Rom. The Gypsies themselves did not take the cards seriously, regarding them merely as props to impress the Gaje and no

substitute for true second sight. Still, it was a reading by the Phuri Dai of his Kumpania that had persuaded Fergus it was time to end his wanderings and return to Blackwood. He could still remember the card that had spoken to him: The Empress. He wondered what question the Ethiope had asked of his cards.

Opening his eyes, the man re-stacked the deck, then turned over the top card. Fergus was drawn deeper into the vision, so that he no longer saw the room or the Ethiope or even the card lying on the black silk; only the image.

A woman stood between what appeared at first to be the columns of an ancient temple, but even as he identified them, they changed into the trunks of trees, silvern with moonlight. Against a twilit sky, the full moon rose behind the woman's head, resting between the horns of her headdress. From the horns flowed white robes, contrasting with the woman's face, which was blacker than the Ethiope's. Her dark hands emerged from winged sleeves, and she held, just beneath her breasts, a round, golden loaf of bread, creased at the center with a cross. Just as the columns had changed into trees, the loaf changed, too, becoming the moon, then, growing larger and brighter, the sun; now the cross at the center blazed in all directions, a star. At last the loaf appeared to Fergus as part of the woman herself, her womb, rounded and rising with life.

Surfacing, Fergus once again saw the card, glowing against the black silk. Above the picture, echoing the temple columns—or trees—stood the Roman numeral II; at the woman's feet, her title: THE HIGH PRIESTESS.

Then, without warning, the Tarot card vanished. Fergus caught the merest glimpse of the Ethiope, a fresh cigarette in his hand, a startled expression on his face—what had he asked?—Then the pond went black.

TODAY
I BAKE 13

ESTHER Peters lifted one perfectly round loaf from the baking sheet and tapped the bottom. The unmistakable hollow sound or feel—she was never sure which—rewarded her. Lifting the loaf to her face, she inhaled its warm, somehow reassuring fragrance. Ah, this loaf was the one baked with rosemary and dill. Setting the loaf on a rack to cool along with three others, Esther stood back to admire her work.

The four loaves sat fatly, radiant in their roundness. Outside the kitchen window lowered a dingy sky, stingy, covered with stubborn clouds that would neither rain nor budge. Her loaves, in contrast, glowed like small suns. For an instant, Esther's pleasure in the fresh baked bread and in herself was so strong that she felt powerful enough to go outside and lift that heavy sky, throw its weight off the world.

Then the phone rang once, twice. As Esther moved to answer it, the ringing stopped. Of course, it was the church phone, too, and Nancy Jones would be in the office by now. Esther glanced at the kitchen clock. It was past ten, and here she was still in her nightgown. A deplorable habit for a clergy wife, not dressing till after breakfast, a vague time period that could and sometimes did extend until lunch. What with getting the children ready for school and fixing breakfast, she found it easier to leave her own dressing until later, unless, of course, it was her morning for the carpool. Still, what if someone came to the door, by no means a rare occurrence in a rectory? Or worse, what if Alan came wandering up in search of a midmorning snack? Was he in his office today? Had he said where he would be? He hated finding her undressed. It was so sloppy and irresponsible; it confirmed all his worst suspicions about her.

Well, that answered the immediate question of what she should do next on this first morning in more than a week that she'd had any time to herself. She headed up the stairs to her bedroom in search of decent attire. First Jonathan, then David had been at home sick with a bad cold and fever. Jonathan had developed an ear infection, too. Colds at the beginning and the end of the Winter season, when the weather was changing and

unpredictable, mild one day, freezing the next, were often the most virulent. In a way, she hadn't minded. Tedious as it was, having sick children
made her life simple. Everything else went on hold.

Now she would have to think again, if it was possible to think about
things you didn't understand: her little shrine in the icehouse, for example,
the whole troubling business of the Lady, which had become a silence between herself and Alan. At least she experienced their careful avoidance of
any reference to the wrangle over the playdough figure as a silence. Perhaps that tension underlay Alan's outburst about Gale, although Gale, as
a topic, was in herself provoking: the surviving Amazon, Alan had
dubbed her.

Esther had invited Gale, and her current lover, Gabrielle—her girl-
friend, Alan said with distaste—to spend Christmas at the rectory. It was
perfectly true, as Alan protested, that Esther hadn't consulted him first. It
was also true that she had acted on impulse.

"I don't understand you," Alan had railed at one point. "You hate going
to the parties we have to attend. You won't take any responsibility in the
parish; you don't even like to pour coffee at coffee hour. But whenever
you get a notion in your head, you act on it, without considering the implications. Like telling Maria Washington about that sexton's job before the
Vestry even had a chance to meet and discuss it. Or like the time in Syracuse you invited the whole Head Start Center and all the parents to
Shrove Tuesday supper."

"Isn't that the sort of thing Jesus was always doing?" murmured Esther,
not quite sure whether or not she intended Alan to hear.

"That was a cheap shot, Esther," Alan shot back; apparently he had
heard. "You're deliberately misunderstanding me. I'm not saying there's
anything wrong with generosity. It's just that you're so undisciplined
about it. Impulsiveness is not the same as generosity anyway. When you
act on impulse, you're usually not thinking of anyone but yourself." He
had stalked out of the kitchen.

Esther had decided not to pursue Alan or the subject. After all, she was
in the wrong, making plans without considering him, and he had not insisted that she cancel Gale. Best to let the matter be. More talk of Gale
could lead to no good. She might let slip that Gale's latest cause was
unionizing street prostitutes; that was how she had met Gabrielle. Of
course, Alan was probably all for prostitutes' rights in the abstract, just as
he was for gay rights. There was no need to get into the particulars with
him. Almost without thinking, she had begun to gather ingredients for
baking bread the next morning. When in doubt, bake.

"Today I bake; tomorrow I brew," Esther chanted aloud as she slipped out of her nightgown. But she couldn't remember the rest of what must be a rhyme, nor its origin. Mother Goose? No, a fairytale. Her memory yielded an image of Rumplestiltskin dancing exultantly around his fire in the deep of the forest, and still she could not remember the conclusion of the verse.

She bet Spencer Crowe knew. Esther dropped her nightgown into the laundry hamper and went into the bathroom to wash. People in that generation had memorized volumes of poetry and Bible verse. Even when they were senile, they could still quote—at length. Towards the end, Esther's grandmother had spoken almost exclusively in verse: whole chunks of Shakespeare, obscure Victorian poetry, and, of course, the Psalms.

Not that Spencer Crowe was senile; her mind was as sharp as the end of her nose. An uncharitable image, Esther chided herself. In fact, Spencer Crowe was one of the handsomest women of any age that Esther had ever met. But she made Esther nervous.

Esther and the children had obeyed a summons to tea last week, just before David had gotten sick. Spencer Crowe had never taken much notice of Esther before, and, on the few occasions they'd met, she'd addressed Esther by the names of several of her predecessors. Esther had supposed they'd been invited because of the flowers and the message about the old estate keeper. Instead, Mrs. Crowe had appeared to be more interested in Esther's habits.

"Tell me, Mrs. Peters, do you often walk in Blackwood?"

Although Mrs. Crowe would not come right out and say: "What were you doing in the woods on All Saints Day?" Esther suspected that's what she wanted to know. Esther's answers had been as indirect as the questions and, she sensed, satisfactorily unsatisfactory. The old lady loved a mystery, it seemed. Perhaps that was why she was so cagey in response to Esther's questions about the Mother Goose Man.

To Esther's relief, Spencer Crowe had finally tired of cat and mouse and had turned her attention to the children, reading to them from an ancient edition of Mother Goose. Esther and Sabine Weaver, meanwhile, had conversed in French. Esther had spent her junior year abroad, becoming fluent in the language and discovering that she lacked the talent to be an artist. As she exercised her rather stiff French, she noticed Spencer's manner with the children, confidential and conspiratorial. It was their shared secret that Spencer was one of them, an ancient child. Their mutual delight was obvious. The boys displayed manners on parting that Esther had not been confident they possessed. She saw Sabine and Spencer exchange approving glances. She had known one of those rare and heady moments of triumph as a mother.

On the way home, David and Jonathan had confided in Esther their belief that Mrs. Crowe was Mother Goose, the real Mother Goose. That was why she had a Mother Goose Man in her woods.

Of course, Esther mused, as she opened bureau drawers considering what to wear, it made perfect sense. She pictured Spencer Crowe in a black steeple hat, mounted on her goose, soaring up to the moon, her profile an image of the half moon's, the lady. And who was the Mother Goose Man but the man in the moon come down too soon, still dazed by his descent. If Spencer Crowe had witnessed her flight into Blackwood, had the old man observed her, too? Perhaps it was time to find out. That she was afraid was all the more reason to go into Blackwood. The old man was looking for the Lady. Well, so was she.

Esther selected the hooded lavender sweatsuit Gale had given her for her birthday in late September. She hadn't worn it then, as the weather was sultry. "The color will bring out that touch of red in your hair and that hint of green in your eyes," Gale had informed her. Esther had teased her about sounding like a beauty columnist in a fashion magazine.

"Hey," Gale had rejoined. "I'm into being beautiful—on my own terms."

Gale had gone through what she called a radical uglification stage, insofar as someone with Gale's natural beauty could succeed with such a plan. Then it had dawned on her that in making herself ugly to spite men she was as much in thrall to them as if she had studied how to please them. Now she enjoyed her beauty. "Because it's mine," as she put it.

Esther studied herself in the mirror with the hood framing her face and decided that Gale was right about the effect the color had on her coloring, then she pushed the hood back and ran a brush through her hair. It was at an awkward stage, not long, not short. For the past few years, she'd kept it cut and styled to keep the kinkiness under control. Frizzy hair was in fashion now, she knew, and lots of people with straight hair were pouring chemicals on their heads in the quest for curls. But when she had come of age, girls with hair like hers were ironing it straight. Her mother had always disparaged her frizz, wondering where it could have come from—not her side of the family! And her father had teased her and taught her brother to do the same: Medusa! Medusa! let down your long hair. Ouch! It bit me! Medusa! No wonder her fingers unconsciously fashioned snakes coiling from the Lady's head.

Esther pulled the brush through her hair once more, brushing it up and out. Maybe she wouldn't get it cut this time, just let it go wild, grow wild. She turned from the mirror and headed downstairs feeling brave and fierce. She would go visit the Lady in the icehouse, ask her what she wanted. She didn't know where else to begin.

She had tried the library, slipping out one evening when Alan was home and the kids were in bed. In the card catalogue, she had looked up the word goddess. She had found one title, *The Goddess Abides* by Pearl S. Buck. She'd stayed up reading it that night: the story of a fantastically wealthy, beautiful, young widow who discovered that her purpose in life was to be a muse to brilliant men. This definition didn't square with Esther's experience of the Lady. The title quotation in the novel had led her to Robert Graves' *The White Goddess,* also in the library. It looked more promising as a source of information, but it was a fat book, fearfully scholarly. So far Esther hadn't gotten any further than the introduction in which the author warned, "This book is not for tired or lazy minds." Esther knew she was guilty on both counts.

As she passed by the kitchen, the scent of her bread wafted over her. She paused to enjoy it, then made a detour into the pantry. After opening and closing a couple of drawers, Esther found at the bottom of one a purple net filet, one of the most useful souvenirs from her year in France. Then she tucked three of the loaves into the magically expanding filet; the bread looked particularly golden against the purple mesh. She might leave some bread at the Gatehouse on her way back. In the meantime, if she encountered anything big and bad in Blackwood, she would thrust a loaf at it. Really, that's what Red Riding Hood should have done: just handed over the goodies. Thus armed, Esther pulled up her lavender hood and went out the back door.

Gathering momentum, she broke into a run in the driveway. With her mind on the Lady and the lurking estate keeper, her eyes on the break in the wall, she did not notice the figure emerging from the office of the parish house.

"Mrs. Peters," someone called.

Esther stumbled to an ungraceful halt, like a kid playing red light, green light. She turned towards the voice and saw Maria Washington's cousin standing at the foot of the steps eyeing her. Did he always look amused?

"Oh, hello." Esther retraced some of her steps until she stood within a few feet of him. "I'm sorry. I've forgotten your name."

But not your face, she added to herself. Nor the disorienting sensations that accompanied her first sight of it. Inwardly, she got a grip on herself, the way she might hold tightly to a child's hand at a dangerous intersection.

"Marvin. Marvin Greene. I don't know your name either."

But he had just called her by it.

"I mean, not your whole name."

She liked that, the suggestion that Mrs. Peters did not entirely explain who she was.

"Oh, it's Esther. Esther Peters. You can call me Esther."

"Well, Esther, look like y'all be seeing my face around here some. Your husband just give me that job you was kind enough to mention. You looking at your new sexton. Starting today," he paused, "if I want. Course I got to get me some work clothes, shoes, gloves, whatnot. I told the Reverend truthfully, I ain't never done no kind of caretaking job before. That don't seem to make no difference. Maria say the word around here, then it be that way."

Esther couldn't help feeling that Marvin Greene's confidence in Maria's control of personnel matters did not reflect well on Alan. She felt embarrassed for Alan and irritated by this cocksure young cousin of Maria's. He could at least have the grace to pretend ignorance of parish politics to the Rector's wife.

"What did you use to do?" Esther asked politely. "In Georgia? Is that where Maria said you were from?"

"In my time, I been in many lines of work." He seemed to be considering. "Most recently I kept a stable."

But he had no work shoes or gloves? Esther felt confused.

"Oh," she said. "Well, there's lots of horses around here."

"Yeah," he suddenly and inexplicably broke into laughter. "It sure is some fine horse country around here."

Esther felt uncomfortable without fully understanding why. She set herself to composing some graceful parting remark; then Marvin engaged her again.

"Where your little boys at today?"

"Oh, they're both in school." This was safe ground at least. "That is, David's in kindergarten, and Jonathan's in nursery school three times a week."

"So what you doing? Jogging?"

With what appeared to be a characteristic boldness, he looked her over from her dirty white running shoes to her lavender hood, from which escaped strands of her frizzy—though lit with red highlights—brown hair.

"Well, yes, sort of. I'd better be—"

"You always go jogging with that fishnet hanging off your arm? What you got in there?"

"Oh." With a rush of relief Esther remembered the bread. "Here." She reached into the filet and drew out the sesame loaf. Open Sesame, she thought absurdly. "Give this to Maria for me."

Maria had greeted the Peters on the day of their arrival in White Hart with sweet potato pie and devil's food cake. When Esther had a Summer flu in July, Maria had brought casseroles for a week.

"Tell her it's fresh from the oven this morning. Well, I'd better go."

But the look on Marvin's face as she pressed the loaf into his hands arrested Esther. For an instant, the ease and arrogance vanished. He looked startled, unguarded, and he stared at her intently as if trying to remember something only she could tell him. For a full moment, she looked back, equally unnerved but fascinated at this unexpected vulnerability.

Marvin recovered first.

"Well, don't let me hold you up, Esther. I be seeing you. Reckon I be starting in on the bushes tomorrow."

Why did everything he said sound like a double entendre, even when she didn't get it?

"Before the snow flies," he added, an obvious statement but somehow cryptic.

"Yes, well, congratulations. On the job, I mean."

Esther turned towards Blackwood, walking until she remembered she was supposed to be jogging.

"Hey, Esther!"

She looked back. He was grinning again, his arrogance restored in full.

"Thanks for the bread. What you gon' do with all them loaves in the woods? Feed the birds?"

"Wolves!" She tossed the word over her shoulder.

He deserved it.

NAKEDLY WORN MAGNIFICENCE 14

NOTHING like having the last word. Esther felt pleased with herself as she jogged down the old carriage road. When she rounded the bend out of sight of the church yard, she slowed to a walk, but she still felt frisky, like a filly given the freedom of the open field after a Winter in the barn. Why had he laughed when she mentioned horses? Well, who cared? She didn't. Despite the dull skies, the damp chill, and the knowledge of November, she felt springy, as if she herself contained that force that could melt snow and resurrect grass.

Esther paused when she came to the choice of continuing on the carriage road or descending some stone steps to the path that led across the stream and up a slope into the deep wood. On All Saints Day, when the weather had been so wet and windy and she so uncertain of her purpose, she'd kept to the carriage road. Now she turned onto the path. It was a more direct route to the icehouse, but that was not the appeal it held for her today. It was the trees that drew her. How had Robert Graves in his dedication—the only part of the book she had read in entirety—described his sense of the Goddess in a November wood? "Her nakedly worn magnificence." Yes, that was the phrase. How perfectly it expressed the beauty of leafless trees.

Esther crossed the bridge, a formality now that the stream had dried to a trickle. Yes, a formality: even if the stream bed were dry, the bridge was a boundary, a threshold. She remembered the first time she had walked with the children in Blackwood amid hot new green of June, the awe the three of them had shared, their whispered certainty that the wood was enchanted. It had struck Esther then that the tangle of vines overhead, the banks of bramble bushes, the odd tree fallen across the path were not just the inevitable results of a neglected estate but somehow artful. It was David who had put the idea into her head. He was convinced that they were on their way to Sleeping Beauty's castle. And the empty Blackwood mansion, past the pond and further up the winding carriage road, easily lent itself to his fantasy.

Esther had assumed that her own sense of magic derived from David's and Jonathan's. So often when she was with them, her perceptions were filtered through theirs. Sometimes she was rewarded by being able to see what they saw, as they saw it—but always at a remove, as if she were watching from behind a window, while they were in the element: their element.

Now as she entered the fastness of Blackwood that sense of enchantment again possessed her. Nothing and no one mediated the magic. She took in lungfuls of damp, loamy air scented with centuries of leaves turned earth. That air sought out her every pore, lifting the fine hairs on her skin. All at once with a shiver almost of fear, she became aware of the quality of silence. She paused a moment to listen, and slowly realized what was strange: she could hear no traffic sound, although the state road was less than a quarter of a mile away, no planes overhead, no noise from the high school that bordered the other side of the wood. At the same time, she became intensely aware of life and activity all around her, squirrels and birds overhead, rabbits in thickets, deer standing as still as trees, and all the silent unseen life underground: insects and snakes, buried, sleeping, small furry animals, burrowing.

Esther walked on, taking in each tree, ashamed of her ignorance; she scarcely knew enough of trees to identify them in leaf. Their barks were a closed book to her. Even without knowing names, she noticed that a wide variety of trees grew in Blackwood. She felt as though she were at an important gathering where gradually, instead of seeing only a crowd, she would come to recognize each entity as distinct.

Here was someone gnarled and knobbly, a little irascible, perhaps, but dependable, not to be budged from any stance. Here was another all curves and arches and quiverings, waiting to be swept into a dance, yes, a waltz. One-two-three, one-two-three, Esther danced a turn or two. Was it her overcharged imagination, or did that tree sway ever so slightly in response? No breeze stirred the heavy air, and yet, as she went on, the feeling overcame her that the trees were alive to her passing, that as she neared one or another there was an exchange of breath. She was almost certain they leaned a little towards her, as if to catch her scent, to sense her intentions.

The old icehouse rested at the rim of the wood next to the pond. As she neared it, Esther's awareness of the trees diminished, and her tension mounted. She could be easily cornered, not to mention trapped, in the icehouse, and it was an unnerving prospect. Before she pushed open the door, she peered in every direction and called upon supposed extra senses to determine if she were being watched. Well, this was her adventure, by definition involving risk. Adventures were rare in the lives of middle-aged clergy wives; when they presented themselves, they ought not to be spurned. Esther gave the door a decisive shove, gazed for a moment into the depths, then followed the lead of the gray daylight she had let inside.

Even before her eyes adjusted and she could distinguish the details of the shrine in the corner, Esther knew that something was different. The musty smell of unaired darkness was overlaid with a smoky sweetness. Approaching the shrine, Esther found the reason. Before the figure of the Lady, where the stone foundation ended and the wooden walls began, lay a half-burned torch, a crude braid of some sort of dried herb. She picked it up and sniffed. Sage, perhaps. As she grasped the implications of its presence, all the chill of the icehouse seemed to concentrate in the pit of her stomach.

"What's going on?" she demanded aloud, setting down the torch and lifting her eyes to the Lady. "Just what the hell is going on around here!"

Esther could hear the anger in her voice, and it startled her. The absurdity of it all, that she should be standing here in an abandoned icehouse asking questions of an "obscene figurine," made her angrier still. She glared at the Lady, daring her to do something, to display the uncanny power to provoke that had sent Alan into a tizzy and had prompted her own ridiculous flight into the wood to build this makeshift shrine where the Lady now sat: smugly, inscrutably. The hollows that served as eyes struck Esther as perversely unseeing. The snake hair looked dried up, lifeless.

"You could use a new perm, Lady," Esther muttered.

Was she imagining it; or did that belly look shriveled? Only the vulva seemed fresh, even saucy, a smirking mouth, or an eye winking surreptitiously. At her? Or someone else? Esther was the joke; of that she was fairly certain. But she didn't get it. Why didn't she ever get it?

"Who are you?" she asked the figure, this time silently.

"I'm playdough, actually," came an answer from somewhere.

In spite of herself, Esther began to smile, just a little.

"Well, what do you want from me? What do you want?"

Esther waited. She had heard of the third eye; perhaps there was such a thing as a third ear. At length the voice spoke again.

"I am your awakening, and you are mine. I brought you here. The rest is up to you."

"I thought I brought you here," Esther quipped.

The Lady, or the inner voice of her third ear, was bringing out a rudeness Esther had never before encountered in herself. She rather liked it. It was nice not being nice.

"Same difference," the voice shot back at her.

"So what do I do now?" Esther asked the enshrined lump of dough. She waited. "Well?"

No answer. Every orifice of the oracle was mute.

"Dumb question, right?"

The rest is up to you, the voice had told her. Did she really have a choice? I am your awakening, the Lady had said. What if she preferred to go back to sleep? Sighing, Esther turned from the shrine and climbed out of the icehouse. Before she closed the door, she paused to wink in the Lady's direction.

Having no further idea of how to pursue her questionable quest, Esther started back down the path. The boys would be back within the hour, and for the rest of the day, for all practical purposes, she would know exactly who she was and what she had to do. Really, she had let herself get carried away this morning, casting herself as some sort of heroine, and in a fairytale at that, not even a spy thriller or a detective mystery. Sheer fantasy. "You're just running away with your imagination," her mother used to say. Or was it "letting your imagination run away with you?" Which was more morally reprehensible, she wondered, the active role or the passive?

Then, rounding a bend, she saw him: the Mother Goose Man. He was standing some distance from the path in the center of what she had failed to notice before as a perfect ring of trees.

Here it was: a clear choice. She could, at this moment, choose to scamper down the path, as fast as she could, out of Blackwood. Forever. Somehow she knew it would be forever. No matter how often she returned, the magic would not open to her again. She could be done with it and go on leading a normal, responsible, adult life. Or she could enter that circle and—

Esther turned from the path toward the round glade. The Mother Goose Man faced her directly, but he was as still and silent as the trees. She could not be sure that he was looking at her or was even aware of her— except perhaps in the way that the trees were aware. Mad, her better judgement muttered over and over. He is stark, raving mad, and so are you. Esther stepped between two trees. Within the circle, she paused.

The Mother Goose Man continued to say nothing, but his eyes met hers. They were very dark eyes. Absurdly, perhaps, their darkness reassured her. Because the eyes of cows and deer and other herbivores were brown? Had she expected an iridescent yellow? A Satanic red? What color eyes did wolves have?

Esther remained poised, her mind frantically running through stock phrases and conversational gambits and realizing that none would suffice.

Yet, she sensed, something was expected of her. All at once, she knew what to do. Reaching into her filet, she closed her trembling hand on a loaf, the one with raisins and caraway seeds, her fingertips told her. Swiftly, Esther closed the gap between herself and the Mother Goose Man and placed the loaf in his hands.

"Lady," he responded.

Esther felt as if one of the trees had spoken.

"Lady," he said once more.

"Why do you call me that!" The words burst from her. Just being able to speak was a relief.

"Because you are the kneader of dough, the loaf giver. That is what the word lady means, you know."

"Well, I only bake bread occasionally." Esther felt flustered. "My name is Esther Peters. I've been told that yours is Fergus Hanrahan. My children call you the Mother Goose Man."

At this the old man bowed, so that the smile she thought she had seen was hidden.

"I am honored."

Esther's fear ebbed. He might be crazy; beyond doubt he was eccentric, but she didn't think he would harm her. Then she glanced at his staff, feeling uneasy again as she remembered the incident with the birds. The carving certainly was exquisite. The stick was alive with figures of birds and beasts. And there was a honey bee, surely, and the flicker of a snake. But no, that was illusory. The figures were carved of wood; they couldn't be moving. Hastily, she looked away from the staff. She couldn't deal with any more animate inanimate objects.

"When you came into the church that day," she began, deciding on the direct approach, "asking for the Lady, did you mean me?"

"You weren't there," he observed, answering and not answering.

"No, but I heard about it from people who mean you no good," she warned. "I wondered, well, if it had something to do with the figure I put in the icehouse." Was she making any sense? "You know about that?"

"I know."

"Was it you who burned the sage?"

"Yes."

He wasn't very forthcoming. Esther was beginning to feel dazed, desperate, as if she were in some terribly significant dream without a clue to its meaning and no means of remembering it when she woke.

"Look," she tried again, "I'm not used to this—whatever it is, what's been happening to me lately. I'm afraid I might be going crazy. To be honest, I'm afraid you already are crazy. That figure I just went to see in the icehouse—which is a pretty strange thing to do—it, she just happened, all by itself. Ever since then, everything has been different, unsettled. I've been different. Whoever and whatever it is, says she's my awakening, but I feel as though I've stepped into a dream. You came into the church looking for the Lady, but it wasn't me you were looking for. Or not really me."

"I was looking for the glimpse of her you gave me on All Hallow's Eve."

The hair prickled on the back of Esther's neck.

"Me? I don't understand."

"You didn't see me," he explained, sounding almost rational for an instant. "But I saw you—or her—holding the snake and the spindle."

No, it was hopeless. He wasn't a little odd, he was a walking psychotic complete with hallucinations. It had been a terrible, terrible mistake to involve herself in this man's delusions. She should turn around and leave right now.

Yet she didn't.

"Who is the Lady?" she heard herself asking.

For an immeasurable length of time, the old man remained mute, neither looking at her nor away from her. She was beginning to think he hadn't heard her question or understood, much less had any intention of answering. Then, although he didn't move exactly, Esther sensed a shift; again, as if he were a tree and the least breeze had stolen into the ring of trees to stir his leaves. And he began to speak.

> *I am she who has no name*
> *and a thousand names.*

Esther shivered as if that breeze had moved into her own branches, with its cold, sensual touch.

> *I am the Virgin, and the Unicorn*
> *sleeps in my lap; the crescent moon*
> *bends to my bowstring.*

What magic was this? Before her eyes, the frail old man, brittle and dry as a November leaf, yielded to a young green strength—a girl's, no less—supple and coursing with spring sap.

> *This is my grove, my sacred grove,*
> *my maiden bower.*
> *Here I hunt the deathless quarry,*
> *Here I run the restless race,*
> *Here you may glimpse my foot,*
> *and dance with my shadow.*
> *Here you may dream.*

Esther closed her eyes, feeling the wild sapling joy of the green girl in herself. She could not contain it. She must burst into leaf or song.

> *I am she who has no face*
> *and a thousand faces.*

The quality of whatever voice spoke through the old man began to change. Esther could feel it in her own flesh as a new richness, a ripening.

> *I am the Mother, and my belly*
> *is big with the moon, live*
> *with the fishes of the sea.*

Ah, yes, she knew about that; to that mystery she was fully initiate; at will she could swell with the memory.

> *This is my grove, my sacred grove,*
> *my birthing bed.*
> *Here I ride the stag into dawn,*
> *Here I blossom to the bee,*

But could she have she missed something? Some fierce sweetness? Some joyous abandon? Doubt came all at once, unwelcome, unbidden, penetrating with one stroke.

> *Here you may drench yourself in my dew*
> *and bathe in a fountain of milk.*
> *Here you may drink.*

She herself had been such a fountain, overflowing, over-abundant, showering the arms of the rocking chair, the bedroom carpet, the surprised and delighted baby's face. Drink, world. But she was thirsty, so thirsty. She could taste that voice; it coated her own throat: milk, honey, wine.

> *I am she who has no secret*
> *and a thousand secrets.*

The voice was a whisper now, a rustling of fallen leaves, a creaking of bare branches.

> *I am the Crone, and the snake*
> *coils round my arm; the sickle moon*
> *lies ready to hand.*
> *This is my grove, my sacred grove,*
> *my burial chamber.*

Someone just walked over my grave, Esther thought, as her spine tingled and her skin puckered, shriveled.

> *Here I gather my harvest,*

Here I draw down the darkness,
Here you may seek me or seek to escape
and still find my gates.
Here you may die.

Esther shuddered and opened her eyes, so startled she almost jumped, for there She was. "A sober suited matron all in black," the line from Shakespeare sounded in her mind. Then Esther recognized Sabine Weaver, standing next to Fergus, regarding her with what appeared to be friendly interest and some concern. Esther's knees almost buckled with relief. Sabine might be post-menopausal but she was hardly a sickle-wielding crone, not with those comfortable cushions of breasts and hips to match, not with her pleasant face, and her sensible low-heeled shoes. In fact only her skirt was black, the severity of its cut merely emphasizing her womanly roundness. Her blouse and sweater were white, at her throat a wine-colored silk scarf.

Esther did not know what Sabine Weaver was doing out in the woods with a mad estate keeper and an unhinged housewife, but she found her presence reassuring. Sabine was homely, nourishing, with an element, perhaps, of practical mystery, just as bread was leavened with the transforming powers of yeast.

"The Lady is here," said Fergus Hanrahan.

"Mais oui, bien sûr, she is always here," Sabine responded matter-of-factly. "Is that not so?"

Esther thought, for just a moment, that she was beginning to understand. She herself was and was not the Lady, just as Sabine was and was not, and Fergus, and even the figure in the icehouse, and the trees of the sacred grove.

"The Lady is here," Esther found herself answering.

Reaching into her filet, Esther lifted out the last loaf and gave it to Sabine. It was the herb bread; its fragrance hung in the still air. Rosemary and dill.

LADY SOUL 15

MARVIN Greene, walking up Main Street, White Hart, turned his cigarette around and cupped it under his hand to protect it from the fat drops of rain mixed with sleet that had started to fall. Just in time to dampen weekend plans—if anyone had any, if it made any difference at this time of year, out here in the sticks. But, yeah, he'd forgotten; it was hunting season or would be come Monday at the crack of dawn. The countryside was already crawling with dudes in camouflage—as like to kill each other as anything else that moved—tracking deer shit, taking the odd shot to scare off stray dogs.

Marvin had done a job of posting for Claire Potter last week. She had no objection to "our local boys" and she gave some of them permission to hunt on her property. It was those "city slickers" who couldn't tell the back end of a deer from a horse's ass—specifically one of her horses—that worried her. Our local boys also knew all of her dogs and wouldn't harm a flea on their hides—if they had fleas, which Marvin could personally testify they did not.

Marvin didn't know, exactly, who our local boys might be—or what color. Mrs. Potter had been very friendly to him, and Maria had more than once hinted that the freezer in her basement could use a haunch or two. But when Marvin had inquired of some poker playing cronies he'd recently acquired about the cost of a hunting license, let alone getting strapped, and what happened to people, particularly of his complexion, who did not have all their little pieces of paper in order, he'd decided against the investment.

Investment, shit. He'd been working three part-time jobs the last three weeks, and what he'd earned just barely covered the cost of the new work boots and clothes he'd been obliged to buy. Then, of course, there was his share of the rent and the groceries. He'd have to rely on poker to keep him in the amenities—that is until some of his other games started paying off. Luckily, his fingers had not lost their touch with the cards. He could win Maria a carcass. Yeah, that's what he would do. And wouldn't she mutter and roll her eyes. She didn't hold with card playing.

Marvin took a last drag on his cigarette and let it drop to the pavement. His hands free, he adjusted his suede cap and his jacket collar. Despite the weather, downtown White Hart was bustling. Like other small towns within a couple of hours drive from the City, White Hart was being discovered by wealthy New York weekenders. But what they found—antique malls and gourmet shops—held little interest for Marvin.

The locals pretty much retreated on weekends to Vinny's Bar and Grill, which was, so far as Marvin could make out, an extension of the all-white fire department. In better weather, half a dozen Black people of various ages and sexes sat on the benches where the County bus stopped. Kids, semi-integrated, hung by the gates to the park, which no one seemed to use except for drinking wine and smoking various substances or littering the goldfish pond, which naturally had no live fish in it. Between trains, the station belonged to a couple of older drunks who went there to sleep it off from time to time. The station master apparently rousted them and sent them back across the parking lot to Vinny's ten minutes before any train was due. The laundromat had the most balanced racial mix of any establishment in town. And you could meet the ladies there—them and their kids who were either whining or had their mouths plugged with lollipops, free from the bank across the street.

And that was White Hart.

Marvin had slept away most of the morning, then he'd wandered uptown with the vague intention of taking the bus to River City where there was a sizeable Black population. Maybe there he could find a congenial place to hang out, music, a party, anything with some life in it. He had a poker game later that night, but many empty hours to fill between now and then. When he had gotten to Main Street, the benches at the bus stop were deserted. With no one there to shoot the shit with him and with no idea when the next bus was due, Marvin had kept on walking just for the sense of motion.

As he passed the hardware store, he noticed a sign for a sale on wall paint, so he went inside. After poking around for awhile, checking out how extensive the sale was and making a note of some prices, he decided to go on up to the parish house. He could take some measurements, do some figuring, make some estimates. He had already put in his fifteen hours at St. Paul's this week, but what the hell, he was bored. He could subtract it from next week. If the P.I.C. or the Vestry or whoever decided those things went for the idea of repainting, he would have something to do in the cold weather. That is when he wasn't shoveling walks, sanding the driveway, fixing roof leaks....

Shit. Mr. Handyman. Sexton of St. Paul's. It wasn't how he had ever pictured himself. So far the work wasn't bad—except for the pay. The job was mostly for show, so people who attended St. Paul's could refer to their "Sexton." It had a high-class sound to it, added some tone.

It used to be that the Sexton of a church was the gravedigger, the P.I.C. had informed him. "Of course St. Paul's doesn't have its own grave yard," The P.I.C. had said in his jokey way, trying to cover up how nervous Marvin made him and how he hadn't really wanted Marvin for the job in the first place. Then the man had attempted to explain what the job did mean: a combination janitor and yardman. "You'll get the hang of it." The P.I.C. had tried out a winning smile. "Look busy and don't bother me with the details," Marvin decoded the unspoken message.

The P.I.C. hardly knew where the furnace was, much less how the heating system worked. Arthur Billings, the money man, had filled Marvin in on what he referred to as "the bottom line and the real bottom line." "And that's really the real bottom line, Marv," he had concluded. "Got it, Art," Marvin had assured him, and the man had looked confused, like he knew something was a little off but he couldn't figure out what.

For the most part Marvin was left to do his job in peace, and that suited him just fine. Much of the time the P.I.C. was off somewhere and when people—which usually meant ladies—came looking for the Rector, more often than not they'd end up talking to the Sexton. Now that was his real talent: putting women at their ease, getting them to lower their guard without noticing it, finding out what was on their minds. Goddamn, with just a few initials tacked onto his name, he could have been a Park Avenue shrink.

It hadn't taken long to find out what was on Alisha Adams' mind. She had given him his third job, and the job description had become clear within a matter of days. Two to be exact. Everything was proceeding according to plan, Marvin reminded himself as he passed the library and the toystore and crossed a side street onto the residential block of Main. Such plan as there was.

The sleet fell thickly, and the pavement of the sidewalk grew slick. The soles of Marvin's new work boots were like tractor treads, and he didn't slip despite the incline. He'd never had shoes like that before; when he looked down at his feet, he just couldn't connect with them. It was like a piece of somebody else—someone he didn't know—had been tacked onto him, confusing his identity, changing it, like in that crazy mix and match picture book Esther Peters' little boy had been playing with. It was a cardboard book with each page divided into three sections. Johnny had come up to him and shown him what he called a gir-be-gator with a giraffe's head, a bear's belly, and an alligator's tail.

Yeah. That's how he felt a lot of the time, like someone or something was trifling with the whole of him, taking him apart, shifting the pieces, shuffling him like a deck of cards. He could hardly recognize himself. Sometimes he'd wake up in the middle of the night with a feeling almost like motion sickness, except it wasn't in his stomach. The more he assured himself that he was in control, the more uneasy he felt: underneath, in his body, in his blood.

Even with Alisha Adams and how smoothly, how predictably everything had gone—the anti-climactic rush of release when they'd done it, standing up in the stables in full view of her horses (her idea)—something was not quite right. That he couldn't place his finger on what it was just added to his tension.

What was he doing here? If he asked himself once, he asked himself a hundred times a day. What was he doing here at Maria's house, in White Hart, hanging around a church yard? After almost a month, he still didn't know. Some of the time, daytime, he almost chose to feel bored, irritable, disgusted with his circumstances. But then there were other times, in-between times, twilight times, when he knew his contempt was just posturing, an attempt to hold on to what he thought he knew. Because to tell the truth, he wasn't bored, he was scared of that deeper pull, like on Hallowe'en night when the earth had reached right out for him, or when Esther Peters had lifted that loaf of bread and had sent his mind reeling into the Tarot card: The High Priestess—the card that had come up in answer to the question: What am I doing here?

Shit. With answers like that, who needed questions? It must be some kind of cosmic rule that a simple question just leads to a complicated one, such as what did the P.I.C.'s old lady have to do with it? 'Course that business with the bread could have been a coincidence. Maybe he wanted it to be a coincidence. The trouble was, he didn't believe in coincidences. Not consistently. You couldn't have it both ways. Mess with the cards, and they were going to do work on your mind.

So what about Esther Peters? She was a woman. At least she had that in her favor. And he was a genius where women were concerned. To have the magic touch with women, you either had to love them—love whatever it was that made them different from men—or hate them. He'd seen it work both ways with the men who had the power. He counted himself as one of the lovers. That was his knack. He could even look at some old hag with shriveled up tits and chins hanging in the breeze, fried hair and a saggy butt, and he could close his eyes and breathe the woman in her. He was like a dowser finding a hidden spring, yes, a spring where all the juices were stored up—still sweet. No woman ever dried up all the way. He had the power to make her remember the woman in herself.

Now with Esther, he certainly didn't have to close his eyes to scent the woman in her. She wasn't bad looking, not pretty but not ugly either, just not his type. She had no edge, no polish. She was, well, nice, and she was a mother, most definitely a mother. He wasn't used to mothers, and didn't have much use for them. Of course, he could have her, if he wanted to. It was obvious to him that his looks and charm had had their customary effect. It was typical of those medium range women that they got all flustered and clumsy when a fly guy checked them out.

On the Street, Esther's type was the easiest to handle: receptive to flattery, grateful for attention, and pre-programmed to please. With coaching, such women could become fine actresses, which is to say excellent whores. You could do amazing things with clothing and make-up with women like Esther. But he looked at them as business prospects, not as women to pursue for personal pleasure.

Marvin turned in at the church driveway. It was deserted this Saturday afternoon. No organist, no Nancy Jones, the church secretary and Marvin's buddy. The P.I.C.'s car was gone, and so was Esther's, unless they were parked down in the garage. He checked his jacket pockets for the keys to the parish house and found that he had them, though he knew where to find a spare key if he didn't.

Marvin glanced briefly at the gray stucco walls of the church, mean and ugly as the spitting sky. The church used to be covered with ivy, Maria had told Marvin. In its stripped condition, she considered it indecently exposed and had formed the habit of averting her eyes as she approached it. One of Marvin's jobs was to make sure the ivy didn't creep back. It had been torn down in the first place because it was undermining the wall, causing it to crack and crumble. In Maria's mind, these practical arguments did not excuse the uglification of her church.

Marvin turned his attention to the rectory as he passed by, taking in the kids' tricycles parked haphazardly on the front porch, and the shrubs—newly pruned by him—squatting like bored guards out front. The windows reflected only the dull glare of the sky. No lights on inside.

He headed on down the driveway towards the parish house. Close kin in looks to the rectory, brown-shingled and shutterless, the parish house was bigger, maybe twice the size. A heating nightmare, Art Billings had commented several times. Another of Marvin's assignments was to search out all the sneaky little drafts and plug the leaks. To help defray the cost of heating and maintenance, the building was rented as a meeting place to a variety of groups: ballet class, senior citizens, weight watchers, AA. Marvin had gotten to know the schedule pretty well. No one used the building on Saturdays.

So what was that beat he could hear as he drew closer, pulsing inside that monster building? Yes, it was definitely coming from in there. Marvin mounted the steps and tried the door. Whoever was inside had locked themselves in; or maybe some kids, finding no one on the premises, had decided to break in and party. Looked like he was going to have to do some investigating.

Sexton Greene on the scene.

Once inside, Marvin paused at the foot of the stairs. The music was coming from the second floor, the largest open space, once intended for seating an audience before the walled-off stage that now stored all the junk left over from the Rummage Sale. Marvin listened; over the music he could hear no voices, no laughter, nothing to indicate a crowd. Just Aretha. Without doubt it was Aretha up there bringing it on home. He knew her voice as well as he knew his own mother's or grandmother's.

Lady Soul. He stood at the foot of the stairs, transfixed. It felt like she was calling to him, like she always called to him, with that voice that grew right up out of the ground, right up through him, till it took off and soared into the blue. Yes, it was her all right. Her voice had aged some since he'd last really listened, like the earth had more claim on it, but that only made it stronger. She was singing to him, singing one of those songs. How can you do me this way, how come you forget where you belong, why you always running, running away, come on home, boy, and see about me. That voice, the sheer sound of it, never mind the words, always acted on him like a rebuke to the white girl runner he had become.

Well, shit, what was she doing here, upstairs in the parish house of St. Paul's, White Hart? Only one way to find out. Marvin climbed the stairs as the song began to soar toward its climax. Life had been so strange lately and his mind so confused, he would hardly have been surprised to find Lady Soul herself, standing in the middle of the room, planted like some big mother tree with her arms outstretched. What he did see when he paused in the doorway made just about as much—or as little—sense.

A woman, with her back to him, danced, making a diagonal slash across the space, sometimes leaping like the ground couldn't hold her, sometimes crouched so low over the floor she looked like some snake or mountain rising up. Yeah, a volcano. Every bit of her was in motion. Even her hair stood on end; he could almost swear sparks were flying. But he couldn't have said what color her hair was or her skin. She danced like the music was inside her and any minute she might burst open.

Just as the music peaked, she whirled around, her arms reaching, head flung back exposing a white throat, thighs turned out, knees bent, back arched so that her round palm-sized breasts spilled towards him. She was open, as wide open as he'd ever seen a woman. But not to him. Not to any man. To a god maybe, like the voodoo dancers who got possessed. Then her hips rolled forward with her head. She lowered her arms to balance herself as she spun while the music wound down, lower and lower, till she ended on her knees, hands and forehead touching the floor.

After a pause the next song on the tape began, but the woman made no motion to get up. He could leave right now, his footfall covered by the music, steal away with his stolen sight. He could, but damned if he would.

Marvin waited, and in a moment the woman sat up and found herself looking straight at him. A white face turning deep red above what he now saw was a purple leotard. Esther Peters. Hot damn! He'd better sharpen up his instincts. How had he missed all that fire locked up inside her? And to think of it wasted on the P.I.C.! Shit, it was a crime, a crime against mankind—specifically him.

Marvin watched her stand up, her movements, so free a few moments ago, stiff with her embarrassment. But he wasn't going to forget what he had seen, and he wasn't going to let her forget, either. He was a witness. Even as she crossed to the table, where she'd set up the tape player, with her head bent like she was ashamed, the heat was still rising off her. It shimmered in the air between them. Heat wave. He would just have to smooth the way for her, make it easy, natural. Yeah, make her feel like a natural woman.

Esther switched off the music, and Marvin greeted the silence with some slow hand clapping.

"Have mercy, lady! I didn't know you was a dancer!"

"Oh, I'm not. At least, I used to take classes in college, but—"

Her response was muffled by the sweats, also purple, that she was pulling on. He was athletic enough himself to know that you didn't stand around in sweaty clothes after a work out, but she was definitely in a hurry to cover it up, like someone who's been caught skinny dipping at the fishing hole—or caught with a lover. Well, she had been making some kind of love, sure enough.

"—and I've taken a couple of exercise classes since the kids were born. I was thinking of maybe getting together a group of mothers to do some aerobic dance. Those ballet classes are too advanced for most of us. They're really for young girls."

That would be some class, Marvin thought to himself. What he had just seen was no exercise routine. Was she trying to throw him off the scent with this talk of a mothers' group or did she really not know what had just happened? She stood by her tape player looking nervous, while he continued to loll in the doorway. There wasn't any other way out, unless she made a dash for the fire escape. One way or another she was going to have to deal with him. Not that he wanted anything specific from her. Not yet. He just wanted to test the waters, to see were they warm.

"I hope I didn't scare you, Esther. I come by to check some things out. Heard the music and thought there was some kind of wild partying going on. And here I find you. All alone. How come you all alone today? Don't seem right."

Esther laughed, and the laughter relaxed her.

"If you were a mother, you wouldn't feel sorry for me. Solitude is solid gold. The kids are with Alan. Sometimes he takes them somewhere on Saturday afternoons, if he's finished his sermon. They went to River City to see a traveling zoo. But I'm beginning to get worried about the road conditions." She glanced out the window. "Was it very slippery when you were out?"

She looked at him, her face drawn into all those mother wrinkles.

"Wasn't bad." He waved away the weather with one hand.

This woman needed some serious distraction.

TAKING MEASUREMENTS 16

NOW, I tell you what we gon' do. If you be so kind as to let me disturb your peace some more, I want you to help me out."

His sixth sense—his woman sense—fine-tuned, Marvin could tell that Esther was both relieved to have him take charge and anxious about his intentions. A promising combination. He wanted her to feel at ease with him, but not safe—only the danger had to come not from him but from inside herself.

That was how it worked.

"You with me?" he asked, half-turning toward the stairs after explaining to her about the paint sale and the measurements he needed. She abandoned her tape player and followed him.

Soon they were standing side by side in front of the office door, going through their keys. It turned out she had a key to the office; he didn't. After rummaging around in Nancy's drawers, they found a tape measure and also borrowed a notepad and a pencil. Equipped with a legitimate purpose, they headed for the basement together.

"These classrooms could certainly use some brightening up," Esther commented as they stepped into the farthest one of the four. "I don't know who is in charge of funds like that. Probably the WOSPs."

"Wasps?" he questioned, wondering if she were talking about some kind of problem with insects.

"Women-of-St.-Paul's," she translated. "Alisha Adams is the president. The WOSPs raise money for things like that. Of course they just spent an awful lot on redecorating the rectory, maybe more than they should have."

Marvin thought about Alisha and Esther and figured Esther probably hadn't had much to say about it.

"But, of course, if there's a sale...."

Conversation lulled as they concentrated on the task: Esther holding one end fast while Marvin drew out the tape, pulling it taut so that it quivered with tension. As a move in the game of seduction, tape measuring had potential, Marvin considered. More than once the tape fell short of the opposite wall. Then Marvin would stand holding the end while Esther walked towards him, reeling in the tape, so that she could reposition her hand where his waited. White on black. Flesh on flesh. An instant of closeness, then a cool matter-of-fact retreat as he stretched out the tape the rest of the way. Finally he would crouch down to scrawl the measurements on the pad, looking up now and then to find her watching him—or pretending not to.

Esther was one of those women who knew when not to talk—like when you were doing figures. He almost wished she wasn't; he had to get her talking. A lot of men didn't understand the importance of words; they thought women wanted some kind of cave man routine, so they just didn't bother to evolve. Marvin knew: words lay down the ground that women believed was solid, where they'd be willing to meet you next time and the time after that—however long it took. If he didn't find a way to get Esther talking, she'd be running scared from all the free-floating vibes. But he'd have to take it slow, play it cool. Whatever happened would have to seem to happen all by itself.

"Well, Esther," he said as they finished the last room, "I thank you kindly for the donation of your time."

"Oh, well." She was flustered.

Marvin turned and headed for the door, standing aside and gesturing for her to pass first. Then he followed her—not too closely—up the steep, narrow stairs, discreetly appraising the view. Not too big, not too small, a little slack, maybe, but not bad, not bad at all.

"Tell me, Esther," he began as they walked side by side back to Nancy Jones' office, "you what they call an at-home mother?"

"Yes, I am. At the moment."

Half the time the woman sounded like she was apologizing for something. Even when she wasn't, she used that tone of voice. When the time was right, he was going to call her on that.

"I'll probably go back to work in a couple of years. I was a Head Start teacher before the kids were born. It seemed kind of silly to find daycare for them so that I could take care of other people's kids. Especially for the money. The salary and the cost of childcare would almost have cancelled each other out. Besides, I want these years with them. It's a very special time."

"More kids have a mother like you, be a better world. I ain't never seen a mother really pay attention to a kid the way you do."

Marvin hadn't reflected on it much at the time, but it was true. He had watched her last week planting flower bulbs in front of the house—crocuses and daffodils, he believed she'd told him. He knew for a fact that she was attracted to him, but when she'd gotten down onto her hands and knees in the dirt, seemed like her mind had gone into the ground with those bulbs. Her attention had been so total, it had distracted him from the hedges he was clipping. When she'd tucked the bulbs in and patted down the earth, he'd almost felt the rhythm of that touch.

Then her littlest boy had come racing around the house from the backyard with some long tale about monsters and whatnot. She had settled her behind right down in the dirt and taken the kid on her lap, and she'd listened to him like that was her purpose on this planet.

"I try," she was saying. "I'm sure I don't always succeed."

He was going to have to teach the lady how to take a compliment.

The tape measure, pad and pencil stored away, Marvin waited while Esther locked the office door. She still had to get her cassette player, then at the very least he'd walk her up the driveway.

"Marvin," she said suddenly, turning towards him, "I was so sorry to hear about your family's land. It's just a crime what's happening to family farms. It must be so hard for you to have to come here and start all over again from scratch."

A wave of that mental motion sickness hit Marvin; the floor shifted beneath his heavy boots, and the walls wobbled. Only Esther remained in focus. He stared at her, trying to hold on to some reality.

"Oh, I'm sorry!" she cried, putting out her hand as if to steady him. "I shouldn't have mentioned it. It must upset you to talk about it."

The room stopped reeling, and Marvin recovered himself, not knowing whether to laugh or curse as the details of the rap he'd laid on Alisha Adams came back to him. That afternoon with Alisha had been the first time he'd tried it out full length.

Now as he looked into Esther's sweet brown eyes—or were they green?—he felt suddenly bored with his rap, impatient. He didn't want to reproduce it. Besides, it wouldn't work with Esther. She would really listen and take it seriously. With Alisha that was not a problem. She was serious about one thing only. Matter of fact, he was surprised she had even remembered as much as she had told Esther, she'd been so intent on figuring out how to undo his belt buckle—the one that told it like it was: Marvelous.

"Well," she said, "I guess I better be going."

Damn. He had to think fast or she was going to slip away.

"Esther," he said, almost touching her arm, the way she had almost touched his before, "let me be real with you."

The words were out before he knew what he meant by them. Tell her the truth? He paused to consider, his arm still hovering, holding her there. Come to think of it, the truth had possibilities.

"You got a minute?"

"I guess so. I mean, I really don't know what time it is—"

Marvin gestured with his head towards twin plush easy chairs arranged next to a glass bookcase that was labeled "parish library" in case anyone failed to notice. The truth was always a risky proposition, but then risk made the game worth playing. You could win; you could lose. And winner take all. He could blow his whole little scene here, if Esther told the P.I.C. he had hired an ex-con to be sexton. Not that he had lied; the question simply hadn't come up. But if she kept it to herself...well, then the two of them would have a guilty little secret, and one guilty secret could lead to another. Winner, loser, at least something would happen; things would begin to move. Yeah, the truth had definite possibilities.

"Esther," he said when he had her sitting down, "my family ain't never own no farm. I come from peoples still own by the land. I'm talking seasonal labor; I'm talking a one room shack sitting up on cement blocks out by the cotton fields. Maybe I got Georgia on my mind from time to time, but ain't no other part of my body been in Georgia, let me see, 'bout fourteen, fifteen years now. Matter of fact, the last five years I been what you might call a guest of New York State. You understand what I'm saying, Esther?"

She shook her head, bewildered. Maybe this was a mistake: too much, too fast.

"Okay," he said, looking away from Esther, studying his own hands. "I better not say no more. This Maria's community. She got a right to hold up her head. She don't need a no 'count cousin to come here and be trifling with her position. See, she don't like my last address. Can't say much for it myself."

"You mean you were in prison?"

Marvin looked at Esther again, and she looked back. He tried to gauge her reaction. Shock? Fear? Curiosity? But he couldn't. He only knew that he had her attention: like the flower bulbs, like her son, like the song she had danced to. Now it was his.

"Where were you before that?" she asked. "And what did you mean the other day when you said you used to keep a stable?"

Marvin laughed. "All right. No more jive. You want it straight, you got it. I live in New York City for maybe seven years before I got busted. I was in the Life, right? You know what I mean by the Life?"

"Prostitution?"

"Yeah." He looked at her with some surprise. "I'm a player, what you probably call a pimp. Only a player generally have more than one game going. Being a player, you might say it's a philosophy. 'Cause, you know, if life ain't a game, then what is it?"

"My best friend, Gale, is trying to organize a union of street prostitutes," she offered.

Hmm. Her best friend might be his natural enemy. What was she doing with a best friend like that? Soon as he thought he had her all figured out, she'd do something or say something that made him have to think again. Well, he preferred to be on his toes.

"You know, that's a good idea, a union. They some unscrupulous players out there. She a working girl, your friend?"

"A prostitute?" Esther smiled. "No, Gale's a lesbian."

More surprises. Did that mean Esther swung both ways?

"Well, lots of girls in the Life be bisexual. You know, your friend better watch herself. She mess with some pimps' ladies, tell 'em they rights and whatnot, she might just wake up one morning dead."

Esther sighed. "I know. I worry about Gale. All the time. She's always said she doesn't feel alive unless someone else wants her dead. She's a walking one woman revolution."

Marvin laughed. "Say, hey! I can relate. I enjoy a little danger myself."

Their eyes met for a second, then she looked away. Was she uptight again? He could hardly blame her. Man, he was playing the fool, going on about pimps and murder. Shit. She probably thought he was talking about himself.

"Esther, I don't want you to be getting no wrong ideas about me. I have live in some violent places with some violent type individuals. But that ain't the way I do business. My girls always had a square deal with me, and I never had no trouble with them. Matter of fact, in the Life, I never even carried a piece. My mother always told me a gun draw bad luck to you. And she was right. 'Cause the one time I did, when me and some of my associates went in on a little sideline venture, that's when I got busted.

"I never had no problem with the police in the Life, except now and then getting the girls out of jail. That's just part of the job. And I had a separate bank account for it and a lawyer on retainer at all times. Hadn't been for my sidelines, I be in the Life today."

"So," she said slowly, "you're not in the Life any more?"

Marvin looked at her and raised one eyebrow. "In White Hart? You think I be running girls from Maria's house? You out your mind? I may be a fool, but even I know better than that. Maria a sanctified lady. She catch me messing like that, she roll me in bread crumbs and fry me with her next batch of chicken."

Esther blushed, then joined in laughing.

"Listen up," he went on. "I'm a sexton in the E-piscopal church now, baby. I'm a honest laborer, understand. Just look here at these work boots. Check out this little blister." He displayed his hands. "That gon' be a callous 'fore too long. You ain't never see no pimps with hands and feets like I got now. Pimps very vain peoples."

He had her out of control now, holding her sides laughing, no doubt partly from relief that he hadn't jumped her bones or whipped anything dangerous out of his pants.

"What made you decide not to go back into the Life?" Esther asked as she recovered herself.

"You know, Esther, that's a question I done ask myself many times, and I ain't had no answer yet. 'Cause that was my plan. Only thing I can figure, being down for so long put me through some changes. All I know is, when I finally hit the Street, I just couldn't make my move. So I decided to come here. Could be for no reason, could be for some reason I ain't understand yet.

"But I tell you, Esther, ever since I got here—Hallowe'en night, yeah— they been some strange things happening to my mind. Sometime I feel like someone trying to tell me something, got some plan for me. Now don't that sound crazy? You probably think I'm some kind of bug, but it's the truth."

"No," she said. "I think I know what you mean. It's funny you should mention Hallowe'en. Something happened to me, then—or started to—and it's kept on happening, and sometimes I think I'm going crazy. I haven't really been able to explain it to anyone. Not even myself. I'm not sure I can."

"Try me."

She looked at him for some time, searching him, like she was trying to decide if she could trust him. Well, he'd told her the truth. What more did she want? He rested his case and waited for her judgment.

"Do you...have you...well, do you know anything about—the Goddess?"

Whew! This lady could sure pitch a mean curve ball! How was he supposed to connect with that? Goddess? Shit. What did she mean? What kind of a preacher's wife was she: with her dyke best friend, her hot dancing, and now—goddess?

"Goddess?" he repeated, playing for time, knitting his brows like he was thinking on it.

Then suddenly his mind's eye flashed him the High Priestess card. He looked at Esther again, picturing that loaf in her hands.

"You know, Esther, I believe you and me got a lot to talk about. You know anything about tarot cards?"

She shook her head but seemed about to speak again when something distracted her. She turned to look out the window. Then Marvin saw it, too. Shit. The P.I.C.'s blue Ford Escort had just pulled in.

"I've gotta go, Marvin. I just realized I haven't even thought about what to make for dinner. 'Bye. I enjoyed talking to you."

Esther was half way to the door. Damn. Well, one good thing: she was acting guilty. Could be she had already sinned in her heart. And like Jesus said: if you've done that, you might as well go all the way.

"Could you lock up?" she called.

She banged the door, but it didn't close. Then, more swiftly than he was accustomed to moving in pursuit of a woman, he followed after her.

"Hey, Cinderella!" He stood in the doorway. "You forgot your tape player."

Halfway up the driveway, she did an about-face, ran back, brushing past him, giving him a whiff of musky woman. She took the stairs, still running, then she was back down and out the door again with the tape player.

"Hey, you done drop your glass slipper, lady!"

He pantomimed bending down and picking it up.

Esther shot him a smile over her shoulder, but she didn't stop running.

Marvin laughed to himself and locked the door. Cinderella, yeah. A little gray ashes girl till somebody got to stirring up those live coals. Whooee! Cinderella. He guessed that made him some kind of prince. Yeah. The prince of darkness.

Marvin ambled up the driveway past the rectory windows, so the P.I.C. could see him, if he cared to. Put that son-of-a-bitch on notice. Then he headed down Main Street feeling hot, so hot the frozen rain was like to sizzle when it hit his skin. About half way home, he realized: he was walking to his own rhythm—never mind the work boots and the sleet—like he was all one piece again, solid as a loaf of homemade bread, hot out of the oven, fresh baked.

BOOK FOUR

ADVENT

AND THE ROUGH PLACES PLAIN 17

SHE undid the buttons one by one, her fingers so deft, so nimble she never once fumbled. No button balked in the tiny hand-sewn button holes. Her fingers commanded, the buttons yielded, melted. The fabric of her clothes did not so much fall away as fly. Airy attendants tore it delicately to shreds, trailing strands of it on the morning breeze, wafting it to tree tops, silken lining for nests. Layers and layers of clothing drifted, dispersed at the touch of her slender hands, hands like white flames flickering in the green shade. And then at last she stood: new, blazing, quite, quite perfect with her red-in-the-morning-sailors-take-warning hair sheathing the naked blade of her body. She had but to raise her eyes, and it would be...

Real. Spencer opened her eyes to plain no-nonsense daylight. No suggestive play of light and shadow; the branches of the trees outside her window were stripped and scrubbed. Sabine had already raised the shades and opened the curtains. Perhaps Sabine's yank of the shade had acted on her eyelids, too. She closed them again, trying to coax back that filtered green light, that delicious moment of impossible youth—for certainly in her real life she had never undressed outside the confines of her boudoir!—when everything trembled on the brink of...well, what was it? She never seemed to be able to stay asleep long enough to find out. Spencer sighed and opened her eyes to the unrelenting blue beyond the naked branches.

At least today waking reality held some promise of diversion. She was having her stair lift installed first thing this morning. And that was just the beginning. Then came the ramp. Her Advent adventure. Make straight a highway in the desert, as John the Baptist always said—or was it Isaiah? Maria Washington had stopped by yesterday after church, and when Spencer had mentioned the ramp, Maria had offered the services of her young nephew or cousin—whatever he was.

Ah, breakfast was ascending, strong tea and fresh croissant. Now the day could begin in earnest. She must have Sabine do something with her hair, and she needed a fresh bed jacket, the dark green satin one today, perhaps. What with workmen in and out installing the lift and perhaps the nephew-cousin coming by later—Alisha Adams had told her he was almost criminally handsome—well, it behooved one to look one's best.

Afternoon found the Lady of Blackwood taking tea downstairs in her front parlour for the first time since her injury last Summer. The parlour window afforded her a view of the front porch and of the gates to Blackwood, which her bedroom windows did not. She relished the change, and she sat as close to the window as Sabine would allow her, facing in the direction of the gates. She had to admit that her view was enhanced by Maria Washington's young relation. He stood staring at the steps of her porch as if by the sheer power of his concentration he could cause a ramp to materialize.

Maria herself sat opposite Spencer. They were sharing a pot of tea and a plate of double fudge brownies that Maria had brought still warm from her oven. Maria had introduced Marlon—was that his name?—but then she had politely and firmly refused on the young man's behalf Spencer's offer of refreshment. She insisted that he step outside and begin making calculations for the ramp so that he could buy the lumber tomorrow. Martin, who had delightful, old-fashioned manners, doffing his rather dashing hat and making her a courtly little bow when greeting her, had several times attempted to speak, but each time Maria had swiftly cut him off—a child to be seen and not heard. Well, he certainly was scenic, although Spencer could not discern that he was making much headway with his design for her ramp.

"Well, Maria, your nephew is quite the Jack-of-all-trades," commented Spencer. She did not add "master of none," but she was beginning to wonder. "I hear he is working for Claire Potter and Alisha Adams as well as serving as sexton. Are you sure he has time for building a ramp?"

"Oh, it's best for him to keep busy, Spencer. I think so. I really do."

"I suppose White Hart must seem a little dull to a young man," Spencer observed.

"He have his entertainments, I'm afraid. Oh, yes."

"Ah," murmured Spencer, debating whether or not to probe delicately for details. "Well, it must be nice for you to have someone handy around the house."

"Oh, yes." Maria sounded a trifle dubious. "It is."

"And how is Raina getting on?" inquired Spencer, remembering that she ought to ask, although she did not quite approve of Maria's daughter.

Spencer had wondered more than once whether or not the several well-to-do WOSPs had not been mistaken in setting up that secret fund for Raina's education. She had been a bright little girl, but look what had happened! She had become such a hardened, militant young woman. Of course, it wasn't anyone's fault that Raina's college years had coincided with all that upheaval. Despite all those riots, she had done very well with her studies and had gone on to become a lawyer. Surely, it would have been more suitable for her to have chosen nursing or teaching as a profession; that was more the sort of thing the WOSPs had had in mind. But they had not had any say in her choice of a career; she had won a full scholarship to law school and had earned the rest of her expenses herself. Then there had been that unfortunate marriage and a child of mixed heritage. The WOSPs could hardly be held accountable for that. But the worst of it all, really, was that Raina had never returned to White Hart and her mother.

"It's been so long since I've seen her," added Spencer with a hint of reproach. "She doesn't get up to White Hart very often, does she?"

"She very busy with her practice." Maria defended her daughter. "Didn't I tell you? She been promoted. She just about running legal services for the whole Bronx. It's a big job. Yes, it is. I be telling her all the time, she work too hard. But you know how Raina is. There ain't no lazy bone in that girl's body. Running, all the time running. And Tana just like her mother—except what she love best is ballet. You remember Raina when she was a little girl; with her it was always books, books, books. They both be here for Christmas. I promise I bring them over to see you. Tana such a grown girl now you won't hardly know her."

"You do that, Maria. I'll depend upon it. You know, it just occurred to me..."

Spencer paused to consider. Yes, why not? Raina Washington was a lawyer. Maybe...yes, why shouldn't she ask Raina's advice? More than that. Why not get rid of Grigson and Bates? Not fire them exactly; Geoffrey might get the wind up. She could simply ignore them. After all, so far she had signed nothing. They had no fresh will in hand that could call into question any document she might choose to draw up with someone else. Such as Raina Washington. Really, that's what she needed: a whole new perspective on her predicament, a fresh point of view. Raina would certainly be fresh, a blast of bracing air. Yes, that might be just the thing....

"Maria, I want to confide in you, but you mustn't breathe a word to anyone of what I'm about to say to you."

Maria did not lean forward, bat an eye or in any way indicate eagerness or curiosity, but Spencer reckoned she was as ready to bite into a secret as into one of her own fudge brownies. Well, Spencer had kept some secrets for Maria—to this day Raina knew nothing about the WOSP fund—now Maria could keep a secret for her.

"I need some help with my will. My lawyers, my nephew Geoffrey hired them, and I don't trust them. Do you suppose Raina could—"

"Now, Honey, hold up, hold up just a minute," Maria interrupted, looking visibly distressed. "Ain't nothing would do my heart more good than to see my girl fix it for you so you could have some peace of mind. Now to me, it seem like the least she could do, but this have happened before. Whenever I ask her to help an old friend with a will, she always say the same thing: just 'cause I work for legal services, don't mean I am one. She tell me she don't do that kind of law. She don't do estates."

Spencer glanced out the window. Young Marlon appeared to have given up. He was sitting down on the steps right where the ramp was supposed to be. And he was lighting a cigarette. Really!

"Now you and me," Maria was going on, "we might think a lawyer is a lawyer is a lawyer, but these days they all got specializations. Just like doctors. Trouble with today, they so much more to know, seem to me like folks know less and less."

"How very, very disappointing," said Spencer crossly.

Now that it had at last dawned upon her that she didn't need to accept the counsel of Grigson and Bates simply because—like Mount Everest and Geoffrey Landsend—they were there, it struck her as cruel and unreasonable, particularly on the part of Raina Washington, that the first course of action to enter her head should prove untenable.

"But I suppose if Raina doesn't do that sort of law, then she doesn't. And I know—don't think I don't!—what a stubborn young lady your daughter can be, Maria. Still, I would like you to mention it to her all the same. Perhaps I could just talk to her about it, and she could recommend someone. Because, you see, I've decided not just anyone will do. For one thing, I want my lawyer to be...well, he must be—a woman!"

Spencer's pronouncement startled both of them. She and Maria stared at one another, each with a brownie suspended in mid-air.

"It is rather shocking to hear that from me, isn't it?" Spencer mused. "Well, if I can still surprise myself that means there's life in the old girl yet."

"Sure enough," Maria chuckled. "Never thought I live to see the day you be asking for woman anything. Wait till Raina hear this. You be in her good books."

"Now this doesn't mean I'm ready for a woman priest, Maria. So don't go spreading any false reports."

"We all know how you feel about that, Dear," Maria said soothingly.

"It's just the way I was brought up, Maria. I was my father's only child, you know, and he adored me. I suppose I've simply assumed that men are there to take care of me—and all the muddlesome things like taxes and investments."

"Why sure you did, Honey."

Spencer glanced at Maria sharply, mistrusting the perfect innocence of her expression. Maria had a long-standing habit of saying whatever one wanted to hear while reserving the right to mean something else altogether. Had she laid rather too much stress on the word you? Nuance could be such a nuisance when other people were employing it. When in doubt, one could always choose to miss the point.

"Of course, I always managed the human side of things," she went on. "And very skillfully, too, if I do say so. But perhaps I should have tried to understand all the money business as well. Not that Geoffrey wouldn't be perfectly happy to take care of everything for me. That's just the trouble. I want to settle things my own way, but I need someone to show me how—not someone who will say: there, there, don't worry your pretty little head about it; just sign here. So it stands to reason that I need a woman."

"Amen, Sister. Set thy house in order, for tomorrow—"

Maria broke off. It was one of the few times Spencer had ever seen her look nonplused.

"For tomorrow thou shalt die?" Spencer finished the quotation helpfully. "Well, really, Maria, perhaps not tomorrow, if you have any influence with higher authorities."

"I'll mention it to the Lord," Maria promised, at ease again. "And I'm gon' talk to Raina, too. If she ain't the woman for the job herself, she sure to know who is. Don't you worry now. Everything gon' be just fine."

"Oh, look!" Spencer's attention was diverted. "There's Esther Peters coming through the gate with her little boys. What's that the children are carrying between them? Why bless their hearts! I do believe they're bringing me a wreath for my door."

Maria and Spencer both turned to watch the approach. The young relation rose to his feet and called out some greeting. Well, of course, being sexton he would have met Esther Peters. Spencer could not hear any spoken response from Esther as she followed the boys, shepherding them and their unwieldy cargo, but she saw Esther's smile, and it startled her for some reason. Could it be that the woman had not smiled during any of her visits to the Gatehouse? That seemed impossible, given how excruciatingly pleasant and polite Esther Peters was. It was more likely, in fact, that she had never ceased to smile from one end of the visit to the other.

What was it about this smile that disconcerted Spencer and made her regard the rector's wife more keenly? She felt almost as though she had never really seen Esther before. Until this moment she would not have been able to pick Esther out from a crowd. Now there was something, well, memorable about her. But what was it? She wished Esther would hurry up and come inside so that she could begin one of the decorous and indirect cross-examinations for which she would be renowned were her methods not too subtle to be detected.

Right now Esther appeared to be caught up in conversation with Marlon, Martin, Mar something. He had advanced a step or two to meet her, stubbing his cigarette out on the carriage road, she noted. The little boys had taken over the front steps, collapsing with the wreath between them. The young man had their attention, too, as he talked to their mother with flamboyant gestures. Spencer couldn't get any of the words, but after watching for a moment she decided he must be recounting some tale, taking the part of more than one character. He kept shifting position, his back towards the window, then his profile visible, alternately.

Spencer glanced briefly at Maria. She was watching the performance, too, with marked displeasure.

"Mmh, mmh, mmh," Maria muttered her disapproval.

When Spencer returned her gaze to the vignette, Esther's smile had stretched beyond capacity. And she was laughing—laughing so hard and so loud that the sound penetrated the glass. Her whole face was contorted with laughter; it was most unseemly. Young ladies in Spencer's day had been warned against giving way to such a degree. Giggling was all very well among the girls, but such hearty laughter was really the domain of men. Hardly the thing for mixed company.

"Well," said Spencer, "I do hope they will let us in on the joke."

"Marvin shouldn't ought to keep Mrs. Peters standing there like that." Maria's tone was severe. "I better be going—"

"No, no. Stay where you are, Maria. She'll be in presently, and I do think you might let your nephew take some tea if he wants to and tell me his conclusions about the ramp. You know, you do enough for me and for everyone in White Hart, Maria. You mustn't make your nephew feel he has to take up carpentry on my account. Gracious heavens! Now what's happening?"

Spencer craned her neck to get a glimpse of Esther Peters dashing off down the carriage road at a run.

"How very odd! Now, Maria, you know I never gossip, but I do feel entitled to say that I think Esther Peters runs off into my wood with rather more frequency than one would expect in a rector's wife. I can't remember any of the others engaging in such pastimes, can you, Maria? Whatever do you suppose she means by it?"

"Spencer, I believe it be best if I just get Marvin and go on home now," Maria said, rising from her chair. "I have him call you tomorrow. You don't want to be tiring yourself too much, your first day downstairs."

"Wait, Maria!" Spencer motioned her to sit down again. "Let's watch this."

Esther disappeared around the bend of the carriage road, and the young relation turned and sauntered over to the steps where the little boys still sat with the wreath. There was a long moment of mutual scrutiny, then Martian—yes, that name suited him; he was so marvelously alien to White Hart—sat down on the lower step, slid the wreath further onto the porch, reached into a pocket and brought out a deck of playing cards, which he proceeded to shuffle with elegant skill. The boys watched the cards arc and fall in total fascination. Maria groaned.

"Lord Jesus, why! Excuse me, Spencer, I got to go. Marvin don't have the sense God gave a billy goat, he—"

"Hush, Maria, he's dealing now. I want to see."

"Spencer, please. It ain't fitting—"

"Maria, I do believe he's dealing seven card stud! Is your nephew a poker player?"

Maria only moaned.

"You know, Maria," Spencer continued as she watched, "when I was a little girl, my father taught me to play. I loved the game. He would even let me play with his friends on occasion. That went on until I developed a real taste for the game—and a certain flair, too, I might add. Then a governess I had for a while, an imported English one who had everybody cowed, found out about it and threatened to quit unless it stopped immediately. My mother never did approve. With the governess on her side, she had my father outnumbered and outmaneuvered. My husband used to play at his club in New York, but he sneered at the very idea of what he called "ladies' games." Of course none of the WOSPs knew anything about poker, nor cared to. So I haven't played in, well, decades, really. I do think it might be diverting to take it up again. A little quiet excitement, you know. Do you suppose your nephew would play with me sometimes?"

"Honey, that boy would play with the Devil himself. And win, too. Yes, indeed. And win, too."

"Well, he's not winning now," observed Spencer. "Unless I've forgotten everything I used to know, little Jonathan's got a Royal Flush!"

Spencer was so engrossed in the game that she did not notice Esther's approach until the Martian stood up, leaving his poker hand face down on the porch. Then Spencer's attention focused not on Esther but on the strange figure she had brought back with her from the wood.

An old, old man with long white hair and a beard to match leaned on a carved staff. Esther Peters appeared to be introducing him to the young relation. The old man kept his eyes fixed on the young man's face even after the younger one looked away and began to talk—judging from his gestures and the direction of his gaze—about building the ramp.

But the motions of the young man's hands became a mere distraction, a flickering at the edge of Spencer's vision. Nor did she register Esther or the little boys. She saw only the old man, the old, old man.

"Who is he?" she murmured. "Who is he?"

"Honey." Someone spoke from somewhere. "Don't you know?"

Father Time, the Old North Wind, voices whispered in her mind. The Hermit, the very Parfit Gentil Knight. She watched the old one inclining towards the younger man the way a plant leans into light, seeking to take in something beyond words, beyond sight.

How well she remembered that stance.

Fergus, Fergus.

Spencer closed her eyes, and the green light seeped in under her lids. An ancient wood shivered, shimmered in the hot chill of their cruel, green youth.

When she opened her eyes again, the old man was squatting next to the steps, his staff laid aside as his hands danced, conjuring a vision of the ramp out of thin air.

She was still separate from him, the window between them. She was still the princess in the tower, the princess under glass. He could not see her watching him, because of daylight reflecting on the window panes. Light concealed her. But night was coming, and she was planning her escape at last.

For the crooked shall be made straight, she reminded herself, and the rough places plain, and the glory of the Lady shall be revealed.

TELL US OF THE NIGHT 1

...For this is he that was spoken of by the prophet Esaias saying, The voice of one crying in the wilderness, Prepare ye the way of the Lord, make his paths straight.

And the same John had his raiment of camel's hair, and a leathern girdle about his loins, and his meat was locusts and wild honey.

ESTHER Peters, sitting in the last pew on the left side, leaned against one of the stone pillars that separated the nave of the church from the side chapel. She closed her eyes, and an image rose up of Fergus Hanrahan scooping honey comb from a hollow tree while enchanted bees swarmed about him in a benign cloud. Of course in Blackwood it was hardly the season for wild honey or locusts, and it wasn't as if the old man had to forage for his food.

In the past few weeks, she had visited his apple-scented loft on several occasions, sometimes with, sometimes without the children. She had seen for herself his shelves stocked with jars of dried beans and grains and garden preserves; braids of onions and bunches of dried herbs hung from the rafters—just like the "rabbit tobacco" in Peter Rabbit's house, as David had remarked. Although the loft was spacious, there was a quality of coziness that did make her think of small animals in Edwardian dress living snugly in well-appointed homes among the roots of trees.

...And now also the axe is laid unto the root of the trees...

The violence of the imagery caught hold of Esther's wandering attention and gave it a yank. She thought of the ring of trees in Blackwood, and her teeth buzzed unpleasantly as if she felt the blow strike her own root.

...therefore every tree that bringeth forth not good fruit is hewn down and cast into the fire.

"The Gospel of the Lord."

Alan lifted the Bible as he bowed his head. Above Alan and the acolyte—a girl today, one of Nancy Jones' daughters—hung the huge Advent wreath with its four purple candles, two lit, two in waiting. "The wreath," Esther could hear Fergus telling her, "is the circle of rebirth. In the dark of the year, the Lady brings forth the sun child out of the womb of night. That is why Christmas is celebrated near the Winter Solstice."

Well, of course everyone knew that, but she had never considered the reason for the wreath. She felt laughter welling in her at the thought of the Lady squatting over St. Paul's, right over Alan's head, in fact, as she readied herself for the birth. Prepare ye the way.

"Praise to you, Lord Christ," the Congregation answered.

Esther's lips moved, and appropriate sounds came out, her irreverence momentarily quelled. Not that anyone would notice her. Only Elsa Endsley shared her pew, and she sat at the opposite end, her attention, like everyone's, on God—or Alan. For all Jesus' admonitions to love your neighbor, in church you didn't even have to look at your neighbor, not face to face, just the back of his head. In the midst of the congregation, Esther felt solitary, anonymous; she found it restful.

> *Watchman, tell us of the night,*
> *What its signs of promise are.*
> *Traveler, o'er yon mountain's height,*
> *See that glory beaming star.*

They sang the second tune, "Aberystwyth." Welsh, no doubt. *With movement*, italic print instructed. And the music did move with the sort of grim joy the traveler might feel after walking all night to find at last the star and the soothsaying watchman.

> *Watchman, does its beauteous ray*
> *Aught of joy or hope foretell?*
> *Traveler, yes, it brings the day,*
> *Promised day of Israel.*

Despite the assurances of daybreak and the switches from minor into major key at the appropriate moments, the tune retained that note of menace, of danger associated with night.

"Please be seated," Alan invited when the hymn was over. They sat, and Alan stood once again beneath the suspended wreath.

"Watchman, tell us of the night!" Alan began. "In today's Gospel, we encounter one of the greatest watchmen of all time, the man who embodies the spirit of Advent, who dedicated his life to preparing the way of the Lord, to making himself and others ready for the one who was and is to come, whose shoes we are not worthy to bear, the one who baptizes us with the Holy Spirit and with fire.

"Now suppose someone were to cry out to you today, Watchman, tell us of the night...."

Tell us of the night, Esther mused silently, closing her eyes once more, feeling the rough terrain of the stone impress her cheek. Tell us of the night.

"Light reveals the earth," Fergus had said. "Night yields the stars."

On that occasion, Esther had been with Fergus and Sabine in the apple barn, two days after her encounter with them in Blackwood. It had been another school day for Jonathan, and after returning from driving the carpool, she had gone straight to Blackwood, hoping to get some light, some plain daylight on what had happened in the Ring of Trees. They had all drunk tea together, black, bitter, bracing tea.

"The circle is sacred to the Lady," Fergus had begun. "It is the shape of the sun and the moon and the earth. It is the roundness of ripe fruit and of the ripening womb. Wherever you find a circle, or make one, there is holy ground. Do you see?"

He paused and looked at Esther expectantly. Well, she did see; that was not the problem, exactly. She saw the fruit and the moon, just as she had seen the Lady that day when Fergus invoked her. But she did not understand. She could not make sense of the images, of their implications for her.

"Do you mean," Esther spoke slowly, groping for the exact question she needed to ask, "that there is a, well, a religion of the Lady with rituals and a set of beliefs and all that?"

Esther looked from Fergus to Sabine, and those two in turn exchanged glances.

"No." Fergus appeared to be pondering. "No, not a set of beliefs, more a set of practices. Worship of the Lady in many times and places has been a practical matter. When practices are separated from their time and place, from their meaning, they are apt to be called superstition."

"Peasant superstition," put in Sabine. "In Europe these words go together. Those who followed the old ways were often called ignorant. Sometimes they were accused of practicing magic instead of religion. Bien sûr, it is not always so easy to tell the difference."

"The word pagan means country-dweller," observed Fergus, "as the word heathen meant dweller on the heath. It was those who lived closest to the earth that the Christians found most difficult to convert to the new religion. As you doubtless know, the Roman Catholic church in many places merely renamed the old gods and their feast days."

"C'est vrai," Sabine nodded. "In my village, Sainte Marie Mauresque, a tiny one in les Alpes-Maritimes, we are under the protection of la Madone

Noire. She has a shrine in a cave, and the spring there is sacred to her as well as the trees, le Bois de la Sainte Vierge."

"I visited it once," said Fergus. "It was there that I first met Sabine. It may indeed have been a virgin wood, which is rare in Europe. It was very old."

"Oui," Sabine nodded. "Et la Madone Noire, elle etait très, très ancienne. She looks a little like your figure, Esther, but she is carved of stone and black as night. Candles are always lit to her, and she shines with their light. It may be true, she has been there long before the birth of Our Lord, but then this is not strange; naturellement, the mother comes before the child. No one knows how old she is. In my village, until the second war, we did not know time in that way. How did you say it, Fergus? It is round, comprenez? It is planting or harvest, full moon or new moon, time for the baby to be born or time to sew the shroud. To l'histoire, les rois, les guerres, we bend like the grass in the wind and take little notice."

The story of Sabine's village, as she then recounted it to Esther, was round—or perhaps spiral—with la Madone Noire always at the heart. Apparently, in the collective memory of the village, which stretched back—or spiraled—at least to the reign of Charlemagne, there had always been a priest of the church, a curé as Sabine called him, and a prêtresse, tending the shrine of the Black Madonna and leading devotions. Sabine also called her la Sage-femme, which Esther knew meant midwife, la Vieille Bonne Femme—Old Witch—and prophétesse. Her functions included general doctoring with herbal remedies and divining as well as midwifery. The curé, who could sometimes read and write Latin, often doubled as a lawyer and judge in property disputes and, being male, served as a liaison with the outside world.

Usually the two came to some kind of terms: sometimes the barest tolerance, sometimes friendly rivalry. There were a few generations when la Sorcière, as she was called then, had to go into hiding. One legendary pair had been lovers. Relations were unpredictable and could be upset at any time, for the church appointed the curé, while la Vielle Bonne Femme always chose and trained her own successor.

"When I was sixteen, la Sorcière chose me."

Esther experienced a roller-coaster jolt as the story spiraled into her own century. It was all very well as a quaint tale, but there was Sabine, sitting across from her, gazing into her tea, giving her words time to settle, as if she sensed Esther's dizziness. Yes, it was like seeing double. As she gazed at plain, sensible Sabine, other images superimposed themselves: stooped green-skinned women, warty and bony, proffering poisoned apples and gingerbread shingles, devouring children or ruining the hopes of beautiful maidens; jealous older women, step-mothers, who could be coldly beautiful until their true hideous selves were unmasked. And there was Sabine, wartless and serene. Had she just said she was a witch?

"Then what happened?" Esther asked, like a child hearing a story, she thought, feeling immediately ashamed. This was Sabine's life.

"Then the war came," Sabine took up her story.

The South of France had been under the rule of the Collaborationist government. Everything was forfeit to the Nazis, if they wanted it: crops, animals, sons, daughters. The peasants had no surplus left to sell and many, like Sabine's parents, were driven off their land, because they could not pay taxes. Some people took refuge in le Bois de la Sainte Vierge, foraging for wild food, sharing the shelter of la Sorcière, thinking that surely between them, la Madone Noir, la Vieille Bonne Femme and le Bois de la Sainte Vierge would protect them.

Then the Nazis decided that they needed lumber. Everyone fled the wood, except la Sorcière and Sabine. In two weeks all the ancient trees had been felled. On the day that they seized la Sorcière, Sabine had been called away to her uncle's farm to help with the lambing. La Sorcière, who was old and little and dark, had doubtless called down curses in old Provençal. Most likely, she had been taken for a gypsy and sent to the camps. Sabine had tried to find her and joined for a time the Gypsy underground where she had re-encountered Fergus.

When the war ended, she returned to Sainte Marie Mauresque with a half-hearted intention to take up her role as Prêtresse. She went first to the shrine of la Madone Noir to ask for blessing and guidance and was astonished to find the entrance to the cave sealed. To all appearances there had been a landslide. She felt bereft, yet also relieved; the shrine had not and would never now be desecrated. Still, with no wood, no shrine, how could there be a prêtresse? Not knowing what else to do, she tried for a time to carry on the ancient tradition.

"But I find I know only little broken bits of something that was one piece. So when the American soldiers came through my village, I meet my husband. My parents, my brothers and sisters have already left the mountains for the city. My world is gone, so I follow him to his world. For all my married life, I try to live like an American, without a past—what a European means by a past. Except for the herbs, which I always gather and grow, I try to forget la Sorcière, la Madone Noir, all the old ways. They have no place in this new world. I have never spoken to anyone, not even my daughters, of my craft, the little I knew of it. I only speak now, because Fergus says it is necessary."

"Necessary?" Esther repeated.

Sabine gave one of her eloquent French shrugs. "Let Fergus tell you about his mother, une vraie prophetesse Irlandaise."

"Long ago," began Fergus, feeling for his tobacco pouch, "one All Hallow Eve, my mother had a seeing. Of Blackwood. That it is one her sacred groves, the Lady's, just as the ravished Bois de la Vierge was a sacred grove. There are not many left in the world. Blackwood is one of the last. You know that, Esther."

A shiver ran through her. Esther nodded.

"Blackwood is in danger."

"Excuse me." Esther spoke as Fergus paused to fill his pipe. "I am very moved by what you've both been telling me, but I still don't understand why you are telling me. I mean, I'm not a prophetess or a...a witch. I'm a Christian. I'm the wife of an Episcopal priest, a priest's wife."

Esther said it several ways to keep a grasp of it—reality—to keep at least one foot on what she knew to be solid ground while the other one drifted, in some unstable barque, farther and farther from the shore, spreading her uncertain legs further and further apart, threatening her balance.

"What could I possibly have to do with witchcraft or the old religion, whatever you call it? I'm still not sure what you mean by it. What do you mean?"

"Some say witchcraft, wicca, means the craft of the wise, like the Wise Woman of Sabine's village who knew the secrets of the wild herbs, or like my mother, who could look into a wash basin and see the shadow of things to come. Some say wicca means to bend, to turn, to shape. Whenever you change one thing into another, that is craft, is it not?"

"Flour, salt, yeast into bread," said Sabine.

"Untilled earth into a garden," added Fergus.

"Sickness into health," Sabine's voice.

"Water into wine."

"Flesh and blood into milk."

"Sorrow into song."

At first Esther looked from one face to the other, the aging woman and the old man, trying to make sense, trying to keep it all straight. Then she just closed her eyes and let their litany act on her.

"Raw wool into spun yarn."

"Yearning into enchantment."

"Seed into fruit."

"Unformed dough into the Lady's shape."

"Cream into butter."

"But—" Esther stopped them, relieved to find that she had the power.

"Yes, that did happen. She took shape, I gave her shape, just as you say. But it was just a bit of playdough, not some ancient and powerful figure, like La Madone Noir, that a whole village worshipped for centuries. And when I went to the icehouse to see my graven image—if you'll pardon the expression—well, that wasn't it, that wasn't what I was looking for. I don't want an idol."

"People who know the Lady have often been called idolators," observed Fergus. "Perhaps rightly, perhaps wrongly."

"Et bien aussi Roman Catholics."

"Papists, pagans," murmured Esther. And because Papists were really pagans in sheeps' clothing, Puritans had gone around smashing statues and windows and outlawing Christmas revels and Maypoles, Esther recalled, not from Church History 101 but from her reading of many romantic historical novels. But then, of course, the good old C of E had found the via media, the Anglican way, Esther reminded herself with a surge of loyalty.

"Those who accuse us say that we worship wood or stone instead of God—as if wood and stone were not of God—instead of the Father immortal, invisible, living beyond this world, who took on flesh once only in all time.

"And it is true, we do worship wood and stone and water and tree, sun and moon, earth. Matter, Mater. It is all She, in us, around us. We rise from her and take on a life, a knowing, as a spring flower shoots from the bulb hidden in the ground. Then we forget our beginning though it awaits us in the end. She claims us; she who gave us form, unforms us. To some this truth is intolerable. We of the old religion seek not to escape the round of life, the roundness. We seek to enter into its mysteries, to be celebrants."

The three sat for a time. The kettle on the woodstove sputtered, drops beading on the hot surface, exploding into steam.

"What you say is all very well," Esther spoke at length. "I mean, it's beautiful. I can see that. But most people don't live close to the earth like that. I have a garden, but this isn't an agrarian society. It's not even industrial; it's post-industrial, whatever that means. The small farmers that are left are going under. Most food production in this country is done by agribusiness. People meet their food for the first time triple-wrapped in the supermarket. People aren't even very aware of the seasons, except in terms of road conditions, sports, school schedules, you know, leisure activities."

Sabine and Fergus made no attempt to concur or dispute. If Sabine and Fergus had rarely spoken of these matters—and then only to each other— their effort to make words for her must be immense, exhausting. Fergus drew deeply on his pipe, then exhaled with a sigh. Esther watched the smoke make the air currents visible. She ought to be going, she thought, not making a move.

"For a long time," Fergus spoke again, "only a few people have known the Lady. She has been in eclipse, perhaps in her own dark moon phase. Her arts have become occult, hidden."

"You don't mean Satanism," Esther said.

"Doux Jesu, non!" Sabine made the sign of the cross.

"The worship of Satan, of which many witches were falsely accused and for which thousands, maybe millions, were tortured and put to death, was a grotesque mirror image of Christian rites with which Christians terrified themselves and terrorized others. The Horned God, which Christians turned into their Devil, is the Lady's son and consort."

"Horned?" Esther repeated, suddenly blushing from head to toe, as she recalled her first sight of Marvin.

"Yes, horned, because in the days which you have pointed out are gone, men could make themselves one with the game. That was their magic, that they entered the mind of the quarry, shared the life that gave them life and knew its death even as they inflicted it. There are still peoples on the earth who know this magic. Where there was no wild game, no hunt, the god was seen in the rising and dying grain. He is the death that gives life and the life that must die. He is the Lady's son, born of darkness, and he is the sun that rises and sets each day, and waxes in strength, then wanes. He shares our life and death, as does your Jesus Christ. In our story, he is the Lady's lover, too, and begets himself before he dies back into her womb. Of course, in your religion he also does that, but you have made him into three persons. Though Jesus is incarnate, Christians for some reason see carnal love as a sin."

Fergus paused to blow a contemplative series of smoke rings.

"It is the darkness that Christians fear or have forgotten, with their worship of the son who is the sun to the exclusion of the mother. And since their fears shape the dark, darkness has become fearful, evil. And the dark is fearsome and also holy. The Lady's darkness is of the womb, of the grave, of the earth, which gives or withholds food. Her darkness is the depths of the sea where men drown and where life begins. And she is one with the moon that draws the tides and rides the night and rules the cycles of planting and harvest, conception and birth. Light reveals the world; night yields the stars. The arts of divination, which are hers, are linked in people's minds with night: dreams and stars."

Esther watched as Fergus wreathed his head with smoke rings that seemed to hold their shape for an unusually long time.

"In a small way, I am a seer," Fergus went on. "There are signs that the Lady is returning, rising—like a full moon rising at sundown—coming to acquaint us with the night. I do not know what this return will mean for the world. I will not live to be part of it. Even now, my world ends at the edge of Blackwood, as you have seen for yourself, Esther. I have given my life and my craft to protecting Blackwood. My sight does not extend far enough to tell you why the Lady has called you here. I have no vision of the future and little claim on the present. I offer you the past, what I know and can teach of the craft."

"And I, too," said Sabine. "I will teach you what I know."

"Why?" Esther turned to Sabine. "Supposing I agree to learn, which I haven't yet. I know about Fergus seeing me on Hallowe'en with the snake and the spindle. But why do you trust me? Do you?"

Sabine considered for a moment. "I think because of your sons, that they are bien élevé. You are a good mother."

"In the name of the Father, the Son and the Holy Spirit, Amen."

Oh, God! Esther came to; she had missed almost the entire sermon. Before she could think whether she remembered enough to offer Alan appropriate "feedback"—by which he meant detailed praise—she was on her feet with the rest of the congregation.

> *We believe in one God,*
> *the Father, the Almighty,*
> *maker of heaven and earth,*
> *of all that is, seen and unseen.*

Esther's voice rolled to a stop somewhere in the middle of the second line and wouldn't start up again; the battery was dead. She stared at the words on the page that she usually didn't read, since she knew them by heart.

> *We believe in one Lord, Jesus Christ,*
> *the only Son of God,*
> *eternally begotten of the Father,*
> *God from God, Light from Light,*
> *true God from true God,*
> *begotten, not made,*
> *of one Being with the Father.*
> *Through him all things were made.*
> *For us and for our salvation*
> *he came down from heaven:*
> *by the power of the Holy Spirit*

> *he became incarnate from the Virgin Mary,*
> *and was made man.*
> *For our sake he was crucified under Pontius Pilate;*
> *he suffered death and was buried.*
> *On the third day he rose again*
> *in accordance with the Scriptures;*
> *he ascended into heaven*
> *and is seated at the right hand of the Father.*
> *He will come again in glory to judge the living and the dead,*
> *and his kingdom will have no end.*

No, Fergus, Esther thought, it will not do, your tolerance of Jesus Christ, your respectful nod to him as a form of your god. That will not work for a Christian, not a Protestant one anyway, she amended, thinking of Sabine, however Romish Episcopalians might be in some of their trappings. For a true Christian, Christ is no myth, no horned magician; He is the one, the only begotten Son of the Father (who never married his mother, who married her off to an old man for appearance' sake. Jesus, do I believe this?)

> *We believe in the Holy Spirit...*

Formerly the Holy Ghost, who had terrified Esther as a child; she had been sure for a time that her grandfather's church was haunted.

> *...the Lord, the giver of life,*
> *who proceeds from the Father and the Son.*
> *With the Father and the Son he is worshipped and glorified.*

Some theologians made a case for the feminine nature of the Holy Spirit, that he was really Sophia, Holy Wisdom. But even in the newly revised prayerbook—

> *He has spoken through the Prophets.*
> *We believe in one holy catholic and apostolic Church.*
> *We acknowledge one baptism for the forgiveness of sins.*
> *We look for the resurrection of the dead,*
> *and the life of the world to come. Amen.*

"We seek not to escape from the round of life, the roundness; we seek to enter into its mysteries, to be celebrants."

How thin, how singular the sound of Fergus' voice in her memory compared to the resounding effect of standing in the midst of a congregation proclaiming as one body, "We believe!" Sabine and Fergus had no idea what they were asking of her. Sabine ought to have had, perhaps, but she didn't. She had always worshipped the Lady and her Son, whether as Roman Catholic or witch. Esther's mind didn't bend that way.

Wicca, to bend, to turn. But the Lord our God wanted the crooked straight and the rough places plain. Make straight a highway in the desert for our God.

"Turn to form five of the Prayers of the People, page 389."

Esther knelt, not bothering to find the page.

"In peace let us pray to the Lord, saying Kyrie Eleison."

Alan was being "high" today, choosing the Greek response instead of the English, Lord, have mercy. Esther caught an echo of Marvin's voice. "Have mercy, Lady!"

Lady, have mercy.

IT'S IN THE CARDS 19

ESTHER squeezed several stacks of Christmas cards in green and red envelopes through the out-of-town slot. She listened to them patter onto the existing pile in whatever receptacle within the mysterious inner sanctum of the post office collected such offerings. Then she stepped back outside into the brilliant morning after the first snow. It had not been enough snow to stick to the roads or to close schools, just enough snow to sugar-coat everything. The Main Street of White Hart, with its Christmas trees strung with lights paid for by local merchants, matched the displays in store windows.

Esther made her way up the street enjoying the strength of her legs, the confidence of her stride. Sun on her face, eyes half-closed to filter the dazzle of the day, she yielded to a sheer animal sense of well-being. It was only mid-morning, and she had accomplished all the tasks she'd set herself: mailing the cards, marinating meat and chopping vegetables for Boeuf Bourgogne. (A traveling bishop was coming for dinner and to spend the night, and as Barbara Pym had observed in one of her novels, the clergy required meat, as opposed to spinsters who could subsist with omelettes and risottos.) Moreover, she had changed the sheets in the guest room and laid out fresh towels. Really, she was a marvel of efficiency and quite possibly gorgeous into the bargain. It was almost frightening, she realized, to feel so pleased with herself.

Alan had wanted her last night, really wanted her, out of desire, not habit or obligation. Whatever she was doing or thinking these days, well, it must be all right if the effect was to improve her marriage. After all, hadn't Jesus said, Ye shall know the tree by its fruits? It would not do to probe too deeply; if you fingered things they fell apart.

For a moment at least, she could rest on her laurels—or, at any rate, rest. Alan wouldn't be home till he returned at dinner time with the bishop, so she didn't have to think about lunch and the kids weren't due back for another hour and a half. She could enjoy a respite from the awkwardness of their wanting to follow Marvin everywhere.

That was the root of the problem. Since the day he had taught them poker, David and Jonathan had become Marvin's devotees. Not that he played with them much or paid them direct attention. When he was at St. Paul's or at Spencer Crowe's, building the ramp, he was working. Usually, he didn't court their favor. "Being good with kids" was not essential to his self-concept the way it was to some men, who, nevertheless, did not seem to know how to relate to kids except by rough-housing, tickling, generally over-stimulating them from a mother's point of view.

Marvin was low-key. He had the rare knack of knowing how to include them in what he was doing. He gave them real jobs, letting them sand or paint, but he didn't push them beyond their attention span. He had no stock of Protestant-work-ethic sayings: if a job is worth doing, it's worth doing well; if you start something, you have to finish it—all of which she had heard from Alan. But then, she stifled the disloyal comparision, Marvin had no stake in the kids the way Alan did. He could afford to be cool when they lost interest, though, granted, he didn't let them get in the way, either, or disrupt his concentration. All in all, he was relaxed, and her sons felt included in a man's world without being under pressure.

What was she to do? Marvin's job description in no way included babysitting. Though he insisted he didn't mind, she did not feel she could just go off and do other things while he watched her children. Forbidding them to spend time with him caused tears and rebellions, though occasionally diversion, bordering on bribery, worked—shopping trips that included the purchase of lollipops and the like. Sometimes—more often than not if she were truthful—she simply gave in, joined in, picked up a paintbrush or a hammer herself and succumbed to the pure (or impure) pleasure of being in his company.

She had, at least, made a rule for herself not to see him alone. Since the day of the dancing, she had avoided the Parish House in off hours. He came to work on foot, so there was never a car to signal his presence on the premises. She couldn't risk a repeat of that encounter, its intensity—intense for her, anyway. Surely for him it was just a game, a diversion. He had been a pimp, she kept reminding herself; seduction had been his profession. By now he probably had women lined up all the way from White Hart to River City. His manner with her was force of habit. She'd be a fool, a naive fool, to take it seriously.

Despite her firm resolve to avoid him when alone, he often happened—coincidentally?—to be out in the driveway just around the time she returned from the carpool. On a cigarette break. Plenty of people smoked inside the parish house, and there were ashtrays scattered about, but Marvin refrained. "God," he said, "had put the fear of Maria into him." He generally sat on the Parish House steps, a gorgeous man with a cigarette

dangling from his lips. His deference to propriety was not readily apparent.

Although it did make sense, on returning from nursery school, to turn
in at the lower end of the driveway, Esther knew she was looking for
Marvin whenever she drove past the Parish House. The other day she had
found a pretext for putting the car down the driveway in the garage. (Oh,
yes, it was supposed to snow.) And she had remembered she had to tell
Nancy something. (What was it?) So she had walked right up to Marvin
as he sat on the steps. (She couldn't very well pass him without saying
hello.) He had watched her approach—she could feel his gaze in the part
of the stomach where butterflies traditionally fluttered—his immense eyes
narrowed to slits. In this mode he always made her think of a cat pretending to sleep, ready to spring.

She was one hell of a stupid mouse.

"Esther. What's up," he had greeted her, not taken in by her blithering
about the weather forecast and a message for Nancy.

"You know, Esther, we never had us that talk. About the Goddess?"

It was true; with the kids underfoot, they hadn't. Esther had assumed
he'd forgotten about it. Hoped. Her mention of Goddess had been rash,
impulsive. She hadn't even talked about it with Alan. Sabine and Fergus
had offered her a handle on the subject, but she was a long way from
grasping it.

"Cat got your tongue, Lady?"

Well, yes, in a manner of speaking, she wished she could say. "Curiosity
killed the cat," he observed.

"And satisfaction brought it back?" She completed the saying. "I'm sorry,
Marvin. It's not that I won't talk; it's more that I can't."

"Yeah? Well, maybe I can. I been doing me some thinking. You know,
when you first say the word Goddess, I asked myself, what the hell she
talking about? What that got to do with anything? Then it come to me one
night, in my religion, we got a Goddess."

"Your religion?" Esther repeated. Was he a Rastafarian or some other
Caribbean or African religion?

"Poker."

Esther laughed. Laughter came easily around Marvin.

"No, I'm serious." Marvin held up his hand as if to put a brake on his
own smile. "I got me a all night poker game Saturday nights. That's how
come you don't see me in church on Sunday morning. I already been."

"But what do you mean, exactly, when you say poker is your religion.
Do you mean it's a ritual?"

"O.K. Hear me out. First thing, what is a religion, anyway? Ain't nothing but a way of trying to make sense of what's going down. So poker, it's like life, right? Life deal the hands. You might get all low cards or all high or something in between. Your hand might be so bad, you be a good player and still lose. Or you might have everything and blow it, 'cause you a fool. If you got the skill with the luck, you can be a king. Or maybe you got just one good card and you slick enough to bluff everybody. Luck and skill, that's where it's at. We all players, and we call the Goddess Lady Luck."

"Dame Fortune," Esther nodded, considering whether or not that was what she meant when she said Goddess. "But, Marvin, wait a minute." Without thinking, Esther sat down on the step next to him and turned towards him. "It just dawned on me what's wrong, what's been bothering me, not just about what you said but about what I know of the Goddess so far, her being, well, like nature, which is another way of saying life. Where does the idea of justice come in? Human justice. Or maybe I mean injustice. The Goddess doesn't explain that."

"Ain't nobody say all luck is good luck. You know the song: If it wasn't for bad luck, I wouldn't have no luck at all."

"But it's not just a matter of luck," Esther persisted. "I mean, maybe if it doesn't rain and the crops fail or if there's an earthquake, that sort of thing, yes. But what about poverty, oppression, wars, racism?" She looked him in the face. "That isn't luck, good or bad. It's what people do to each other. What about that? Maybe that's where Christianity comes in."

"Ain't no religion I know of ever make sense of injustice—or put a stop to it neither. But folks sure enough have use religion to make the wrong they determine to do look right. Ever hear of the children of Ham? Bible story, right? That's how white people done try to prove the righteousness of enslaving the Black race."

"But then," Esther countered, "what about Martin Luther King, Jr.? He was a Christian if ever there was one. In his speech, I've been to the mountaintop and I've seen the Promised Land, he's quoting Moses. He's identifying with Moses. That's a very different use of the Bible. For the cause of freedom and justice."

"That just prove my point. People use they religion for they own purpose, so life make sense to them. With the Bible, it ain't the scripture, it's who's quoting make the difference. They say the Devil can quote with the best of them. Dr. King—and I got every respect for the man, believe me—he wanted justice; whether it was on account of him being a Christian or being a proud Black man or both beats me. All I'm saying is Christianity, right, it still don't explain why I was born Black in Georgia and you born white in—"

"New Jersey," Esther supplied.

"That's where the deal come in. The luck of the draw."

"But people make choices," Esther argued. "And it's more complicated than making the best play, because you're not just in it by yourself, for yourself, the way you are in a poker game. You're in families, communities. And injustice is not as simple or straightforward as cheating so you can win. I mean, there's more to life than self-interest."

"Yeah?" Marvin shrugged. "Like I say, ain't no religion make sense of it all."

"But Jesus," Esther struggled to express what she meant. "Jesus himself. It's not so much that he tried to make sense of life as that he entered into it, suffered it."

"Excuse me, Esther." Marvin dropped his cigarette and ground it under his boot, though he made no move to stand up. "I don't mean no disrespect, and I know you the preacher's wife. Lots of people get mad with me when I talk this way. Maria? Whew! I know better than to let my lips get loose. But Jesus? Yeah, he suffered. The man got himself nailed up. And one of his best friends turned evidence on him, and that's cold. But he ain't never been lynch for looking sideways at no white woman. His peoples abandon him, but he ain't never been bought or sold away from them. They been so much evil going down B.C., A.D., I never did understand how one man dying was supposed to make everything all right. You? If we saved, I missed something. Bible say Jesus rose again. What about the rest? We sure could use a glimpse of Dr. King right now, another forty days of Malcolm. Where they at? Where's Jesus, come to that. If he's coming again, what's he waiting on? Who gonna see justice get done? Shit. Excuse me."

He turned his face away and reached into his pocket for his pack of cigarettes. Lucky Strikes. Esther watched him light up. She had never seen this aspect of him before, anger, bitterness. His surface was so beautifully smooth; here was a hint of something jagged and unfinished underneath.

"But, Jesus, yeah." Marvin took a drag on his cigarette, recovering his composure, exhaling his customary cool. "He was all right. I got nothing against the man. And he was a man—you know—the only man, for some. Where I grew up, my grandmother and the other old sanctified ladies, seem like they got disgusted with they own men after awhile and turn to Jesus. 'Cause he ain't never gonna let them down." Marvin laughed. "Jesus, yeah. He had a way with him. Bible don't like to spell these things out, but you can read between the lines. All those women hanging around him all the time. Word made flesh. Why go to all the trouble of getting born and dying, if you ain't got no plan to enjoy the finer things of life in between? What kind of man he be if he ain't taste the fruit?"

He was playing with her again, rolling his eyes at her.

"Oh, Marvin!" She got to her feet; the conversation was getting out of hand. "Only you would think of that."

"Yeah? Well, you tell me, Esther, what else is there?" He got up and stood over her on the top step. "Talk about religion now. That's where it all begin. Garden of Eden. Adam and Eve, right? Don't give me no jive about the Holy Spirit and the Virgin Mary. Any time a man and a woman make love, I mean really make love when they both want it, that's the Holy Spirit right there."

Esther mumbled something about his rather liberal interpretations of scripture, and turned to flee towards Nancy's office.

"You and me, Esther," he called after her, "we have us some more talks. You got a lot on your mind. Might be I can help you out."

In the day and a half since then, Esther had held some of those conversations in her head; or rather they held themselves while she sat back and listened. She found out that it was true: the Goddess did have something—everything?—to do with that yoking, no, fusing of flesh and spirit that had led her to put on the Aretha tape and dance. That dance had been an explosion of sorts or a stone breaking the smooth surface of a pond, the ripples expanding out and out, long after the stone submerged. All because Marvin had seen her: so exposed, so vulnerable she might as well have been naked. But then, he had made himself vulnerable to her, too, telling her the truth about his life. Was that what made it so difficult to dismiss him from her mind, that mutual witness?

But she must dismiss him, Esther told herself, as she started up the last block before the one the church property dominated. He was definitely not the one to help her sort out her spiritual crisis, if that's what it was. There were no safeguards with him, except the children and the fishbowl existence of a church yard. No fifty minute hour, no clearly defined roles or rules. That's what she should do: see a shrink or a priest or one who was both. There were plenty around these days. Alan would know whom she ought to see. And if she ever managed to talk to him about this...whatever it was, he would undoubtedly urge her to get professional help. She should talk to him. He was her husband, and the more she didn't talk, the vaster the silence became, the harder to bridge or break. At least they had made love last night. Had the Holy Spirit been involved?

Esther crossed the last street, and she did not permit herself to consider turning right and going up the back way which would take her past the Parish House. Steadfast in virtue, she continued to trudge up Main Street past the two other houses on the block, only to spot a familiar figure in a jaunty hat, assisting two workmen with stringing lights on the community Christmas tree smack dab in the middle of the rectory's front lawn.

Now Esther remembered. Gwen Owens, the organist, had told her that the three churches of White Hart rotated the privilege of having a town-sponsored Christmas tree and the responsibility for holding an ecumenical carol sing. This year it was St. Paul's turn. Well, she couldn't have known they'd be putting it up this particular morning. It would be absurd to go around the block again, just to avoid seeing the sexton of her own church. She would just walk past quietly, with dignity. Very likely no one would notice her.

"Hey, Esther!" Marvin called as she turned into the driveway, having eschewed the option of cutting across the lawn right past him. "You know if they's an electric outlet outside anywhere?"

Esther let out the breath she didn't realize she'd been holding and called back, "I think there's one on the front porch."

Surely the men could have figured that out for themselves and would have if she hadn't appeared at that exact moment. Esther reached the porch before Marvin, who was uncoiling wire along the snowy ground. The outlet was self-evident. She could just go inside, but that might seem rude.

"Here it is."

"All right."

Marvin, all business, proceeded to connect the cord and flick the switch. Relieved, disappointed, Esther headed for the door.

"Esther." Marvin spoke without turning towards her, just as her hand touched the doorknob. "We just about done with stringing lights. I got something I want to show you. You got a minute?"

"O.K.!" He waved in answer to the other two men. "Later."

The two men got into a town pick-up truck. Marvin turned to Esther. "Tell you the truth, reckon I mean more like an hour."

Say no, her better judgement instructed.

"That's about how long it is till the kids come home." Esther spoke slowly, glancing at her watch.

"Come on, then." Marvin made one of those motions with his head that so unnerved her, and he began to walk off the porch.

Dear Goddess, how do you say no to someone who commands so easily and assumes your delighted compliance?

Esther followed. In the driveway he waited for her, and they walked side by side towards the Parish House. Why didn't he say something? More to the point, why didn't she?

"Where are we going?" she attempted, biting her lips to keep the nervous laughter in.

"Some place quiet where we can concentrate."

"On what?!" She'd better start offering some resistance.

"Ain't gonna tell you, gonna show you."

Turn around right now, better judgement hissed. Esther kept walking.

Inside the Parish House, they mounted the stairs, then crossed her erstwhile dance floor and proceeded up the steps to the walled off stage. Marvin produced his keys and unlocked the door. Feeling powerless to argue with someone who hadn't said anything yet, Esther stepped backstage and tried to hide her panic at the sight of some cleared floor space—(Marvin must have cleared it; the room had been wall-to-wall junk the last time Esther had seen it)—with some old sofa cushions—strategically?—placed.

Adultery in the Parish House? Right over her husband's office? And if she said no, would he....No, she couldn't bear to believe it of him. She would make him understand; they could talk—

"Take a load off your feet, Esther. Get comfortable."

"Marvin, I—"

"Don't look so scared, Lady. I ain't gonna bite."

Esther sat down cross-legged on one of the cushions, ashamed, for an instant, that she'd let her doubts about him show. Then she experienced a refreshing surge of anger. He knew damn well what she was thinking. And why shouldn't she! The way he acted with her, carrying on about Jesus Christ's sex life. She had every reason to be suspicious of him. And he knew it. He was playing with her. Well, she wasn't going to play along anymore. And if he tried anything—

Marvin, still standing, opened a drawer of a dilapidated bedside table and took something out of it. Then he sat down on another cushion. He sat cross-legged, too, at a right angle to her. No part of his body touched hers, but they were close enough that she could feel the electric charge in the inch and a half between her right and his left knee.

On the floor before them he began to unwrap something covered in what looked like black silk, whatever it was he had taken from the drawer. Then he spread out the cloth. In the center glowed a deck of cards that looked as though they were backed with carved gold.

"My Tarot deck," he introduced the cards.

CELTIC CROSS 20

ESTHER was so relieved a tear slid out of the corner of each eye. She brushed them away swiftly.

"Lady name of Selena, a genuine Gypsy fortune teller, give me these cards. This an extremely rare deck. Dude who design it base it on a very old Spanish-Moorish deck hardly anyone know about. He ain't never put it on the market, just pass a few decks to peoples he trust. That's how Selena come by it.

"Selena, she teach me to read the cards, too. On the Inside, I had me a lot of time to practice, so I ain't half bad as a reader. But don't be expecting no you-going-on-a-long-journey shit. You know, fortune cookie stuff. Selena say that's only for the gaje. Gaje, now that be Romany for white fool, sort of like calling somebody a cracker.

"To me what the cards do is show you what's on your mind, your deep mind, you understand? Things you might not know about with your daytime mind. Sometime they show you where your deep mind want you to go."

The arts of divination which are hers are linked in people's minds with night, Esther remembered Fergus saying. Stars, dreams.

"Not too long ago," Marvin was saying, "these cards done give me a little glimpse of you—you with your loaf of bread. I ain't understand the card at the time, but it put my deep mind on alert. When you hand me that loaf, suddenly the High Priestess Card come to life. Tell the truth, I still don't know what it all mean. Then you start talking about the Goddess. My daytime mind don't know what hit, but something in my deep mind click. And lately seem to me like you been troubled in your mind. I think to myself, maybe the cards tell her something she need to know. So I'm offering you a reading free of charge. You ain't even got to cross my palm with silver. We got just about enough time. You up for it?"

He was actually seeking her consent?! As for his designs on her, he'd just made it clear that the reading was the main event. There wasn't time for anything else.

"Sure," she said gamely.

"All right. First thing we got to do is relax your mind."

Trusting now, Esther closed her eyes and let Marvin's voice make pictures. She was sitting in the midst of dense, swirling fog. "The worries mystifying your mind." Then the cloud formed rain which began to fall and soak the ground, softening it. Gradually, the fog lifted, the rain ceased. Stars shone through, and the moon rose.

"Ain't nothing between your mind and the whole sky."

Now Marvin directed her to fix her mind on what she wanted the cards to tell her. He shuffled steadily, rhythmically, and the patter of the cards sounded like rain, soothed like rain. But overhead in a clear sky wheeled the heavenly bodies. Esther waited. The strongest image was of herself, standing poised on the bridge in Blackwood, the boundary, the threshold, her stillness a form of camouflage. Why was she hiding? From whom?

"Since Hallowe'en," Esther found herself speaking with her eyes still closed, "something has been happening to me that seems beyond my control, even against my will, my conscious will. Yet it also seems to come from inside me, some deep place that is me, really truly me, yet more than me. I've been calling it the Lady, the Goddess, because that's the form it takes, and because it demands my attention that way—the way God does. It's confusing the faith I've always accepted. It's shaking everything up. It has something to do with femaleness, but not just gender, some whole other level of femaleness. Yet it's also very ordinary, down to earth—making bread, giving the children a bath. I know I'm not making sense. How can I when I don't understand? But I do know that it also has something to do with the woods next door, Blackwood, and with Fergus, the old man who lives there."

And I fear it has something to do with you, an inner voice added.

"So I guess my question is, what does it mean—the Goddess, these changes? Where does it lead?"

Esther stopped speaking and listened again to the cards, dividing, arcing, falling, going through their changes, her changes.

"Tell me when you ready to cut the deck," was all Marvin said.

She waited for another few moments, as if counting breakers, waiting for the one she would ride to shore.

"Now."

The shuffling ceased. Esther opened her eyes and looked at the deck, which Marvin had placed before her on the silk.

"Cut with your left hand to the left," Marvin instructed. "Cut as many times as you want from the first pile, till it feel right to you."

Esther took a deep breath, then cut once, twice, and sat back. Moving so that he was kneeling next to her, Marvin restacked the deck and began to lay out the cards.

"Name of this spread the Celtic Cross. Cross in the circle, circle in the cross, whichever way you look at it, it's a powerful shape. Selena done explain it to me, one of those male-female things. It's how life work, what give the universe its juice."

Esther watched as, counter-clockwise, Marvin placed three cards in the center of the silk. The last of these three lay on its side to the right of the second. Then, beneath this central trinity, he laid another card; moving clockwise, he set cards at what would be nine, twelve, and three. Now the shape of the cross became apparent to her; the three within the four must represent the circle. To the right of this configuration, in a vertical column beginning from the bottom, he dealt another four cards. Setting aside the remainder of the deck, he sat back again cross-legged beside her, his knee a hairsbreadth, yes, a little electrified hairsbreadth from hers.

But the cards commanded Esther's attention now. Before she fixed on any one of them, the richness of their colors overwhelmed her along with a dizzying sense of motion in the patterns, the shapes. Each card was a world; the rectangular outline defining only the limits of her vision.

"Marvin," she marvelled, "they are so incredibly beautiful!"

"Study on them awhile, before I explain anything. Then tell me which one draw you the most."

Esther let her eyes roam. Looking at the cards was like dreaming the sort of deep dreams you knew must be trying to tell you something: the secret, the clue to the mystery. Each card had its own quality, though some seemed related, as though they shared a landscape. Some were night scenes; some shimmered with heat. Some frightened her, and some made her want to weep. Finally she returned to one of the cards at the center.

"This one." Esther pointed to a card entitled The Star. A woman with purple-black skin knelt next to a pool, an oasis, for the vast emptiness of terra-cotta hills beyond suggested a desert. On the other side of the water from the woman was a palm tree in black silhouette. The sky and the water were almost exactly the same color, a dusky violet with hints of silver in the water that gave the pool a shimmering quality. In the sky bloomed a multi-pointed star; the water answered with a lotus. The woman kneeling had curling hair, just blacker than her skin, trailing towards the water. She was in the act of lifting a pitcher, colored the same earth-red as the desert. Any moment cool water would cascade down her neck. Overhead, a golden bird with a wide wing span, hawk or eagle, floated on the wind, balancing between earth and star.

"Well, that's you." Marvin sounded pleased. "What you call the significator, the essence. Same card don't turn up for every reading, but that's you, right now, in relation to your question."

"That's amazing!" How could something so lovely be her, be hers? "Did you know that my name, Esther, means star? Do you think the cards are making a joke, a play on words?"

"The cards be known to have a sense of humor, but I believe they serious 'bout this one. How the card make you feel?"

Esther considered. "Reborn. Refreshed. Like I'm baptizing myself."

"Yeah," said Marvin. "Seem like you got a natural feel for the cards, 'cause that's what the Star mean. It's the sign of hope, a new day coming, a new way opening. It also mean healing after a hard time. The star woman there, she be a link, just like the eagle, between the heavens and the earth. She between the waters. You know, the waters over the heavens and the waters under the heavens, like they done believe in Bible times. She connect them; they flow through her. She open a way, not just for herself but for other peoples, too. She see the star and she be the star."

"Whoa!" said Esther. "Slow down. I mean that's beautiful, but I just don't feel equal to it."

"That don't make no never mind," said Marvin. "It's still there. Deep, you know. Ain't nobody said you can always get down to it. Now let's take a look at the others. This one here be the atmosphere."

He pointed to another of the inner three, one of the hot cards, a translucent egg riddled with cracks nestled within a flame; within the egg, ready to hatch, a coiled snake.

"Atmosphere mean the mood of the reading, where your question come from. This be the ace of wands. Ace mean a beginning. Ace of wands is a whole lot of energy busting loose, new life that make the egg crack or the grass split the earth in Spring. Springtime energy. Wands be fire."

Marvin paused; Esther could feel him glance at her.

"Fire mean a lot of things. Spirit, a flash of lightning when suddenly you see it all, intuition. It also mean sex power, power to attract, like the flame draw the moth. And the snake, too, a sign of knowledge and a sign of sex."

Esther felt her face growing hot and red as the background of the card. Maybe this reading had been a serious mistake. Obviously, if the cards were going to reveal her deep mind to her, Marvin was getting more than a glimpse as well.

"This one," Marvin continued, sparing her further interpretation, "this called the obstacle or the challenge; that's why I lay it crosswise. Could be something you got to overcome—or it could be what you got to become. Let's turn it upright, so you can get a better look."

When Esther looked at the card called The World she felt a shock of recognition that she could not immediately place. Then with one of those lightning flashes Marvin had described, she knew: it was her figure, the playdough woman, only in the card instead of squatting to give birth, she was dancing. Yes, she danced; Esther could hear the rhythm pulsing, roaring in her ears like surf. Esther could feel the fall of the woman's feet, the shifting of weight from hip to hip as she danced, an ageless woman the color of fertile earth, her powerful breasts and thighs draped in a tunic that was both blue and green, like the mantle of the Madonna in the sacristy. In each hand the woman held a flowering wand, one blossoming red, the other white, roses and lilies. The same flowers, strengthened by dark green leaves, formed an ellipse around the dancing woman. Esther knew all at once, without knowing how, that the ellipse was a vulva; the woman, the World, was birthing herself. Outside the ellipse, each one weighting a corner of the world, were four creatures: dolphin and bull at the foot of the card, eagle and lion at the top. And beyond all the figures the sheerest coating of sky blue over beaten gold.

"What does it mean?" Esther asked, afraid that she knew.

"The World is when it all come together. This card the last of the Greater Trumps, the big twenty-one. They's really twenty-two Greater Trumps, which mean the big secrets, but the Fool be zero, the egg, the end in the beginning and the beginning in the end. The Fool and the World very close—the Fool is like the child mind, knowing everything without knowing. The World is when you get beyond your own little mind, you know, your personality, who you think you are, to the deep mind of the world."

"It's a dance," said Esther slowly. "It's a heart beat."

"That's right." She heard approval in his voice. "See these wands she holding? They the poles of existence, whether it be north, south; male, female; active, passive; you know, the yin-yang thing. It's all here. And the animals, dolphin signify water; the bull, earth; lion be fire; and the eagle, air. Everything come together in the dance. Look to me like that be your challenge, Esther. The cards saying: get it together, Lady. What you think?"

"A whole lot easier said than done is what I think. But you know, Marvin, the way this card affects me, what you said about it, well, it's pretty close to what I mean by Goddess. So maybe the cards are saying, one way or another, I've got to deal with it, come to terms with her."

"One thing for sure," said Marvin, "you onto something big. That's why the cards give you so many Greater Trumps. You got another one down here at the root." He pointed to the card at six o'clock called the Tower. "Life be putting you through some changes. Make no mistake about that."

"It scares me," said Esther, looking at a crumbling gray tower against a blood red sky. From the top, stones were falling and the middle seemed about to buckle. Human figures tumbled, too, their mouths gaping in horror. Only one figure seemed exhilarated. Dancing or leaping, arms upraised, the naked figure appeared to be a human lightning rod, drawing the shattering bolts to the tower. Esther was uncomfortably reminded of herself, rushing from the rectory in a rage on Hallowe'en night, screaming and raising her hands to the sky. Had she brought down destruction on herself in that rash, uncharacteristic act?

"I hear you," said Marvin. "Tower of Destruction name of this card in some decks. But listen up, we used to thinking of destruction as something bad, but sometimes it's necesssary. Me, I have always like this card, because to me the Tower look like prison. Matter of fact at Greenvale they got towers almost exactly like this one, only they ain't freestanding, they built into the wall. That's where they keep the search lights and the machine guns. They's always guards on duty, watch command. They the ones in the card screaming as they fall. I got the lightning in my hand, and I'm jumping free."

Esther found no comfort in his words; she wasn't like Marvin, bold, free. Her hands were trembling.

"Understand," Marvin went on, "the tower represent something you think is solid, an institution, a way of life..."

The Church, Esther thought, my marriage. No. No, she wouldn't accept that. It didn't have to mean that. It didn't have to mean anything, really. It was all random. The cards were powerful, she supposed, because they were Jungian archetypes or something. But to give weight to how they fell out was sheer superstition.

"...and all of a sudden, it crumble under your feet. This card be your root, the ground, what you standing on."

"Great." A little anger leaked into her tone. "So you're telling me I'm standing on an earthquake."

"Ain't me telling you; it be the cards. You say it yourself before. You all shook up. Now hear me out: all the power that done hold up that tower for so long, it's loose now. It's yours, if you want it."

And if I don't? She wondered silently.

"Remember now," he added. "You got to read these cards in relation to each other. You still the Star Woman. Tower fall, but you gonna kneel by that water and wash all the dust and grief away."

Tears threatened. It was too much, the terrible beauty of the cards and Marvin so close to her, his words like touches on her bare soul.

"What else?" she asked, her voice tight.

"Well, over here," Marvin pointed to nine o' clock, "in the recent past be the High Priestess card I mention. Recognize yourself?"

Esther gazed at the serene, moon-crowned High Priestess standing between the silver trees with her round golden loaf marked with the cross. Cross in the circle; circle in the cross. She remembered standing in the ring of trees offering her loaves. A ritual act? Take, eat....

"Sometime a card in the past position mean over and done with. When the card be one of the Greater Trumps, it more likely mean: you got that. Could have been your significator or your challenge before. Now it's part of you. High Priestess signify the power of intuition, that's how come she wear the moon for a crown. She also mean secrets. Changes you can't see how they happen."

Whenever you change one thing into another, Fergus' voice came back to her, that is craft.

" 'Course if you gon' be changing them dry little wafers into a chunk of some man's body, sure enough help to have some folks ready and willing to believe." Marvin laughed.

"I think I'll stick to yeast bread for my miracles of transubstantiation." Esther attempted levity.

"Now up here is your sky." Marvin went on pointing to the card at twelve o'clock, all business again. "Sky mean what's on your mind, what you think about what's happening. This here the four of pentacles. Pentacles the earth suit, the material world."

Esther found this card, in marked contrast to so many others, restful. A robed figure crouched in a shady corner of a walled garden. There was rambling rose climbing the wall and lilies blooming at the base of a fountain. The shadow of the wall formed a diamond or square, and the crouching figure, in the act of tracing the encircled star in the dust, appeared to have drawn pentacles in the other three corners as well, as if marking boundaries or the points of a compass.

"Four a very stable number. Sometime it be a gateway, like in the four of wands, but more often it signify a need to feel safe. Some people say the four of pentacles mean greed, holing up behind walls with your wealth, like in a castle. According to Selena pentacles don't always mean money—just whatever you need to be secure."

Solitude, Esther thought, some time to breathe. Taking refuge in a fortress was not a bad idea.

"You got the Tower falling under your feet. Make sense that your mind be looking for some solid ground."

"Then this card doesn't mean that I'll find it," Esther queried, "just that I want it?"

"Tell the truth, Esther, look to me like they ain't too much chance of any grass growing under your feet. Check this one out. Coming right up. Your near future."

Marvin directed her attention to three o'clock. The Chariot. Once again Esther felt a jolt of recognition, not of herself or of the playdough woman. The charioteer, well, the artist could have used Marvin as a model. She stole a glance at him, wondering if he saw the resemblance. When he met her eyes, she quickly looked back at the card. Their mutual focus on the spread was at least a veil of modesty, however gossamer.

"This a very strong card," Marvin commented. "It represent will, what you might call ego."

Surely Marvin was an expert on that subject, Esther considered. Studying the card, Esther found that it held for her much of Marvin's appeal. The young Black man, holding no reins, stood balanced in a rather sleek looking chariot, perhaps the ancient equivalent of a sports car. He wore a pale golden tunic fastened at the shoulders with silver crescent moons, waxing and waning. The wheels flamed, small suns, and the canopy of deep blue cloth embroidered with constellations rippled with wind and speed against a clear daytime sky. Strangest of all were the steeds: a white unicorn with its head raised, horn pointing to the heavens, and a black winged horse lowering its head, nostrils flared. Both appeared to be galloping, but it was not at all clear that they would pull in the same direction. There was a sense of dynamic tension in the card that hinted at the possibility of everything flying apart and crashing to ruin. The charioteer seemed exhilarated by the danger, willing to take a chance, to try his luck, trusting in grace—his own.

"Do the cards always represent the person who asks the question—"

"The querent," Marvin supplied.

"—or can they show the querent a picture of someone else?"

"Who you see, Esther?"

His tone was suggestive. Esther knew that he wanted her to say it: that she saw him, shining there in her near future, riding towards her, right out of the card, at full speed. And she would have to yield to the roll of those fiery wheels, crushed by a will stronger than her own.

"It's just that I don't see myself. I don't identify with the card." An evasive answer but a true one, nonetheless. "I can't relate to ego in any positive way, not for myself. I can't separate ego from being egotistical, which

I've always been taught is bad. I mean willfulness is really the Original Sin."

"Yeah?" Marvin sounded surprised. "Ain't no more to original sin than that? Here all this time I been thinking it was what the preacher call carnal knowledge."

"Well, I suppose they're related." Esther felt confused; theology was treacherous ground, and she was, after all, a seminary dropout. "I mean they both have to do with wanting something for yourself. Desire."

She should have bitten her tongue till it bled before she let out that word desire. There it was, hanging in the air between them, shimmering with heat.

"I reckon I ain't saved no matter how you look at it, 'cause personally I can't see nothing wrong with desire. To me it's the life force, you know. As for ego, it don't have to be a bad thing. Take a look at the card again. See? Charioteer ain't got hold of no reins. Ego don't mean you force life to go your way. It mean you respect yourself enough to want to win. Say you need to roll a double six, you put your whole mind on it, and let the power flow through your hands. It's not like you in charge of the universe, just willing to jump on and go for a ride."

Esther suddenly remembered a particularly blood-thirsty round of parcheesi with Mary, a childhood friend. Esther had rolled double after double, exhilarated by her rare run of luck, riding high. Then, when she had sent another of Mary's pieces home, Mary had burst into tears, and the energy that had surged down Esther's arms and through her fingers turned off like a tap. Marvin was wrong; ego was harmful, inherently.

"See how you relate to this one."

Marvin pointed to the card at the base of the column, The Hanged Man. "This the self-image card."

Oddly, despite the title, this card was not frightening to Esther. It was one of the cool moonlit cards. She gazed at it dreamily. Full moon in Blackwood. The figure hung upsidedown by one ankle from two intersecting bare branches, suspended over a void that could have been moon-flooded ground or water or nothing at all—moonshine. The arms of the figure were not bound but fell freely over its head. Fanning out around the head was a purple glow, and as she looked more closely, Esther saw that the ankle was bound to the branches by a golden snake. She shivered, remembering the purple aura and the snake in Fergus' Hallowe'en vision of her.

"Let me show you something." Marvin turned the card upside down, and Esther laughed: the figure upright was clearly dancing, just like the

World. Then Marvin put the card back so that the blood rushed to the Hanged Man's head once more.

"So what does it mean? That I see myself as hanging in there? Or maybe that I'm all hung up." She sought refuge in flipness.

"Hanging in there is close. One thing the card mean is suspense. What's gon' happen. Your fate, hanging in the balance. It also mean surrender, letting go your idea of what's supposed to be, losing control."

"It's almost the opposite in meaning to the Chariot," Esther remarked. "It's sacrificing ego. It's a sacrifice."

"That's right," Marvin agreed, unperturbed. "The Hanged Man signify initiation into the mysteries."

Esther thought again of the Ring of Trees, Fergus and Sabine.

"Initiation always involve some kind of death and rebirth," Marvin explained. "You know, like Jesus say: if you lose your life, you find it."

"But how do you reconcile this card with the Chariot?"

"Excuse me, Esther. You the querent. Question is: how do you? That be your challenge."

"And this one?" She pointed to the next card up. She was beginning to feel anxious about time. She also had to pee. That was the Original Control Issue.

"Your house," Marvin said without elaboration.

The card, the Seven of Swords, spoke rather plainly for itself. A castle under siege. No, not under siege; for the defense had not been successful. The enemy was inside the wall. Three figures in full battle dress pressed themselves against a turret, either hiding or waiting to make a surprise attack on four others who roamed the battlements searching, swords at the ready. For the moment action was suspended. (Another form of suspense.) But any minute all hell would break loose. She did not need interpretation from Marvin; she did not want it.

"Marvin, I'm afraid I've got to go—"

"Relax, Lady. By my watch we got us ten more minutes and just two more cards. Look-a-here at your hopes and fears."

He pointed to the card second from the top.

"Hopes, fears, they go together. What you hope for, you afraid you might get, and what you fear, you want."

The two of cups, Esther read, and she recognized the image as her favorite one after the Star. Two naked figures on moonlit sand, male and female, fair-skinned and dark. They leaned towards one another, arms linked, as they raised loving cups to their lips. Each of the lovers balanced on one foot, lifting the other in a dance step. Their free arms, flung wide and high, arced skyward. Together they formed a chalice. Between silver sand and black sky a wine-colored wave curled, pale green foam at its crest. A black dolphin leaped in the wave and a white bird swooped down to greet it. Over all a half moon presided.

"Twos be about balance," Marvin was saying. "And the element of cups, naturally, be water, which signify emotion. You ever hear the old saying: opposites attract? That's what this card about."

Esther was so deep inside the card, practically tasting the salt spray on her lips and how it contrasted with the sweetness of the wine—it must be wine!—in the cups, that Marvin's voice came to her disembodied. Yet that quality made it all the more intimate.

"Black, white. Man, woman. Moon, sea. Dolphin, bird. Two different things draw each other, like north and south on a magnet, two different things connect. And it all happen, not in the mind, but deep down. That's why the wave rising over them."

And what would happen when the wave broke? Would it shatter them? Would it sweep them out to sea beyond all hope of rescue? Esther felt herself struggling for breath, for control.

"So what the card say to you, Esther?"

Esther surfaced from the card and became aware of herself in the stage-storeroom, sitting next to Marvin, the card now lying flat and innocent.

"Just what you said." She tried to sound off-hand. "You know, hopes, fears."

" 'Bout what?"

Do not let him win, a surprisingly fierce inner voice commanded.

"Well, since you say it's about opposites attracting, north and south poles and all that, I expect it has something to do with my challenge, the World Card, maybe putting together the Chariot and the Hanged Man, or—this could be it!—the Goddess and Christ," Esther concluded triumphantly, having just about convinced herself.

"Mmm," Marvin made a noncommittal, possibly even nonplused noise. "Well, you know, there be many layers of meaning to each card. Now check out this last one, your outcome card. Outcome mean, if this pattern you in now continue and work itself out accordingly, then you gon' end up here." He pointed to the card at the top of the column.

Esther gave her attention to the card called Strength. Strength? She had always thought of herself as despicably weak. Here was a woman—Black, naked, with a halo of jet hair alight with hints of every color—astride a massive, golden lion. Esther found herself imagining the warmth of the lion's flanks against the woman's thighs as she rode the magnificent creature. One of the woman's hands rested caressingly on the side of the lion's face, almost in his open mouth. The other arm, encircled with that ubiquitous golden snake, was raised, hand-cupped, as if she had just set the full moon in the purple sky. Yet the light in the card seemed to have another source, warm and golden like the lion's mane. Of course, it came to Esther, the sun was setting as the moon rose. Here again was balance: sun, moon; day, night; roses and lilies, red and white, springing in the path of woman and lion.

"This card sometime called Force, sometime Lust. You say before that what all been happening to you got something to do with being female. Well, this card mean Woman Power. That lion she riding, he represent nature, you know, wildlife, danger. She tame that. Now that don't mean she turn the lion into a pussycat. She take that force and shape it, become a link, like the Star woman. She bring that power to the people and teach them how to use it. Like fire. Fire can destroy, but when it's under control, it's a source of heat, life. That's what I mean by tame. And sex. This woman got sex power. She understand what to do with it; she use it for healing."

For once, Esther sensed, in talking about sex, Marvin wasn't being suggestive or manipulative. He seemed to be concentrating on getting across a concept, a concept she must grasp, not for his purposes, but for her own. She was touched by his seriousness—and disarmed.

"It's a tall order," Esther sighed. "All of it. I'm just amazed, and I know I don't understand it all. But I'll tell you, my deep mind has gotten a workout. The images are so powerful..." her voice trailed away, as she realized she didn't want to say more. Enough had been revealed, too much. She should just thank him politely and go—

"So, what you think, Esther?"

"I just told you, I don't know. I really—"

"Esther."

Her body answered, turning towards him. There. His face. Lost, she was lost again in its perfect planes. His eyes, questioning, questing, the danger of being drawn inside them. The same magic as the cards but more potent. Potent.

"What you think it all mean?"

The wave was rising, breaking. Salt ran into her mouth. The world was dissolving before her eyes, in her eyes. Then somehow she was on her feet, stumbling towards her memory of a door.

MINDING HIS OWN BEESWAX 21

THE windows in the loft of the apple barn were opaque with steam and the air as fragrant as deep noon in May. Fergus Hanrahan, having fired up his woodstove, was melting beeswax. One batch of wax was already hardening in various candle molds. Now Fergus was making dip candles, two in each hand, connected by the wick. He would dip one pair and pace, and then the other, giving the wax gathering on the wick time to cool between dips. He paced a figure eight, a loop for each pair, the point of intersection being the pot of hot wax.

Birthday candles, these were, for the Lady's child who was now drawing near to term. On the longest night, Fergus would light all the candles, dozens of them, and make his loft a birthing chamber for the sun. Time was when he would have lit a bonfire, sparks dancing with stars in the open night, light calling light. He was old now, as he sometimes remembered, and need not keep watch in the cold. Candles would suffice, and his mother did not even trust him with them. No, not his mother: Sabine, of course. She would watch his watching, and he would not put it past her to use her magic to lull him to sleep. He knew she would not leave till she had snuffed every last flame.

Still, the honey scent would linger and sweeten his dreams. Candles of beeswax were as good, maybe better than bonfires for the birth, the wax being the work of the turning year, the foundation for new life, and the bees themselves sacred to the Lady. He had encountered people who feared bees, not only as stinging insects, Fergus suspected, but because of the structure of the hive: the large, dominant queen, the sacrificial drones, the unsexed worker bees.

Ah, but what those people did not see—or did see and dreaded—the bees were not sexless; they were sex itself, not in their single being but as a manifestation of the lust of life for life. The myriad blossoms with their colors, shapes, and scents, all to entice the bees inside to drink the sweetness, to dust their legs with sticky gold. And the bees flying, drunken, laden, bearing all possibility from bloom to bloom.

And everyone craved a taste of honey, the sweetness on the lips, even as they feared the Lady, without knowing her name, feared the lust that offered up the drones and drove the bees miles into orchard and field, the lust that opened blossoms and turned the very air into a love potion. Because that yearning of life for itself was also merciless to men—and women—and they did not want to know it.

Pacing his figure eight, the infinity sign, Fergus slipped backwards in time, always pausing by the pot, inhaling the steam as he dipped the candles, lost in a honeyed fog. No, not lost, for did he not eternally move from the eve of November into that May dawn? Surely, he would find his way there again. Why else could he still hear the wild song of the Lady in his blood? Shrill as peepers in a spring bog, insistent as the mating calls of bird and beast, loud with the million beating wings of swarming bees. Sweet, sweet. And then, the sting of her slap, still ringing in his ears, and the words she sobbed over and over: brother and sister, brother and sister.

Fergus paced the words, round and round, across the world, down the years, back to Blackwood, deeper. Then he laid down two finished pairs of candles and took up more wick. Even as he focused on his immediate task, something flickered at the edges of his vision, a delicate tremor, such as only the most finely tuned instrument could detect. He consulted the melted wax, waiting for an image to form, but the warmth of the heavy air was dizzying. His second sight steamed over like the windows; a sticky film coated his psychic powers.

Fergus dipped the naked wicks and returned to his path. After a few turns around eternity, he felt himself entering a treacherous, shimmering stretch of time, riddled with mirage and quicksand. Here past and future eyed one another warily, attempting to strike a bargain—and anything might happen. Groping his way through the miasma, he found the going rough, the terrain unfamiliar. But then, it was not his turf, not really. Yet perhaps he had some business here. He proceeded with caution.

Then she came into focus as he looped around her where she stood alone in the Ring of trees: Esther, Astarte, as he named her to himself, she of the purple lights, who received the gifts of snake and spindle, who offered the loaf, she whom the Lady had called to Blackwood. Slowly, so slowly, petal by petal, the motion invisible to the naked eye as the blossoming of a rose, she opened to her power. Nothing and no one must force that unfolding. She was so vulnerable now to anything sudden: heat or cold, hailstorm, passion.

Danger, that's what he had sensed, that was the tremor. One false move and—Fergus tiptoed, as if his own careful steps could guide hers.

The candles thickened on the wick and he walked on. On one loop, he spied the Ethiope, likewise alone in the Ring of Trees. The Marvel, Fergus called him, because he was a marvelous surprise to Fergus, a sudden strong color, a bold streak in a fading pattern. For the Lady had called the Marvel to Blackwood, too. Fergus had known it the moment he recognized the man from his vision, the Tarot reader, that day outside the gatehouse. He had seen the Marvel's soul lights then, too, a hot red overlaid with a cool green, an unusual and magnetic mix. Though he lacked the rigorous training Fergus had received, the Marvel was a Seer, a Diviner. The question was: did the Marvel know? Did he know what he knew? A young man like that could be dangerous, if he did not recognize himself.

The vision faded into the warm fog. Fergus waded on across a spit of sand, little wavelets rushing towards each other, meeting around his feet. The tide must be coming in, past rising to meet the future. He must find his way back to Blackwood.

Blackwood. The Lady liked a play on words: calling a Black man to Blackwood, as he himself was Black Irish, a descendant of Spanish sailors. Was that how the salt got in his blood? Other dark blood ran in his veins, too. He had finally opened his mother's Pandora's box, long after her death, when he had returned to Blackwood. Carefully wrapped in a lace handkerchief was an old photograph labeled Joseph Blue Eagle de Chenaux, whose face, eerily familiar, he recognized at last in his own. He connected bone structure with the bare bones of his mother's biography: her arrival in Nova Scotia where she worked as a laundress in a logging camp before she somehow made her way South to effect her mysterious appearance in Blackwood.

Brother and Sister. Brother and Sister. The discovery of his mother's secret came too late to change the course of his unfathered youth. And really, what did paternal blood matter when he and she had sucked milk at the same breasts? Brother and Sister.

The Marvel, with his black skin that held a subtle gleam of red—(another sign of kinship between the young man and himself)—and Astarte, her pale cheeks so easily stained with a blush, had no such taboo between them. Ah! Fergus stopped in his tracks. Of course, that was it! That was the seismic signal he was receiving. Yes.

The Lady had set her hand upon them. With her breath, she fanned the flames, raised the seas, and the ground shifted beneath their feet. Ah, the wanton. Oh, the poor mortal fools. The Lady cared nothing for convention, except perhaps to violate it. That Astarte was married to a priest of the Father-Son only added to the merriment. And she whose womb contained the constellations laughed at distinctions made by the races of the human race.

Should he warn them? But of what? What vision of danger lurked around the corner of his second sight? That they might not survive the storm, not know when to resist, when to yield. Timing was crucial in love. It was like catching a wave: a moment too late and you missed the wave and slid into the trough—unharmed but also unmoved; an instant too soon and the wave broke over you, boiling you in its furious foam with other bric-a-brac: pebbles, shells, driftwood, till it tossed you up, one more bit of wreckage on the beach. Passion demanded the same daring and precision: only then the ecstasy, the perfect ride on the crest of the wave.

How could he tell them, Astarte and the Marvel? And was such cautioning his task? Was it for this purpose that he had all but outlived himself? All at once he could not bear it, this picture of himself as an old man, standing in the wings, an observer only, wagging his tongue or finger at the principals, the players. And all because he had missed his own moment. How had it happened? Had he waited too long or reached too soon?

A warm rain was falling, salty, sweet. Fergus could not see, but he knew where he was. He walked through Blackwood in May. The rain only made the scent of the blossoms thicker, gave it substance, texture. He was swimming to the Ring of Trees, flying. She guided him with her fragrance, for his eyes were blind with the hot rain. There. She drew him in, soft folding and unfolding of petals, and he drank deeply of her nectar.

When he came to himself again, Fergus was standing over the pot of hot wax, his face bathed in steam, another two pairs of candles complete.

She had answered him. He curled into his own moment, content to wait. It was warm and black; he had been floating there with his twin since the beginning. The end was now in sight. Deliverance.

No. It was not for him to cry 'Look out!' as their wave swelled. He would only throw off their rhythm, break their concentration. He would just have to trust the two the Lady had called into Blackwood.

Cutting two more lengths of wick, Fergus returned to minding his beeswax.

WET DREAMS 22

MARVIN Greene woke languorously, reluctantly, as if parting from a lover. Some people opened their eyes first, then figured out they were awake. Marvin clung to the darkness behind his lids, even after he had admitted to himself that he was conscious. Rolling over onto his stomach to give sleep one last embrace, he encountered a damp sticky spot on the sheet.

Shit. What was that all about, he wondered, finding dried traces of the same substance on his thighs and groin. He wasn't some horny virgin kid or some sex-starved inmate. He was getting some every two or three days, two or three times an afternoon when he worked for Alisha. Why'd he have to go cream on his sheets? Damn. He was going to have to do the laundry again. Well, maybe he'd cultivate some new ladies at the laundermat. That's probably what he needed. A little variety. Hadn't God said it? All the fruit in the Garden was good, especially the forbidden kind. Most especially.

Marvin rolled over onto his back again out of the damp, but left one hand resting near his crotch. He put his other arm over his eyes, barring the light of day as he tried to coax back whatever dream had aroused him. He couldn't see anything clearly, but there was a scent—in his dreams he could smell—of earth and leaves, a feel of sun-soaked warmth that he connected with Esther. Yeah, Esther. A smile tugged at the edge of his lips. That's what Esther smelled like: sweet hay, new grass, something you wanted to lie down and roll in. Just thinking about her made his sleepy, sated snake begin to stir, old snake in the grass. Esther, yeah. One way or another it had to be her fault, that dream.

He was going to have to see about her. She'd been hiding out on him the last few days, since the Tarot reading. Not that he was sweating it. Talk about fruit: the woman was ripe. He didn't even need to reach. All he had to do was hold out his hand, and she'd fall.

Marvin opened his eyes, motivated now. Time to get up and moving. If he remembered right, it was a school day for both Esther's kids. In one fluid motion, he swung his legs out of bed and followed them onto his feet. Stretching, he considered the sheets. Could he just throw back the covers and let the spot dry? But if he did, Maria was sure to come up and make the bed. Cleaning-and-tidying was the name she gave to her investigations; she just had to know did he have any wine, women, or dope stashed away in those dresser drawers. These sheets wouldn't do his reputation any good, he decided, stripping the bed and stuffing a few other items into a pillow case. He'd leave the bag at the laundermat on the way to work and do the wash on the way home. The advantages of small town living: no one would steal your dirty laundry.

When Marvin arrived at St. Paul's, Esther's car was not in evidence. Most likely she was driving the carpool this morning. If she ran an errand or two on the way back, she'd pull in about ten. Just the right time for him to be taking a break outside on this fine sunny day, warmer than the past few, that little baby snow all melted now. Meanwhile, he'd get to work on painting the trim in the nursery room in the basement.

As Marvin mounted the steps to the Parish House, he heard the Rectory door slam followed by the sound of steps on the gravel driveway behind him. He didn't need to turn and look; he knew it was the P.I.C. on his way down to his office in the Parish House. The P.I.C. would sit at his desk for an hour or so, playing like he worked here, while he drank the coffee Nancy Jones would make for him and took a couple of phone calls. Then he'd go off somewhere and Nancy Jones would cover his ass for the rest of the day. That was her job description. All of which suited Marvin's purposes to a T.

"How you doing, Reverend?" Marvin called a greeting over his shoulder as he got out his keys and unlocked the front door of the Parish House.

Nancy Jones had once attempted an explanation—Marvin suspected at the P.I.C.'s request—about how it wasn't "correct" to address Father Peters as Reverend, Reverend being a title for use on envelopes or church bulletins as in The Reverend Alan Peters. Marvin chose to ignore the hint. Shit. He knew about titles; he had one himself. The Marvelous. But that didn't mean people couldn't call him Marvelous or even Marv if they were tight with him. No way was he going to call this baby-face white boy Father— or even Mister for that matter.

"Oh, hello, Marvin. How are you?"

"All right."

One of these days he was going to say: Hey, Rev! Or maybe Al. Yeah.

As Marvin headed downstairs to the basement, he speculated on whether the P.I.C. had any suspicion at all that the Sexton was about to seduce his wife. Marvin decided he didn't. He wouldn't know what was going on right under his nose, because he couldn't see that far. Of course,

Marvin knew he was nothing to the P.I.C. but a glorified janitor, a favor he had to do for Maria. Marvin didn't give two shits what the P.I.C. thought or didn't think of him. But the man didn't see his own wife; his blindness had all but made the woman invisible.

To think that he'd almost missed it himself, Esther's attraction. It had been sleeping when he met her, but then her dancing had awakened them both—or at least swelled that sleep with dreams. She was dreaming of him now; he'd lay odds on it. He was going to wake her with a whole lot more than a kiss. Soon. Hadn't the cards predicted it? He was the "someone else" she'd seen in the Chariot card, sure enough. And what was more, she knew that he knew it, too. She was just running scared, running in circles. Sooner or later, she was going to run right into him.

Marvin painted for a while on the trim—fire engine red, Esther called this color. The work was both mindless and meticulous; he liked the combination. He could be absorbed in the task while his mind roamed free. A little later some commotion overhead drew his attention to the time. Must be the Senior Citizens arriving for their weekly meeting; that meant the P.I.C. would be on his way out. Marvin glanced at his watch, ten of ten. Time for a smoke. Definitely.

Marvin put his paintbrush to soak in a pan of water and stepped out of his oversized coveralls. Pulling on his jacket and checking the pocket for his cigarettes, Marvin headed for the stairs. Just at the turn in the narrow staircase, Esther and Marvin collided. Marvin had heard footsteps, but she, coming from the din upstairs, must not have heard his. Thrown off balance, she stumbled. Marvin caught her and steadied her in his arms.

Mmm. He breathed her. That was the scent; his dream surged back. Only now it was real. And she had fallen—for real. Right into his hands. Just like he predicted. Ripe. Sweet.

Then she stiffened and stepped back. He had to let go of her or feel like a fool.

"Marvin, I have to talk to you."

Shit. Marvin barely suppressed a groan. Worst thing about women: they didn't know when to stop running their mouths and just let it happen. Now some men, at a moment like this, would try to press their advantage, even use some masculine force to overpower the woman. But that wasn't Marvin's way. He stepped aside. With a swift, invisible motion, he put on his cool.

"All right," was all he said.

She was flustered, but he wasn't going to help her.

"Were you on your way outside for a cigarette?"

Marvin shrugged. "Don't make no difference to me. Depend on how public you want this meeting to be. We can stand right here on these stairs, if that's what you want."

"Okay. Let's go outside," she said, suddenly decisive. "We can go sit on my back steps. Then you can smoke, and the Senior Citizens won't have to step over us."

Marvin raised one eyebrow, the facial gesture intended to invite her to consider the appearance of Mrs. Alan Peters and Sexton Greene hanging out together on the back steps. But his subtlety was lost on Esther, who had turned to lead the way. He found himself confronted at eye level with her curving hips in worn, soft-looking jeans. Her hips were shaped like an upsidedown heart, a valentine in motion.

When they reached the back steps—a more secluded setting than Marvin had realized, the shrubs and trees in the back yard sheltering them from the eye of a casual observer—they both hesitated. Then Marvin sat down and took out his cigarettes. Let her choose where to sit in relation to him; the choice might be revealing. After a moment, Esther sat down next to him on the third step from the bottom, leaving about two feet of empty space between them. Their charged energy fields—that everyone had, like the glow from a candle's flame—were just a hairsbreadth out of each other's range.

They sat there in silence side by side for half a cigarette. Marvin could hear Esther breathing, each breath deeper and slower than the last, quieter. He toyed with the idea of saying what's up, what's on your mind, but decided not to. She was the one who had to talk. Let her talk. Meanwhile he watched the two streams of smoke from his flared nostrils. They rose in the air, momentarily clouding the strong light. It was so warm today; the cement steps, southfacing, had lost their chill. It seemed more like the beginning of March than December, like this whole mess of Winter they had to go through was already over and done with.

"This is where it all started."

As intensely aware of her as he was, Marvin was surprised when Esther spoke.

"Where what started?" He'd never sat with her on the back steps before.

"Maybe I never told you about it. I was sitting on the back steps with the kids playing with playdough, and she just took shape in my hands, the Goddess."

Not the Goddess again. Shit. She hauled him out here to talk about the Goddess? Hadn't they talked about her enough already? Marvin took a deep drag on his cigarette and exhaled his displeasure audibly.

"That's not why I wanted to talk to you." She answered his loud lack of comment. "It just occurred to me, that's all. And maybe that's why I wanted to talk here instead of somewhere else. Anyway," she took a deep breath, "there's two things I need to say."

She had rehearsed whatever was coming, laid awake nights memorizing; he could hear it in her voice.

"First of all, I never did thank you for the Tarot reading. So, thank you. I was very affected by it. I'm embarrassed that I just ran off that way. You probably wondered what was going on—"

"Maybe I know more than you think I do," he interrupted, more to confuse her, to make her lose her place in her planned out speech than for any other reason.

"Maybe you do." She came back more quickly than he thought she would. "So maybe what I have to say won't surprise you."

She paused. Waiting for him to say it for her? No, she was doing her breathing thing again; this time it sounded a little more jagged. He turned to look at her face. He knew women in general and this one in particular well enough to tell when there was a struggle with tears going on.

"Take it easy, Lady. It's gon' be all right." He murmured reassurance, realizing only now, as he softened towards her, that he had been angry. Maybe he still was.

"Marvin, I can't see you anymore." She finally got it out. "You understand that, don't you?"

Esther turned towards him now, her face seconding the appeal of her words. But her almost-tears had lost their effect on him, because it was clear that she was holding out against them. And she was going to try to hold out against him. Damned if he was going to make it easy for her.

"No, I don't understand, Esther. You gonna have to explain it to me."

Her blush was almost painful to behold. Her skin got all blotchy. He had to ask himself: what the hell was he doing here with this middle-aged wife and mother who didn't even wear make-up? What did he see in her?

"Okay." She turned her face away again. "I guess for you it's all a game. You probably act this way with all women, and I'm making a colossal fool of myself. I just don't have the kind of detachment you seem to have. So I can't handle this—I don't know what to call it, exactly—flirtation. I feel out of control and very, very vulnerable."

"Let me get this straight, Esther, put it in my own language. You think I'm playing with you, and you, I mean we—I got some stake in this— gonna go too far?"

She met his eyes, and her blotchy skin didn't matter anymore. The look she gave him was naked enough to make him blush. She nodded and looked away.

"What make you so sure I'm trifling with you?" he demanded.

Yeah. That was the way to go with her: flatter her and at the same time let her know that he was offended.

"You're right," she said after a moment. "It's not for me to tell you how you're feeling. I can only truthfully speak for myself. That's what I'm trying to do."

"Okay. Then tell me some more truth. You saying you attracted to me, right? Enough so you feel like you in trouble. Got to be a reason this happen."

She turned to him with a half smile. "You want a list?"

She was being more difficult than he ever could have anticipated.

"Come on, now, Esther. Get real. You know what I'm talking about. Married woman like you get restless, start looking at other men...well, maybe something wrong at home. No, I ain't asking you to tell me no details. All I'm trying to say is: maybe you got a right to be looking some place else.

"And check this out, Esther. I ain't asking you for nothing you don't want to give. 'Cause they ain't nothing I need. What's going down between you and me? Its name desire. Now, I know you got responsibilities to other peoples. Believe me, I got every respect. But that ain't no reason why you and me can't relate, and nobody know but us two. Think about it, Esther. Ain't nobody's business but your own."

"No, Marvin."

No! He'd just made her an offer no woman could refuse. No?

"What you mean, no," he heard himself saying. "You mean flat out no? You ain't even gonna think on it?"

This was getting ridiculous. Look at him sitting here pleading with the woman. How had he let that happen? What did it matter to him anyway? What did she matter? His cigarette had burned out, but he still held it cold between his fingers. He ought to toss it away and walk, his cool intact. Let her beg him to come back.

"You fighting the cards, Esther," he said instead, not moving.

"No, I don't think so, Marvin," she said slowly. "I really don't think I am. Listen, I want to try to explain something, not just to you, but to myself."

She gazed down into her cupped hands as she spoke.

"I'm not made that way, so that I could keep things—feelings, people, parts of my life—separate."

"Got nothing to do with the way you made," he objected. "It's a skill, and I could teach you."

"Marvin, you're not hearing me. I don't want to learn not to be, not to be...whole. You said it yourself, my challenge is to put it all together."

"Then how come you cutting me loose?"

"All my life," she went on, talking to herself now as far as he was concerned, "I've just gone along with things, let other people decide for me, carry me. I wanted to be an artist or a dancer, but I didn't think I was talented enough—or nobody else did—so I gave up, gave up even the wanting. Then I thought: well, I like children, maybe I can teach. But in my family that wasn't professional enough, teaching the primary grades, or teaching anything less than college level, really. You were supposed to be a doctor or a lawyer or an architect or maybe a priest—or at least marry one.

"Anyway, I went to Seminary. My grandfather had been a priest, and women's ordination was a hot issue at the time. I had visions of myself as a pioneer, but really I was just lost in the wilderness. Then Alan came along, and he seemed so understanding. He had this whole mystical thing about priestly vocation, and pretty soon he convinced me that I didn't have one. So I dropped out of Seminary and married Alan. Since I was married to a priest, my father became more or less reconciled to my being a Head Start teacher. Then, when I had the kids, well, for the first time ever, everything was crystal clear, what I was supposed to be doing all day, what my life was for."

Marvin shifted position, scanned the sky and got out another cigarette. He didn't understand what she was driving at or how any of it changed the simple fact that she wanted him and he wanted her.

"But now," she went on, "everything's all murky again. I can feel all these currents pulling me one way, then another. The thing is, I don't just want to drift any more, yield to whatever or whoever is strongest, most forceful. I want to find my own strength, my own will. That's what the Chariot means. Yes, I know, I thought it was you at first; the figure even looks like you, maybe it is you partly, but it's also me, what I have to find in myself."

Damn. Why'd she have to take all that shit so seriously, turn it against him. He was the one who explained the cards to her. Where'd she get off being such an expert after only one reading?

"Excuse me, Esther, but you ain't making no kind of sense. You say you trying to find your will. By your own account, what you want is me. How come the first thing you do, when you find out your will, is to go on and deny it?"

"I'm not denying anything; I'm admitting it."

"You denying yourself, you denying me."

They were both silent for a time, the air between them charged with anger.

"Marvin." She spoke first. "Don't you see? I could just yield to you so easily. Maybe I do have problems at home. I could let you or my own feelings carry me away. Then I wouldn't have to decide anything. Marriages blow up that way all the time. Instead of trying to figure out if you can rebuild something or if it's worth it, you just close your eyes and fling a hand grenade. Then the decision is made for you. There's nothing left.

"That's probably what would happen if I, well, if I became your lover. Then there I'd be with my two kids—and I sort of doubt that's what you had in mind."

"I thought we agree you ain't gon' try to tell me how I feel or what I want."

"Sorry, I know you—"

"Hear me out." He cut her off. "You been telling me how I feel, what I want and don't want. But you know what I think? You ain't thought about me at all. You ain't thought of nobody but yourself. That's right. You selfish. Selfish."

He ground it in. Most nice women crumpled when they heard that word selfish. They would do anything to deny the charge.

"Let me tell you something else," he went on when she didn't respond. "You have way overestimated my cool, just because it suit you to think I'm some kind of black ice. Talk about cold. You say you out of control, but you made up your mind to say no before you even hear what I got to say. You sure ain't got to worry about going with the flow: that river done froze."

Marvin stood up and crushed out his cigarette with his boot. Walk, he told himself. But Esther's stillness, as she sat with her cupped hands not looking up, held him. Without intending to, he sat down again.

"You're angry," she said, "because I'm imposing my decision on you."

"Yeah." He let out a long breath he didn't know he'd been holding. "Yeah."

Now that she had named it, given his anger its due, Marvin felt it ease out of him—not like before when the possibility of tears distracted him, but cleanly, completely, like it was done. He found himself looking into his own cupped hands, into a well of deep silence where they both could drink.

"Esther," he said after a time, "I want to ask you one thing: could you ever be in love with me?"

He wasn't sure why he wanted to know. Always before he had associated love with trouble: a woman trying to stake a claim, make demands, a sure sign that it was time to cut her loose. Now, well, maybe he wanted to know just exactly what it was he could or couldn't have, what were the stakes.

"But I am in love with you!" She sounded surprised. "That's what I've been telling you. That's why it can't be a game for me."

"It ain't no game, Esther. Sure ain't no game."

Marvin turned to look at her: her wild hair that she'd stopped trying to tame, it looked like wind was whipping through it or lightning had just struck. Her eyes, a mixture of brown and green, put him in mind of the pond where he used to fish back home and the peaceful excitement of lying there dreaming in the shade of a live oak, waiting for a fish to bite. All of a sudden, he knew: he wanted her—how had she put it?—wanted her whole. Not in snatches in the storage room of the Parish House or even for a few hours in some motel in River City, if she could find a babysitter and an alibi. He wanted all of her: Priestess, Star, Strength. All.

"So what we gon' do? How we gon' work this thing, being as you live here, and I work here? You want me to quit?"

She looked so relieved and so sad, Marvin had all he could do to keep himself from reaching for her and pulling her onto his lap.

"I don't see why you should have to give up your job. I'm just going to stay out of your way, that's all. I wanted to tell you why, so you'd know and wouldn't need to wonder why I was avoiding you all of a sudden."

Marvin nodded, then asked, "What about David and Jonathan? They used to spending some time with me."

"I know," said Esther. "And it's been great for them. Look, if it's all right with you, maybe we can agree that they can still see you now and then, as long as you know you can send them home when they get in your way. And one other thing." She paused, searching out the words. "I need to know that you won't use them, use them to try to get to me."

Marvin felt a flicker of annoyance that she didn't seem to know for certain that she could trust him. But then, in all honesty, he hadn't really known it himself until just now; how trustworthy he was—or could be.

"It's a promise," he said.

Marvin didn't know which of them had made the move, but all at once they were both standing, facing each other, with their last words waiting in line. He might as well get in as many as he could.

"And I promise I'll keep my distance—leastways for the time being. But Esther, I'm gon' be straight with you: I ain't gon' promise to give up for good. So don't ask me to."

The way she looked at him, any cool he had left was rising from his body in steam. And he had called this woman cold?!

"Marvin."

Esther turned and walked up the back steps into her house. Unmoored, Marvin drifted back to the basement. He pulled on his coveralls and stared at the paintbrush and the pan of red water as he tried to think what it was he was doing. But all he could see was Esther, standing in the river, swaying but rooted while the waters swirled around her.

DAMN! Unless he was very much mistaken, that woman had just pinched his ass. Hard. Marvin forced himself not to react in any way, as he continued tying one of the small cedar trees to the altar railing. All the while, Alisha Adam's mouth kept running as she explained to the P.I.C. just exactly how it was and always would be at St. Paul's Christmas Eve Manger Service. In the meantime, Jack Farmer—whose name went with his trade; he was the manager on one of those big tax loss estates that kept a herd of beef cattle—finished stapling the black cloth over the frame of the stable they'd built just inside the opening of the altar railing.

Jack, by tradition, always played the part of Melchior in the pageant and had to blacken his hands and face for the role. He'd been joking that Marvin should take his place as the Black king and had tried to teach him to sing Melchior's verse in We Three Kings. Their carrying on had made Alisha mad, because it had interfered with her telling them how to do what they were already doing. She'd been diverted when the P.I.C. came in. Marvin had never been so glad to see the man before. It had been a pleasure, too, watching Alisha put the P.I.C. through his paces.

Then Alisha had gone and goosed him. And it wasn't playful. Marvin could feel that. The gesture didn't mean: you and me got a love secret. It meant: your ass is mine, boy, bought and paid for; I can grab it anytime I want, and don't you forget it. Marvin knew, because to be truthful he'd made that gesture many times himself, a crude but effective reminder: I control the cash flow. I state the rules of the game. I pick the tune: you dance.

"Frankincense to offer have I," bellowed Jack, helping Marvin tie the last of the trees to the railing so that the front of the church looked like a miniature forest. "Incense owns a deity nigh. Now your turn, Marvin. Let's hear it."

"No, man, I told you; I deal strictly in gold. You get me that part, and you got a deal. I put on the pancake, you put on the soot, and we be a team. Otherwise, no dice."

"Aw, you'll never get Art Billings to give up the filthy lucre. He's played Gaspard even longer than he's been treasurer."

"Marvin." The P.I.C. was addressing him from the side of the church. "We're going to need a new light bulb for the star." He came and stood beside Marvin and pointed to the star-shaped floodlight in the rafters over the manger. "Can you take care of that?"

"And Marvin," Alisha called from the sacristy, "I'll leave the fresh candles for the sconces on the counter in here. Don't forget to clean out the old wax first."

"Looks like you got your work cut out for you," said Jack. "Say, Marv, I'd stay and give you a hand, but the wife is expecting me home for lunch. I could come back later—"

"Naw, man. You got to rest up for the big performance. And remember now, I'm gonna get me a front row seat."

"Say you don't mean it!" Jack protested. "You know I'll never make it through with a straight face if I see you there three feet away giving me the hairy eyeball."

They both cracked up.

"Now, now, boys, behave yourselves." Alisha sashayed towards them trying to insinuate herself into the joke.

The P.I.C. forced a laugh. "Well, thanks a lot, Marvin, Jack. Looks great."

The P.I.C. turned and started down the aisle.

"Oh, wait a minute, Alan, I'll go with you." Alisha's high-heeled boots tapped out the rhythm of pursuit. "There's something else I have to talk to you about." She caught up with him and took his arm.

Jack rolled his eyes and whistled softly a bar of "Here comes the bride." Then he headed for the side door.

"Take it easy, Marv."

"Later, Jack."

And Marvin was alone.

With a sigh of what he suspected might be relief, Marvin sat down on the railing cushion and, closing his eyes, inhaled the pungent smell of fresh sap. What he needed was a cigarette, but it was nasty outside: a raw wet wind gathering meanness along with moisture, looking for some place to wring itself out. Be a shame after all this work if foul weather kept people away from the Manger Service, especially Old Lady Crowe who was planning her big St. Paul's comeback. It would take more than a little ice or snow to stop her from sliding down her new ramp, hell on wheels in her wheel chair. But then that French womann, Sabine, generally kept the old girl out of mischief, including calling her on using a marked deck before she fleeced Marvin of his life's savings. Naturally, they played for high stakes; neither of them would have it any other way.

Marvin opened his eyes and gazed down the nave of the church. Then he took in the sconces: three candle holders to each sconce and six sconces on each side of the church. Shit, he better get to work. Forget about the cigarette. He could smoke later on his way down to the Parish House to check out the light bulb situation and find a step ladder. He might have to make a quick trip to the hardware store. No time to hang out on the steps. Besides, he didn't want Esther to look out her window and see him there, like he had no other purpose in life than to cause her pain.

Marvin stood up, stretched, then went into the Sacristy where he found the candles and a large piece of heavy plastic for covering the pew cushions, which he would have to stand on in order to reach the sconces. He hoped Alisha wasn't planning to come back to lock up. That woman was so freakish, he'd bet anything it would turn her on to do it in a pew—or even on the altar. Lord have mercy! The Sacristy would be child's play to her. She just loved those we-might-be-caught-any-minute-doing-it-in-public kind of fantasies.

At first Marvin had been impressed with the range and detail of the scenarios she insisted on—until he'd discovered that she got them out of books. One day, looking for cigarettes while he waited for her to get into one of her costumes, he'd found her pornographic stash in the drawer of her bedside table. Amused, he leafed through one of the books, recognizing scene after scene until he hit one entitled: *The Fantasy of the Big Black Cock*. Feeling almost sick at his stomach, he'd shut the book and shoved it back in the drawer, fighting a powerful urge to grab his clothes and get the hell out. But the next minute she'd appeared, all tarted up and ready for action, and he'd gotten hold of himself.

Of course he was a fantasy for her, just like white women had at one time been a fantasy for him before they became just business as usual. Hell, he'd dealt in fantasy all his working life. That's what was bought and sold on the Street; that's what he'd taught his girls to create and manipulate. So? What else was new? If Alisha was willing to pay, he was willing to play. Still, he drew the line at videotaping himself with her. That was his one rule: leave no hard evidence. As it was, he'd picked up a new skill, learning to operate the camera, filming her, at her request, in a variety of poses.

Marvin set down an armload of candles on the first pew. Then he spread out the plastic to stand on, got out his pocket knife and began easing the old candles out, scraping away the wax. If Alisha came back and started purring and rubbing up against him, she'd just have to learn: he was for hire, but not for sale. At the moment he was in the pay of the Episcopal Church, thank you, Jesus.

After a time, Marvin relaxed into the painstaking but mindless task of replacing the candles. Beeswax, he could tell by the smell, though he might not have known it for a fact if he hadn't visited Old Man Fergus the other day and seen his candles all over the place. Strange old dude, but not a bug, as Marvin had first thought. Just a man who knew how to be with himself, the way most people didn't, the way Marvin hadn't, until, well, just the last few days as a matter of fact.

Marvin was aware now of being alone in the church. He liked the sound of it: the odd syncopated rhythms and whistlings of the radiators, the racketing of that wicked wind as it circled the building, finding chinks in the caulking, seeping in under the doors, forcing the heat high up in the rafters where it didn't do anyone but the bats any good—he'd better remember to turn on the ceiling fans before he left. Before, he'd never given much thought to being alone, whether he liked it or not. Of course in prison it was a relief; you could let down your guard, stop watching your back for a minute. But mostly solitude had been an inbetween state: time for a catnap or for planning the next move in whatever game he was running.

Now, suddenly, solitude was something in itself, something rich. Yeah, rich. For the first time in his life, Marvin felt that he possessed riches. He needed time, time alone to examine his wealth, all the more so because he didn't understand its nature. It had to do with Esther. He knew that much; he just couldn't make sense of it. She'd said no to him, after all. He hadn't even seen her since that day, except from a distance. But there was no denying it: he'd been walking around on a high, hugging his little secret to himself—(But I am in love with you!)—like some fool woman who'd just found out she was pregnant. Yeah, it was like that, like there was something alive inside him, that was his and more than his, growing in its own hidden place. It made him feel bigger.

Marvin brushed the loose wax that had fallen onto the plastic into a waste basket he'd brought along for that purpose, then he moved to another pew and started on the next sconce. Outside, the wind rose to a howl. If it got much darker, he'd have to turn on the lights in order to see what he was doing. Seemed more like the Crucifixion than the Birth with all that shrieking and groaning, though come to think of it, Mary had probably done her share of hollering in that stable, Jesus being her first baby and all.

A blast of wind shook the West windows, blowing right through Marvin's cotton work shirt. Now it sounded like the wind was working the doorknob, trying to get in all the way. Be enough to spook you if it wasn't high noon. What did that wind want? Whoosh! A gust of cold and damp rushed in and made straight for his spine. Must be Alisha and the

P.I.C. hadn't closed the door tightly enough. Sometimes it stuck and didn't latch. Marvin was just climbing down from the pew to go shut the door when he heard it close and the latch click.

And then, there she was: striding down the aisle in knee-high lace-up boots, long blonde hair streaming out behind her. He could swear he glimpsed a bow and a quiver of arrows slung over her shoulder, a bright shield blazing across her breasts—at least for an instant. But then maybe he was seeing things. Whoever or whatever she was did not appear to notice him as she marched down the aisle, until, abruptly, she stopped by the pew where he was standing and turned to face him.

"I'm Gale," she announced, as if that explained everything anyone would ever need to know.

"Well, Gale, that's quite a storm you raising out there."

Marvin knew he was losing it, but that was the only sense he could make of her: that the wind had just walked in and apparently had some business with him.

"You're Marvin," she informed him. "You and I are going to talk."

"All right, Gale, why don't you start, since you seem to know what this is about and I ain't got a clue."

"You don't know who I am?"

Marvin shook his head. He wanted to sit down, but he wasn't going to have this six-foot blonde with her ice-blue eyes looking down on him like he was some kind of insect she might or might not choose to squash.

"Ah," she nodded. "That's what I told her. She kept saying: But he does care about me." Her contempt could have refrigerated a morgue. "And I said: He doesn't know or care a thing about you or your life. And he doesn't want to, except insofar as it enables him to manipulate you—"

"You Esther's best friend," Marvin interrupted. "You a dyke and you organizing a union for hookers. Pleased to meet you."

Marvin extended his hand. Gale studied him for a moment, then she held out hers, and they shook hands briefly. He was her enemy, but he'd won that round, and she was honest enough to admit it.

"All right. Now that we both know who we're dealing with, let's get down to business."

"Why don't we sit down first." Marvin indicated the pew.

"I don't think that will be necessary."

"Then if you don't object, I got to get back to work. You can stand there and talk as long as you want."

Marvin climbed back up on the pew and opened the blade of his pocket knife. That's what Gale was like: a blade, a switch-blade, sudden and shiny and dangerous. He couldn't let her gain the upper hand. "But I do object. I want to see your face."

"Gale, I got a lot of work to do."

"All right. I'm sitting."

Marvin climbed down, closing the blade and pocketing the knife. Gale was liable to get more wrong ideas about him than she already had.

"So." Marvin looked her in the eye. "Esther been talking to you about me?"

"Who else would she talk to? I'm her oldest friend."

And who else could he talk to? All at once Marvin realized that he was hungry for talk of Esther. Next to Esther herself, it was the only thing he wanted.

"And talk is hardly the word," Gale added.

"What you trying to say, Gale?"

"I mean she's breaking her heart over you, you callous son-of-a- bitch—"

"Hey, let's leave my mother out of this."

"—You never thought of that, did you?" She stayed right on track, oblivious of his attempt to derail her. "You never considered the consequences for her. Well, get this, brother. I'm here to tell you that there will be consequences for you, too. Understand me: your balls are forfeit—"

"Gale!" A voice from the back of the church startled them both. "I knew you were up to something."

"Gabrielle!" they both said, then turned to stare at each other.

"You know her?"

"You know her!"

"Hi, Marvin sweetie. Long time, no see."

Gabrielle, short, plump, sleek, her head covered with black curls, slipped into the pew behind them.

Marvin, standing now, leaned over as Gabrielle reached for him, and he returned the kiss she planted on his cheek. Then Gabrielle turned to Gale, burst out laughing at the expression on her face and kissed her, too. Marvin remembered; Gabrielle had always been hugging and kissing on everyone, even the Johns.

"Put away your razor blade, honey. I been in both your beds, you know. I guess that sort of makes you in-laws." Gabrielle cackled. "Or maybe outlaws."

Marvin stole a glance at Gale. There was a definite possibility that she might vomit any minute.

"Marvin's the one I told you about, Gale, the one that went to the slammer."

"Ah, yes." Gale recovered herself. "The one you said—and I quote—wasn't so bad for your basic scum-of-the-earth pimp."

"Words to that effect," Gabrielle admitted.

Marvin shrugged. Gale was going to have to do more than call names to get a rise out of him.

Gabrielle began to giggle again. Her sense of humor had always been a little out of control, Marvin recalled. Used to get her in trouble from time to time. She'd be in the middle of a blowjob, something would strike her funny, and she wouldn't be able to stop laughing. Man would shrivel right up. On one occasion a John got violent with her. He guessed he earned that "all right for a pimp" then. Most players would have beat the woman themselves for acting the fool with a date. Instead Marvin had hunted down the man and threatened him with arrest. He'd always liked Gabrielle. For all her joking around, she had a good business head. Twenty-two when he'd known her, she'd been outgrowing her need of him. He'd been considering going into a partnership with her, opening a house, when he'd lost his head over that stupid car.

"This is so cute." Gabrielle was still laughing. "A Presbyterian dyke, a Jewish whore, and a Black pimp all in church together."

"That's a race, Gabrielle," Gale corrected, "not a religion."

"Which? Black or pimp?"

"Hold up now, Gale, Gabrielle, hold up. I be Black and that's a fact, but I ain't no pimp no more. Let's get that straight. And what about you, Gabrielle? I can't believe you still on the Street. You open that travel agency yet?"

"Not yet. Besides, owning a business is so bourgeois. Gale prefers her proletariat lumpen."

"Gabrielle!" Gale protested, then actually blushed. Maybe she was human.

"And as a matter of fact," Gabrielle added. "I am still on the Street. I'm an organizer."

"Right on. You was always organizing everybody anyway as I recall."

"Yeah, well, now I'm getting paid by the union. Not much money in it, but what the hey." She shrugged. "So Marvin, what about you? I mean...church? I have to confess, that's about the last place I would have looked for you. What happened to you? What are you doing here?"

"Me? Just so happens I'm the Sexton of this joint."

"The Sexton?"

Gabrielle lost it again, and Marvin did, too. It felt good to let loose. That's why he'd wanted to keep Gabrielle around; she was better than reefer.

"Pimp. Sexton." Gale's voice cut through their laughter and killed it. "I don't care what you call yourself. Just leave Esther alone. She's not your kind."

"Gale!" Gabrielle sounded shocked.

"I guess that sounded racist. Maybe it was. Sorry."

Gale looked him in the eye; he had to admire her nerve.

"Let's put it this way: she doesn't come from the kind of world you know. Call it the Street, whatever. She doesn't know the rules of the game. She doesn't even know it is a game. And she has everything to lose, while you, frankly, you have nothing. Nothing to lose. Nothing to offer."

Nothing to offer but himself, nothing to lose but Esther. Well, he sure wasn't going to waste his breath arguing with her assessment of character. But there was something about her attitude that bugged him, something she had gotten dead wrong.

"You know," he began, calling on the words to come to him, "you say you her oldest friend. You say I don't know or care nothing about her. You know what I think? You the one don't know the woman. You ain't see her for who she really is."

"And you do, I suppose?"

"Yeah. As a matter of fact, I believe I do. You talk like she some kind of dumb little sheep, walk right up to the Big Bad Wolf and don't even recognize him. Don't know what a wolf is. Little Red Riding Hood, right? So good, so nice, she stupid. Her husband don't see her neither. None of y'all do. Maybe she don't see herself.

"Let me tell you something: this little lamb you think you got to save from the Big Bad Pimp, she strong. And she ain't nobody's fool. She done handle me herself. She may want you to hear her out. Like you say, who else she gon' talk to? But she don't need you to hunt me down and threaten to cut off my balls. The lady turned me down and left my manhood in one piece. That's a powerful woman. Yeah. A priestess."

"Just what do you mean by priestess?"

She spit out the word like it had a bad taste.

"I mean she belong to herself," Marvin answered, surprised that he knew. "Herself and the Goddess."

"Jesus H. Motherfucking Christ."

"Gale!" Gabrielle put her hand on Gale's arm and glanced nervously towards the Cross.

"Not this goddess shit again. Well, I guess I owe you an apology, Marvin. You have been paying attention to her—more's the pity—and obviously you've been encouraging her. I suppose it's too much to expect you to see that this goddess trip is just one more rip-off. Only this time women are doing it to themselves. Telling each other how powerful they are, so they don't have to face their powerlessness and do something real to change it—"

"Calm down, Gale."

"No, Goddamn it, Gabrielle, I am not going to calm down. That is not my purpose on this planet. Just stop with this priestess crap. She is not a fucking priestess. She is a woman with two kids who hasn't held a paying job in the last four years, whose skills qualify her only for low-paying work, who is, in fact, totally economically dependent on her jerk of a husband, and who is now pregnant with a third child, which, in all likelihood, said husband is going to resent like hell...."

"She's pregnant?" Marvin felt like Gale had just clubbed him. "Why ain't she tell me? Why ain't she tell me herself?"

"Oh, Christ. Now I've gone and stuck my foot in it. Listen, she just found out this morning. She hasn't even told Alan yet. If she finds out I told you, she'll probably never forgive me. So pay attention: I'm renewing those threats. If you tell her, I told you—"

"Gale." Gabrielle's voice was soft but commanding. "Leave the man alone. He's had a shock. Can't you see? He's in love with her, too. They're just going to have to work it out for themselves. Come on." Gabrielle pulled Gale to her feet. "You've caused enough commotion. Esther's going to be wondering where we are. She's probably got lunch on the table."

Marvin sat in the pew, barely registering Gabrielle's parting kiss or Gale's end-of-round-one nod of the head. Outside, the wind dropped. In the absence of drafts, the air inside the empty church became thick with scent: honey and sap. It was too much.

Hell with it. Climbing back up on the pew, Marvin took a cigarette out of his breast pocket and lit up. What Maria didn't know wouldn't hurt her. And as for Jesus, he knew how it was. He'd been a man.

CASTING THE CIRCLE 24

ESTHER sat in St. Paul's church, breathing the scent of beeswax and cedar, turning herself into a birch tree—the tree of the first moon, Fergus had told her. When she was rooted in earth and extended to the heavens, she turned her attention to the East, as Fergus had taught her. There were traditional correspondences of elements, human qualities, animals, colors, with each direction, but Fergus had urged her to explore the directions for herself. In the East, Esther had found Water.

How bright appears the morning star.

Silently she sang the words. Gwen Owens was playing the Bach chorale prelude on the organ. Esther followed the melody through the intricate variations.

In the East the star had appeared, the star over the stable, the star of Isis, the five-fold star of rebirth. In one of the East windows of the church, Christ stood in the fisherman's boat, calming the waves.

Esther closed her eyes and stepped through the star onto a beach at dawn. At the horizon, Venus emerged from the water, Stella Marina. Esther waded into the surf. Dark waves curled and broke, swirling around her as they rushed to sweep the beach clean of her footprints. Salt water surged in her blood, rocked in her womb, coursed down her cheeks. She roared with the surf, and her cries rose, grew wings, caught the wind. Deep within, a tiny fish swam in her vastness.

> *How bright appears the morning star,*
> *With mercy beaming from afar;*
> *The host of heaven rejoices;*

Esther stepped back through the pentacle and turned to the South where she had discovered Fire. In the South of the church was the Sanctuary. The altar was obscured tonight by the stable, but Esther could see the Cross and Christ victorious suspended in perpetual noon.

Closing her eyes once more, Esther traced the star and stepped through it into her own South: blaze and shadow, thorn and bloom. And he was there; she couldn't help it. His body was the terrain: mountain, valley, plain, jungle, fountain. He is black and comely, O ye daughters of Jerusalem, as the tents of Kedar, as the curtains of Solomon. And green. Greene. Southern exposure. Greenhouse. Like the tender green shoot, probing towards light inside her.

> *O Righteous Branch, O Jesse's Rod,*
> *Thou Son of Man and Son of God,*

Esther retreated from the South and turned to the West where she had seen the curve of the Earth as the continent spread out before her to an unseen western sea. Opening her eyes once more, she saw in the West of the Church the window of Jesus the Good Shepherd, his crook in one hand, twin lambs in the crook of the other arm.

Esther closed her eyes and the pentacle appeared. Through it she entered a thick golden light where St. Francis preached to the birds. Then Francis became Fergus with the mourning doves circling him, only he was not outside the Parish House but in a desert, rolling away in earthen waves to mountains that pierced the sky, making it run with red. Herds of cloven-footed creatures—goats, antelope, deer—converged on Fergus, drumming the earth with their hooves. Then Fergus raised his rod and shifted his shape: now bear, now bull, now bird. And the life within her shifted shape, gathering earth, making her round as a world.

> *We, too, will lift our voices:*

Esther withdrew from the West. North was behind her, the home of the Wind. She did not need to look to see the organ pipes rising in the back of the church: immense and gleaming reeds, making music with the wind.

Esther felt rather than saw the invoking pentacle behind her; it sucked her through into a cold, glittering night. The Old North Wind sang its death song; feathered seeds rode its currents, dancing the double helix. The end in the beginning, the beginning in the end. Alpha and Omega. Ashes, ashes, we all fall down. There was the old woman with her broom sweeping the cobwebs from the sky. Mother Goose, Spencer Crowe. And then, at midnight, the child is born, out of the ocean—mare, Mary—into the air.

> *Jesus, Jesus! Holy, holy, yet most lowly,*
> *Draw thou near us; Great Emmanuel, come and hear us.*

Esther, borne on the wind, returned through the pentacle. Now the circle was cast, the sacred ground prepared for the coming of the Goddess. Though really, Esther reflected, opening her eyes as the prelude ended, the circle had always been here. What was a church but a womb space?

Esther glanced around her as the congregation rose to the chords of the opening hymn. The church was quite full; a forest of people had grown up as she'd sat with her eyes closed. She and Gabrielle were sitting in the last pew on the left, near the aisle, where they could see the shepherds and angels gathered and waiting for their entrance cue.

David and Jonathan were both among the shepherds. At St. Paul's, Alisha Adams had made clear, only girls could be angels, the archangel Gabriel's seminal role in the story notwithstanding. Jonathan had been disappointed; he'd wanted to wear gold wings. Even Alisha Adams could not persuade him to carry a toy sheep instead of Ellie the Elephant.

"The snow lay on the ground," everyone sang, although it didn't, not yet, at least.

> *The stars shone bright*
> *When Christ our Lord was born*
> *On Christmas night.*
> *Venite adoremus Dominum,*
> *Venite adoremus Dominum.*

As the hymn continued, Esther turned and sought her sons among the waiting flock of children at the back of the church. There was Jonathan, near the front since he was one of the smallest, clutching Ellie and looking bewildered. David, old enough to have the idea that something definite was going to happen, stood on tiptoe trying to see whatever it was. Neither of them had spotted her or Gabrielle, and Esther made no attempt to attract their attention. Jonathan was apt to break ranks and was certain to make a fuss if anyone attempted to restrain him.

In fact, it looked as though he had found someone or something of interest to him and was wandering towards it with a tentative sense of purpose. Esther turned to see where Jonathan was headed, and saw Spencer Crowe sitting in her wheelchair in the back of the church near the Baptismal font. Resplendent in a black velvet cloak fastened with a diamond brooch that matched her diamond earrings, Spencer transformed her wheelchair into a throne fit for the Queen of the Night.

Attendant on Spencer was a couple Esther did not recognize. Both members appeared severely sleek in full length fur coats, and it was difficult to guess their ages. They had a polished quality, so smooth and hard, their faces looked almost removable, Esther considered, objects to be laid aside on the night table along with eyeglasses and false teeth. The two attempted to smile as Jonathan, who had reached his destination, leaned against the wheelchair, fingering its controls, but it was difficult for them. The mold of their faces did not permit much range of expression. Spencer, on the other hand, appeared delighted with Jonathan's attentions and was bending forward to whisper in his ear.

> *And thus the manger poor*
> *Became a throne;*
> *For he whom Mary bore*
> *Was God the Son.*

The closing verse began, and Alisha Adams, who had spotted Jonathan's defection, came to lay claim to him. When she took hold of his shoulder, he immediately stiffened.

"Jonathan!" Esther caught his attention with a loud whisper and motioned for him to join the others, but it was Spencer's regal nod of dismissal that did the trick.

Before Esther could turn around again, Spencer caught her eye and held it. Her expression was curious; it was not a greeting, nor an isn't-your-son-a-darling-little-boy sort of look. Her gaze seemed to have no reference to Jonathan's excursion. Really, Esther felt, Spencer seemed not to be looking at her at all, but through her and beyond. Yet it was an intent look, as if Esther were a window that afforded a particular, if limited, view of something she wanted very much to see. At last, as the hymn ended, Spencer looked away, and Esther turned around again, wondering why she had submitted to Spencer's strange scrutiny.

In the front of the church, from the lectern to the left of the Manger, half visible above the trees, Alan, robed in a plain white cassock, welcomed the congregation and asked parents to please refrain from taking photographs during the service. All over the church, babies were crying, toddlers were clambering on and off laps, standing on pews, staring at the people in the row behind. Shepherds and angels, still waiting in the back, had the jitters; they shifted from one foot to the other, poked their neighbors, and giggled. Alan began to read the opening prayers and collects. Parents tensed. It was all taking too long. No miracle could support the weight of all this waiting.

Tomorrow, Esther thought, not attending the prayers, tomorrow, she would tell him. She would wake him in the morning dark, before the children started battering down their door. It would be her Christmas gift to him: their unplanned miracle. It would make the crucial difference in their marriage, turn the tide. And her pain, her private pain, would seep invisibly into the ground, like melting snow, become a hidden spring, a source of life, nourishing the sacred child, a daughter this time.

And it came to pass in those days, that there went out a decree

from Caesar Augustus that all the world should be taxed. And
all went to be taxed, everyone into his own city.

Alan began to read the First Lesson, raising his voice to be heard over the fractious babies and whining children.

And Joseph went up also, out of the City of Nazareth into
Judea onto the City of David, which is called Bethlehem, to be
taxed with Mary his espoused wife being great with child. And
so it was that while they were there the days were accomplished
that she should be delivered. And she brought forth their first
born son, and wrapped him in swaddling clothes and laid him
in a manger, because there was no room for them in the inn.

Out of the North, a bell gave tongue. All at once everyone, even the babies, hushed.

Ave Maria, Gracia Plena,
Dominus tecum, Virgo Serena.

One female voice sang the archangel's greeting to the Virgin. Esther did not look to see who was singing. Born of woman, the voice floated out into the vastness of the church and filled it wholly.

Benedicta tu in mulieribus,
Que peperisti pacem omnibus,
Et angelis gloriam,
Et angelis gloriam.

Then in the South, answering the voice that hailed her, she appeared. Entering by the choir room door with the babe cradled in her arms, Nancy Jones' younger daughter, Mavis, cloaked in a blue bedspread, laid the plastic Jesus doll in the manger, took her place in the stable with this year's Joseph, and made the Goddess manifest.

Et benedictus fructrus ventris tui,
Qui coheredes ut essemus sui,
Nos fecit per graciam,
Nos fecit per graciam.

Esther closed her eyes and saw blue. Deep blue, heavenly blue, blue as the Virgin's mantle, blue as the sea, the deep blue sea.

She appears, she appears.

Stella Marina.

How bright.

BOOK FIVE

CHRISTMAS

CHRISTMAS 25

"ALAN?" Esther spoke his name tentatively, softly. "Alan?"

No response from the familiar mass beside her in bed. She reached over his bulk to turn his digital clock towards her. At night, before she went to sleep, she usually turned the clock away; those discrete, insistent units of time gave her insomnia. Now the digits flashed 7:03, then 7:04. It was only a matter of minutes at best before the boys woke up and remembered what day it was.

"Alan."

The dim glare of the red numbers made an artificial dawn, just enough light to reveal the geography of Alan, the ranges of hip and shoulder, ravines in the folds of quilt, crags of nose and brow. Inert. Real dawn seeped in around the window shades, climbing Alan's Eastern slopes. If she rose now and lifted a shade would she see Venus rising and fading into day over the church? Or was it not the right time of year? Fergus would know.

"Alan." Esther moved closer, pressing the length of her body against him, breathing in his face. He rolled over. "Alan, Merry Christmas," she whispered in his ear.

"Five more minutes," Alan mumbled. "Just give me five more minutes."

She could understand his craving for sleep. They'd both been up for the midnight Eucharist, which didn't end till nearly one. Esther had been able to attend, because Gale and Gabrielle were here to stay in the house with the boys. She waited. 7:10, the clock flashed.

"Alan." She spoke more urgently. "Wake up. I have a present that I want to give you. Now."

"Can't it wait?" Alan groaned. "The kids aren't even up yet."

"That's the point."

"I get it." He rolled towards her, sighing, and put one arm around her, while with the other hand he fumbled for her crotch.

"Not that," she said. "I mean I'd be happy to, in a minute, but first I want to tell you something."

Alan withdrew his hand, but generously—affectionately?—moved it to the curve of her waist and let it rest there. Yes, it was going to be all right. After she told him, they would make love.

"Well?"

"Alan, we're going to have another child."

He remained motionless for a moment, staring at her, then he rolled over onto his back, saying nothing. The ceiling might have been able to fathom the look on his face. Esther couldn't. She forced herself to wait a decent interval, to give him time to take it in, form a response.

Nothing.

"Alan," she began to blither, "I know this must come as a shock. I mean, I know we didn't—"

"I can't believe you did that." His words stopped her cold. Her heart started pounding.

"Did what?"

"I can't believe that you would actually stoop to that kind of behavior. A high school girl's trick."

"Trick? What trick? Alan," she attempted humor, "if you're worried about a shotgun wedding, relax. It's too late. We've been married almost eight years. Remember?"

"This is not a joke, Esther. It's serious. Very serious."

"Of course it's serious. Having a baby—"

"You wanted a third child." He cut her off. "I never said I did. As a matter of fact, I don't. So did you discuss it with me? Did we come to a mutual agreement? No. You just took matters into your own hands. Your own hands—ha!—That's putting it politely!"

"Alan, wait a minute. Are you saying that you think I got pregnant on purpose? That I'm presenting you with a fait accompli and expecting you to go along with it? No wonder you're upset! I'm sorry, Honey. I should have made it clear. This is as much a surprise to me as it is to you. And I guess, like you say, it's something I've wanted. I only found out about it for certain yesterday. I really should have told you as soon as I suspected and not made such a big deal surprise out of it. I'm sorry. I know you're ambivalent, Alan. I should have been more sensitive. I'm sorry, Alan. I'm sorry."

She was pleading now. He still hadn't moved. She didn't dare touch him.

"You expect me to believe that, Esther?"

"Believe what?"

"That you got pregnant accidentally."

"Well, of course I expect you to believe it. Why shouldn't you believe it? It happens all the time."

"Not to responsible people."

"Yes, to responsible people. It's just happened to us!"

"It's happened to you."

Without warning, Alan flung away the covers, got up and stalked to the bathroom. Shivering, Esther sat and pulled the covers up around her shoulders. She didn't know what to think; she couldn't think. She felt sick.

A moment later, Alan returned. He switched on her reading light and turned it so that the naked bulb glared at her. Then he held up her diaphragm. Yes, the rubber had worn thin in one place, and a pinprick beam of unfiltered light shone through.

"Mama! Daddy! It's Christmas! It's Christmas! Come on! Get up!"

Alan dropped the diaphragm into the wastebasket.

"A very Merry Christmas, Esther."

*   *   *   *   *

"A very Merry Christmas to you, Aunt Spencer," said Geoffrey Landsend, bending to kiss Spencer's cheek.

"Merry Christmas, Aunt Spencer." Jessica Landsend repeated the gesture.

Their kisses were dry and—what was that word with the string in it?—astringent. Had she an oily complexion—which she had never had—the kisses might have done her cheeks some good. What her skin required, especially in her old age, was moisture. Sabine, that darling witch, gave her facial masks of honey, fennel and yogurt and baths steeped with orange blossoms, rose petals and white willow bark. Geoffrey and Jessica both looked as though they could use a thorough soak in something. What was that dreadful modern thing that was done to everything to make it instant? Freeze-drying, yes, that was it. Geoffrey and Jessica looked freeze-dried. Just add water.

"We'll just go check in with Sabine and get our instructions for the day," Jessica excused herself and Geoffrey.

Instructions! They made it sound as though they were minding the baby on Nanny's day out! How very insulting. As if there were anything remotely useful for them to do. Sabine had already prepared an entire Christmas dinner from pâté to roast goose to plum pudding. She had been bustling about in the kitchen since well before dawn. In a few minutes, Sabine would leave to spend the day in her own old house with her son and his family. Meanwhile Spencer was stuck with a nephew by marriage and his familiar—it was difficult to think of Jessica as something so robust sounding as a wife.

"Don't worry." Spencer could hear them in the kitchen reassuring Sabine. "She'll be fine. Spending the day is the least we can do."

Spencer shuddered to think what the most might entail.

After a formal exchange of meaningless gifts—well, perhaps not quite meaningless: Spencer had given them a set of expensive bath oils—the three of them sat down to the exquisite feast Sabine had left in readiness. As Jessica was clearing the soup course, a lovely shrimp bisque, preparatory to bringing out endives with a French mustard dressing, Geoffrey, by a pre-arranged signal, Spencer surmised, brought up what he referred to as a "minor little detail."

"I saw Thurston Bates at the Club the other day. He said that you hadn't felt up to another appointment since he went over the estate plans with you. You know, Aunt, the changes involved are really very insignificant, but these lawyers with their legalese, well, frankly, some of them forget how to speak any other language. They think they're explaining something to you, but all they're doing is making it sound much more complicated than it really is. Perhaps later on, if I looked things over with you, I could make some sense of it for you, put it into plain English. I'm sure once it's done, you'll feel easier about it. You'll know everything's taken care of and won't get bogged down in the courts. We don't want the lawyers getting any richer, now do we, Aunt Spence?"

Geoffrey attempted a conspiratorial wink, at least she thought that's what he was doing with his right eye, but perhaps he had something lodged in it? A beam, for example. What was it Jesus had said about that?

"You're so right, Geoffrey," she said agreeably. "You know, so many of my friends think it's dreadfully morbid of me to be so concerned about my will. You'd think death was one of those—-what do you call them?— four letter words, when in fact it's got five letters, I believe. D-e-a-t-h. Yes, five. Just the same as money. Funny, isn't it? Then there are some other words I can think of that have only three letters. Well, never mind, it all evens out in the end, I suppose.

"In any event, my friends say to me: Why, Spencer, you're still so young! And it's true, come to that. I could easily live another twenty years. 'Nothing wrong with that ticker of yours, old girl,' Dr. Haywood was saying to me just the other day. 'You've got a constitution like a horse. We'll have you back in the running in no time.' I am making marvelous progress. Soon I'll be able to get about without my walker. But I always say: Set thy house in order, don't you know. We never know what's going to happen, do we? Why, just think, Geoffrey, you and Jessica could have a fatal car accident on the way back to—"

Geoffrey suddenly started coughing violently into his napkin.

"Vinegar," he gasped, reaching for his water glass and gulping. "Just a touch too much vinegar in the dressing."

Geoffrey let the matter of her will drop for the rest of the meal. Had he been reassured by her answer, Spencer wondered, or did he guess that she was playing with him? She had better be careful. An image of Raina Washington's stern face came into her mind. Raina had come for a tentative consultation two days ago; she'd made no commitments, but she had warned Spencer that Geoffrey could contest any secret will she might make on the grounds that Spencer was not compos mentis. She mustn't blither too blithely. She must at least appear to understand what it was Geoffrey desired of her. Perhaps she'd better humor him, let him explain the will—his will—to his heart's content.

But not until after she'd had her nap. There was no hope of even approximating a state of compos mentis until she'd had a little snooze. Odd, she'd come to enjoy these interludes of afternoon sleep. She'd never allowed herself naps before; she'd looked on such indulgences as silly and weak, like swooning or having the vapors, as too tightly corseted or cosseted ladies used to do in her youth. Now she looked forward to her naps. She had the loveliest, most tantalizing adventures; or at least she woke feeling that she had. She could never fully remember the dreams; nor did they ever come to a definite end. She looked forward each day to resuming them.

Also, she'd found on more than one occasion that if she wanted to remember something that eluded her when she was awake, whatever it was would come to her in her sleep. Right now, for instance, Geoffrey and Jessica were a surface distraction. Demanding her deeper attention was a bit of poetry—Biblical most likely—that kept wafting through her mind like the scent of blossoms on a breeze. "O that thou wert as my brother that sucked the breasts of my mother." The scent was so fresh and inviting, she wanted to follow it, track it down to its source.

Perhaps she was not compos mentis? Surely that was her privilege. But Geoffrey and Jessica mustn't suspect.

The plum pudding and the hard sauce were both heavily laced with brandy. No one should be expected to remain upright after consuming it.

"If you'll excuse me, children, I'll let you clear up. Feel free to have a liedown if you like. There's the couch and the reclining chair. Though, of course, at your age a brisk walk might do the trick. I'll look over those papers with you when I get up, Geoffrey."

"Let me help you to bed, Aunt Spencer." Jessica rose.

"No need. No need. I'm quite independent these days."

Holding on to her walker, Spencer maneuvered her way to the stairlift, then ascended bodily, like the Virgin Mary. Happily, these days she could get herself on and off the commode.

*   *   *   *   *

"Shoo, Maria, shoo! Now I mean it. You go lie down right now or I'm gonna take this frying pan to your head. Marvin and I can take care of this little old stack of dishes."

Marvin wished Raina would just speak for herself. Maria had used every dish in the house and then some. She'd only fed half the neighborhood, gathered in kith and kin from as far away as Cleveland and as near as River City. She'd been baking pies and cakes and cookies and biscuits non-stop for the last three weeks, not to mention roasting turkey, ham, venison, frying chicken and ribs, stewing beans and greens, steaming rice, baking candied yams. Throw in the odd lasagna and hot potato salad, and you had a serious mess of dishes. Don't even talk about the pots and pans! Matter of fact, she'd used up her own supply of pie tins, baking sheets and roasting pans and had had to borrow some from the church. He knew, because he had been the one who transported the extras for her.

"Marvin?" Maria hooted with laughter. "Dishes? He don't know nothing 'bout washing no dishes. A dish? That's something with food on it. You get the food off the plate into your mouth, and it's over!"

Another woman making assumptions about him. Did they bother to ask him anything? Find out what he would or would not do, what he did or did not want? He might as well sit back and drink some more of this rot gut wine some old biddy aunt of Maria's had brought. Let them settle it. What was this stuff? Dandelion? Elderberry? Put him in mind of the hooch on the Inside. They made wine out of anything there, potato peelings, floor sweepings. He remembered a preacher down at the Protestant Center carrying on about Jesus changing water into wine. "Hell," someone had piped up, "there's a guy over in H block can do that."

"Besides, it ain't fitting, Raina," Maria was saying. "Marvin's a good boy. He do whatever I ask him to do. Right now, he probably want to go be with the other mens."

Yeah, agreed Marvin silently, have a smoke, pass a bottle of something more than four percent, start a card game, that is, if Maria would ever allow herself to become unconscious.

"Come on, Marvin." Raina collared him, literally. Talk of male and female roles was a red flag to her. "You're going to show everybody how a Real Man does dishes. Now I mean it, Maria, scat! Time Marvin and I had us a little cousin to cousin rap session. Tana!" Raina called after her daughter who had just bounced in to the kitchen only to turn tail when she heard the sound of dishwater running and saw her mother rolling up her sleeves. "Take Gran up to her bed."

"All right." Maria surrendered to Tana's tug of her arm. "I'm gone."

"You want to wash or dry?" Raina asked.

"You mean to tell me I actually got a say in the matter?"

"I'm being nice to you, fool."

"I'll wash." It was easier than trying to remember where everything went. "Where's them rubber gloves Maria use sometime?"

Marvin rummaged around under the sink, finally finding some aqua-colored gloves that were too small for him. When he finally forced them on, his pinky ring stretched the rubber so thin that it almost gave way.

"Still vain about our hands, I see," commented Raina. "I would have figured with all that painting and hammering and shoveling shit, you would have given up on your manicured look. Now that you're an honest laborer."

Marvin ignored her as he tossed silverware into the bottom of the basin to soak and lined up the glasses to wash first. He'd show Maria and Raina who knew how to do the damn dishes. Shit, when you'd had as many women in and out of your apartment as he'd had in the old days—damn! the old days—always having their little bedtime snacks, their friends, his friends always stopping by, looking to party, you learned about dishes. Talk about men's and women's roles! It had always seemed to him like women were the natural born slobs.

"So, what's eating you, baby? You haven't said more than three words to me since I got here. I've had to hear about your doings from Maria. You haven't asked me how I am, either. You've been acting like some damn ostrich with your head stuck up your ass!"

" 'Scuse me," he muttered.

Then he glanced at Raina in her deep red caftan with a gold belt that matched her dangling gold earrings, her beautifully shaped afro, which she'd worn since high school in varying lengths, adding three or four inches to her medium height. Her features resembled Maria's, skin a shade or two lighter, maybe, but she was younger, tougher. The set of her mouth said: Better not mess with me.

"Well, you looking good, Raina."

"You think so? Look again, boy, look again."

Marvin rinsed a glass instead. He didn't know what she expected him to see. He was tired of this guessing game women insisted on. They spent all this time making up their faces, doing their hair, choosing their clothes, then they wanted you to see through it all and read their minds.

"So, you got man trouble?"

Raina made a noise that sounded like it could have led to a hundred dollar fine, if she'd made it on the subway.

" 'A woman without a man is like a fish without a bicycle.' "

She'd said that to him many times before, specifically when he asked about her love life. He'd never gotten it.

"Even if a man came along," she continued, "Mr. Right, you know, whose existence I find about as plausible as Santa Claus', I wouldn't have the time to give him the time of day. And that's the truth. Do you understand what I'm saying? I'm getting tired. Burnt out.

"You know what hit me today, Marvin? Might even be funny if I had the energy to laugh. I spent all the time I did in school, college, law school, moved to the city, married Tana's father, got me a high power career, all because I was going to be different from Maria, have a different life. That's what she wanted—she said—and that's what I wanted.

"But you know, looking at this crowd she's got here, all the people she's feeding, not just today, but all the folks she looks out for when she can hardly look after herself, the way she's always been? It occurred to me today: I'm doing the same exact thing. Yeah. I have the same job description. Trying to make sure people have homes, have food, have what they need, what they deserve. Only I'm called a lawyer, and I have an office. And at least I get paid. Some.

"But it seems to me, no matter how hard I work, it doesn't get any better, not really, not for long, not for most of the people I see. In a lot of ways it's getting harder and harder. And I ask myself, where is this Promised Land, when are we gonna get there? Seems like we've been wandering in the wilderness forever. Lord, I'm tired."

"That's why you need a man," said Marvin, knowing he would infuriate her. "Somebody to give you something back, meet your needs." He began washing the utensils, carefully putting knives and forks in the drainer with their points down.

"Meet my needs!" She snorted. "Child, most of the men I've ever known think the definition of a woman—that is, if they think at all—is: created by God from my rib to meet my needs. All I do not need is one more person in my life with needs. I'm already a single mother working doubletime!"

"So why don't you quit, then?" challenged Marvin. "Come on back to White Hart, set up a private practice and get yourself a mess of rich clients."

Raina laughed. "That seems to be your line, Marvin. But you're a man, and you weren't raised here. Me? When I come back here, I'm Maria

Washington's little girl, and everybody thinks I owe them a favor. But you know what? If I decide to meet with old Mrs. Crowe again? I'm gonna charge her full price. And I told her that, too. Just wait till Maria finds out! And she's bound to. But I hope I'm long gone back to the Bronx before she does."

"What Old Lady Crowe say to that?" Marvin was curious.

" 'Well, young lady,' " Raina did a passable imitation, " 'you drive a hard bargain, but I believe you might be worth it.' You know, it's not like I have a whole lot of time to sit around just filing my nails while I wonder what to do with myself. I told her that, too. But I just might take her on for the pure D. hell of it. I haven't made up my mind yet. The situation tickles me. Here's this woman, this WOSP, you know about the WOSPs yet, Marvin?"

He nodded. He sure did. Their president had her stinger stuck in him good.

"This WOSP lady who about had a cow right at the Communion rail the first time a woman tried to hand her a wafer, talking about how she needs a woman to represent her interests. Her trouble is, she doesn't know what her interests are. I'm not even all that sure she's dealing from a full deck, to use an expression I'm sure you can relate to. Well, she is over eighty years old. She keeps talking about waiting for some kind of sign. I didn't mince words. I told her to watch it around that nephew of hers. She says he wants to turn the whole property into luxury condominiums. Well, I'm with her there. One thing this world does not need is more housing for the rich!"

"Rich got to live somewhere." Marvin moved a stack of dishes into the sink.

"Give me a break. By the way, that old lady has taken quite a shine to you, boy. You know what she said to me? 'If I were twenty years younger, I'd marry that handsome young cousin of yours for the sheer fun of it.' Play your cards right...."

"Luxury condos."

Raina took the dish towel and snapped it across his butt.

"Not while I got breath. Don't forget, I'm her attorney."

"It ain't official yet."

"Well, you just motivated me. It is my civic duty to protect innocent old ladies from predatory young boys like you. It is my duty to my sex."

"What about your race?"

"Ha! You're one to talk. You and your white women, never mind if they're eighteen or eighty. You know, cousin dear, correct me if I'm wrong, but it seems to me like you haven't changed your basic game plan. So what gives? Why are you so down in the mouth? Maria says you're doing fine. Three or is it four jobs? Some low-life poker-playing friends for your free time. Women, I would assume. So?"

"I been thinking I might head on back to the City." Marvin moved another stack of dishes into the sink.

"Don't you think you ought to change that water? It looks awful greasy."

"Mind your own business," he growled.

"About the dishes or your life?"

"Both."

"Sorry, baby, but you're in the wrong family for that. I do not have a mind-my-own-business gene, and I intend to mind yours if I think you're slacking off on the job. What do you mean, go back to the City? Haven't you been hearing me? The City is becoming a disaster area! You cannot afford to live in the City on any kind of honest wage you could make. Hustling? Any kind of hustling, the competition is deadly, as in you could wind up d-e-a-d dead. I thought you knew that. I thought that's why you came up here.

"So what did you have in mind? Drugs? Prostitution? What? Or maybe something more ambitious, shining shoes outside of Grand Central, escorting folks to their taxis, washing windows during traffic jams, hanging out next to potholes and changing tires? Of course there's always mugging or straight out begging. But just about anything you do to survive is going to land you right back in Greenvale or some other lovely State residence. So what is bugging you? Just what is your little problem?"

The last of the dirty dishwater disappeared down the drain. Marvin rinsed out the basin and started filling it with clean, scalding water. Squeezing out of the plastic dispenser a generous amount of detergent, he watched the bubbles multiply.

"Woman." He had to say something or she'd never get off his case.

"You can run, but you can't hide: we are everywhere. So, what else is new? Who is she?"

"Can't tell you."

"Married," Raina deduced. "And someone I know—or someone Maria knows. White?"

He didn't answer.

Raina sighed. "Goddamnit, Marvin. You have the nerve to tell me to find a man. Do you know how many beautiful Black women are alone because of all the Brothers running after white women every chance they get? No wonder Black women are bitter. Look at you! Young, working. You could be a dream come true for some Sister. Save some money, get married, have a couple of kids. But no. Instead you're sulking, threatening to blow your whole scene because of some married white bitch. Excuse me a minute. I'm gonna have to go and be sick."

Raina actually left the kitchen, whether or not she carried out her intention. With the amount they'd all eaten and drunk, it wouldn't be surprising if she did get sick. Marvin slowed his pace a little so as not to overfill the dishrack while she was gone. He couldn't justify himself to Raina; he wasn't even going to try. How could he? The situation didn't make any sense to him either. You just want her because you can't have her, Raina would say, if he tried to explain. Might even be true. Oldest story in the world, oldest trick in the world. Except that with Esther it wasn't a trick. He knew that much. And it wasn't a game; he'd said that to her himself. So why was he involved? Why should he care? No game, no stakes, no chance to win. No point. Why not just quit?

Raina stalked back into the kitchen, opened a drawer or two and located a dry dish towel. Neither of them spoke for a time.

"Marvin." Raina broke the silence. "I've decided not to waste my breath on advice you don't want to hear, let alone take. I'm just going to say something to you up front: I want you to stay here for the Winter. There is nothing for you in the City, whether you believe me or not. Come my vacation this Spring, I'm gonna spend some time here to see if I can move Maria to a better place, closer to the Village, smaller, easier to heat, no stairs. Meanwhile, someone has got to look after her this Winter, make sure that walk is sanded. The ice never melts in this hollow. Make sure the oil gets delivered on time, and she's got enough groceries when the weather's bad. You're the one, Marvin.

"Just stick it out for the Winter, and I promise when I get Maria settled, I'll help set you up wherever you want to be. Even in the City, if you're still crazy enough to want to go back there. You know, you really owe it to Maria to stay at least that long. She's the one who introduced you to all those people and got you all those jobs. If you just up and leave everybody in the lurch, it's gonna shame her, and I won't stand for that. You hear me?"

"I hear you," he answered, strangely relieved to have it settled for him. He owed Raina, too; he knew that.

"And Marvin, I've got to say this much. This Miz Ann, if she belongs to Saint Paul's—and it wouldn't surprise me at all if she did—well, all I can say is, you just better keep it cool."

"Cool," Marvin repeated. "Yeah, cool."

His mind took him back to the sun-warmed steps, the heat in Esther's eyes. He had told Esther he wouldn't give up, but that was before he found out she was pregnant. Jesus. A married white woman with two point something kids. Raina was right. He was a fool. No, he was The Fool. The Cards hadn't lied. Lady Luck had landed him here, and he still didn't know why. Well, he'd stay the Winter, but that was it. Over and out.

"Cold," he added. "Gon' be a long, cold Winter."

"Hey, I do believe you're hurting!" Raina sounded surprised.

Then she surprised him; she laid down her dishcloth and wrapped her arms around him.

*   *   *   *   *

"Christ it's cold!" Gale took Esther's arm as they walked together down the driveway.

"It's going to start snowing any minute," Esther predicted. "Then the cold won't feel so bitter. Snow softens it."

"Have you heard a weather report or do you speak in your capacity as witch—or is the correct term priestess?"

Esther ignored the bait as they stepped through the gap in the wall into Blackwood.

"One advantage of being pregnant in the Winter is that you don't feel the cold."

"The incubator effect?" Gale queried.

"Of course, I've timed this one all wrong," Esther continued. "With the last trimester in the Summer. Do you know, I looked at that Women's History calendar you gave me, and according to my calculations my due date is Labor Day."

"Cute," commented Gale. "Although how you can say you timed or even mistimed a totally accidental pregnancy escapes me."

"Well, according to Alan I did it on purpose. At some level. Maybe unconsciously. He might give me that much benefit of the doubts he has about me. If it's a benefit. I mean, the way he sees it, I've either been dishonest or pathologically irresponsible. And I guess I have been irresponsible. I haven't replaced my diaphragm since after Jonathan was born. You're supposed to do it every two years."

"That fucker! If a diaphragm leaks, who the hell does he think the drip is! Is that what he—"

"Ssh!" Esther hushed Gale as they rounded a bend in the carriage road and came upon a couple Esther recognized as the man and woman who had been with Spencer Crowe in the church; it was the full length fur coats that alerted her.

The pair were standing at the top of the stone steps that led down to the bridge and over the stream into the deep wood. Intent on their own conversation, they seemed unaware of Gale and Esther's approach. Esther yanked Gale's arm and pulled her back around the bend, just out of sight.

"What are you doing, Esther!" Gale hissed.

"Ssh. I want to hear what they're saying."

"Good grief," muttered Gale, but she obliged.

"But you do see my point, Jessica." The man was insistent. "This whole area should be filled in, leveled off."

"Unless, as I said before, Geoffrey, we want to leave it as a scenic area. That could be a selling point, part of the attraction of the overall package."

"Well, obviously, Jessica." The man sounded exasperated. "Obviously, we're going to use the old private estate concept, the landed gentry thing. But this area right here, this stream you're so irrationally attached to, well, it's simply too much of a swamp, a petrie dish for all sorts of undesirable life forms, mosquitoes for one. I know for a fact, because I've seen it, that in the Spring there are skunk cabbages here. Skunk cabbages, Jessica! That is hardly the kind of nature people have in mind when they're looking for a 'beautiful natural setting.' "

"Really, Geoffrey, there's no point in arguing about it now, anyway. We have to get Benson here for a look. We're not landscape designers. We don't have to concern ourselves with the sordid details. Let him worry about the skunk cabbages, for Godssakes. We have to look at the big picture, and I still think we should at least consider a castle motif. That stream bed could be turned into a moat. We could even have a draw-bridge, which would heighten the atmosphere of exclusivity, not to mention increase security. We could call it Camelot Condominiums...."

"Jessica, please! This is not Disney World. What we're after is under-stated elegance, flawless taste...."

"Who are these people?" whispered Gale.

"I don't know; they're related to Spencer Crowe in some way. She owns this estate. She's a parishioner."

"Well, unless you want them to find us skulking here and eaves-dropping, let's start walking."

Esther and Gale moved back into the middle of the road and rounded the bend, just as the man and woman turned their way. "We'd better be getting back to your aunt," the woman was saying. "She did say she'd go over those papers with you. Whatever you may think of my taste and my social background—"

"Jessica, I didn't say—"

"Oh no, of course not. You would never be so crass as to say anything! Not when you can imply."

"Jessica, I merely—"

"Oh, shut up, Geoffrey, and listen to me for a change. We'd better not count our condos before they're hatched. Why haven't those papers been signed before now?"

"Really, Jessica, there's nothing to worry about. She's—"

"I'm telling you, Geoffrey." The woman lowered her voice, but Esther could still hear. "I smell a rat!"

The two pairs passed each other without so much as a Merry Christmas, just a suspicious glance from Jessica.

"We're going to have to step up the security around here." Gale articulated Jessica's look. "You can't have just anyone wandering in and out."

"Hush, Gale, they'll hear you."

"Well, let them! Assholes. Fucking Camelot Condominums. Give me a break."

"Oh, no, Gale. Everything will be done with elegant understatement, flawless taste...." Esther's voice quivered, then broke. When they reached the stone steps, she sat down and sobbed. It was too much: all of it, everything. Too much.

Gale sat down next to her and encircled Esther in her arms and had the rare good sense not to say anything. After a while, tears spent, Esther quieted.

"Esther," Gale said. "I'm glad you had yourself a good cry, but it is, pardon the expression, colder than a witch's tit. Can we start moving again?"

Esther stood up. "I'm not ready to go back to the house yet. You can, if you want—"

"As long as we can keep the blood circulating, I'm with you."

"Good, because I want to show you something. Then I've got to go and find Fergus."

"Fergus? Oh, yes, your warlock or whatever he is."

"I've got to tell him what we just heard."

"Excuse me, Esther. Reality check. Just what do you think either of you can do about it? Black magic? Voodoo dolls? I don't much care for exclusive high-income housing either, and come the revolution, those two will be near the top of my list of who's gotta go. But Esther, in the existing order, if the old lady wants to leave them her estate, that's that."

"But she doesn't."

"How do you know?"

"Well, you heard them. She hasn't signed any papers. Blackwood is her life."

"Not once she's dead."

"Look, Gale, I know you don't understand. But it's more than not wanting condominiums and yuppies. Blackwood is important in itself. It's a sacred grove."

"Do you want to know what I do understand, Esther?" demanded Gale as they crossed the bridge. "You, Esther, you yourself, are between a rock and a hard place. You are pregnant. Your marriage is on the fritz. You are in love with another man, one, moreover, who can do nothing for you if you do leave your marriage. You are in trouble, woman. But instead of dealing with your own situation, you are obsessing about a bunch of trees!"

Esther stopped for a moment as they left the bridge and began to climb the wooded slope.

"Gale. Be quiet. My life is a mess. Yes. We'll talk about it later. I promise. But just for now, please shut up and pay attention to the trees."

Esther resumed walking, leading the way. With Gale out of sight behind her, she gave her attention to the dreaming trees, their sap slowed, their seasonal death upon them. Their trunks looked black, solid, but the tips of their branches grayed, melting into the early twilight, smoky, ghostly.

Esther entered the ring of trees and went to stand in the center, slowly turning in greeting. Now she knew each tree by shape, by bark, most by name: ash, oak, maple, birch, beech, locust. She sent down her roots; her branches stretched skyward, reaching through the cloud cover to the setting new moon. As Esther raised her arms, the snow began to fall. Closing her eyes, she felt the first flakes land on her face; then she opened them again and looked across at Gale, standing just inside the circle, her long hair gleaming. Gale stood unusually still, a tree woman.

"You're right," said Gale. "The snow does make the cold softer."

"Gale, do you see now? Do you understand? Look!"

Gale only looked at Esther. After a moment, Gale crossed to her and took Esther's hands.

"All right. I'll tell you what I do see. I see you, Esther. I won't say that I understand, but I see that you draw strength here. And from this goddess-priestess..."

"Crap," Esther supplied.

"Thank you." Gale laughed. "You know, the pimp actually called me on that. Got on my case for not seeing your strength—"

"You talked to Marvin? Gale! When! What did you—"

"Um, sorry. Can't answer. Mouth full of foot."

"Gale!"

"All right. All right. All I did was threaten to castrate him. But Gabrielle came along and said: Down, Girl! before I did any permanent damage."

"Thank Heavens for Gabrielle."

"Amen to that, sister. By the way. Gabrielle knows him. She was one of his—" Gale grimaced—"girls. You know what that means, don't you. She didn't just work for him, she, ugh! slept with him."

Esther nodded.

"Well, doesn't that gross you out, Esther? Anyway, I have to admit they greeted each other with more friendliness than I could have wished, given the nature of their connection. The whole thing took me by surprise, threw me off stride."

"But why didn't you or Gabrielle tell me?"

"You have enough on your plate, not to mention that I figured you'd be pissed."

"I'm mortified. Gale, I spoke to you in confidence! I trusted you! Now tell me the whole truth. Just what did you say to him? What did he say?"

"I told him to stay the hell away from you, that he had nothing to offer you but trouble, which is the plain truth, as far as I'm concerned. As for him, well, he's a cool customer, I'll give him that much. He wouldn't get into it with me, wouldn't justify himself. The gist of what he said was that you didn't need me to protect you—"

"That is correct."

"He said you'd already dealt with him yourself, leaving his rather robust ego intact. That really impressed him, that a woman could actually say no to a man without being a ballbuster."

"So he wasn't offended? That you threatened him, I mean."

"No, on the whole I think he was flattered. I was stupid enough to say you were breaking your heart over him. Jesus, I can't believe I said that."

"Gale!" Esther wailed.

"I'm sorry, Esther. I was just so angry, I wasn't thinking straight."

"Oh, well," Esther sighed. "I guess he already knows that. Anyway it's true."

The surge of energy she'd experienced when she raised her arms to the sky seeped away, leaving her pain exposed.

Marvin, Marvin.

"Since we're into true confessions," Gale went on, "I honestly didn't mean to do it. I got carried away. He started in on how you were a priestess, and I saw red. Anyway, I spilled it about your pregnancy. And that got to him. Even I could see that it did. Gabrielle told me to lay off him. We left after that."

Esther didn't respond. She was trying to imagine what Marvin must have felt at that news. The last straw; it felt like the last straw. He would give up on her. He'd be a fool not to.

Esther started to weep silently. Snowflakes melted into hot tears.

"Oh, Esther. Esther. I'm sorry. I'm so sorry."

Gale held her in the center of the circle.

"It's all right," Esther said at length. "It doesn't matter that you told him. He'd have found out eventually. Everyone will. Because I'm going to have this baby, Gale. That's the one thing I do know. So don't even talk to me about abortion. I'm having this child—with or without Alan."

That was all Esther could say. She didn't know how to express to Gale or to anyone this sense she had of carrying the sacred child. All she could do was warn people off her turf, keep them away from her nest.

"Esther." Gale spoke after a silence. "It is getting seriously dark. But I want to say one thing to you before we leave your grove. And I don't want you to answer or argue. Just hear me, tuck the words away in case they might be of use to you someday. Listen: What you want to give birth to is yourself."

Gale turned, then paused. "Which way is out?"

"Come on." Esther took Gale's hand. "Oh, I forgot. Fergus."

"Esther, it is no longer getting dark. It is dark. Moreover, I would like to get back in time to save Gabrielle from slow but certain death by Parcheesi. If this Fergus character you've described is for real, he already knows what's going down. It would be much more to the point for you to speak to the old lady. She's the one with the signature in question. But for that you're going to have to wait for the turkey vultures to leave town."

"That's true," agreed Esther as they made their way out of the circle. "To be honest, I guess I've always been a little intimidated by Spencer Crowe, but there's so much at stake now. I'll have to risk her displeasure. And yes, let's rescue Gabrielle. I can't believe she actually got Alan to play Parcheesi with her and the boys. She's amazing."

"She's a professional," grumbled Gale. "She's used to jerks like him."

"Well." Esther let the slur on Alan pass. "I don't know how I would have gotten through this day without the two of you. I'm so glad you're here. Both of you. I've been meaning to tell you, Gale, I think you and Gabrielle are wonderful together. I'm so happy for you."

"That's sweet of you, Esther," said Gale as they slid down the slope on the new snow. "To be happy for me when you're so miserable."

"I don't begrudge you joy, Gale. I don't begrudge anyone joy."

"Except yourself."

"No, not even myself." They paused for a moment on the bridge.

"Joy to me," Esther proclaimed. "Joy to the world."

*   *   *   *   *

Joy.

> *I sleep, but my heart waketh: it is the voice of my beloved that*
> *knocketh, saying, Open to me, my sister, my love, my love, my*
> *undefiled.*

Fergus slept but his heart waked.

> *Awake, O north wind; and come thou south; blow upon my*
> *garden that the spices thereof may flow out.*

His left hand was under her head, and his right hand embraced her.

> *I charge you, O ye daughters of Jerusalem, by the roes, and by*
> *the hinds of the field, that ye stir not up nor awake my love,*
> *till he please.*

They were sleeping together after all these years, sleeping while their hearts waked. It had happened slowly in these latter days, insofar as dream time may be measured. At first he caught only glimpses of her: the maiden in the grove, the birds tearing away her clothes to line their nests. Sometimes she was an old woman with a bundle of sticks bound to her back. Once she had stood looking at him from across the pond, her belly round as the moon with child.

She took other shapes, too: the doe, the dove, the crow. Once she was a weaving spider, once a startled hare. He always knew her, no matter her form, even when she did not see or know him. Sometimes he would match her shape. A wild creature, slow to trust, she had come closer little by little, till at last, trembling, she fed from his hand—or he fed from hers.

> *My beloved is gone down into his garden, to the beds of*
> *spices, to feed in the gardens, and to gather lilies.*
> *I am my beloved's and my beloved is mine: he feedeth among*
> *the lilies.*

The ancient words sang within him, but she was their source. They emanated from her like scent. The scent of her body, her breath, her dreaming. She gave off poetry; she called forth lilies and spice and heat, a dreamscape for their loving.

His left hand was under her head, his right hand embraced her. Her eyes opened to him: the rounded blue of perfect Summer sky.

No more fear.

> *O that thou wert as my brother that sucked the breasts of my*
> *mother! when I should find thee without, I would kiss thee; yea,*
> *I should not be despised.*
> *I would lead thee, and bring thee into my mother's house, who*

*would instruct me: I would cause thee to drink of spiced wine
of the juice of my pomegranate.*

No more fear.

Open to me, my sister, my love, my dove, my undefiled.

His left hand was under her head, his right hand embraced her. He kissed her with the kisses of his mouth. The sky over them was love. Her eyes. He dove; he soared into the curve of the blue.

"Aunt."

*I charge you, O ye daughters of Jerusalem, that ye stir not up,
nor awake my love, until he please.*

"Aunt? Aunt Spencer. Jessica's brought you a nice cup of tea."

Fergus plummeted. He hit the ground hard. Stunned. Blank. Except for this horrible, insistent voice.

"Aunt. Aunt."

Then Fergus saw her: wrenched suddenly, cruelly from his arms, wrenched from endless Summer into time. She stared about her, aged, bewildered, clouds drifting across her eyes. He could not see the faces of the two who had broken into her joy, his joy—only their backs, lean, predatory, as they bent over her, pressed in on her. His sister, his love, his dove, his undefiled.

"Well, Aunt, I thought we'd just take a look at those papers while you have your tea. And if you would just sign one or two things, I could go and see Bates myself, save you the trouble of having him here."

Fear. Fear was in her eyes and confusion. They were crowding her, cornering her, and she hadn't the strength to gather her limbs and leap clear. He must do something. Go to her. Cry out a warning—

"Wake up, Fergus, wake up. It's all right. You're all right."

Darkness again. Someone was touching him, hand on his shoulder, waking him from a nightmare. His mother.

"Fergus. It's me. Sabine."

He opened his eyes to gaslight. She'd lit his lamp. It was the scent of apples that told him where he was.

"Joyeux Noël, Fergus. I am sorry if I startle you. I heard you calling in your sleep, so I think you are having bad dreams. I have made you some tea and brought you some dinner. If you like, I will stay for awhile before I return to Madame. The Landsends are still there."

"No." Fergus spoke with effort, his strength nearly spent in straddling the worlds. "Go to her. At once. She is in danger."

Sabine cast him one sharp glance, nodded; then, without a word, she turned and went to heed his warning.

*   *   *   *   *

"Help!" said Esther. "We need help, Alan."

She had followed him into his study where she perched on the edge of one of his two leather chairs, like a parishioner. Only she hadn't made an appointment. She hadn't even knocked. She was breaking the rules. Breaking and entering.

Alan, sitting behind his desk, did not respond. He was leafing through his clergy directory. The flip of the pages, the angle of his head said: You are disturbing me; you are a disturbance.

Esther decided not to take any hints. She waited, listening to the hot water pipes clank and groan in familiar protest as they yielded water to the tub upstairs. Santa's offerings this year had included bubble bath. Esther pictured the hard jet of water from the tap meeting the water in the tub, churning it, generating a frothy landscape of bubbles. Gale and Gabrielle would each have a boy in hand, a little over-excited boy, naked and sleek. A screech followed by a thud meant the tap had been turned off. Then came galloping feet as one, maybe two boys raced down the hall, insisting on being captured.

Esther and Alan continued to sit, not part of the comforting chaos, their silence loud in contrast. It struck Esther that she and Alan had evolved no nightly rituals with each other, no habitual reassurances. Nothing she could count on. So here she was, a supplicant, an intruder.

"I've been going through the directory." Alan finally spoke. "I think Ed Thompson at the Cathedral would probably be able to refer you to a therapist in the area. With the boys' schedule, I don't see how you could go to the City on a weekly basis. And clearly you've got to see someone as soon as possible."

"Alan!" She was almost too amazed to be angry. "Didn't you hear me? I said we. We, as in you and me. We're in trouble. Together. Our marriage is in trouble."

Alan laid down the directory and looked at her blankly, with a sort of brutal pleasantness. Like a doctor: What seems to be the problem here?

"Well, isn't it fairly obvious?" Esther persisted. "We can't even talk to each other."

"Oh? What are we doing right now?"

"I mean we haven't, for a long time, been able to talk to each other about what matters to us. What we want, what we think, feel."

"Really?" The blandness of his tone had an edge. "I think you should try speaking for yourself, since it's your perception. What else haven't you told me?"

Did he mean Marvin, she wondered? Her stomach clenched. Did he suspect something? Had there been rumors? She couldn't tell him about Marvin. She wouldn't. There was nothing to tell.

"Alan, I haven't kept the pregnancy a secret from you." She answered the implied accusation. "Whether or not you believe me, I didn't deceive you. But there are things I haven't told you. Things, well, that are happening inside me." An unfortunate choice of words perhaps; she hesitated, then took the plunge. "Changes in my thinking, in my theology."

"Your theology?"

His tone said it all, the slight but pointed emphasis on the word your. Who are you to suppose you even have a theology? Dietrich Bonhoeffer? Karl Barth? Hans Kung? How dare you call your emotional upheavals by the name of the Queen of Sciences, the systems of thought that formed the first curriculum for all modern universities? And perhaps he was right. Knowing the Goddess was not the same as knowledge of God. You would not study her religion at seminary. What if someone were to found an ovarium? Imagine the curriculum: myth, divination, erotic poetry, lewd dancing, graven imagery. Abominations 101?

"Listen, Esther." Alan interpreted her lack of response. "I am not interested in discussing a lot of voodoo, Roman Catholic, right-to-life hair-splitting about the sanctity of unborn life and when the immortal soul comes into existence, if that's what you mean by theology."

It hadn't even occurred to her; among all the changes in her thinking, her conviction that each woman must decide whether or not to bear a child remained unshaken, strengthened even. She stared at Alan, feeling as though she was losing a grasp of the reality of their conversation.

"Because I'd much rather debate how many angels can dance on the head of a pin," he concluded.

"Oh, do let's!" she said wildly, feeling a desperate desire to giggle.

"If you're not willing to be serious, I see no point in continuing this discussion."

"But I am serious, Alan, It's just that I'm...."

She stopped herself before she could say overwrought. She would not allow Alan to dismiss her as an hysterical female. Though she supposed that was exactly what she was, given the derivation of the word hysterical. She was one of those people with a womb, a womb, moreover, with a mind of its own. Did that make any sense?

"Then let me say this to you in all seriousness, Esther, for the sake of our marriage, which you say is in trouble. I want you to consider an abortion."

"No."

"Why won't you?"

"Why do you want me to?"

Alan sighed, as though infinite patience were being exacted of him. "I guess I have to believe you when you say you didn't plan this pregnancy at a conscious level, but I think that unconsciously, you did. I think you want to hide behind it, to avoid making decisions about what to do with your life. That's a very selfish reason for having a child, Esther. Not to mention the fact that you have two children already, more than enough when you consider the population crisis. Also, I shouldn't have to point out to you what it will cost to raise them to middleclass adulthood. Finally, if you're so concerned about our marriage, you might take into consideration the added strain of another child."

Esther sat in silence, knowing she was guilty on all counts: cowardice, selfishness, irresponsibility on a global scale.

"I am asking you at least to get counseling before you make any final decisions about the pregnancy," Alan pressed. "You've still got time to work it out. Nobody will ever need to know about it."

"No, Alan," she said again.

Where was this willfulness coming from, she wondered? It was a refusal to be bullied any longer, an answer came from somewhere within her. Bullied, she queried? Alan? Sensitive, liberal, enlightened Alan a bully? Yes, the voice was emphatic, a bully.

"I'll go to marriage counseling with you gladly, but I am not going to therapy for the purpose of being talked into or talking myself into an abortion. No, Alan, no. It's out of the question."

"So, what it comes down to is that you're forcing your decision on me!" Alan exploded.

She supposed that was true; men didn't like that, she'd noticed.

"I don't get you, Esther," he went on. "You don't add up. You don't make sense. Here you are with your militant lesbian best friend, your subscription to Ms. Magazine, and last year you went to a reproductive rights conference—for which occasion I had to babysit, I might add—all of which led me to believe that you were pro-choice!"

"I am," she said quietly, and then again, "I am!"

The words resounded, waves of power rippled from her womb.

"I AM."

BOOK SIX

EPIPHANY

NEW SNOW 26

SPENCER Crowe set aside the latest manifestation of the everlasting sock and took mental command of her various parts, carefully thinking through the maneuvers necessary to get all of them together out of the wheelchair and into a standing position. There was second infancy for you! Walking, which in the intervening years had been as natural and unconscious an act as breathing, had become once more a feat requiring attention, precision, and daring. Grasping her walker, she got her balance, then she inched her way without the walker across the parlor to inspect the new snowfall from the North windows.

New snow for New Year's Day struck Spencer as appropriate, and she took pleasure in it. Adding to her pleasure was the image she had entertained during the storm last night of Geoffrey and Jessica back in New York, battling the elements in full evening dress, unable to find a cab as they hopped from party to party in a desperate effort to appear at each gathering where it was de rigueur to be seen. Spencer blessed the New York Season. Due to storm warnings, Geoffrey and Jessica had left a day earlier than planned. Being snowbound in White Hart on New Year's Eve would have amounted to social suicide, apparently. It was not to be contemplated.

The departure of the Landsends had been a tremendous relief, both to herself and to poor Sabine. Not only had Sabine had the extra burden of feeding the guests in the manner to which they were accustomed, she had also appointed herself Spencer's bodyguard. Or so Spencer fancied; she and Sabine had never discussed the matter in so many words. Since Christmas, when Sabine had returned to find the pair of them advancing on her with those papers, Sabine had not left Spencer alone with her young relations.

Spencer did not think she would have been imbecile enough to sign anything. She might not understand legal folderol, but she knew human nature and had no illusions about it whatsoever. It would have been as much as her life was worth to hand over her signature to Geoffrey. Sabine must have sensed the menace behind their cloyingly correct bearing towards dear old Aunt Spence. In addition to protection from the Landsends' potentially murderous intent, Sabine also helped cover Spencer's lapses of compos mentis. If Sabine had not appeared when she did on Christmas afternoon, Spencer might have given Geoffrey and Jessica grounds for their dearest suspicions.

When she had opened her eyes that day to the pair of them looming over her, Spencer had not had a clue as to who they were. Worse, she had not been sure of her own identity. In her dream, which, insofar as she could recall it, had been of a delightful but indelicate nature, all the trappings of Spencer Crowe had been stripped away. There was heat; there was youth; there was yearning and an exquisite sense of being on the verge of...melting. It had taken time for her to congeal again into her present, recognizable self.

Even now, as she stood at the window, looking out at the brilliant cold of the day, the heat of the dream rose from some deep place, spread out into her limbs, stained her cheeks as if with juice from a pomegranate. Pomegranate? Now whatever had made her think of pomegranates? Had she ever eaten one? Yes, long ago, on a trip to the Mediterranean with Mama and Papa. The juice had been deep red and the seeds profuse. They had made her think of caviar.

Spencer pressed her cheek against the window pane and the hot languor of the dream receded as the cold captured in the glass invigorated her. New snow, a new day, a new year. How she wished she could go for a tramp in Blackwood as she and Fergus used to do when they were children, walking out early in the morning before any other human footprints scarred the snowscape. They would visit all their favorite places, made new and mysterious by the snowfall; they would follow the ordinarily invisible tracks of mice and rabbits, the delicate hieroglyphics of bird feet. Then later the games: sledding, skating, and in deepest Winter a bonfire on the ice. She was the Snow Queen as she was Queen of all the other seasons in turn, each one peculiarly her own; each one, in passing, her favorite.

Now, in sober honesty, each season could be her last. If only her wheelchair had runners, if only her feet had wings, she would rush out into the clean emptiness of snow, and it would all come clear to her. Well, at least she could make a New Year's resolution as she stood here watching the snow in her tiny yard blow and drift against the stone wall and the branches of the Rowan tree—the tree with eyes—springing skyward whenever a gust of wind released a branch from the weight of snow. Resolved, then, to find the heir to Blackwood, to make her last will and testament, to track black ink across white fields of legal paper.

*   *   *   *   *

Esther Peters stepped over the gap in the wall, having slipped out the kitchen door with only a shawl thrown over her shoulders, and hurried towards the gatehouse. As she made her way, she ate a whole wheat cracker, insurance against succumbing to morning-noon-and-night sickness in Spencer Crowe's presence. She was nervous enough as it was, but she had resolved to tell Spencer what she had overheard in Blackwood on Christmas day at the first opportunity.

Opportunity had presented itself this afternoon when the boys had spied Marvin shoveling the church walk and had actually gotten themselves suited and booted, so motivated were they to go out and "help" him with their new half-sized shovels. Apparently, the sight of Marvin hefting snow had aroused in Alan some atavistic urge to prove his own manhood. He'd decked himself out in full L.L. Bean regalia and started in at the other end of the walk. Esther had left the grounds unseen by any of the males. She had not wanted to explain her errand to Alan, and it was time she summoned the courage to face the old lady without Jonathan and David for distraction.

"Ah, bon! Esther, Happy New Year!" Sabine answered the door, kissing Esther, first on one cheek, then the other. "Madame will be glad for your company." Then, in a lower voice, Sabine added, "She is very restless today."

"Have they gone back to the City?" Esther inquired in the same tones.

Sabine nodded, then made a gesture which Esther interpreted as a sign warding off evil, such as a werewolf or vampire.

"Madame is in the parlour. I am sure she is waiting for you without patience."

"Who is that you're talking to, Sabine?" Spencer called. "Who's there? I didn't see anyone come in through the gate."

"I'll go right in," Esther said to Sabine, who returned to the kitchen.

"Happy New Year, Mrs. Crowe," Esther greeted her, stepping into the small round room.

"Ah, Mrs. Peters." Spencer turned from the window to face her and began to progress slowly across the room.

"No walker, Mrs. Crowe? Congratulations!"

"Sit, sit." Short of breath with the effort of her journey, Spencer gestured to the chair next to hers.

Esther sat, and Spencer reached her destination, lowering herself into her chair with careful grace. Then, allowing herself a moment to recover, Spencer turned toward Esther with a sort of verbal pounce.

"I suppose you came the back way this time. You are the most enigmatic creature with your mysterious comings and goings. Once I saw you walking up the street to my gates, and I thought to myself, well, she must be coming to see me, and you never appeared. More than once I've seen you rushing off wildly into the Wood—and in all weathers, I might add. Now you sneak in the back way and take me unawares. Do you care to explain yourself, Mrs. Peters?"

Esther considered for a moment. If Spencer Crowe were a cat, she would be sitting perfectly still, perhaps even purring, while her tail belied her calm and lashed a warning.

"No," she said at length.

Spencer laughed with apparent delight. "Good for you. Never explain anything. That's my motto. Keep them guessing."

"Well, perhaps I ought to explain why I've come today," Esther began.

"Do you mean to say this is not a purely social call?" Spencer raised her eyebrows in mock—Esther hoped it was mock—reproach. "Oh, but I see you've left your house in some haste." She took in Esther's shawl; snow that had fallen on her from a branch was now melting on it. "Forgive an old woman her foolish prattle. Nothing is wrong, I hope? Where are Davy and Jonny?"

"They're out shoveling the walks with Alan." Perhaps not a strictly accurate statement. "They're fine. I'm going to take them tobogganing in a little while."

"Ah, wouldn't I just love to go with you!" Spencer cried.

Esther saw that she would. She felt for a moment the frustration of all that outward thrusting energy trapped in a broken body, in age, in time itself. How could you shut up a blustering March wind? Or a stream swollen to Spring flood? Young, riotous forces surged in her. No wonder children responded to Spencer Crowe, claimed her immediately as one of their own.

"Now then," Spencer resumed. "You have something to tell me. I do hope it is scandalous or at least diverting."

"It may be something you already know," began Esther, feeling unequal to meeting Spencer's expectations for entertainment. "And in either case, it's probably none of my business."

"Ah," nodded Spencer. "You are meddling."

"Yes."

"Good. Go on."

"On Christmas afternoon I went for a walk in Blackwood. I recognized the couple who came to church with you on Christmas Eve. Your nephew—?"

"Nephew-by-marrriage and his wife—what-is-her-name—Jessica."

"I saw them standing by the steps that lead down to the bridge, and I happened to overhear—"

"Happened to overhear?" Spencer raised one eyebrow.

"I eavesdropped," Esther amended; Spencer seemed to prefer brazen candor. "In fact, I went so far as to conceal myself around the bend."

Spencer clapped her hands with pleasure.

"And so—"

"Wait," Spencer interrupted. "Before you reveal more, you must satisfy my curiosity on this point: What prompted this foray into amateur espionage? Why didn't you simply continue walking, exchange greetings, introduce yourself as the rector's wife, observe the usual niceties?"

Esther blushed, seeing her behavior from the outside, from the point of view of social convention. Eccentric would have been a kind word for it. Childish was the one that sprang more readily to mind.

"Because when I saw them with you on Christmas Eve there was something about them I didn't like." Juvenile, definitely.

"Yes?"

"They, well, they didn't seem to belong with you. When I saw them in Blackwood, I felt that they didn't belong there. I know it doesn't make sense, and it's certainly not my right to object to anyone's presence in Blackwood, least of all your guests'. It was an impulse. I acted on it."

"And what were the fruits of your efforts?"

"I heard them talking. They were planning what they would do with Blackwood, arguing about the best way to develop it. Your nephew was for leveling the stream bed. His wife was for turning it into a moat. But they both want to build condominiums."

Spencer was silent for a time, the stream frozen over, the wind stilled.

"What happened after that?" she asked at length. "Did you meet them? Did they see you?"

"My friend—my old college roommate who was visiting for Christmas— insisted we walk on so they wouldn't find us spying. I don't think they knew we were listening. They didn't speak to us at all. In fact, as we passed them, they were still arguing—about you, I think. Your intentions. The woman said she smelled a rat."

"What a disagreeable, not to say hackneyed, turn of phrase. But tell me, Esther, if I may call you that, what is your motive for recounting this tale?

Neighborliness? A sense of Christian duty? A moral conviction that one ought to warn an old woman about her avaricious young relatives?"

"Well, they do strike me as rather predatory."

"But I do not, I hope, strike you as easily preyed upon."

Esther smiled and shook her head.

"What I am attempting to divine is this: would you have a personal objection to seeing Blackwood overrun with condominiums? That is, supposing it was my will?"

"Oh, but it's not!" Esther blurted out.

"You are so sure. Explain yourself."

"You told me never to do that."

"Cheek!" Spencer exclaimed with obvious approval. "Old age confers the privilege of contradicting oneself with impunity. I intend to enjoy it. Let me rephrase my question: Esther Peters, what is Blackwood to you?"

How to answer. Esther pictured the ring of trees. Blackwood is a sacred grove, the sacred grove of the Goddess, Goddesswood. Spencer must know that, but she would never use those words. Spencer Crowe, pillar of St. Paul's Episcopal Church, who objected vehemently to women's ordination to the priesthood. Briefly, Esther closed her eyes, seeing the circle again, feeling herself take root among the trees, twining her roots with theirs in the earth. The ground, it was not just the trees but the very ground that gave them life. She drew a deep breath.

"Sacred ground." Esther opened her eyes and looked directly into Spencer's. "Blackwood is sacred ground."

Now Spencer closed her eyes and let out a sigh that seemed the release of Esther's own indrawn breath.

"Does Fergus know you?" Spencer asked.

It was an odd way to put it, Esther thought. Not "Do you know Fergus?" but "Does Fergus know you?" Yet somehow apt.

"Yes."

"Good."

Spencer opened her eyes. "I am very grateful to you for coming, my dear. You must come and see me often."

The audience was over. She was being dismissed, but kindly, almost with a benediction. Esther rose, stood for a moment uncertainly. Life had not taught her how to take graceful leave of a Grande Dame. Well, she would wing it. Not allowing herself time to think better of it, Esther knelt swiftly on one knee, took Spencer's hands in her own and raised them to her lips.

"Happy New Year." In one fluid motion, Esther rose and left the room.

*   *   *   *   *

Spencer Crowe gazed after Esther, bemused. What an extraordinary gesture for a young woman to make! Even in the more courtly days of her youth there had not been much formal hand kissing. And the girl had had the good sense to leave at once before either of them could be embarrassed. That mouse-colored exterior—but no, that description was not just; the woman's eyes were quite stunningly green—hid a good deal: eccentricity and spunk. Yes, she would do. Admirably. After all, it was not necessary that she should be a classical beauty, just a lady. A loaf giver.

Spencer could hear Esther saying goodbye to Sabine in the hall. Apparently the two women were friends. Well and good. Better and better. Now there was something else she must do. What was it? But she was so sleepy, deliciously so, as if she had been out all day tramping in the snow, and Moira had given her hot chocolate and a hot bath and was tucking her into bed, the sheets white and fresh, trackless as new snow. And Moira, who wasn't much of a one for caresses, would nonetheless let Spencer lean against her breast while she sang. She would place Spencer's ear right over her heart, and the steady pounding would soothe her, wave after wave washing over her, taking her far, far out to sea....

The thud of the front door closing jerked Spencer awake. She peered out the East window, which gave onto the porch and steps, trying to see what was going on. Ah, there was her young friend, the Martian, as she called him to herself. Bless him, he was clearing her walk. Now he straightened and looked in the direction of the porch, leaning slightly on his staff—no, his shovel, of course. And there she was. Why couldn't Spencer remember the woman's name? She had just seen her; she had just chosen her. Star. Her name had a star in it. Ishtar, was it? No, that couldn't be right. Ishtar was a heathen goddess, the Whore of Babylon, or some such.

What were they doing, those two? Standing, leaning. The Star woman's head was bent. Now she lifted it, and his face shone. Or was it just the air? The bright air, snow bright, star bright. Spencer could see the air; it danced between the man and woman; it became a breeze. Ah, now she could feel it on her own face. Spencer closed her eyes and breathed. The air was so warm, warm and scented. What was that fragrance? Apple blossom. Then it must be time, time to meet him at midnight, midnight at the ring of trees on the eve of May.

The harsh sound of metal scraping ground startled her eyes open. The Martian was shoveling with a sort of fury, and Spencer caught a glimpse of plaid shawl as the woman hurried down the carriage road. Now she remembered: her name was Esther. Of course, Esther Peters, always dashing off to the woods without explanation. Her own darling Esther, lady-in-waiting.

Whatever was Esther up to, standing and stirring up Spring breezes with Spencer's Martian? Was that quite proper? Didn't the woman have some sort of formal connection with someone outside of Blackwood? The Rector's wife, that was it. She was the Rector's wife, what's his name.

Oh dear, that was a small fly in the ointment. She didn't want any rector involved in her business pre or post mortem. Only Esther. A pity she had married the man; it complicated things. But surely something could be done to make it clear that she wasn't including Father So-and-so in her will. That's what lawyers were for. One paid them to be clever and devious. Lawyers, yes, that was it. That's what she had been trying to remember before. Raina Washington. The Martian, almost invisible at the moment in his self-generated storm, the Martian could get Raina for her.

"Sabine!" she called. "Sabine!"

"Madame?" She appeared in the doorway.

"Maria Washington's nephew, or whatever he is, he's outside clearing the walk. Call him for me please."

"Ah, Marvelous!" she greeted him as he entered the room.

"That's me," he acknowledged. "What can I do for you today, Lady?"

"Apart from what you are already doing, just this: Get your cousin for me, Raina, I need to see her right away."

"You just in the nick of time. She's leaving today on the 5:09. Hadn't been for the snow storm, she be gone yesterday."

"I must see her before she goes."

"Show me a phone, I'll call her right now."

"In the kitchen, Marvin," Sabine answered.

The Martian left the room. Spencer waited, feeling light, light-headed, light-hearted. She gripped the arms of her wheelchair to keep from floating away. A lady did not perjure herself: until she met with Raina and made her last (her very last) will and testament, it was strictly compos mentis, all the way.

YOU know what beats me?" the Marvel called to Fergus.

It was a mild afternoon, the beginning of a January thaw. Sabine, it seemed, had contracted for the Marvel's services to help Fergus clean the gutters and clear the porches and balconies of what the servants had always called the Big House. The Marvel was poised on a very tall ladder, tending to a clogged drain while Fergus, close by, shoveled snow from a third-story roof terrace.

"How come they ain't been no vandalism here? The high school ain't but a half mile away cross-country. I don't know if you aware what generally go down this half of the twentieth century, but I am amazed. I don't see no graffiti, no works, no beer cans or wine bottles, not even cigarette butts. I ain't seen a broken window yet, and they's got to be more glass from one end of this place to the other than the stockroom of Tiffany's. So what gives? Can't tell me y'all ain't got no hoodlums in White Hart. I seen 'em myself and I seen what they done to them gardens down the end of Main. They really falling down on the job here. Don't seem sporting, waste an opportunity like this one for devastation and general nastiness. And this place been empty how long?"

Fergus paused for a moment in his shoveling, all his concentration required for the shift to chronos. The view didn't help him: the squat forest of chimneys, the roofs sloping at a multitude of angles, meeting in gullies, rising in peaks; a run of gable windows here, a turret there. It was the same fantastical roofscape he and Spencer, as children, had sneaked out to explore on moonlit Summer nights. There were the same trouble spots every Winter and Spring where water pooled or ice didn't melt; the same gutters clogged with Autumn leaves; the same seasonal round of work to keep the roof in repair, the chimneys clean. No, that was a difference: the chimneys were cold, no dance of smoke, visible spirit of a living house. No, not for—

"Twenty years." He answered the Marvel at last. "Twenty years it's been empty."

"Whew! So what you do, put some kind of charm on it? Or a curse fall on anybody who mess with it? Or maybe the sight of you, walking around with that long hair and beard like Old Father Time, waving that wicked looking stick do the trick."

"I am not without powers," Fergus observed somewhat testily. "As for vandalism, the house protects itself. It's haunted."

Or at least that was how people who had only a linear concept of time experienced it.

"That right? Who all be doing the haunting?"

"Any house that has seen more than one generation has its Dead and calls upon their services when necessary. My own mother, Moira Hanrahan, was head housekeeper here for more than thirty years. I believe she still keeps house when necessary."

"Yeah? Well, I sure hope she ain't working days no more."

Fergus felt something strange and uncontrolled bubbling up out of his throat. It took him a moment to identify it: laughter. It had been so long since he'd passed the time of day in this way, tossed words lightly back and forth, played with them. It was refreshing, exhilarating, and also tiring—as any unaccustomed exercise would be. Or as the first warm days of Spring were tiring. Or, so he understood, as giving birth and suckling young were tiring.

New life was tiring. New life had entered Blackwood. And the Marvel, with his irreverence and his restless energy, was part of it. Something of great moment had occurred. The year had turned, and even as woodchucks and snakes, seeds and bulbs slept in the earth, Blackwood was wakening from its long enchantment. Yet he, Fergus, keeper of time, guardian of the Sacred Grove, did not know the exact nature of the change he sensed. In his last days, the Lady mocked him, robbed him of second sight. He nosed along in the dark, like a mole, like other mortals. As light waxed, and the sun journeyed North, even his dreams were blind. She no longer met him there. He slept now like a baby. He slept like the dead.

"Hey, man. Check this out. My gloves was soaked, right? So I took them off. Now they standing up by themselves. Sun's going down. What you say we call it a day, old man?"

Fergus scraped the roof once more for good measure. Straightening up, he looked West to the mountains on the other side of the River. Today they were a milky blue, not as sharply defined as on the coldest Winter days. Then you could actually make out the trees against the snow. The sun was indeed on its way down, withdrawing its warmth as it went. The trees surrounding the Big House began to creak with the change in temperature. The night would be fine enough so that everything that had melted today would freeze over. Later, the full moon would rise, the moon of Birch, the first full moon of the year.

"Indeed, day is done," Fergus agreed. "Unless the world beyond calls to you, come back with me to the apple barn for a while. I've got stew on the stove and a keg of mead that's been ripening."

"I thank you kindly," said the Marvel, backing down the ladder. "Don't mind if I do."

It occurred to Fergus as he descended the ladder in turn, the Marvel holding it steady for him, that perhaps the younger man knew something about the changes Fergus sensed but could not see. Or perhaps he could know, if encouraged. The Marvel had a gift for divining. Now was the time for the gift to be consciously cultivated. Now was the time for Fergus to recognize his heir.

*   *   *   *   *

Maybe the old man could teach him something, Marvin speculated, as he leaned back in a rocking chair, his feet propped up on a polished tree stump table. Stocking feet. In fact, he had on a pair of Fergus' socks, Marvin's work boots being insufficiently water proof and his own damp foot gear drying by the woodstove. Fergus' socks were warm, genuine wool, thick and lumpy, obviously hand-knitted by some female, old lady Crowe most likely. Whenever he came to play cards with her, she set aside some kind of knitting.

Marvin drew on a corn cob pipe, also supplied by Fergus, then reached for the matches again. How did you keep the damn thing lit long enough to have a decent smoke? There. He puffed and exhaled a series of smoke rings. That was more like it. If he could get the hang of this pipe smoking thing, he might just give up the butts. He had found he just couldn't smoke them in Blackwood; they didn't go with the surroundings. Maybe it was the chemicals in the paper that made cigarette smoke. so nasty. Pipe tobacco seemed to blend right in with the smell of apples and whatever was in the pot that the old man was stirring and tasting, adding a pinch of this, a squeeze of that. More than once he picked some leaves from one or another of the bunches of dried herbs hanging from the rafters, grinding them between the heels of his palms to a fine powder right over the pot. Marvin reached for his mug and took another sip of mead, the fiery sweetness blazing a trail to his gut, then spreading out from there almost to his fingertips and toes. He was drinking fermented honey, Fergus had told him. About forty proof, Marvin estimated.

As he set down his cup, Marvin's gaze lit on the old man's stick propped up against the kitchen table—a hand-hewn table with birch legs, the bark still on them. Maybe it was the effect of the home brew or the gas light, but suddenly the stick seemed alive or crawling with life: owl, snake, mouse, rabbit, bee, spider, buck deer, fox, fish, frog, crow, more figures than he could count or name. The shapes kept shifting, changing, flickering like flame or sunlit water, dissolving, then taking form again. Marvin stared, fixed by fear and fascination. Because damn! either he was going bugs or there was some kind of power here.

"Soup's on," announced Fergus, setting the bowls on the table.

The carving stilled, releasing its hold on Marvin's mind. He eyed the stick for a moment with suspicion and respect. Then giving it a nod, he set aside his pipe, which had gone out again, and joined Fergus at the table, shifting his curiosity and wariness to the old man.

"Thank you, Lady," said Fergus casually, as if whoever she was that Marvin couldn't see was standing right there.

"Uh, likewise," Marvin put it. When you didn't know what was going down, it was generally a good idea to fake it. Just imitate the native.

For a time they ate in silence. The stew had about ten different kinds of beans in it, along with some grains, rice and barley maybe, and something crunchy. Lots of garlic and a touch of something hot, probably a chili pepper from that string of them hanging up there with the herbs. They also had pan bread made with cornmeal and molasses.

"This a fine spread, old man," said Marvin. "You got the good life here. Snug as a bug in a rug."

"Why, yes." Fergus looked up and gazed around him, a little surprised.

"Tell me something. You do the carving on that stick of yours?"

"I did."

"You work some magic into it? Spells and what not?"

"What did you see?"

Marvin eyed Fergus, and the old man eyed him back. He had spooky eyes, so black you couldn't see where the iris left off and the pupil began. Black like a moonless night, like deep, still water. Marvin wasn't sure he wanted to wade into that Deep; might get in over his head.

"I seen them move." Marvin stuck a toe in. "All them creatures you carve on it."

Fergus nodded and went back to spooning his stew. Marvin kept eating, too, just to show he was cool. Pretty soon his bowl was empty. Without a word, Fergus got up to refill it.

"You ain't gon' tell me nothing about it?" Marvin broke down and asked as Fergus set the steaming bowl in front of him.

"About what?" Fergus sat down again.

"The stick, man, the stick. Either you doing work on my mind or I'm losing it. I seen the stick come to life."

"Well, and it is alive. That's what you saw. The reality."

"Run that by me again."

"Most people, most of the time, even seers, such as you and I, see only the surfaces of things, the appearance. The stick, for example, under ordinary circumstances, appears to be fixed, immutable. In reality, it is moving, changing, dancing, as everything dances, as the universe itself dances. As you should know, Young Marvel. That is also how and why the cards work."

"The tarot pack or the playing cards?"

"Both."

"You know I read tarot?"

At this point, Marvin was hardly surprised; he just wanted confirmation.

"The very first time I saw you, you were face to face with the High Priestess," the old man answered.

The back of Marvin's neck prickled, not exactly with fear, but with something older, that had no name.

"I was scrying," Fergus added. "Water gazing. There are many ways to see."

Fergus, who had not had a second helping, leaned back in his chair. A pipe materialized in his hand and ignited spontaneously—or anyway it looked that way to Marvin. The old man puffed away peacefully, exhaling fat smoke rings that he arranged in various configurations: spirals, pyramids, figure eights. Marvin finished his stew, pretending indifference to this display of smokey prowess. Finally, he had to give it up. Dammed up laughter busted loose. He laughed at himself, the situation, the old man showing off for him.

"All right," he applauded, still laughing, while Fergus smiled in happy bewilderment. "First off, I want you to teach me how to smoke a damn pipe, starting with keeping it lit. Then how 'bout we move on to wood carving? I hear what you saying about appearance and reality, how everything move and change. But you can't tell me they ain't no magic going down here. Stick didn't carve itself. Maybe you don't want to tell nobody your secrets; I can relate to that. But if you do, I'm all ears."

"Listen then: magic is art and art is magic."

Marvin waited for more and met with silence. He was going to have to dig for it. Like the old man was a mine, and he was the miner.

"I been called a con artist from time to time, but I don't know much about no other kind of art. I don't know much about magic neither, except in the same way. Street magic, three card monte, confusing folks' minds so they don't know what it is they seeing."

The old man nodded. "It all hinges on the same principle. The huckster, the carver, the magician, all practice craft. For different purposes perhaps. Sometimes the desired end is to create illusion, to trick people into taking it for reality, and sometimes the purpose of craft is to reveal what is not apparent. The artist is a seer first, then a medium, taking a vision that only he sees and making it manifest in some form—song, image, dance, carved stick—that other people can then touch or see or hear. The seer is also a lover; the vision is the beloved. He enters into it and becomes one with it.

"That is the only secret I can tell you about the carving on the stick, the only secret I know. I have seen those creatures by becoming one with them. When I carved, I did not just carve their likeness but their essence. Do you understand? I saw from the inside as well as the outside. I looked through their eyes. So the carving is alive, and its life is magic. When I lift my stick and call to a creature, it answers, not because it recognizes the carved shape but because the life within the shape calls to it. Then, too, there is power in the wood itself: oak. Some call it the tree of life."

Fergus fell silent again, and gave his attention to his pipe, reviving it just before it went out. Marvin rose and fetched the pipe he'd been smoking before they ate. He dumped the charred remains of his earlier efforts into an ashtray on the stump table. As he sat down again, Fergus handed him the tobacco pouch, and Marvin concentrated on refilling the bowl.

"As to what I can teach you.... Don't tamp it down too much; it has to have room to breathe. There. Now light the whole surface. Gently does it," he instructed as Marvin drew deeply and coughed. "This is not your mother's teat, though I suppose it is reminiscent," Fergus mused; Marvin spluttered again. "It's a very delicate thing, the draw of a pipe. You don't want to take the smoke into your lungs, just taste it on your tongue and your teeth. Think of a cumulus cloud, think of thistledown seed and puff, not too fast or it will get too hot, not too infrequently or it will go out. Yes, that's it. Good.

"Now, as to what else I can teach you. I can teach you the craft of woodcarving, carpentry, blowing smoke rings, whatever you desire to learn. I can teach you various techniques of divination and help you to hone your skills as a seer. But I can't give you vision. The vision must be yours.

"A word of caution, Young Marvel. Seers are people who open themselves to great power. A seer who seeks power for its own sake, to have it, to manipulate other people with it, mars his vision. It becomes distorted, or he loses it altogether, though he usually won't admit it. He ceases to be a lover, a lover being one who is willing to risk all for the beloved. He rejects risk and begins to crave absolute certainty—or the illusion of it, for it is illusion. Do you understand?"

"Can't say that I do." But he was beginning to get the hang of pipe smoking; he ventured a few smoke rings. "Not all of it. I ain't thought about it this way before. Power," he mused. "Here's what I know about power: I want it. To me power mean my manhood. If I ain't got my manhood, I ain't got much. They be plenty of people, not to mention institutions, don't like to see a Black man have power, do whatever they can to deprive him of it.

"Far as manipulation is concern, well, I guess you could say at one time my livelihood come from controlling women. Tell you the truth, I enjoy that power. And you know what? That power, part of it anyhow, come from the enjoyment. You understand what I'm saying? I enjoy women, and they enjoy me. Because I'm a powerful lover. I reckon you could argue that once I got that power, I abuse it—or use it for my own purposes. I don't know. Can't see my way clear. It's all mixed up together, good and bad."

Marvin looked across at Fergus, trying to read his reactions. The old man had let his pipe go out. He was frowning, not with judgement, Marvin sensed, but with concentration. Marvin waited.

"In the end as in the beginning," said Fergus, "the seer's vision, the lover's beloved is a mystery. To keep your sight true, your love steadfast, it helps to have names, names to remind you of the reason for the risk. I myself call the great mystery by the name of the Lady."

"The Lady," Marvin repeated. "That be what Esther mean by the Goddess?"

Esther.

"She has many names and myriad forms. Come." The old man stood up, leaving his pipe in the ashtray and motioning for Marvin to do the same. "Enough talk. Let us go and see."

*   *   *   *   *

Marvin saw: the full moon rising free of the naked trees. Their branches stretched, reaching after her, like kids holding out their arms for their mother, or men hankering after a cool beauty. She. Now he was doing it, too. This goddess shit was getting to him. The full moon was bringing out his craziness. Of course everyone knew the full moon stirred up trouble: high tide and homicide. All that salt water inside coming to a boil. Given a choice, he'd rather make love under a full moon. Any place men were locked up with other men was no place to be at full moon time.

Now here he was stalking through the snow with old man Fergus. But that was all right. For the time being, they were both lunatics, crazy in love with the Lady, like everything else out under the sky tonight: hoot owls and rabbits, rabbits he could swear he saw dancing in the orchard under trees, trees dripping with moonlight, moonlight like milk spilling all over creation. And the snow on the ground lapped it up and gave it back to the sky: earthshine, snow crystals, standing out more clearly than stars. Full moon in Winter, trees and snow, moon and sky, gave black and white a whole other meaning: they were made for each other, a lovesong, a lovescape. Like the two of cups.

> *She walks in beauty like the night*
> *of cloudless climes and starry skies.*

The old man startled Marvin by breaking into chant as they left the orchard, coming into a clear view of the moon over the pond.

"Tell it," Marvin murmured.

> *And all that's best of dark and bright*
> *meet in her aspect and her eyes.*
> *Thus mellowed to that tender light*
> *which heaven to gaudy day denies.*

"A-men," put in Marvin.

Past the pond, they entered the oldest part of the wood. The contrast of light and shadow were as sharp, sharper than day; the wind picked up, and the twisted shadows of the bare branches came alive, gliding over the snow, riding the dips and rises of the stark ground. The whole wood moved to some rhythm he could not hear, and the wind howled after the moon.

Now the old man left the path and led Marvin to a moon-drenched clearing, round and ringed with huge trees. And in the center—No. No, his mind protested. No, he didn't want to be a seer. Forget about it. Just cancel that shit. He did not want to see this: The Lady, the Lady herself. Hair he did not know he had stood up along his spine. He froze at the edge of the circle, staring.

She was wearing acres of white, moonlight. The wind lifted her robes like a sail. Her long, wild hair floated, too. Silver. No, red. Dark as blood. She was old. She was a girl. She was beautiful. She was terrifying. If she looked his way, he'd lose what was left of his blown mind. But she wasn't looking at him. Her eyes were fixed on the old man. Marvin glanced at Fergus; he was looking right back. No doubt about it, he saw whoever, whatever she was, too. They were both crazy. Marvin looked back at the Lady, hoping maybe she'd disappeared. She was still there, slowly raising her arms, reaching for the old man.

"No, wait, man," Marvin called out a warning as Fergus stepped into the circle. Marvin started after him, then stopped cold. The man who walked, careless of warning, into the Lady's outstretched arms, wasn't any old man: he was young, straight as a blade, tall, with hair blacker than night. He walked fearlessly, eagerly, breaking into a run. Where his feet touched the ground snow melted, and darkness grew green and warm. Marvin's heart began to pound as if he was the one rushing towards joy.

Then just as the man reached the woman, grasping her hands, she crumpled. A cry of alarm cut through the wind, and a very real looking woman in a bathrobe and boots ran into the circle to the old man crouching and cradling an old woman in his arms. Marvin's legs unfroze, and he ran, too.

Holy shit: Old lady Crowe, out in her nightgown, in the middle of the night.

"Sainte Marie, Mère de Dieu," wept the woman in the bathrobe who turned out to be Sabine Weaver. "How could I let it happen! But I never dreamed she could—! Come, we must get her warm! Fergus, no. You cannot carry her yourself. Let Marvin—"

But the old man had already lifted her in his arms. She opened her eyes once and gazed at him, then nestled against him, turning her face to his chest.

"Fergus!" Sabine tried again. "You can't carry her down the steep part."

But he was already on his way.

"Doux Jesu." Sabine and Marvin hurried after him. "I don't know how she got herself all the way here. I wake up and feel a draft. I go to the door, and I see the footprints. The moon is so bright. I thank all the saints you shoveled those steps down to the bridge, Marvin. She got down them with her walker. No sign of a fall; then she leave the walker by the bridge.

"Fergus, please! I beg you, let Marvin carry her here. If you fall, you will break every one of both your bones. Please!"

Fergus paid Sabine no mind, just walked on steadily.

"Nom de Dieu," Sabine despaired. "Marvin, walk on one side of him. I'll walk on the other. Try to catch him if he slips."

"I'll be right with him," Marvin reassured Sabine.

But Marvin knew: Fergus wouldn't fall. This wasn't some frail old man carrying a crazy old lady with brittle bones. This was a sixteen year-old blood, rippling with muscle, agile as a buck deer. In his arms was the sweet, slim body of a young girl.

Fergus was her lover.

Back at the gatehouse, Marvin followed the pair up the winding staircase at Sabine's request but retreated as soon as Fergus had laid his lady gently on the bed. Downstairs, he waited for a few minutes while Sabine lamented and boiled water for brandied tea and hot water bottles. Then Marvin remembered the old man's stick. He must have dropped it at the edge of the circle. It wouldn't do to leave it lying in the snow.

Silently, Marvin slipped out of the gatehouse and walked back into Blackwood to retrieve the stick. Lady moon walked along with him, lapping up the warm salt tears she drew from his eyes.

BOOK SEVEN

CANDLEMAS

JUST AROUND THE CORNER 28

BUT where is the corner that Spring is just around?" Jonathan persisted.

He was not satisfied with Esther's explanation of the prophecy, nor with his father's argument that if he didn't see his shadow, the groundhog wouldn't either. Jonathan wanted to catch the groundhog—or anyway a woodchuck—in the act of looking for its shadow. After they had seen David off to kindergarten, Esther and Jonathan, who was at home that day, had headed for Blackwood with the intention of ferreting out Fergus. If anyone could call forth a woodchuck from its Winter hibernation to do its prophetic duty, Fergus was the one. On their way home, Esther had planned to stop in briefly and see Spencer Crowe, who had come home from the hospital two days ago.

"Where is the corner? Depends on how long the block is," answered Esther unhelpfully.

Marvin might have said something like that, Esther reflected, which was probably why she had. She hadn't talked to him, really talked, for almost two months, but she still heard his voice in her head.

"What block?" demanded Jonathan as they rounded the bend in the carriage road. Did that qualify as a corner? "My color blocks that I build with?"

"No, sweetie, I'm sorry. I was just being silly. Just around the corner is an expression, a saying. It means it could happen anytime; we don't know when." Which was why it was such an effective prophecy, she considered. "Sooner rather than later, we hope. If it was sunny, and the groundhog did see his shadow, that's supposed to mean more Winter."

"Why?"

"I don't know."

It was the truth, but her voice held an edge, a frayed edge. Jonathan must have heard it; for once he seemed willing to accept "I don't know" as an answer.

She didn't know. Let other people read the oracles. Today was Brigid's day as well as the groundhog's, Fergus had told her. Brigid, goddess of poetry, smithcraft and healing, whose feast marked the waxing light, the quickening year. Candlemas, the feast of flame; in churches candles were blessed. Mary had been purified after childbirth on this day, and Jesus had been presented at the Temple. It was a time of naming and initiation, of vision and prophecy, as the second moon of the year waxed. The moon of Rowan, the tree with fire-berries, also called quickbeam, the seer's tree.

All this lore that she'd gathered from Fergus seemed meaningless today. The sky was overcast, the whole world void of color. For three days she had been spotting, traces of rusty blood. She had called the midwife at the clinic in Gilead, Connecticut. Gilead was a few minutes closer to White Hart than River City, and there was a small hospital there, where Spencer Crowe had been treated for pneumonia. Esther had an appointment for her first prenatal check-up at the end of this week.

"Probably just implantation bleeding," the midwife had said. "Come in sooner if you want, but unless the flow increases or you experience cramping, there is probably no need. Just get all the rest you can."

Esther had decided to wait until her scheduled appointment on Friday when both boys would be in school. She had not mentioned the spotting to Alan. She did not think she could bear the hope she might see in his face.

"Let's keep to the carriage road, Jonathan," she called as he ran ahead and turned to the steps.

"But, Mama! I want to go across the bridge!" he protested.

"I'm sorry, sweetheart, I know you do. But Mama's very tired today. The trail on the other side is too steep and slippery."

"You're always tired," he said angrily.

She took a deep breath, to keep from snapping back at him, to keep back the tears.

"I know it must seem that way to you. I guess it's true lately. Remember I told you about the little baby growing inside me? It's a lot of work to grow a baby, and sometimes the mother gets tired."

"I don't want any little baby!" He kicked at the stone wall, still refusing to budge from the steps. "I want to go on the bridge."

"I'll tell you what," she said torn between irritation and guilt. Wasn't it her fault that sunny little Jonathan had turned so sullen? Alan was right; she was selfish, imposing her irrational decision on all of them. But right now she was too tired to care about anything. "I'll sit here on the steps, and you can spend as much time on the bridge as you want."

"But, Mama—" He started to whine.

"Take it or leave it," she said sitting down, heedless of the damp ground, the traces of old snow.

"Okay," he conceded, seeing that she meant it. "But you watch me. All right? All right, Mama?"

"All right."

He turned and trotted down the steps, running and sliding toward the bridge, a semblance of his more cheerful self. On the bridge, he soon became absorbed in throwing twigs, slush, dead leaves into the rush of the melting stream. The day was mild, at least.

Esther leaned against the stone wall and tried to rest in the moment, not thinking about anything, not the future—she didn't want to know—not even how long the block was and whether Spring was around the corner. Just rest.

Then it happened: starting in her rectum and squeezing upward. Cramp did not do the pain justice; what she was having was a contraction. It was followed by a gush of warm blood that quickly overflowed the mini-pad she was wearing. Gripping the wall, she pulled herself to her feet. In the graying snow where she'd been sitting was a spot of bright blood. Another contraction took hold.

"Jonathan!" she called. "We have to go back. I'm not feeling well." Anticipating his wail of Why! she added, "I have to go to the doctor to be checked. Now."

"But Mama." Good, he was running up the steps; she turned and began to walk slowly. "We haven't seen the groundhog!"

"I know. I'm sorry. Come on. I'll take you to Nancy. I bet she'll let you use that typewriter." An old manual relic.

"I want to go with you!" Tears threatened.

"No, Jonathan. I'll probably have to wait around and have some tests at the hospital. You need to be here with Nancy to meet David when he comes home."

"I want to see the hospital!" He was working up to a full-scale howl.

"Ssh! Jonathan, look!" Esther whispered, pointing. "It's the groundhog."

Thank you, Brigid. A lean oracular woodchuck sat in the middle of the path that led from the carriage road to the break in the wall. Jonathan gazed in silent awe.

"No shadow," he pronounced solemnly.

The woodchuck slowly swiveled his head, and then, as if he concurred, turned and ambled toward the stone wall, where he disappeared down a hole.

*　　　*　　　*　　　*　　　*

Marvin, in the P.I.C.'s office next door to Nancy's, was fitting a window pane to replace one that had been broken in a Sunday school snowball fight that had gotten out of hand when the older boys started packing theirs with ice. Hearing Jonathan's voice, he looked up to catch a glimpse of Esther, because damn! he couldn't help himself. She was heading for the door to Nancy's office, and something was wrong. He could tell by her face, and she was walking funny, too. He heard the door open and close; he stilled his own activity in order to listen.

"Hi, Esther! Hi, Jonathan!" Nancy greeted them, happy as always to stop what she was doing and just be folks. That was her real job; typing and mimeographing were just something to do when she was bored.

"Nancy, where's Alan?" Esther's voice was urgent, cutting through the preliminaries.

"He's on his way to New York. There's some big deal meeting at the Cathedral today. He left about half an hour ago. Didn't he tell you?"

"I don't know; he may have. Listen, Nancy, I have to ask you a big favor."

"Sure, Esther. By the way, you don't look too good. Is something wrong?"

"I seem to be, I think—" He could hear the tears she was holding back. "I'm almost sure I'm having a miscarriage. Could you keep Jonathan with you for the rest of the morning, then go up to the house to meet David at noon? That's when he gets home. I've got to go to the clinic. I don't know how long I'll—"

"Honey!" He could hear Nancy getting up out of her squeaky, swivel chair. "Of course, I'll stay with the boys. Look, are you going to be okay? I didn't even know you were pregnant. Wait a minute, how are you going to get to Gilead? You can't drive yourself! Listen, why don't I just take Jonathan and drive you there, then—"

"No." Esther cut her off. "I can manage. You wouldn't get back in time to meet David. I'm just going to go. Try to reach Alan at the cathedral. Jonathan—" Her voice was lost.

Marvin laid down his tools and stepped into Nancy's office. Esther had knelt down to give Jonathan a hug. The kid was putting up with it, but he appeared to be more interested in opening an old typewriter case.

"Oh, Marvin!" Nancy made silent gestures in Esther's direction. "I forgot you were still here."

"Come on, Esther," he said. "I'll go with you."

"Thanks, Marvin." She stood up again. "But I couldn't ask you—"

"You ain't asking. Asking ain't got nothing to do with it. Let's go."

"Mama! Mama!" Jonathan suddenly abandoned the typewriter and flung himself around Esther's legs, almost knocking her off balance. The woman looked like she didn't have any blood left in her face. "I want to go, too!"

"Hey, Sport, you're gonna stay and help me run the office." Nancy knelt beside Jonathan and tried to put her arms around him, but he shook her off.

"Jonny," Marvin said, walking past Esther and opening the door. "In about an hour, maybe a little more, maybe a little less, I be calling you on the phone, tell you what's happening. You gonna be here to receive my call?"

"Yeah," Jonathan released his mother and looked at Marvin.

"All right. Tell David I be speaking to him, too. Later, Alligator."

"In a while, Crocodile," Jonathan answered, almost smiling.

As they walked down the steps, Marvin struggled against his desire to put his arm around Esther. He could feel her fighting for control. She'd made her hands into fists, and she was knuckling back the tears.

"Where's your car?" he asked.

"It's in the barn," she said. "But I've got to go up to the house and get my keys and my pocketbook."

"If you tell me where they at, I go get 'em, then bring the car right here. You look like you in some pain, Lady."

"Yeah," she let out a long breath. "But I really want to change my clothes, maybe call the clinic to let them know I'm coming."

He glanced at the length of her body and took in the blood soaking through her jeans.

"Listen, Marvin," she said as she walked up the driveway. "It's kind of you, but you really don't need to—"

"Now look-a-here, Miz Lady," he could feel himself getting angry. "You carrying pride and righteousness a mite too far. Goddess know, you a powerful woman, but you in trouble right now, and it ain't nothing to mess with. Maybe you wish it was someone else, but I'm the one here, and I don't want to hear nothing more 'bout you can manage by yourself. It ain't necessary."

"You're right," she said as they reached the porch of the house. "And I don't wish you were someone else." She opened the door, got her pocketbook from under the hall table, and rummaged for the car keys. "By the way, I know you know, because Gale told me she told you."

It occurred to Marvin that only he, and possibly Gale, of all the people in the world could have understood the context of what she'd just said. Months of silence and distance melted away like snow in the soft rain that was beginning to fall outside.

"That mean my balls safe again?"

"For the time being." Esther smiled, just a little. "You know Gale would never admit it, but I think she liked you." Esther handed him the keys.

"Yeah? I kinda liked her, too. Okay, I be back in a flash. You ain't gonna pass out on me, now?"

"I don't think so."

She looked a little better than she had in the Parish House, Marvin reassured himself. Out of her sight, on the way to the barn, his own anxiety surfaced. It had been a helluva long time since he'd operated a vehicle. He hoped he could get the damn thing into reverse. Of course, the license he had gotten so that he could buy that Jaguar he never got to drive had long since expired. But Esther didn't need to know about that.

*   *   *   *   *

The pain had eased somewhat, Esther considered, as she eased herself out of her blood-stained jeans and dumped them into the bathtub under running water. The nurse at the clinic had instructed her to bring any clots or tissue she might have passed; it seemed simplest just to put her ruined underwear into a plastic bag and carry it in her pocketbook.

Naked from the waist down, she joined her jeans in the tub and splashed water over her thighs. The blood, someone's life blood, flowed freely and brightly. So did her tears, but without wrenching sobs. The fatigue of the morning seemed to have drained away with the blood, replaced by what she supposed was a surge of adrenaline. Or maybe all the energy that had been bound up in waiting and wondering what would happen was released now. It flooded her; it flamed in her.

Esther turned off the taps and left her jeans in the tub. Let Alan suffer a queasy moment or two. She dried herself, then tossed the stained towel into the tub, too. She put on clean underwear lined with two pads, then pulled on soft, ancient, stretched-out-of-shape red sweat pants that had seen her through two pregnancies. After tucking an additional change of clothes into an old shopping bag, she paused and looked in the mirror, running a brush through wild snaky hair. Her reflection startled her; for someone in the midst of a miscarriage, she looked vibrant.

"Esther?" Marvin called. "You all right up there?"

"Yes!" she called back, setting the brush down. "I'll be right there."

At the curve in the staircase, Esther encountered Marvin. They both paused, and he looked up at her. His face was naked, and she saw: he loved her. He loved her.

"You ready?"

It was not just adrenaline; it was Marvin. Marvin, her lover. She was losing the baby and losing control. Sorrow all tangled up with a wild, unseemly joy.

"I'm ready."

Marvin waited for her, then turned and walked beside her, close but not touching, down the stairs and out to the car.

YOU know the way to Gilead?" Esther asked, as Marvin tried to keep his cool while getting the car into first gear. He didn't want to put her through any sudden jerks.

"Turn right at the end of the driveway and keep going East," he said, doing just that after glancing to the left and deciding he could stay in second gear as no cars were coming. "I went there last week with Maria and Claire Potter to see Old Lady Crowe in the hospital," he added, shifting up to third. "You seen her since she been back?"

Ah, now he was in high gear, and the way was clear. With any luck, he wouldn't have to stop and start again for the rest of the way. Good thing they weren't going to River City, too many traffic lights there. He relaxed a little and glanced at Esther. She was sitting with her body inclined toward his.

"No, I haven't yet," Esther answered. "I was going to stop in today. I saw her in the hospital, too. She seemed awfully weak."

"Yeah. That's why I ain't been by her house yet. She see me and her fingers start itching for the cards. She owe me a lot of money, and she hellbent on winning it back. Sabine say she don't want her overexcited right now."

"I love her!" Esther laughed. "She's such a child, yet at the same time such a grande dame, the belle of the ball."

"I know exactly what you mean," said Marvin, thinking of the vision he'd had of her, wondering if he could tell Esther. It would ease his mind, but maybe now wasn't the time. "Did Sabine ever tell you what happen? How she got pneumonia?"

"I heard she just got up one night and went for a walk. I can imagine her doing it. It was the night of the full moon, I think."

"That's right. And I was there."

"You were? Tell me!"

"I was with Old Man Fergus. He took me to that ring of trees. You know where I mean?"

Esther nodded.

"Well, there she was, right in the middle of it, but I ain't recognize her at first. This gon' sound crazy, but I thought," he hesitated. "Tell you the truth, I thought she was the moon. Do you understand what I'm saying?"

"Yes," said Esther, "I do."

"Then she collapse in the snow, and the old man pick her up in his arms, like he was a young man—hell, he was young; he change right before my eyes, and she did, too. He carry her all the way back to the gate-house. You know, I do believe she went up there looking for him."

"They were lovers!" Esther cried out, like she was seeing it, too, just the way he had seen it. "Or they were meant to be."

"Yeah," he agreed. "That's how it appear to me."

*   *   *   *   *

They were lovers, Esther repeated to herself, breathing the charged silence. They were lovers, even if one never laid so much as a finger on the other's body. All it took was a glance.

She looked away, out the window. The rain had turned to mist as they wound down a hill into a valley. They were driving through a cloud, the bleak landscape shrouded, greyed. Inside, the car seemed warm, glowing, lit with dancing flame, with sun flares. If only there was no need to arrive, if they could just keep wheeling through the fog in their golden chariot, their pumpkin coach.

Then Esther gasped, seeing red for an instant, as pain, with renewed force, ripped through her. Then it was gone. Rest for a moment; time to breathe. It stabbed again, a silver blade of pain, releasing the red.

"Esther." Marvin sounded scared. "What's happening?"

"Contractions," she answered between them. "They're for real. It's basically labor on a smaller scale."

"What you want me to do? Slow down? Speed up? Stop for a minute?"

"Only for this red light." They were in Amesville, a small town between White Hart and Gilead.

"Motherfuck!" He slammed on the brakes; luckily there were no cars ahead or behind. "Sorry, Esther. You all right?"

"I'm fine." She started to laugh helplessly. "Don't worry, Marvin. It's only another ten minutes from here. Green light."

The car stalled, and then Marvin jerked it into gear. "Damn," he muttered. Then he started laughing, too. "Esther, I'm sorry. I didn't want to tell you this, but by now, I reckon you done figure it out for yourself. I don't know what I'm doing. I ain't drive a car in, must be six, seven years, and I never done much driving before then, neither."

"Oh, Marvin, I love you!" The words spoke themselves before she could stop them.

Their laughter ebbed, and another pain gripped her fiercely. Blood gushed. Her thighs felt sticky with it.

"How you doing now?"

"It's pretty bad." She clenched her teeth.

"You go on and cry or yell, if you want to. You ain't got to hold nothing back on account of me."

"I can't let go yet. If I do, I'll just turn into a puddle."

"Do what you got to do. I'm here."

They were silent again as Esther concentrated on breathing, and Marvin concentrated on shifting between third and fourth on the winding road between Amesville and Gilead. At last Marvin made a smooth and graceful left onto the Main Street.

"Where the clinic at?"

"Oh, go right here. The parking lot's in back."

Marvin parked as close to the entrance as he could. Esther opened her door and tentatively got her legs out. Before she tried standing, Marvin was already there, searching her face.

"Say what you need, Lady. Want me to go tell 'em you're here?"

"I think I can walk. Just be there to steady me."

Esther stood up, and Marvin took her arm. They had taken only a few steps when she felt it: her womb opening all the way, the birth sack at its mouth, ready to slide free. She stopped.

"Hold me up."

Marvin put both arms around her. Supported by him, she let her knees bend, let her weight go, and with one push, released the tiny death from her living body.

She stood up straight again, hugging herself to herself. Then she turned to Marvin and buried her face in his shoulder, the flannel of his work shirt—he hadn't bothered to get his coat—soaking up her tears.

*   *   *   *   *

Baby-step by baby-step, they made their way down a corridor to the OB-GYN area. Marvin would gladly have picked Esther up and carried her, the way Fergus had Spencer, but he sensed she did not want him to. She wasn't looking to be rescued.

In the foyer, the receptionist took in Esther's condition at a glance.

"Mrs. Peters," she said, grabbing a folder from her desk. "Sit down. I'll tell the doctor you're here. And if you wouldn't mind, just fill this out for us." She handed Esther a form attached to a clipboard.

"Isn't the midwife here?" Esther asked. "She's the one I was scheduled to see."

"This is her day off. But the midwife can't treat problem pregs. Dr. Perkins is expecting you. I'll be right back."

The receptionist disappeared through a doorway and returned a moment later with one of those clean-shaven, baby-face white men, like the P.I.C..

"Hi, I'm Dr. Perkins. Come right this way, Hon."

"I'll take that," the receptionist took the form, tucking it into her folder. "Can you walk, Dear?"

The receptionist or nurse, whichever, supported Esther on one side. Marvin didn't know what he was supposed to do, and nobody was giving him any cues, so he held her other arm, and they all squeezed through the door and then squeezed again into an examining room. Another nurse was there with the doctor; she took Esther behind a screen, presumably to change. Marvin could hear Esther explaining the details to the nurse. He was just about to beat a retreat when the doctor, who been examining the folder the first nurse had handed him, spoke to him.

"Are you, uh, Reverend Peters?" the man asked without looking at him.

"No, man, I'm the Sexton," Marvin heard himself saying. Jesus! Why'd he have to make himself even more a fool than he already felt.

"There's a waiting room down the hall, second door on the left." The man dismissed him still without looking him in the face.

"I'll wait by the front desk, Esther."

Marvin stalked down the hall, nervously escorted by Nurse One, ignoring the waiting room full of pregnant women and toddlers. Son-of-a-bitch had a nerve telling him where to sit. Shit, it wasn't like he wanted to stay and watch Esther being examined by some boy doctor who thought her name was Hon. But the incident rankled; if he had been white, the man would have taken it for granted that he was Esther's husband.

Marvin sat down in the foyer and took out his cigarettes. Just before he lit up the nurse cleared her throat in a pointed manner. Glancing towards her desk, he saw the sign: THANK YOU FOR NOT SMOKING.

"Don't mention it," he muttered aloud. "My pleasure."

About ten minutes later, Esther reappeared, walking more easily, accompanied by the second nurse. Marvin rose and went to Esther, and the nurse went behind the reception desk and started dialing the phone.

"He thinks the miscarriage is pretty much complete," Esther explained as they sat down again. "Out in the parking lot? That was it. Even so, apparently it's routine to have a D&C afterwards. They're scheduling one." She indicated the nurse, who was on the phone. "I'm supposed to go check into the hospital now. The doctor will be over when he finishes his appointments. I should be able to go home late in the afternoon."

"You're all set," the nurse said, heading back to the door. "They have a bed for you right now. Can you make it over there on your own?"

"I be going with her," Marvin pointed out, feeling angry again. Were they blind or was he invisible? He stood up. "Ready?"

"Wait, Marvin. I want to call the kids before we go to the hospital."

"Let me make the call," he offered. She looked exhausted. "I told Jonathan I would."

Esther closed her eyes and nodded. "Thanks, Marvin. Just make it collect from you. Nancy knows to accept."

The nurse-receptionist saw him plainly enough at least to hand him the phone. When he had talked to both boys, Esther took a turn.

"Okay." She turned to Marvin when she hung up the phone.

" 'Bye now, Hon," said the receptionist. "Now don't you get discouraged. You're sure to have better luck next time."

Hey, this ain't no numbers game, Marvin felt like saying.

"Thanks," said Esther. She couldn't be rude to save her life. "Nancy said she reached Alan at the Cathedral about ten minutes before we called," Esther told him, as they walked back down the hall. "He's on his way back."

They paused by the door and looked at each other, the same look, that said the same thing: two more hours, maybe three.

At the hospital, Marvin sat with Esther while she filled out forms and answered questions with answers that were fed into a computer. Most of the shit had to do with insurance. A person could die during this process. Every now and then, someone tentatively shoved a paper in his direction, asking: Are you the Husband? He felt worse than useless. Finally when four different people seemed satisfied that someone would pay, an orderly—the first Black person Marvin had seen in Gilead—arrived with a wheelchair for Esther. At the entrance to the maternity wing, the head nurse greeted him:

"Are you the Husband?"

Marvin felt the top of his head growing hot. In a minute the lid was going to fly off.

"Only family members may accompany patients to—"

"He's my brother." Esther cut her off.

Mad as he was, Marvin almost burst out laughing at the sight of the nurse's mouth opening, then closing, while her face tried on different expressions.

"He's my brother," Esther repeated. Quiet. Powerful.

"Whatever you say," the nurse sighed, then turned and led them down the hall to the last room on the left.

*   *   *   *   *

"They so concern with covering they ass," Marvin commented as yet another doctor left with Esther's signature in hand, "it's a wonder they can find they hole anymore to take a crap. Excuse me."

"You don't have to excuse yourself every time you say something crude, Marvin. I like it. Besides it's true."

"Yeah, truth be pretty crude sometime."

Esther nodded, then leaned back against her pillows. For the last half hour, the traffic in and out of her room had been constant. The nurse, who had decided to accept Marvin as Esther's brother, had been kindly in a brusque head nurse sort of way. She had taken her to the bathroom and helped her wash and change into that ridiculous hospital johnny coat that always made you feel that your ass—unlike the doctors'—was uncovered. Then another nurse had come to take her temperature and blood pressure. A lab technician had taken a blood sample. The radiologist had been in to see her, and the anesthesiologist, with whom she'd had a long discussion of her options. She had chosen to have local anesthetic instead of general, and within moments of her decision a third nurse had come in with pre-op sedatives. Then Dr. Perkins had arrived, and she had insisted on a thorough explanation of the procedure and the forms. She was through with being a "good girl," docile and obedient, who submitted without question to what her "betters" thought was best.

Now the sedatives were taking effect. Esther closed her eyes. She wanted a little uninterrupted time before they came and took her away to the operating room where they would scour her womb. She wanted time to realize what had happened, to say good-bye within herself to what was already gone: the little pink-gray birth sack that had slipped to the floor when she undressed behind the curtain in the doctor's office. The nurse had retrieved it with tongs and put it in a jar to be sent to some lab for analysis.

She was glad she had seen it: this being—no, you could not call it human yet—too tiny to be distinguished from what doctors called the products of conception. Her body had made the sack and the nest of blood to nurture the little fish or whatever it was at this point, and she was moved by its efforts. The little sack bore no resemblance to the full-blown daughter she had conceived in her mind. They were different forms of conception, both real, both lost. Yes, the truth was crude sometimes, and she wanted to know it, to touch it and to let it touch her. Sealed in her own darkness, Esther began to drowse with the drugs. Now she was the little fish, swimming, floating, suspended in wombspace, awash in the salty, salty sea.

Then the sound of Marvin shifting in the chair next to her bed penetrated. She remembered again where she was and that time existed. And time was running out. There was Marvin, sitting with her, honoring her silence, just there, as he'd said he would be, taking his direction from her, waiting for her to say what she needed, what she wanted. Oh. What she wanted.

"Marvin." With her eyes still closed, she reached out her hand in his direction. "Marvin."

"I'm right here, Sister." He took her hand in his own hands. "I'm here."

"Marvin." She rolled over toward him, and a big wave of grief curled and broke. "Oh, Marvin, I was going to have a girl."

All that salt water began to pour from her eyes.

"I know, Baby, I know."

His arms were around her. He cradled her head against his heart. She listened to it pounding, and the waves rushed in, then out, in, then out.

"I was going to give birth to the goddess. That's what I wanted. I wanted to be Mother of Goddess." She laughed at herself as she wept.

Marvin held her close.

"Girl, don't you know?" he murmured into her hair. "You are the goddess."

*   *   *   *   *

"There's just no way to know what the sex was, Honey," Alan explained. "The doctor says it was just too early to tell. But statistically speaking, most spontaneous abortions are of males."

Esther believed that Alan was attempting to comfort her. He had arrived when she was in the recovery room. Marvin must have driven her car back to White Hart. Alan had said nothing about him, and she had not asked. Somehow, even in her drugged stupor, she knew better than to speak Marvin's name. It would come out as a wail of grief. Now she was doubly bereft. They had come so suddenly to take her to the operating room. She and Marvin had barely said good-bye, had not prepared themselves for the likelihood that Alan would return before she was out of recovery.

Now she and Alan were back in her room. He was holding her hand and trying to make eye contact with her. But her eyes felt glassed over.

She could see through them, but she couldn't connect. She turned her face to the window. The raindrops were having the same difficulty, spattering on the glass pane that was invisible but impenetrable.

"And, Honey, I talked to Bill Perkins about how it happened? That it was unplanned? The result of a leak in your diaphragm?" He paused, as if waiting for some response from her. What could she say? "Anyway, he told me that we're really very lucky. If the baby had come to term, there might have been serious birth defects. The spermicide that's used with diaphragms can cause them. So that's probably why it aborted, and it's for the best."

He waited again. Esther kept her eyes on the window. She imagined the glass dissolving and the wet wind rushing into the stuffy room.

"And it really is best for us, Esther, don't you see? We can start over again. Start fresh."

Start over again, start fresh, Esther mused, picturing the bright red blood on the dingy snow, the leanness of the hungry woodchuck. Spring is just around the corner. Start over again. Start fresh. At the edge of her vision, Esther caught the flicker of Brigid's flame, felt the heat radiating from her forge. Start over again. No form withstands the flame. Below the surface of the earth, there are rivers of molten rock.

"Can't you say something, Esther!" He was losing patience. "If we're going to work on our marriage, communication is very important. Look, Honey, I know how upset you are. But, you know, none of this is my fault. Using silence as punishment is very destructive. It's very passive-aggressive. If this marriage is going to grow, we've got to start sharing our feelings."

He left a space. As if on a form, she thought. Fill in the blank.

"Now I know you're holding it against me that I didn't want another child. I admit that. I've been upfront about that. But that doesn't mean I'm not sorry you had to go through this. And I'm really sorry I wasn't here. You should have told me you were having complications. I could have canceled the meeting, and then you wouldn't have had to go through this all alone."

I didn't go through it alone, she almost said.

"Come on, Esther," he pressed her. "Let's try to share this."

"There's been a death, Alan." She spoke at last, turning to look at him. "Do you understand? There's been a death."

PENCER Crowe sat propped up in bed knitting rain-
bow socks, socks of many colors, like Joseph's coat. There was no
point in sending Sabine to buy more wool when she had a bagful
of loose ends to tie together—with rather ungainly looking knots, she had
to admit. She was enjoying this random selection of color and thickness,
thrusting her hand blindly into the bag and incorporating whatever she
pulled out. Uneven, shapeless socks were the warmest, she believed, and
if one was a little vague about turning the heel, they could fit almost any
foot. So Spencer knitted blithely, wondering why, until now, she had been
so constrained by convention in her choice of color.

The click of her needles kept time—more or less—with Sabine's. Sabine,
who was sitting in a chair near the foot of the bed, was a show-off. She
was knitting another of those complicated Irish fisherman's sweaters, the
kind of which, originally, no two were alike, so that a mother or widow
could identify the drowned by the knit if nothing else remained. In a chair
just to Spencer's right, Maria Washington silently tatted lace. Two cups of
tea sat on a small table between Sabine and Maria; Spencer's rested on her
bedside stand. The steam spiraled gracefully into the air. A pyramid of
butterscotch and chocolate brownies remained inviolate beside Spencer's
cup. For the moment, all three women were content to let the tea cool and
the brownies wait as they kept to their rhythms. Spencer tired first, coming to the end of the red. Setting the sock aside, she reached for her tea.

"Maria," Spencer said, sipping her tea and gazing in aesthetic fascination
at the lace, flowing from the dark, gnarled hands, pooling in Maria's lap.
"Where is your young nephew? I've been back almost a week now, and he
hasn't showed his face. I'm beginning to think he has designs on my fortune. I owe him almost that much, and it's not sporting of him to deny
me the chance to win it back."

Maria and Sabine exchanged a look.

"I saw that!" Spencer cried. "Come now. Tell me whatever it is you're
keeping from me. If you don't, I'm warning you, I'll put aside the niceties
and simply read your minds. I've developed the most uncanny abilities

since I was delirious. I have been doing my best to exercise a well-bred and ladylike restraint, but if you expect me to go on behaving myself, don't put temptation in my way!"

"Marvin be glad to come, Honey, when you feeling up to it."

"Who says I'm not?"

"Like I say, he be glad to come. Now the Lord knows, Marvin don't know any better—or he don't want to, but I am surprised at you, Spencer Crowe. Card playing be bad enough, why you got to go and make it gambling?"

"It's more exciting to play for high stakes!"

"Pardonnez moi, Madame, but that is the point." Sabine looked stern. "You have been gravely ill. The doctor say you are to rest. No excitement."

"Excitement be Marvin's middle name," Maria put in.

"You know how you are with the cards, Madame. You forget yourself. You—"

"Ah, my dears," Spencer interrupted. "It all becomes clear. You're afraid I'm going to—what is it the children say?—croak. Yes, that's the word."

Sabine looked at Maria; Maria looked at Spencer; Spencer looked at Sabine. There was a pregnant pause, then all three burst into wild gales of laughter.

"It is funny, isn't it?" said Spencer, brushing the tears from her cheeks and taking another sip of tea. "At least in my case. I mean no offense. I know that in many other instances death is very sad, tragic at times. But, girls, don't you see? I am ready. Yes, Maria, my house is in order."

Spencer smiled to herself. Even Sabine did not know the contents of her will. It was a glorious secret, a delicious secret, known only to herself, and Raina, of course, who was bound by professional discretion not to reveal what she knew. Spencer's only regret was that she would not be present in person when her will was divulged. She was counting on some sort of afterlife, so as not to miss the fun altogether.

"And here is the beauty of it: I am free. Do you understand? Free. And you are not to hedge me about with restrictions and precautions. If I wish to play cards feverishly with a handsome young card sharp, well then, I will, so long as he will oblige me. If I take it into my head to go out this afternoon and search for the first snowdrops—which you keep insisting are not up yet, Sabine—then I will. If I die tonight, I die happy. And if I die three months or a year from now, I hope I may say the same. Darlings!"

Spencer looked from one face to the other, their tears running in deep channels cut by the years. But Spencer, merely by closing her eyes for an instant, could call up each woman's youth.

"Darlings," she repeated, seeing Maria with Raina on her hip, pregnant with the baby who had died. And Sabine, barefoot in the Spring grass, hanging out laundry, two children playing at her feet, and a baby sitting in the laundry basket. And she recalled herself, too, fifteen years older than one woman, twenty years older than the other, heavy with the pain of childlessness. Only now she was delivered! And pain had grown into something else altogether.

"Darlings, how I love you!"

That was the sweetness of near death, that she knew at last what mattered and what did not: that socks need not match; that the people one had always known and taken for granted were astonishing in their beauty; that passion was mighty, mighty. It was a river, and if you surrendered, it would bear you all the way back to the sea.

Spencer spent a lot of time on the river these days. It was usually Summer, and the breeze was warm and steady. She had a little boat—or she was a little boat—with blue and white sails that had a trick of turning into sheer sky. Quite often the river was the Hudson, with its long rolling slopes on the East side, its palisades, its sudden mountains that looked like the ones on Chinese scrolls, on the West. But then, sometimes, the river was wide and muddy, the land stretching out on either side barely higher than the water level. And sometimes the river was overhung with dense jungle. All the rivers of the earth opened to her now. And when she lay in Fergus' arms, they were each other's vessel, and their love was the current—swift or gentle or wild. She might say dangerous, except that there was no more fear.

And sometimes, when the sails gave way to sky, she did, too, and then she saw the river, a snake shimmering. She even held it once, feeling it slip through her fingers, a silver thread, moon-spun. There it was now. She followed its gossamer brightness through trees. As she walked she wound the thread, gathering it into a ball.

"Ah bon," Sabine whispered. "She sleeps."

"Sleep be the best thing for her now," Maria agreed.

The needles began to click again, keeping time with Spencer's steps. Lace grew on the North side of the trees, and she kept winding through the wood. Blackwood, of course. She hardly needed this river of thread to lead her to the ring of trees. Here the labyrinth ended or began. Spencer held the bright ball in her hands. Shouldn't someone put it back into the sky where it belonged? Well, she was Lady of Blackwood, so she supposed it was her task. There, she set it in the southern curve of the sky. Ah, here was Esther, her sweet chick, her hatchling. Before she left for good, she must speak to Esther about tending the moon. But wait! Something was wrong. Esther could not see her—this must be one of those delirium dreams—and the child was weeping; she was alone in the circle weeping.

"What is wrong with Esther?" Her own voice brought her back to the room and opened her eyes. Sabine and Maria were exchanging another look.

"I don't know who suppose to know and who ain't," began Maria, "but since Nancy Jones know, I reckon everybody will sooner or later, and I know you close to her heart. Esther done miscarry a baby. Just a few days ago."

"Ah." That explained why Esther hadn't visited. "And who was the father?"

Two pairs of eyebrows rose toward the ceiling. Maria looked particularly distressed.

"Madame, really! She is a married woman."

"Oh, yes. I keep forgetting."

And she kept forgetting that such things mattered to other people. In fact, they had mattered to her until recently, until she'd learned to sail. What a lot of things used to worry her! How ruled she had been—despite her willful eccentricities—by conventions. How absurd it all seemed now.

"Well, never mind. Poor girl. She is grieving alone. Sabine, Chérie, you are the most able-bodied of us three. Esther is at the ring of trees. Would you go to her and bring her back here? That is, when she has completed her rite, of course."

"Bien sûr, Madame." Sabine rose to go.

"And we thought you was having yourself a innocent little nap." Maria chuckled. "My, my! We are busy!"

"Now, Maria. I don't need my new powers to know what you are thinking. I know people have always called me a busybody and a snoop behind my back. Just count yourselves fortunate that until now my investigations have been confined to conventional methods."

"A-men."

Spencer closed her eyes. She didn't see Esther now; Esther was taken care of. But she did see, quite distinctly, a riot of snowdrops blooming in the Southern lap of a great oak at the ring of trees.

"But will my powers work with the cards, I wonder," Spencer murmured. Then she opened her eyes all the way and hissed to Maria, "No fair warning the Martian."

*   *   *   *   *

Esther had come to the ring of trees, mourner and priestess. She had looked through the *Book of Common Prayer*, the old one and the new; there were prayers of thanksgiving for birth and adoption but no mention of miscarriage.

The 1928 prayerbook entitled the rite "The Thanksgiving of Women after Child-birth, Commonly Called the Churching of Women." The service began with the woman entering the church "decently apparelled" and kneeling. Then the priest admonished the woman to give thanks to Almighty God who, of his goodness, had given her safe deliverance and preserved her in the great danger of childbirth. The woman, still kneeling, repeated the prescribed psalm.

In the new prayerbook, the whole family was to stand at the altar and say together a prayer of thanksgiving—to the Heavenly Father—for the birth of the child. There was no mention of the woman's part in it at all, except, at the end of the rite, an optional prayer of thanksgiving for a safe delivery. Great Danger, Esther noted, had been reduced to "pain and anxiety." How vulgar and modern, she could almost hear Spencer Crowe complaining.

Esther did not like the tone of either version, not the 1928 with the woman kneeling alone, that is, if her apparel passed inspection, nor the contemporary indifference to women's central role in childbirth. The 1928 seemed almost punitive in its focus, the 1977 belittling in its vagueness.

"Well, what do you want!" Alan had been exasperated when she tried to express what she felt was lacking.

"R-E-S-P-E-C-T." She reflected later, hearing Aretha Franklin belt it out in her mind.

First she had to find out what it meant to herself. As she'd stood alone in the Ring of Trees it had begun to come to her. She wanted her experience, the experience of women, to be acknowledged. She wanted rites of grieving; she wanted rites of celebration. These rites did not exist. In a church whose central rite was the eating and drinking of one man's body and blood, there was no place for the celebration of women's bodies and blood.

In response to her suggestion that the miscarriage could be mentioned in the prayers for the dead, Alan had said, "It wasn't a baptized Christian. It didn't have a name. It wasn't a person yet. Really, Esther, there's plenty of room in form IV for silent prayer. That would be more appropriate. No one even knew you were pregnant. Do you really want people coming up afterwards, asking for details?"

She had to admit, on reflection, that she did not want that. But part of her pain was loneliness. This fleeting life had been real to her alone. No one else had experienced it. Yet here was a vicious irony: if she had had an abortion, many people would have called her a murderer, and, of those, some were campaigning actively to change the law, so that a woman could be tried as one. No rights. No rites. The two were connected somehow. And this obsession with the personhood or lack of it of the tiny being in the pink sack seemed just that: obsession; it served other people's needs, not hers. She wanted only to name her grief, grief for what might have been and now would not be, and, in a way she did not quite understand, she also wanted to honor the mystery of the event, her own intimate bodily knowledge of life and death.

So Esther had slipped out of the house that afternoon, a Sunday, while Alan was reading *The New York Times*, and the boys were having quiet time, theoretically, in their rooms. She'd worn her priestly purple sweats, and on her way out, she'd picked up a child's tambourine, belonging to Jonathan, that happened to be lying on the floor in the back hall. It was made in the shape of a koala bear, but was quite serviceable as an instrument.

Standing in the center of the ring of trees, she had sent her roots down and her branches skyward, trusting that what she needed to do would come to her. The sun shone, warming her back, melting the earth. Most of the snow had melted; she could almost hear the new life, tentative, stirring beneath decaying leaves. Protected from the north wind by an old oak, a cluster of snow drops bloomed, thrusting old leaves aside, even piercing through some of them. Esther closed her eyes and breathed the rich scent of death and regeneration.

As she stood, swaying slightly, catching the subtle rhythm of the trees, Esther understood that she must dance. Both dance and the bloody mysteries of women's bodies had been eschewed by her church. Only voices flying from the body had been allowed to praise and—until recently—only men's voices, boys serving as sopranos and altos. Women shall keep silence in churches; they shall cover their heads and come decently apparelled. Their bodies shall be for the service of others only, not for their own pleasure, not for praise, not for grieving, not for rage.

Esther pulled off her wool cap and freed her hair, shaking it loose, feeling the sun catch its lights, letting the sparks fly. Then she shed her coat as if it were an old outworn skin and stood, face to the light, arms to the sky, listening for the rhythm of her dance.

When it came to her, she followed it with her tambourine and began to move around the circle. In the East she did the dance of the waters, of conception, of the primal fish. Then she danced South and became flame, quickening. In the West she danced the roundness of earth, of a woman gravid with gravity. And in the North she bore down, released, let go, let fly. Her voice joined the dance, keening.

Esther turned to the center, still dancing, eyes closed. There she saw the sacred child, her daughter, a little elf between two and three years old with black curls and green eyes. The child was dancing, skipping, jumping, turning in circles, till she fell down laughing. When she stood up again, she reached out her arms to Esther, and they sprang together. There was a rain of kisses, a warmth of sun on dark earth, and everything grew and bloomed around them as they danced.

Then Esther felt others entering the circle. A young girl with her mother, celebrating the first blood. An older woman, circled by sisters, celebrating the last blood. A young woman stepped into the circle, cradling her own loss as she honored and mourned her choice of abortion. Other women came to stand with her. More and more women sought the circle: women with children in their arms or holding their hands; women alone; pregnant women needing nurture; abused women seeking healing; homeless women searching for shelter; women who were each other's lover came for blessing of their union. And these were not all, the circle thronged with women: artists, activists, fighters, peacemakers. And men, too, began to find their way in, because the circle was big enough; it expanded out and out, rippling, every pair of arms widened its embrace, and those within it did not need to see eye to eye, only face to face. All other life: trees, birds, bees, beasts, rocks, mountains, rivers, seas, life itself was already there, the common ground of the round earth.

The dance went on, gathering power, circle within circle, spirals and double spirals, and all the breath of all life met and mingled, and the many voices rose and arced, curving into the curve of the sky.

When silence fell, Esther lay down full length on the ground, returning the power of her vision to the earth along with her tears. Then she felt warm hands on her shoulders, soft, full breast pressed against her back. She rolled over and sat up, finding herself in Sabine's embrace.

"Ma petite chou," Sabine murmured. "If you are ready, come. Madame waits for you."

"Sugar." Maria Washington greeted Esther when she entered the gatehouse, and she was again enveloped. "Come on in now. You ain't got to grieve alone no more. We know. We know. I done lost a child myself. Come on upstairs. Got a plate of brownies that's just going to waste."

Esther followed Maria upstairs, with Sabine bringing up the rear. How did they all know? Well, of course, Marvin might have told Maria. (Marvin....No. Even thinking his name threatened floods; this grief was simple compared to what she felt for him.) But how had they known where to find her? How had they guessed what she was doing there? Well, you called them, didn't you, a voice inside herself answered. You called them, and they were there. Even before you called. They have always been there.

"Esther, Sweet." Spencer Crowe laid down a dazzling sock. "Come give me a kiss."

Soon they were all sitting down, telling their stories, weeping, laughing.

They had always been there, just hidden, sometimes, sadly, self-hating, but always there. The women, the church within the church, like Mary in the Sacristy, with their own secret rites. The thread wound back through a labyrinth, through thousands of years, into a ball, round and bright as the full moon.

BOOK EIGHT

LENT

ACE UP HIS SLEEVE 31

IT was as clear a reading as he had ever done for himself. Marvin wandered through the landscape the cards laid out for him, nodding to the images: Yeah, I know you. How you doing? There was the Star, not in the sky where you might think a star would be, but at the root, deep, the deepest part of deep mind, the wisdom of his body, the ground of his being. Esther, of course. Hello, my Dear. But it wasn't just Esther, it was himself, too, the changes he was going through. Esther had taught him that about the cards, when she'd understood that the Charioteer was not just him, like they'd both thought at first, but something she had to find in herself.

The Empress was in his house, the Queen of Life, a massive Black woman enthroned among green and red pillows, the horn of plenty overflowing in her lap. Marvin gazed at the image, seeing quite clearly: Maria; the ghost of his grandmother; and, though she was old, white, and way too thin, he also recognized Spencer Crowe. Ladies, he nodded his head respectfully.

And there was the old man—how could he mistake him—leaning on his carved stick, cloaked in the night, carrying a lantern that lit his face from beneath. Fergus, my man. The Hermit. The card had come up as Marvin's challenge. Selena had once explained to him the connection between the Fool and the Hermit, how they both knew the secret. The Fool knew blind, like a child, without words, without thinking. The Old Man had his eyes open, he could see in the dark. It was time for Marvin to know what he knew.

Time, too, to pare himself down to the bone. That was the other meaning of the Hermit. Selena had laughed at his puzzlement when she first tried to explain this card to him. "It doesn't mean being a monk the way you are thinking it does. It means being complete, contained. You have heard the expression hermetically sealed? You focus the energy, the life force, the sex force within, you create out of your own substance. You are sexual but not defined through a lover. It is what the word virgin used to mean."

Virgin, shit. However you defined it, that was sure enough a major challenge for him. But it appeared that it might be worth his while to meet that challenge, to learn what life wanted to be teaching him right now, because there, in the outcome position of the spread of cards, was the World, the Big 21. A snatch of song went through his mind, the Black man's answer to the saying: free, white, and twenty-one. The figure in the world card, the cosmic dancer, seemed to catch the rhythm.

> I'm three times seven,
> And that makes twenty-one.
> Ain't nobody's business what I do.

If the truth be known, he was closer to thirty-one, but he could still take care of business. Tomorrow, for starters, he was going to Alisha's to call in the chips, take his ass back into his own custody. Be a free man. That's what the Hermit was. Free. With the World waiting for him like a lover. All at once, he remembered the fall he had taken last Fall, head over heels, like a fool in love, like the Fool, how he had landed on the ground and felt it alive and female and knowing. His body had understood and responded. Now he was beginning to know what he knew.

He gazed at the round breasts and belly of the World. The image reminded him of something else. Yeah, that figure he had found in the icehouse when he'd been exploring in Blackwood one day. It had done some work on his mind. He'd picked it up to have a closer look, and he swore, for an instant, she came alive. He had seen Africa stretched across her belly. Mother Africa. Later he realized that the figure must have been the playdough Goddess Esther had told him she'd made. Maybe he'd mention it to her next time he saw her, ask her why she'd hidden it in the icehouse.

He and Esther had given up on the idea of avoiding each other, and Marvin was glad, even though it was hard for him, the way things stood right now.

After her miscarriage, several days had passed before he'd seen her. He had begun to feel concerned, but he didn't know if he should seek her out. Then, suddenly—it had seemed sudden; he hadn't heard her footsteps—she had appeared beside him in the basement classroom where he was fixing one of the radiators. He'd laid down his tools and had stood facing her. They had looked at each other for a long time without speaking. Just looked. That look was a revelation. It had taught him things about sex, him with all his expertise, that he had never even dreamed. Gave the word a whole new meaning. Looking at each other that way—he had felt like they were old, old lovers, and at the same time new. Totally at ease, and trembling.

"We can't go back to pretending like we don't know each other, Esther." He'd spoken first.

They had a bond now, a blood bond.

"No, we can't."

The current flowing between them was so strong. If he fought it any longer, he'd lose his breath and go under. Yet there she was, still struggling.

"Marvin, I love you, and I'm not ready yet to be your lover."

"We already lovers."

Jesus, her eyes, now green, now brown, now almost gold, the color of a slow, snaky, Southern river. Hair the color of the earth back home, brown with some red in it, like his own skin. Sweet palm-sized breasts. How had he ever called this woman medium-range? How had he ever missed, for one second, her beauty.

"I know."

So what was the point of this foot of air between them?

"I can't go to bed with you..." She spoke slowly, like her words had to move through water instead of air to reach him."...even though I want to."

"You could." His words swam, too, his head, his eyes.

"But I won't, not until I have a bed that's mine to take you into."

Marvin closed his eyes. When she said bed, the way she said bed, he didn't see sheets, he saw moon-colored petals on lush moss; there were leaves overhead, branches, stars. Bed, her bed. Take me into your bed. Without meaning to, he groaned.

"I'm sorry."

He opened his eyes; hers were wet.

"I want to belong to myself, before I give myself. I want to belong to myself."

"You telling me you planning on leaving your husband?"

"I don't know what I'm telling you, except the truth of where I am right now. I can't promise anything. All I can do is be honest with you from moment to moment, so you know. So you can decide to do whatever you need to do. Stay. Leave. Find someone else...." Her voice trailed off.

"I don't want nobody else."

They looked at each other again. This was crazy. He'd never had to deal with a situation like this one. He didn't know whether to get angry or burst out laughing.

"Come on, Esther. Sit down and tell me some more truth."

They each took a child-sized chair, and Marvin took care to leave two feet between them. Sitting down made it a little easier to resist the current; it was like being anchored.

"Well, here's what's happening." Esther seemed steadier, too. "I'm job hunting. I've put Jonathan into the five-day nursery program already. If I—" She hesitated. "If I did leave Alan, I'd ask for child support, of course, but I'd want to have an income of my own. So I'm thinking about all these issues, but to be truthful, I haven't talked to Alan about the possibility of a separation. I'm too confused and scared, about too many things. I want to give the marriage a chance, but I don't know. I just don't know. Alan still refuses to go to counseling with me. He says I'm the one who's unhappy, so I'm the one who needs help. I do need help, but there's something in me that resists being labeled the problem."

"Takes two," Marvin muttered, aware of feeling a little sick. He almost couldn't stand hearing about it, this life she had that didn't include him, these loyalties she was struggling with, but it was part of who she was.

"Let me ask you something, Esther. You still love your husband?"

"I don't know."

"You think you ever love him?"

"I don't even know that."

"Why you marry him?"

She thought for a moment. "I guess I didn't know what else to do at the time. My whole life was one big question. He looked like the answer. It was probably something like that for him, too, what he saw in me, I mean. I don't think we saw each other, just our own needs."

"What you think holding you up now?" he probed, not looking at her.

"The kids."

Naturally. He had really known that without even asking.

"That's the scariest thing for me, how it would affect them. I mean, if I did leave, I'd have to come to terms with a whole lot of guilt about sacrificing my children to satisfy my own selfish..." She was struggling. "My own selfish, well, desires, I guess. I'm still hung up on that."

"Okay. I hear you."

He looked at her again. She stared at her own lap where her hands clutched at each other for comfort. He could argue with her. He might even have the power to move her, wide open to him as she was. He could do it, damn it, but he wasn't going to. He had too much at stake. He wasn't what you might call a disinterested party. He wouldn't use his power to force her hand.

"You worried about custody, too, ain't you? Wouldn't do you no good in court if anybody find out the preacher's wife been sleeping with the sexton. The Black sexton," he added.

"Oh, Marvin." She sounded miserable.

"Listen up," he went on. "You looking at a man, understand. I ain't gonna be begging and pleading and making things harder on you. You do what you got to do. Just like you say, I'm free to make my own decisions. I can't make no promises neither. But I'm here now, and that's where I'm gonna be, till something tell me it's time to go. Till one or the other of us can't take it. Till then, I rather see you when I can than not see you."

"But what do you get out of it besides...frustration?"

"What do I get out of it?" he repeated, gazing at her face. How could she ask? "What do I get out of it? This." He made a gesture that encompassed them both. "This."

He couldn't make it any clearer than that, but he knew what he meant. She seemed to understand, too. The lines in her face eased, and she smiled.

"And if we can't touch each other, leastways we can talk," he said. "One way or another, I want to know you, Esther. I want to know you."

And that was how it had been the times they had met since then. And he wanted her so bad, he ached. And at the same time he was content. Wanting her didn't make him feel a lack. There was more to himself than he'd guessed—or less. Their talks surprised him. Her listening made him see himself, as much as his listening revealed her.

Marvin stood up and stretched, deciding to leave the cards spread out overnight. In the morning they could give him a little nudge towards meeting his challenge. Alisha might feel obliged to give him a hard time. She'd been dropping hints lately—well, she thought they were threats—that she might just turn him loose, that he was getting too "uppity," and she had other fish on the line; or was it other fish to fry. He suspected what had her really ticked was that he didn't care who all she was screwing or how many. She knew her attraction for him had been money, and he didn't need it any more, what with his poker winnings and Old Lady Crowe hiring him half-time to help the old man. Since Alisha had no hold over him, she could get vicious: accuse him of stealing or even of rape. Easing himself out from the grip of those nasty red nails was going to take some tricky maneuvering, but when need arose, he could be one slippery dude.

And he needed to be free. Now. Regardless of whether or not he and Esther ever got it all together. He needed to know he belonged to himself.

*   *   *   *   *

Late the following afternoon, when he'd finished checking fences at Claire Potter's, Marvin turned up his collar and started the mile or so walk to Alisha's place. The air was cold, but the light was strong. With March beginning, the sun didn't set till nearly six, which made all the hiking he had to do more pleasant. He had to admit that he was in better shape these days than he'd ever been. Since he'd given up cigarettes for pipes, he had more wind. Right this second, he felt good, striding along with his shadow stretched out before him. But damn! he still wanted a car. Since that less than smooth ride to Gilead, he'd gotten his learner's permit and was scheduled to take the road test this week. He wanted to be ready when Lady Luck saw fit to roll some wheels his way.

Tuesday was not one of Marvin's regular days with Alisha, and he had not let her know that he planned on paying her a call. She generally didn't like anyone messing with her schedule. If she had known his intention, she would either have refused to see him or would have gotten herself all ready for him, like she usually did, selecting an outfit, a fantasy, a pose—and whatever he had on his mind could wait. He had no desire for a farewell fuck, and whatever advantage surprise gave him, he could sure enough use. In case she wasn't at home, he had come prepared with a discreet typewritten note that she would understand, but that gave her nothing she could pin on him.

Marvin turned into the long, crescent drive that curved toward the big white house: Greek revival, Alisha had informed him. Looked to Marvin like a movie set for *Gone With the Wind*. Trouble was, it was a new house, imitation Greek revival, so those big old spreading trees that should have lined the drive just weren't there.

Her Volvo was not out front, but that didn't mean anything, since she usually parked it in the four-car garage out back by the stables. As he came nearer, Marvin caught sight of the tail lights of some car parked behind the house almost completely out of sight. Curious, he walked around back to see if he recognized it. Mmm. Mmm. Mmm. If it wasn't a certain blue Ford Escort with clergy plates, one of the P.I.C.'s perks. Too bad the congregation didn't see fit to provide the sexton with subsidized transportation, too. He would have taken a cut in pay in exchange for a car, maintenance included.

A glance in the direction of the garage told him that Alisha was here. Her husband's BMW, which Marvin had long since identified as belonging to the commuter he'd spooked the night arrived in White Hart, was gone, though the two other vehicles, a Rover Jeep and Mercedes Convertible, remained. So it appeared the P.I.C. was paying a little pastoral call. Marvin knew Alisha and the P.I.C. were tight. Alisha had to have lunch with the man on a regular basis or the church would definitely collapse.

At least that was how she saw it. Might be interesting to find out what all they talked about.

Today was Mardi Gras, Marvin remembered. The Episcopals called it Shrove Tuesday, Maria had explained to him, because they were supposed to shrive themselves of their sins, which, loosely translated, meant something like: no more jive, time to shrive, almost Lent, time to repent. Lent, as far as Marvin could make it out, meant giving up anything you enjoyed, which must include pancakes, because there was always a pancake supper at St. Paul's on Shrove Tuesday put on by the men of the parish. (Flipping pancakes was something Real Men were allowed to do, like cooking barbecue.) Marvin had no intention of attending the St. Paul's pancake supper, but the P.I.C. would have to be there.

If Alisha Adams had decided to do some shriving with the P.I.C., they'd better have gotten an early start. If she went into any detail, it could easily take all night to get through her list of sins. Well, he sure didn't want to interrupt her private confessions. With any luck, she'd already decided to give him up for Lent.

Marvin went in through the mudroom, which was full of the riding boots and crops that had a way of winding up in her bedroom on certain occasions. From the back hall he'd have access to either the kitchen or the living room. Depending on where they were, he'd leave the note by the microwave or the VCR controls. If they were talking, they wouldn't hear him; he could move like a cat when he needed to. He might just overhear something that would give him some insight into the inside track. You never knew what information might come in handy one fine day.

Marvin opened the door to the back hall soundlessly and stood listening, his hand still on the knob. Definitely nobody was going to hear anything with the stereo blaring like that; Alisha had speakers in every room. Now why did she have the volume up so loud when the P.I.C. was—

Wait a minute! Jesus mother fuck! Excuse me, Jesus, but are you aware of what's going down here? Mardi Gras. Yeah. Jive Tuesday. Right now, Marvin had to decide what he was going to do about it. He listened again, carefully. He knew this piece of music by heart—well, heart wasn't exactly the part of anatomy that had been most involved. This routine was one of Alisha's standard ones. She'd gotten it out of some movie she'd seen about ten years ago—he'd seen it, too. It involved timing your climax and hers, too, to match the climax of the music. A long slow build up to the Big O. By Marvin's estimation there were about eleven and a half minutes to go. Suddenly, he knew just exactly what he would do.

Calling on his carefully honed criminal talents and tendencies, Marvin moved into the living room, left his note by the VCR controls as planned, and grabbed the video camera, loading it with a blank cartridge. Then he stole up the stairs. It was a risk, sure. But if they caught him catching them, whose problem was it, really?

By the time he opened the bedroom door, the volume had increased with the intensity of the music, obliterating any sound he might make. A glance confirmed his suspicions. They were in bed—the bed being to the right of the inward opening door, which gave him some cover—and they were hard at it. Six and a half minutes left; no time to lose. Marvin positioned himself right next to the door, so that he could move behind it in a flash, and started the camera rolling.

Too bad he couldn't move in for a closer shot. The P.I.C., whose back and head Marvin could recognize since he knew the man's identity, was on top. The way the son-of-a-bitch was grunting and straining, he appeared more like he was having a tough time taking a crap than enjoying a good screw. He was off the beat, too, Marvin noticed. Alisha, bucking from underneath, seemed to be trying to get him back on it. Damn! he couldn't see her face either, but he could tell by the slackness of her legs that she was getting bored and frustrated. Five minutes left to go. In his former profession, Marvin had more than once witnessed other people in the act. From the observer's point of view, he had to admit, sex usually looked kind of dumb, but this had to be one of the stupidest fucks he'd ever seen.

Suddenly, there was a scuffle in the bed. Alisha was taking charge. She flipped him over like a Shrove Tuesday pancake, and straddled him with her war cry, which was not her come-cry, but meant: Goddamnit, you'd better see to it that I come. And thank you, Jesus, because of her angle—arched, head tossed back, big boobs flapping, while she rode him at a full gallop—Marvin finally got a good shot of the P.I.C.'s face. Anyone would recognize him.

Then, with two and a half minutes left and Alisha still hanging fire, the P.I.C.'s eyes rolled up inside his head and he grimaced like Christ crucified on the cross. Okay, enough.

Marvin withdrew, retraced his steps, unloaded and replaced the camera, and was out the door just as the music ended. Not wanting to chance the driveway, he cut through the stables and took a cross-country detour back to the road where he strode off into the sunset. Free.

And not only free but with an ace up his sleeve.

ASH WEDNESDAY 32

I invite you, therefore, in the name of the Church..." Alan read to his congregation.

> ...to the observance of a holy Lent, by self-examination and repentance; by prayer, fasting, and self-denial; and by reading and meditating on God's holy Word. And, to make a right beginning of repentance, and as a mark of our mortal nature, let us kneel before the Lord, our maker and redeemer.

Esther bowed her head, but her knees wouldn't give. What was going on with her, she wondered, as she managed to sit down. She shoulddn't have come. She could have pleaded the need to prepare for her job interview at the women's shelter this afternoon. Now, in a moment, everyone would go up to the Communion rail to receive the Imposition of Ashes. What would she do? She couldn't decide or predict.

At least she'd had the sense to sit in the very last pew close to the door. The other congregants were clustered in the first five or six rows. "The faithful women," Alan had dubbed those who attended week day services. Esther could recognize all of them from the backs of their heads. Maria Washington, Elsa Endsley, Claire Potter, Nancy Jones, up from the office, Alisha Adams, of course, some half a dozen others. Once Spencer Crowe would have been among them, but her health, since her wild night flight, remained extremely fragile.

"Almighty God..." Alan read on.

> ...you have created us out of the dust of the earth: Grant that these ashes may be a sign to us of our mortality and penitence, that we may remember that it is only by your gracious gift that we are given everlasting life; through Jesus Christ our Savior. Amen.

Maria and Nancy, in the second pew, rose to their feet and led the way to the rail, Nancy holding Maria's arm as she bent arthritic knees.

"Remember that you are dust, and to dust you shall return."

The dust that was Esther—but, no, she was not ash yet, she was fire!—refused to budge. Don't make a scene, an inner voice rebuked her. Don't draw attention to yourself. For God's sake, don't make a scene! Esther ignored the voice. She spoke to herself, silently, clearly. No, I will not go to the rail to receive the ash. I know I am earth, living earth. I am not ashamed. I will not be shamed. I do not repent.

"Have mercy on us, O God..." the congregation stood and began to recite.

*...according to your loving-kindness; in your great
compassion blot out my offenses.*

*Wash me through and through from my wickedness
and cleanse me from my sin.*

*For I know my transgressions,
and my sin is ever before me.*

*Against you only have I sinned
and done what is evil in your sight.*

*And so you are justified when you speak
and upright in your judgement.*

*Indeed, I have been wicked from my birth,
a sinner from my mother's womb...*

Mid-psalm, Esther rose and left the Church, heading for the Wilderness. If it was good enough for Jesus, it was good enough for her.

*　　*　　*　　*　　*

Fergus opened the door to his woodstove and shoveled the old ash into the metal bucket, raked the coals, then broke up some kindling. He'd already fetched three logs from the stack the Marvel had made against the West wall of the loft. The Marvel had gotten into the habit of bringing more wood from the lower barn every week. Fergus had grown weary and wise enough to be grateful that he no longer had to haul wood up the stairs. The day had not warmed up as he had imagined it might—or his body had not. Even as the sun waxed in strength, his own internal fires seemed to wane. He was using more fuel this Winter than he ever had before.

Now Fergus balanced the logs on the kindling that was already beginning to catch. He knew the wood: ash, tree of the third moon, the tree of birth, following the trees of quickening and conception. The after-birth, in older times, was often buried beneath the ash, and in the lap of the ash tree people had set forth bowls of cream for the Good People. It was under the ash tree that the three Fates sat spinning their threads and dispensing justice. And it was well known that the ashgrove was sacred to the Unicorn.

There was no ashgrove in Blackwood, but there had been a number of ash trees. Now they were dying. Fergus did not know the exact cause, but he had suspicions. In the past few years, when he'd entered into communion with an ash tree to try to divine what was wrong, he could sense a burning, an eating away of vitality at root and leaf, a sensation he traced to the water, the rain. Something was wrong, and the ash trees, the most sensitive to the imbalance, were dying first, their death a silent warning: Something is wrong. Even in Blackwood, something is wrong. Fergus' powers were not strong enough to shield Blackwood from poisoned rain.

As Fergus gave the log over to flame, he remembered the living tree. It had grown by the stream bed, taller than any tree near it, slender, supple in its strength, with a beauty of line that moved him, even in memory. And he remembered the small, delicate, pentacle clusters of leaf, turning dryer and browner each year, still yearning after the upper reaches of air, unfiltered light of sun, moon, stars. Fergus thanked the tree for this last gift of heat.

Ash was a hot-burning wood and would heat the loft quickly. Later he might look for an oak log, slow-burning, to last the afternoon. Fergus sat back in his rocking chair, leaving the door to the stove open to give the fire air till the logs fully ignited. Once the leaping dance of flames might have spoken to him, revealed some telling image, as water used to, or wind, or the subtle quiverings of earth. But the second sightlessness that had overtaken him at the turning of the year continued to deepen. Yet, though he grieved at times, this new blindness was not without sweetness.

He understood that he, Fergus, guardian of Blackwood, keeper of time, had come to the place where time turns, the heart of the double helix—or its outer rim. So he moved counter to the sun on this last journey home. Home. Already She had opened her arms to him and taken him as the lover of her youth. Soon, no doubt, he would suckle at her breast. And then the final mystery.

The ash logs caught and flamed, burning, turning to ash. Buried in the wood: a sapling, a seedling, a seed. The fire warmed an old man, whose body curled and dried and disintegrated, another dying leaf on the Tree. Who knew what his own last gift might be? Did not the blackest night blaze with stars? Embracing his blindness, he yielded to flame. He burned. He burned. And from his willing ashes what phoenix might not arise?

"Fergus? Are you home? Fergus?"

In one of her forms, She was calling to him.

"I am."

The trap door creaked open, and she of the snake hair appeared, head first. Esther, of old Ishtar and Astarte, the latter his own favorite form of the name. She lowered the trapdoor and stood for a moment, gazing at him from across the room. Then she astonished him by rushing to him, flinging herself at his feet, burying her face in his knee. Astarte, Queen of the Stars, and a mortal woman weeping in his lap.

His hands remembered an ancient gesture; he laid one hand on her head and felt her hair curling, coiling round his fingers. Slowly, rhythmically, he began to stroke her hair, her neck, her back. She quieted under his touch. In a moment, she rose to fetch her favorite stool. He closed the stove door and put the kettle on for tea. Then, knocking the old ashes out of his pipe, he refilled it and lit it, while Esther filled the tea ball and hotted the pot.

"Tell, me, Astarte," he invited when they were both settled with their steaming mugs. "That is, if you wish to speak. Sometimes to sip hot tea is enough."

Esther nodded, doing just that.

"I almost think it is," she said. "I am not giving up anything for Lent," she added, with a touch of defiance. "I've just come from the Ash Wednesday service," she explained. "Well, actually, I walked out in the middle of it.

"You know what's the worst of all this whatever it is I'm going through? I embarrass myself. What a self-dramatizing gesture, walking out of church. I feel like a middle-aged adolescent. What could be more absurd?"

Fergus noticed that as she spoke, her tears had begun to fall again.

"Don't mind me." She brushed them away. "I'm just overwrought."

Fergus fetched a clean cotton handkerchief. He seemed to have little else to offer. He sat down again and puffed helplessly on his pipe, wishing that words would come to him, but he exhaled only smoke. It danced in the air between them, coiling, uncoiling, like her hair. Then an image began to form.

"It is not easy," he began, "for the snake to shed skin. The new skin underneath is extremely sensitive, tender to the slightest touch. The snake at this time has a tendency to heightened temperament. It is all in the natural order of things."

"For the snake, maybe. But, Fergus, I can't shed Christ like a skin. He's too deep, more like bone marrow. Yet I can't deny Her, either. It's tearing me apart. It feels more like drawing and quartering than shedding skin. And it's affecting my whole life and, well, other people's lives, too. I have decisions to make, big ones. I'm hardly even used to the idea of having a will, much less asserting it."

"And you believe there is deadly enmity between Christ and the Lady in this matter of choosing?"

She sipped and appeared to ponder for a time. Hot tea not only soothed but, in Fergus' experience, the clear dark liquid in the cup made an excellent scrying bowl.

"I'm not very sure about anything, but I've always thought that following Christ, the way of the Cross, you could say, meant self-denial, self-sacrifice. Self-will or self anything else or just plain self is selfishness. Jesus says something about losing yourself or your soul in order to save it. So what that has meant to me, at such a deep level I've never even questioned it till now, is: if I want something, anything, for myself, it's dangerous. If I know I want it, then it's probably selfish and I should sacrifice the desire. And if I can't, but go on wanting it and willing it, I'm almost sure not to get it; that's the punishment for wanting. The only way to get what you want is not to want it—but unless you're sincere in your sacrifice, then you're being manipulative, which is even worse. It makes me tired just to try to understand it. Unless you really are a Saint, you get involved in this convoluted kind of double-think, or just plain self deception. And you do feel guilty all the time."

Fergus, on the other hand, felt confused. Denial of the obvious generally did result in confusion.

"Astarte, are you telling me about wanting the Marvel as your lover?"

Fresh tears answered him. "But it's not as simple as that," she insisted.

"It never is," he agreed. Then added, "Although perhaps it should be."

Esther looked surprised, and Fergus knew the moment of pleasure reserved for the old when they find they have managed to shock the young.

"So, Astarte, as I understand it, you believe that Christ wants you to deny your selfish desires and the Lady wants you to indulge them? To put it crudely, that is."

"I guess it is pretty crude," she allowed.

"Well then, I suggest you tell them both to mind their own business."

"Fergus!" She was further shocked. "I thought you believed in the Lady. I thought you were her priest."

"Belief has little to do with it. It is a matter of practice, a practical matter. I am not so presumptuous as to suppose I have fathomed the exact nature of the Mystery. Remember, Esther, we create the gods in our own image, after our own likeness, male and female created we them."

Esther laughed. "Now I understand the saying the Devil can quote scripture—or misquote it."

"I am not misquoting, just restoring the original, if unintended, meaning."

"But, Fergus, are you an atheist, or an agnostic or what?"

"I am that I am. And so are you. And so is She and so is He. No one knows the secret name of Mystery. The ancient Hebrews were right about that. It can't be pronounced."

Esther refilled their cups. They were silent for a time.

"I don't suppose any of my palaver has helped at all," Fergus sighed. "I'm an old man, and I've lost such powers as were mine. I can't see the way ahead for you, Astarte."

Esther rose and stood beside him, stroking his hair. His vision blurred. Ah, tears. Well, let them fall.

"But that's the adventure," she said, "that I don't know what's around the corner or beyond the next rise. I don't need to be told, just encouraged to go on and find out for myself."

"The Lady is a mischief-maker, that much I know. She enjoys a good laugh at our poor mortal expense."

"And Jesus was a trouble-maker," Esther mused.

"Don't force your decisions, Astarte, or let anyone else force them. Learn from an old fool who most of his life has been young and impatient. Shakespeare said it best: Ripeness is all."

"Jesus spent forty days and forty nights alone in the wilderness," Esther observed.

"The Lady is the wilderness. Or that is one of her names. Lady of the Beasts, who tames and is untamed."

"That's like the Strength card in the Tarot deck!" Esther said. "Marvin explained it to me once."

The pleasure in Astarte's voice as she spoke her beloved's name was almost enough to restore his second sight; the whole room seemed to tremble for an instant with sympathetic passion. Passion.

"Astarte." Something important had come to him; he closed his eyes, feeling in the dark for the words he needed. "When you ponder the Passion of Christ, remember this: sacrifice and denial are not always one and the same. The word sacrifice means to make sacred. Life is sacred, and sacrifice is returning to life what life has given. A sacrifice might be something offered or relinquished. Something dies and becomes the ground of new life, and both the life and the death are sacred. Until you know what it is that must die, don't kill anything. Sometimes you won't know, till after it's happened. You see the old skin on the ground and the snake glides away; you see the broken shell, and the bird has flown; you seek Christ in the tomb and find it empty. I tell you Astarte, it is in the nature of things. Offer yourself to life. Let be."

"Fergus."

There was a sudden, sweet darkness and the softness of lips on his brow.

"I have to go now. Thank you."

"Blessings on your way, Astarte."

"And on yours, Fergus."

*   *   *   *   *

"And Sabine," Spencer called, as she took out her deck of playing cards and began to shuffle, "if Father Peters comes with Communion, tell him I'm not at home—or, no, that I'm simply...incommunicable. Is that the word I want?" Spencer queried the Martian.

His only response was to raise one of his smooth elegant eyebrows, while he kept his beady eyes—well, no they weren't at all beady, really— on her shuffling, ever vigilant for her attempts at cheating.

From Sabine came no answer at all, which either meant that she hadn't heard or that she didn't wish to hear. Sabine, that Papist pagan, walking around with the ashes on her forehead, had been scandalized to discover that Madame had no intention of canceling her Wednesday afternoon poker game, simply because today was the beginning of Lent.

"You see, Sabine," Spencer had endeavored to explain, "I am repenting. I am repenting most particularly of all the sins I never committed. You must admit that in the past I have been altogether too good for my own good. And I am heartily sorry."

Sabine had attempted to maintain a disapproving silence in the face of what she considered Madame's naughtiness, but her best efforts were undermined by occasional, uncontrollable bursts of laughter.

"My deal, I believe," said Spencer.

Spencer and Marvin played several hands with Spencer concentrating her newly acquired powers of clairvoyance on Marvin's cards with such passionate fury that she almost bored smoking holes in them. To her great disappointment, her efforts yielded no results, though she'd somehow dealt herself rich enough hands that she had won back a couple of hundred of the thousands of dollars she owed the Martian. Now close to the end of the hour that Sabine allowed them, she was losing again. She was about to fold her hand when at last an image formed in her mind.

An ace, yes, an ace, though she was not sure which one, spades or diamonds, she was inclined to think. She had the ace of hearts and the ace of clubs in her hand, but no way to play either. Hadn't the Martian already played the other two aces and one of them high at that? Now what was he up to? Wait! The image sharpened. Why the devil! The scoundrel! She never would have thought it of him—of herself, perhaps, but not her Martian. With natural-born luck like his, he had a nerve trying to cheat! But that ace, whichever one it was, was decidedly concealed in his sleeve. Well, he wasn't going to get away with it.

"Take off your shirt, young man."

"Excuse me?" The Martian's already immense cat-shaped eyes widened even more.

"You heard me. Take off your shirt."

Leaning towards her, he spoke in a low voice, "You feeling all right?"

"I'm all right, all right. Take off your shirt!"

"Now just hold up a minute. When a woman ask me to take off my shirt, I'm generally pleased to oblige, but I like to know her intention towards me first. Come on, now, why you want me to take off my shirt?"

"Don't play the innocent with me. You and I both know you have an ace up your sleeve. Strip!"

"You bugs, Miz Lady? You know I ain't got no ace up my sleeve. If anyone holding on to any ace it's you, girl."

"Bugs yourself! Then you've got the bug." They allowed the joker in the game to serve as a wild ace. "And you were about to slip it out and beat me with a straight flush, you skunk. But I've caught you—what is it—flagrante delicto. Off with your shirt!"

Marvin shrugged, then started to unbutton his shirt. "I didn't know we was playing for stakes like these! What you gon' take off?"

He was down to his last button, trying to keep a straight face, a poker face, when he suddenly burst out laughing.

"Take it all the way off!" she commanded.

Spencer couldn't help herself, laughter was so highly communicable. Her laughter began silently inside, where she tried to keep it, while Marvin clowned, slowly withdrawing one arm from a sleeve and then the other, rolling his eyes in mock seduction, until her whole body shook with laughter and she had to let it out.

"See?" He shook out his shirt, then held out his gorgeous bare arms towards her. "I done told you. I ain't got nothing to hide."

"But I swear I saw an ace up your sleeve!"

"What you mean you saw an ace? Even if I had one, which you can see for yourself I don't, how you gonna see it if it's in my sleeve?"

"Oh, don't be a young idiot! I had a vision, of course. You know, a vision. What do you call it these days? E.S.T."

"Oh, a vision. Why you ain't say so in the first place? A vision!"

They looked at each other, then simultaneously burst into laughter again. Like fools. Like children. She laughed so hard, she couldn't breathe.

She couldn't breathe! All at once she was gasping, choking, wracked with coughing. Tears .streamed from her eyes as she coughed and coughed, fighting for breath.

"Easy, girl, easy."

The Martian was at her side, making her sit up straight, supporting her against his chest with one arm, patting her back with his other hand. She continued to cough for a long, long time. Gradually her breathing eased, and the Martian's patting changed to soothing strokes. She leaned back against him, breathing his scent, feeling the heat of his bare skin.

Ah. To think that she had missed this pleasure most of her life—when it could have been hers!—this deep delicious pleasure of warmth, of flesh, of touch, of touch. That was indeed cause for regret. She nestled closer, and closed her eyes.

Maybe it was the tobacco scent that hung about the Martian, the same brand, surely, that Fergus smoked, that called up the apple barn where Fergus lived. She was receiving such a clear image of apples all of a sudden, bushel baskets of apples, stored in the lower barn in Blackwood. The vision honed in on one basket in particular. Something was concealed there. What was it? Her inner eye looked beneath a layer of apples and descried a black object about the size of a book, but it wasn't a book. It appeared to be made of plastic, and it enclosed something resembling scotch tape. She hadn't the least idea of what it was. Now why on earth should her mind give her a picture like that?

Really this E.S.T, this clairvoyance business was vastly overrated. It seemed to have little or no practical use. She couldn't even win at poker! Ah, well, he smelled so good, and the beat of his heart was soothing. She hoped he wouldn't go just yet.

"Madame?"

With immense effort, she opened her eyes.

"I thought your game might be finished. Father Peters is here—"

"Send him away, Sabine. Can't you see I'm busy?"

Her eyes closed again.

"You can give me the ashes yourself, Sabine, if you feel it's so important. You're a witch, I mean a Catholic. Which is it? Ha! I made a pun. Which witch is which? Fergus left a pipe somewhere. Use those ashes. Fergus... Fergus...."

But Fergus was here with her now, wasn't he? She breathed his scent. He was holding her in his arms, and the River was waiting for them. The Euphrates or was it the Nile....

*   *   *   *   *

The old lady had fallen asleep in his arms like a baby. What was it about someone sleeping that always made you think of babies? This was one old baby here, and that cough of hers was bad news. Sounded to him like she really hadn't shaken that pneumonia. Her head against his chest felt hot, heavy. He wouldn't be at all surprised if she was running a fever.

Marvin listened to the murmur of voices downstairs; then the door closed, shutting out the P.I.C., much to Marvin's satisfaction. A moment later, Sabine returned. Marvin held his fingers to his lips. Sabine nodded, then gestured to him to keep holding her while Sabine fixed the pillows. With a cough like that, it wouldn't do to have her lying flat. When Sabine had helped to ease the old lady out of his arms, she took the steamer from the bedside stand and went to refill it.

Marvin stood, then bent to pick up his shirt. As he leaned over, his pipe fell out of his pants' pocket, scattering some ashes on the floor. Ashes to ashes. Dust to dust. On impulse, Marvin bent and put his forefinger in the ash; then he turned and approached the sleeping woman. He'd never been to one of those Ash Wednesday services, so he didn't know what all the priest was supposed to do with the ashes, but he could see that Sabine had a smudge on her forehead.

So Marvin leaned over and gently traced a circle of ash between Spencer's brows, a circle: for the moon, for the sun, for the world.

Then he put on his shirt, pocketed his pipe, and went on his way.

ESTHER sat at the foot of her bed, a mug of coffee in one hand, the telephone receiver in the other. She listened to Gale's phone ring, visualizing Gale and Gabrielle's tiny apartment on the lower East Side, one room, essentially, but shaped more like a rhomboid than a square, with odd little triangular spaces, one of these triangles a miniature terrace jutting out over the street, another a tiny loft Gale called the perch. At the same time, Esther gazed out her own bedroom window, registering the roof of the church and the trees of Blackwood beyond, their branches tossing in the erratic March wind.

Four rings; that meant no one was there. In an apartment that small, you were never more than three rings away from the phone. Well, she'd hang on for six or seven, and the machine would pick up. Almost everyone had an answering machine these days. Alan had just bought one for the church office.

"Hello," came Gale's tape-recorded voice, severe to the point of sounding menacing; you'd think twice about harassing this person over the phone— or anywhere else. "You have reached..." Gale's voice gave only the phone-number and the barest instructions. Esther duly waited for the beep.

"Hi, Gale, it's me," Esther began; Gale would of course know who me was; that was how they identified themselves to each other over the phone.

"Hello, you." The real Gale picked up. "Hold on. Just let me put these groceries down on the counter. "Hey, I oughta make an exercise video," she said when she returned to the phone, still out of breath. "I could call it Gale's Sixth Floor Walk-Up with Groceries Work Out."

"Well, I hope you're wearing your designer sweats."

"No, I'm in paramilitary drag. Later this afternoon Gabrielle and I are meeting with some women from Avenue C who are trying to form a new local. There've been a few hostilities over there on the part of, uh, management, to use a polite word."

"You and Gabrielle are both still in one piece?"

"We're fine. Don't worry. I almost hate to admit this, but I'm beginning to suspect Gabrielle of having a good influence on me. There's a distinct possibility that I might be mellowing out—just a little. She tempers my tendency towards direct and violent up-against-the-wall-mother-fucker confrontations. She's got street smarts and common sense. Mother wit, you could call it. I don't mean that she cramps my style or controls me or anything, it's just that when I take myself or life too seriously, she laughs at me. She finds me wildly funny. You know, I never got the joke before. I still don't, sometimes. But when Gabrielle laughs, it's almost impossible not to laugh, too."

"Yes, I noticed that at Christmas, Gale. You've got a good thing going with Gabrielle." Esther paused for a moment. "And I bet you're scared to death."

"How did you guess?"

"You could call it mother wit."

"You know, Esther, it's actually getting pretty serious for a relationship that's a laugh a minute. We even mentioned the M-word the other day."

"You mean that outworn, oppressive, patriarchal institution?"

"Yeah, that one. The hets-only club that gives members tax breaks, better insurance deals, the right to visit your spouse in the Intensive Care Unit...."

"And gives you a new cause."

"True. But how else besides espousing a cause can I deal with the embarrassment?"

"The embarrassment of what? Wanting a life with Gabrielle?"

"Eating my words."

"Oh, Gale!" Esther laughed. "Eating your words is good for you. It's nourishing."

"Yeah, right," grumbled Gale. "Like spinach and liver. But what about you, Esther? Here I am kvetching—as Gabrielle would say—about my humiliating happiness on your phone bill. Esther! You didn't call to talk to me about the D-word, did you? Or maybe the S-word?"

"I assume you mean divorce and separation, not death and shit? No, actually, the word begins with a J."

"J." Gale ran through mental files. "J. Job? Esther, you got a job?"

"Yes."

"Tell me all about it."

"I'm going to be working at a battered women's shelter in River City. They just called me this morning. I'm going for training next week. I can hardly believe it."

"Esther, that's fantastic! I'm so proud of you. What will you be doing? What's your job description?"

"Child counselor is my official title. I'll be running children's groups, also working with women and children on family issues, and I'll be doing advocacy work, going to court and social services with women."

"You'll be superb, Esther. What about pay, benefits? Is this full-time?"

"Half-time. That's one of the best things about it as far as I'm concerned. I'll be working from nine to one every day, so most of the time that David and Jonathan are not in school, I'll be with them. There's also health insurance, if I want to sign on. Paid sick days."

"But, Esther." Gale sounded concerned. "It can't pay very much, a half-time job in human services."

"No, it can't and it doesn't. Just a little more than minimum wage. But, Gale, it's a start. And it's really important to me to have the time with the boys."

"I'm not arguing that, Esther. Let me be blunt. Should you decide you want to leave Alan, well, have you thought about it at all, Esther, how you would manage? I was under the impression that the possibility of separating was part of the point of finding a job. Have you and Alan talked about a separation?"

"Oh, Gale." Esther took a sip of her coffee and almost spat it back into the cup; it was lukewarm and bitter from too many re-heatings. She reached back and set it on her bedside table, then she curled up on her side. "It's hard to think in dollars and cents when nothing makes emotional sense. No, we haven't talked about separating, or about anything else, for that matter. You're right; I wouldn't be able to support the kids on my earnings. I'd have to have a generous amount of child support. Maybe I could support myself, pay rent on a small place. But housing could be a problem. White Hart is expensive. If I could, I'd like to keep the kids in the same schools, minimize the changes in their lives."

Esther registered the familiar panic that mounted in her whenever she considered the consequences to her children. She curled tighter and clutched her stomach with her free hand.

"Gale, I don't think I can even consider a separation till June, if then. I've just got to take it a step at a time. First of all, I've got to learn this job, get used to working again."

"Of course you do. I'm sorry, Esther. I don't mean to pressure you. You know me, it's just the way I am, always charging the barricades, trampling everything underfoot with my size nines. You're really upset about the kids, aren't you? How are they? Are they picking up on any of this?"

"It's hard to say. It's not like they're overhearing huge fights all the time. Alan and I aren't really communicating at all. He's hardly ever around, but that's not really new. And, Gale, as confused and scared as I am, I'm also really happy sometimes...."

"I take it that means you are still in love with the Pimp, excuse me, the Sexton, and he is still on the scene. Esther," Gale addressed her lack of response, "I can hear you blushing over the phone. Quite distinctly. I am not entirely without mother wit myself, you know. All right, maybe you don't want to talk about it, but you know you have to deal with it."

"Are you kidding? I'm dying to talk about it. I could talk your ear off. Dealing with it, that's something else again. I can't deal with it."

"Not that it's any of my business—but since when has that ever stopped me from butting in—are you sleeping with him?"

"No."

"No? Then what are you doing with him?"

"Nothing, everything. I don't know, Gale. That's just it. I love Marvin. I want to leave Alan. But I don't want to leave Alan for Marvin. You of all people should be able to understand that."

"You would think so, wouldn't you?" Gale spoke slowly, abstractedly, as if there was something else she wanted to say but couldn't quite remember.

"If I leave Alan, I want to leave him for myself, because it's the right thing to do."

"Wait a minute. Stop right there. The first part, yes. Whatever you decide to do has to be for yourself, not for the Sexton or Alan. But don't try to second guess yourself. Don't get hung up on the purity of your motives or you could become paralyzed. To make any move, you might just have to give up this notion of yourself as a good person who always does the right thing."

Give up. The words caught Esther's attention. Sacrifice. Something must die.

"To quote a favorite expression of Gabrielle's: the Virgin Mary you're not."

In fact she did want to be a virgin, Esther realized, whole in herself, complete. But she could not be; she was a mother, by definition not intact. Flesh of her flesh and bone of her bone existed separately from her, outside the sacred precincts of her body. However Mary had conceived her son, she was not a virgin after the birth, no matter what anyone said. Her heart had been pierced and broken.

Esther sighed. "I suppose I want my decision to be right and good, to be morally justified, because I won't be the only one suffering the consequences."

"Could you be a little more specific?"

"The kids, Gale, the kids. I thought you understood; that's what's holding me up."

"Explain."

"What's there to explain? Everyone knows divorce is devastating for kids. It tears their whole world apart. Mother. Father. That's the very stuff of the universe. That's what it's made of. I don't want them to be torn."

"Like you are."

"What?" Esther uncurled and sat up again.

"It just hit me. You're talking about yourself. Yes, you are. At least as much as you're talking about the kids. You're the one who's torn between your sense of obligation—okay, commitment—to the marriage and your need—yes, I said need—to be free. And there's something else you want, Esther, that you're not getting in your marriage. The polite word for it is intimacy. You want it, but you don't think you deserve it."

While Gale talked, Esther got up and began to pace. Now she stood, with the phone wire stretched taut, in front of the window, focusing again on the Church and Blackwood, one juxtaposed against the other, a single view, a double image—or double message. It was true what Gale said: she was the child; she was torn. Mother. Father. God and Goddess. She didn't want her parents to get a divorce. But she wasn't a child. Maybe that's what Fergus had meant when he advised her, in effect, to tell the deities to buzz off. Maybe it was her innocence, her helplessness that had to die.

"Are you still there, Esther?"

"Yes."

"I just want to say one more thing, then I'll shut up. Scout's promise." Gale had been a girl scout in one of her former incarnations. "My parents never got a divorce. You've met them. They're still married, till death do them part. They've got a death hold on each other, as in teeth stuck in jugular. Togetherness, right? Do you think my world was whole? Do you think I wasn't torn apart? They were so locked into their struggle, I couldn't get close to either of them. Maybe if they had gotten divorced, become two people instead of one monster, maybe then the poles of the universe, far apart as they might have been, would at least have been accessible to me. You know, that was their excuse all along, staying together for the sake of the family. Well, you know family really meant my grandfather, that patriarchal old fart who had everyone bound and gagged with the purse strings." And who, as Esther recalled, had disinherited Gale when she came out as a lesbian. "Well, from the point of view of the child, thanks but no thanks."

"Oh, yes, Gale. I do understand. I guess part of my problem is that I don't know what my parents' marriage was really like. Just when everyone else was starting to rebel and question and figure out what was wrong with their parents, my mother died. That's probably why I got married as soon as I had the chance. Being a wife, a mother, was a way to try to get my own mother back. It didn't have a whole lot to do with Alan. He was just there. I used him, Gale."

"You don't think he used you the same way?"

"I don't know. I've never really understood what's in it for him."

"May I be frank?"

"When have you not been?"

"Esther, you cut me to the quick! You would not believe the restraint I've exercised the past however many years it's been, starting with your wedding day when I had to be your maid of honor instead of voicing my objections. Forever holding my peace has been pretty tough. Believe me, I've regretted that decision."

"Okay, Gale, shoot."

"In my analysis, Alan chose you because you didn't threaten him the way the others did, those rowdy seminary amazons hell-bent on being or-dained father-mothers. On some level—I don't say consciously, because I don't think Alan has much consciousness—he figured you'd be a good prop, a helpmeet, as they say. My guess is that he's furious with you now, because you're supposed to be an extension of whatever his ego requires at the moment, whatever is in vogue in a wife. Instead, you turned out to be a separate human being, and a rather quirky, surprising, and original one at that."

"Is that a compliment?"

"It's all yours."

"Well then, thank you."

A big station wagon pulled into the driveway below and discharged Jonathan. A moment later, he disappeared from sight, and she heard his feet pounding on the front porch, then the doorbell pealing wildly. He still couldn't open the heavy front door by himself.

"I'll let you go, Esther. I can hear Johann Sebastian on the chimes. Jona-than home for lunch, I presume. Hey, Esther, what are you going to do about that hour or so when they're back but you're not?"

"I don't know. I'll work something out. Alan can probably manage lunch."

"Well, good luck, Esther. I'll call you next week to hear how it's going on the job."

"Thanks, Gale. Love to Gabrielle."

"Definitely. Take it sleazy, Esther." Gale used a parting phrase from their college roommate days.

"You, too, Gale."

*   *   *   *   *

"Look, Esther, it's not going to work," stated Alan.

The children were in bed, and Esther and Alan were in the kitchen where Esther was emptying the dishwasher and putting away pots and pans.

"It's only an hour a day, Alan! Could you at least take care of them until we can make other arrangements?"

"Who's we? This job of yours wasn't my idea. You didn't consult me before you accepted it."

"Alan, I don't believe this! You knew I was looking for a job. I told you about the interview. You weren't around when they called to offer me the job. And even if you had been, what was I supposed to do? Say excuse me, I have to go ask my husband?"

"I don't see why not."

"Why not! Because I applied for the job in good faith with the intention of accepting it if it was offered. You knew that!"

"No, I didn't. I didn't know you had already made up your mind. I guess I was under the mistaken impression that in a marriage the couple talks things over first. If you had asked me, I would have told you what I think. The job isn't worth it for the amount of money you're going to make. If you want to do that sort of work, you'd be better off volunteering. At least then you could choose more convenient hours."

"I don't understand you, Alan. I thought you wanted me to go back to work, have outside interests, build a career of my own."

"You call this a career?"

"In case you've forgotten, I do have a degree in early childhood education. This is my field. It may not be much money, but it's not bad for a half-time salary. And most of the time, I will be able to take care of David and Jonathan."

And do all the cooking, shopping, and cleaning, as usual, she almost added, but stopped herself in time. Even if she did end up doing it, she no longer wanted to define it as her part of the bargain. A devil's bargain, she was beginning to think.

"Okay. Okay." Alan held up his hands, clearly having just mentally washed them—like Pontius Pilate, she thought. "Pardon me for having your interests at heart. Don't let me talk you out of taking a low-paying, dead end job taking care of other people's children when you can afford to stay home and take care of your own or go back to school and get a more useful degree. Never mind that we agreed that you would take primary responsibility for the children until they were both in school full time. If you must take this job-hobby to be fulfilled, far be it from me to stop you. But don't assume that you can interfere with my career in order to do it."

"Interfere with your career? Alan, we're talking about lunch. One hour a day. Quality time. Lunch, Alan. We're talking about lunch."

"Lunch. Yes. Lunch. And haven't you ever heard of the Power Lunch?"

"The Power Lunch!" Esther burst out laughing. "Alan, this isn't New York; this isn't L.A. This is White Hart!"

"No, Esther, this is the Church. Do you think I want to be stuck in White Hart forever? Think again. How do you suppose you get anywhere in the Church? The same way you do in other organizations. Connections. Networking. It's very important that I be able to spend at least two days a week in New York City or Westchester. Not to mention that there are some parishioners who are only able to meet with me for lunch."

"Oh, like Alisha Adams? Come on, Alan. Give me a break."

"Leave her out of this." Alan's skin turned blotchy. "The point is, Esther, I have work to do. I am a priest of the diocese, not your babysitter."

"This is not babysitting. You're their father, Alan. Their father! And all I'm asking is that you care for them an hour a day until I—as you put it—can make other arrangements. And I thought you were my husband. But I don't know anymore. Maybe my definition of marriage, of what I want from marriage, is changing. Maybe I'm changing, too, or anyway challenging the unwritten rules we've always accepted. Maybe it's time to renegotiate the terms of this marriage."

"Stop spouting jargon, Esther. You sound like a women's magazine, a second rate one at that."

Esther's eyes stung; she saw red. Tears. Tears of rage, a red, salt tidal wave. She stood still for a moment, trying to contain herself. Then she slammed the door of the dishwasher and whirled around to face him.

"Listen, Alan, if you won't start looking at how our marriage works—or doesn't work, if you won't look at us, if we can't go through change together, well, I'll have to do it alone. I'll have to come to my own conclusions."

"Is that a threat?"

"It's a fact."

They stood facing each other. The distance between them, no more than three feet, seemed cavernous with deadly cold. He hated her. Suddenly, she felt appalled, terrified.

"Alan!" she cried out, reaching towards him. "Alan! How did this happen? How did this happen to us?"

"I don't know," he said dully.

She took a step towards him.

"You'll have to come to your own conclusions." He turned away. "Right now I have some calls to make. I'll be down in the Parish House."

And he was gone.

FRUIT 34

ESTHER sat in the church, inside the circle she had cast. She had called the four directions and the elements. She had called the Goddess, Eve, Mother-of-all-living. According to the Lessons for today, Eve had succumbed to seduction by the serpent, disobeying God as she bit into the forbidden fruit, corrupting Adam as she tricked him into doing the same, thereby bringing sin and death into the world. Then Jesus, born of an obedient woman, had managed to resist his own temptation by Satan, and, through his death, had restored the hope of everlasting life.

At least that was how St. Paul and subsequent church fathers interpreted these events. Esther still remembered reading Tertullian in Seminary—just before she dropped out. His attack on Eve's daughters had been so virulent that it had made a lasting impression on her.

> You are the Devil's gateway; you are the unsealer of that forbidden tree; the first deserter of divine law; you are she who persuaded him whom the devil was not valiant enough to attack. You destroyed so easily God's image, man. On account of your desert—that is death—even the son of God had to die.

Alan stepped forward to preach, and Esther sank back, drawing the circle closer around herself. Alan's voice remained: audible but beyond the circle along with the sighings and creakings of a congregation in varying degrees of restlessness and resignation. Within the circle was silence, and when Esther closed her eyes, the walls of the church gave way to a vast empty space she had never seen before but recognized as her own wilderness.

She had learned from Fergus not to be afraid of the images that rose in her mind—or came through her fingers, as the playdough woman had. Most of the time, Fergus had explained, people did not know what to do with the images. They barely registered them and could not remember them when they were gone. Fergus had taught Esther how to hold an image, to deepen her focus, so that she could not only see but hear, smell, touch, taste. Now she resolved to explore the landscape surrounding her.

It was not a desert, like the one where Jesus encountered Satan, but more like a moor, or down, those places she'd read about in English children's stories. The ground, though firm, suggested motion. The hills rose and fell. They swelled. The air was fragrance. With each step, however light, her bare feet bruised aromatic herbs and released their scent. Flowers blossomed in constellations, galaxies; roses and lilies, and every kind of tiny five-petaled flower: purple, white, and the milkiest of blue, blue-white like breast milk, a milky way of flowers. The sky seemed to blend and reflect all these shades.

Esther reached the top of one rise and turned around slowly in a complete circle, the curving body of the Earth surrounding her, the curve of the Heavens holding the Earth. A full moon was rising, face to face with the setting sun. The light of both flooded the landscape and bathed her body, which, she noted without shame, was naked.

Then, out of the South, a huge graceful motion came towards her at a bound. She did not have time to be afraid before the great beast came to stillness in front of her: a lion, fiercely golden, the embodiment of fire. Meeting the creature's gaze, she understood that she was to ride its back. She mounted from his left, sinking her hands into his mane in order to pull herself up. When she was astride, the lion moved again, slowly at first. Riding naked, she could feel the strength of his magnificent muscles. When they became attuned to each other, the lion quickened his pace, covering vast expanses of ground with great gathered leaps. Esther held on, leaning into the lion's mane, breathing the scent of heat and fur.

Then her ride on the lion ceased like a wave curling and breaking onto shore. She tumbled from his back, and the lion receded in a golden rush. She was alone again, lying face down on the sweet earth. When she sat up, she saw that she was in an orchard or garden. There was no enclosure of any visible kind, and yet it felt contained. It was sheltered from the North by a hillside from which a spring gushed, forming a pool in the garden.

Esther approached the water. A many-pointed flower, maybe a lotus, floated in the pool. Someone had placed an earthenware jug on a flat rock. She filled it and poured the spring water over her back, her breasts, her thighs, her feet. Then she bent over the pool and drank. It was like drinking stars: cold, burning, pure.

When she had drunk her fill, she turned to the trees and wandered through the orchard, recognizing apple, pear, plum, cherry, peach, quince, all manner of citrus, fig, olive, date, pomegranate, trees from all climes, all bearing, with vine fruits twined in their branches. At last she came to a tree whose fruit she could not name, though it seemed somehow familiar to her. It was round as an orange but more tender looking, with skin the texture of an apple's or a plum's. She had never seen fruit of this color, the color of dusky sky or of water reflecting that sky. It had a shine to it, Earth shine.

She began to reach for the fruit, when the sight of a snake, thick as her arm and wrapped around the trunk of the tree, arrested her. It was a beautiful snake, black and golden diamond-backed, with a flickering tongue and glittering eyes. She was terrified.

Take, eat.

Esther could not tell if it was the snake who spoke, or the tree, or herself.

This is my body.

Just say no, another voice prompted her. Or anyway, no, thank you. It would be polite and much safer. Nice girls said no. This was a trap, a trick. As soon as she touched the fruit, the snake would strike. Or maybe the fruit itself was poisonous. Hadn't someone said: "In the day thou eatest thereof, thou shalt surely die." Better to be safe. Better to be safe than sorry.

This is my body, which is given for you.

The fruit was ripe, glistening. On its roundness, seas rolled and continents rose.

Take, eat.

And what if she did die? The Son of Man had given his life for the world. Would she, the Daughter of Eve, withhold her own life out of fear?

This is my body,

She reached out and touched the fruit. It was tender, firm, as a tautened testicle, as a milk-swollen breast.

which is given,

Its weight gathered itself into her hand. She held it.

given for you.

Yes.

Mouth, teeth, tongue, juice, flesh. Fiery sweetness spread out from her center, suffusing every sense, opening her all the way. She knew. She knew the rising snake, twining the tree. She was the snake, and she was the tree, and she was the ripened fruit falling to the ground that fed the tree; she was the ground. She was the blossoming earth, laying herself bare to the sky. She was the cleft in the rock and the source of the spring. All life rose from her and died back into her. She was the rotting fruit and the seed of new life borne within it. She was the gateway, mother of all living and all dying. And her body gave and received and gave again.

"In the name of the Father, the Son, and the Holy Spirit, Amen."

Alan closed his sermon.

Esther opened her eyes and opened her circle.

Dazed with joy, Esther floated through the rest of the service. David and Jonathan arrived with the rest of the Sunday School in time for the Eucharist. She went to the rail with them, for once receiving the wafer and the wine without confusion or constraint. It was all communion. When the Bach postlude burst from the organ pipes and her sons burst from the pew, she flowed dreamily down the aisle, startling Alan by standing in line to shake hands with him. She startled herself by being able to look Alan directly in the face with friendly detachment. Here was more of Her flesh. Esther looked on his form with interest. He looked away and abruptly dropped her hand, reaching for Elsa Endsley's.

As she started down the driveway to the Parish House, she was nearly toppled by her sons, who each seized one of her hands, then pulled her along at a break-neck pace. They were chanting something esoteric and, no doubt, of mystical significance but with a meaning she could not fathom.

"Marvin's got a mustang, Marvin's got a mustang."

In her mind's eye, she pictured him riding bareback on a wild horse. Then she saw Marvin himself, as her sons led her to him, where he stood around the bend in the driveway, leaning against a bright red car. Her subconscious made the connection before the rest of her did. The song "Mustang Sally" began to resound in the jukebox portion of her brain.

"Mustang Marvin," she sang in greeting. "Boy, you better slow your mustang down."

"Check it out." Marvin stepped aside and gestured.

"Marvin, can we get in? Can we sit in it? Please?" David and Jonathan begged.

"Well," Marvin hesitated, glancing at their boots. "Just don't be getting no mud on the seats, hear?"

"We won't. We won't." They scrambled in.

"No fighting about who in the driver's seat. Y'all got to take turns. Understand?"

"So, Marvin, where did this car come from?" Esther asked.

"Lady Luck."

"You mean you won it? Playing Poker? You're kidding."

"Nope. I just complete the transaction: papers, registration, whole deal. Don't know if you notice, but this car practically antique. This dude I done win it off, old cars be his hobby. He got some cars more valuable than this one in terms of make, year and what not. But this one runs. It's in good condition. If I can keep it that way, be worth even more in a few years."

The grin on his face threatened to take over his whole body. He looked about as old as the mean age of her sons.

"Does this also mean you have your driver's license?"

"Just this week."

"Congratulations!" She wished she could fling her arms around him, or at least grab his hands and dance a jig.

"So tell me, Esther, I ain't seen you for a few days, how you doing?" He leaned a little closer to her. "You look like you high on something, Lady. What's going down?"

"It would take some time to explain about that," she said, marveling at Marvin's face, at the texture of mud and gravel in the driveway, a flock of starlings peppering the sky.

How to explain that nothing appeared solid to her; there were only varying degrees of permeability. Nothing was separate; everything quivered with connection. Nothing was permanent, just part of shifting patterns in a universe that danced. And yet at the same time every single thing struck her as wonderfully significant, completely itself. The frost heaves in the driveway, the curve of Marvin's cheek bone, the murmuring of the pigeons, the lingering chill in the air. Yes, she was high. In this moment, she could see. Everything. Not forever, but for now: she could see.

"Oh, but I do have something to tell you," she remembered. "I got a job."

"All right!"

"I'm going to be a child counselor at a battered women's shelter in River City. Half-time. I start training tomorrow. Oh, that reminds me, I've got to hit coffee hour and find someone to babysit for me at least for tomorrow."

"What kind of hours you working?"

"Nine to one, which means I can't be back till around 1:30."

"Kids get back around what? Twelve? Twelve thirty?"

"Roughly. Someone really needs to be here by twelve. Nancy could probably do it till I can find someone permanent—"

"I can meet them."

"Marvin, that's really sweet of you, but I couldn't ask—"

"Seem like we been through this before. You ain't asking. I'm offering. Listen up. I work here every morning till around twelve. So I can stay with them, give them lunch here, or take them to Maria's house, now that I got me a car. Bring them back at 1:30. With wheels, I got plenty of time to get to Claire Potter's if I'm working there. Besides, about three days a week I'm working in Blackwood with the old man, not to mention my card game with Old Lady Crowe. So I got to come back here anyhow."

"But Marvin, wouldn't that really tie you down? It's your lunch break."

"So I eat lunch with the boys. It ain't no big thing. Think on it, and let me know later on. Right now, I got to go find Maria and break it to her easy the kind of style she gon' be riding in. Don't want her to have no heart attack on me."

Marvin started to walk away.

"Marvin! Marvin!" Two boys scrambled out of the car in hot pursuit. "Give us a ride! Give us a ride!"

"Not now," said Esther. "Marvin's got to take Mrs. Washington home. But maybe tomorrow. Tomorrow Marvin's going to be taking care of you after school for a little while."

Marvin paused and turned around to look at her.

"Goody! Goody! Goody!"

"Thanks, Marvin!" she called over the cheers. "I'll talk to you later and give you all the details."

He smiled, then nodded and walked on. The boys shifted the focus of their joy, grabbing her hands and spinning her around.

SPRING 35

THE first day of Spring, the whole world balanced, for one day not tilted towards dark or light, just spinning, spinning in space.

Marvin and Fergus had spent the afternoon cleaning up after old man Winter, removing fallen branches from the paths and the orchard. They'd made a pile of brush by the pond where it would be safe to light a fire. It was a good time to burn, after all the rain they'd had in the past couple of weeks. Fergus had invited Marvin for supper, followed by a bonfire: to celebrate the Spring Equinox, Fergus had suggested. The old man had invited Esther, too, but the P.I.C. was just coming back from some conference and she'd figured she'd better be there.

Marvin didn't even want to think about that.

He hurled a couple of heavy branches onto the pile with unnecessary force. He was on edge; he could feel it in his muscles. There was too much hanging in the balance, and he was sick of hanging. He had an image of himself, dangling and spinning like a yo-yo that's just lost its bounce and is all strung out. It was tension that kept things spinning. One rainy lunch time at Maria's house, he'd showed David and Jonathan how to spin dimes and quarters. First the coin spun so fast, it was a gyrating silver blur. Then it would start to wobble; the edges would come into focus, finally it just fell flat. He was beginning to wonder: how long he could hold the tension?

"I'm going to go warm the stew and put on the kettle," said Fergus. "Come in when you're ready."

"All right," Marvin nodded, wondering how the old man had known he needed to be alone for a little while when Marvin hadn't known it himself till just this minute.

Marvin watched Fergus blend in with the orchard. The apple trees still had that gray smoky look that leafless trees took on at dusk. Only the swamp maples—Fergus had been teaching Marvin the names of trees— had buds yet. You noticed those buds because they were red. The grass was still mostly brown except for the onion grass. New grass, flowers, leaves, all waited, invisible but coiled, ready to spring. It made Marvin feel jittery, agitated, all that energy pulsing just below the surface. He believed he might be coming down with a serious case of Spring fever. How long before the spring coiled inside him busted loose and went haywire?

Marvin turned and walked to the pond where the water was doing mirror tricks with the sky. Some geese honked by overhead. He couldn't see where they were, but he thought he caught a reflection of wings in the water, just before a breeze raced across the surface blurring everything. The geese called again from farther away. Their cry stirred the restlessness in his blood. He wanted to be on the move. Instead here he was standing still like some damn tree with his sap rising, swelling into bud.

*   *   *   *   *

Later, inside the loft of the apple barn, Marvin brooded his way through two bowls of black bean chili, without pausing to exchange a word with Fergus.

"If I still had my sight," Fergus broke the silence, leaning back and lighting his pipe, "I would tell you what I could."

"What you mean?"

"I mean that I have enough ordinary perception to sense that you are impatient."

"Tell the truth, you reading my mind."

"No, just your body. It's plain enough to the naked eye that you're yearning so you can hardly stand it."

"Hardly stand what?"

"That if you want her, you have to wait for her."

"Seem like I been waiting five minutes less than forever. What I want to know is, what's she waiting on? She got a job, almost three weeks now. That man she still live with ain't hardly home no more. I'm the one watching her kids. Shit," Marvin concluded, reaching for his own pipe.

"It's hard on your manhood isn't it, Young Marvel? Waiting, not being the one to—what's the expression?—call the shots."

"That ain't got nothing to do with it." Marvin waved away the suggestion like so much smoke.

Fergus started to laugh, not just a chuckle, a big old belly laugh.

"You laughing at me, old man?" Marvin demanded testily, trying to keep hold of his bad mood.

"It's within the realm of possibility."

"Well, I done miss the joke. S'pose you just explain it to me."

"If you don't see it, I can't, that's just the trouble. I hope you don't have to grow as old as I am before it strikes you funny. Life, that is."

"Shit."

They smoked in silence for a while.

"Old man," said Marvin, "if you can't tell me nothing about the future, how 'bout you tell me something about the past. Your past. Specifically about you and Old Lady Crowe. Now I know there's a story there, and I bet you ain't never told it to nobody before."

Fergus didn't answer but just stared for a moment—a look Marvin couldn't read.

"Hey, just tell me to mind my own business, if that's how you feel."

"No," said Fergus. "I think the time has come to speak. The past, for what it's worth, is something I can offer. Vision has failed me, but so far memory has not."

"Go ahead," Marvin encouraged.

Fergus closed his eyes and leaned back again.

"She was beautiful," he began. "In all my years of wandering the world, I never saw her like. Her hair was thick as a horse's mane, and, before she grew up to be a young lady, as wild; a true chestnut color. When I think of her eyes, I see birds soaring in them; they were that immense and blue. When she was a girl, she spent most of her time outdoors, riding and hunting or rambling the countryside with me. She had the bearing of a Diana.

"Perhaps, if we had not been forced apart into separate worlds, as master's daughter and servant's son, if we had been truly brother and sister, as it seemed we were as children, perhaps familiarity would have blinded me to her beauty. As it was, I was blinded by her, dazzled. In short, I was in love with her.

"Just as I entered upon my manhood—and a restless, angry, impatient youth I was—engaged in scrying with my mother on All Hallow's Eve, I had a vision—we both did, but only I remembered it afterwards. It was vouchsafed to us that Blackwood is one of the sacred groves, a place of power, but that it was in danger of being defiled, destroyed. If that destruction occurred the healing power held in that place would be lost to the world. Then my mother cried out that the Great Rite, the Sacred Marriage, must be performed in Blackwood in the Ring of Trees. Do you know what that is, Young Marvel?"

Marvin shook his head.

"It is the union of the Goddess and the God. Their lovemaking restores balance and harmony and brings fecundity to the Earth. In ancient times, the Great Rite was celebrated on the Eve of May. That is why the Puritan Church banned Maypoles. The pole is the erect member of the God, and the weaving of the ribbon around the pole is the caress of Her sex. Traditionally, on May Eve, there was a great deal of what Church Fathers called ungodly fornication, a remnant of more ancient times when a priest and priestess would open themselves to be the vessels of the God and Goddess; the sacred powers would enter the mortal pair and unite in their union, assuring the abundance of the Earth.

"The vision of the Great Rite in Blackwood took possession of me, and I brooded on it all through the dark of that year. On the May Eve that we were both sixteen, I sent her a message, beseeching her, calling on all our childhood pacts, to steal away and meet me in the Ring of Trees at midnight.

"We lay side by side looking up at the budding branches and the stars with long silences between words. I did not know how to say what I wanted, what I believed was destined to be. Between vision and flesh yawned a great chasm. I did not know how to bridge it.

"At dawn, she rose to go. We stood facing each other. Desperate, I took my chance and seized her, trying to plant kisses on her mouth. Then, with all the passion she might have given as a lover, she rejected me. Sometimes, I can still feel the sting of her palm on my face. My young man's pride was ground to dust; the bitter dust of humiliation was in my mouth.

"That very day I left Blackwood for the wide world. It took me long years, long, lonely years to understand you cannot force the Spring, you cannot pry a bud into flower. I roamed for forty years, just as the Israelites wandered in the desert. I found, at last, that the world is round, and all paths lead back to their beginning."

The old man came to a stop. His pipe had gone out as he spoke. He knocked the dead ashes out.

"All right now, you left when you was sixteen," Marvin did some mental arithmetic, "gone forty years. That mean you come back when you was fifty six. What happen then? Appear to me like you got another thirty some years to account for. 'Cause, you know, it ain't over till it's over."

"When I first returned," Fergus went on, "the one called her husband still lived, though seldom in Blackwood. They had an arrangement, common among people of their social class, of separate households: his in the City, hers in Blackwood. He died some years later," Fergus paused.

"And then?" Marvin prompted.

"After forty years, silence is not lightly broken. Such silence has its own weight and substance."

"Hold up. Let me get this straight. You telling me that in all that time you was never her lover? Man, that blows my mind."

Marvin felt out of his depth, over his head, out of his time. This kind of heavy-duty love jones was serious business, too serious for him.

"I'm telling you that in all that time I was her lover. Listen, young Marvel and understand: passion is a power. From it springs life. And if passion cannot create, it lays waste. A child is born of passion. A great work of art takes form or a great act of mercy or courage. Or passion dissipates, sometimes in violence: a murder committed, a city sacked, a war begun— or thwarted passion turns inward and a life destroys itself.

"I took my passion and sowed it in the very earth of Blackwood. Enchantment grew up. I did not fulfill the vision of the Sacred Marriage, but my passion has held Blackwood out of time, until time could begin again. Now it has begun, but not for the old lovers. For us, time is not beginning but unraveling. We grow young together, she and I, and everything that was lost to us is restored."

Marvin shivered, remembering his vision of the black-haired boy and his lover in the Ring of Trees and how the snow had melted in the middle of a January night and for a moment everything had smelled warm and green. He had seen something real. He didn't understand it, but it had been real.

Fergus rose. "Let us go light the bonfire. And let me tell you something, Young Marvel. As you know, I have lost my second sight. But you yourself have the makings of a seer, and tonight is a night to look. Watch the reflections of the flames in the water. If there is anything you need to know, you will see it there."

* * * * *

It took Marvin and Fergus some time to get the fire going, because the wood was damp. When the fire finally did catch, the flames reached for the sky. The air was still, no distracting wind. It seemed to Marvin that the sparks were determined to fly straight up and join the stars. He and Fergus spread out some thick canvas covered with blankets close to the water's edge and near enough to the fire to get the benefit of its warmth. The old man stretched out on his back, blinked a few times at the sparks and the stars, then closed his eyes. Marvin lay down on his stomach, cupped his chin in his hands, and gazed at the water, as instructed.

He had no great expectations but was a little disappointed at first when he saw what anyone could see: the reflection of flame in water, the heat of its color cooled by water, its jumpy motion slowed by the water's smooth, unhurried flow. The combination of those elements, water and fire, reminded him of music, where maybe the bass guitar was doing something smooth and relaxed against a funkier drum or vocal. Music made him think of dancing, where maybe your arms followed the melody while your hips swayed to the beat. Dancing led his mind to lovemaking, two rhythms melding into one.

After a time, Marvin no longer saw the movement of light on dark water as the reflection of flame, but just as changing pattern. He didn't try to see anything else. His mind emptied out and opened up. When the light on the water shifted its shape into an apple orchard in full blossom, he simply let it. After a time, the image changed to black branches in new leaf stretched against a sky full of stars, and that image gave way to white petals on thick moss. Then he saw the curve of a new moon nesting in the tree tops. In a moment, it was no longer branches that held the moon but hair, snake hair. Esther's.

Now he saw clearly: Esther was wearing the new moon in her hair, just like the High Priestess in the Tarot deck. She was naked, and he was there with her. He could feel that he was there; for an instant he caught a glimpse of his own reflection shining in the depths of her eyes. He could feel the Maypole rise, and the power between the two of them making the air spark and shiver until the trees around them swayed and groaned.

Then the flame died down and the water darkened, dissolving into night along with his vision. But it was enough. He had seen. He knew what he needed to know.

EESE," said Spencer without opening her eyes. Esther hadn't heard them herself, but at Spencer's naming the sound, she listened. Spencer was right.

"Go to the window," Spencer directed, "and see if you can see them."

Esther complied, peering out each of the windows in the turret room.

"No, I can't see them," she reported. "They must be high overhead."

"Open a window," said Spencer. Apparently aware of Esther's reluctance, she went on, "I know. I know. Sabine wouldn't like it. Well, bother Sabine. You would think I was an infant who had to be guarded against catching cold!"

Whereas in fact, Esther added silently, she was merely an eighty-six year old woman, who only last week had been in the hospital once again having her lungs pumped out.

"Go on, child! Just for a moment. I want to hear their voices clearly. Who knows, it may be my last chance. I've always loved the cry of wild geese. It makes me feel that I'm going somewhere even when I'm not. If I close my eyes, I can fly with them."

Esther gave in and opened the window a crack. The sound of the geese filled the room. They seemed to be circling over Blackwood, forming, re-forming their ranks, debating, perhaps, whether to spend the night on Blackwood pond or fly further North in the last hour or so of light. Esther closed her eyes, too. The calling of the geese, the flow of fresh air into the tiny room made it easy to imagine the walls and ceiling dissolving into wild, wide sky. Esther could understand Spencer's yearning for wind and wing. She'd been confined to this room, most of the time, since August. It was almost April now, nearly a full gestation.

Esther sat down again beside Spencer's bed, blocking the draft from the window as best she could. Spencer appeared to have dozed off, perhaps dreaming of the geese. Esther would just make sure to close the window before she left to pick up the boys at the Rectory. Spencer wouldn't mind her waiting here while she slept. Esther picked up the everpresent, ever-lasting sock of many colors, as it had become the custom for Spencer's visitors to do, and she began to knit a lavender stripe. The communal knitting had been instituted by Spencer as a way of soothing the nerves of her well-wishers, giving them something to do so that they would not feel obliged to chatter at her.

It was restful to be in the turret room, in the late afternoon light, with the dreaming Spencer, listening to the click of the needles and the call of the geese. Some of Esther's tension began to ease. The geese knew when it was time to go. The slant of the sun's rays told them. On the wing, they could see the lay of the land. And their direction was always clear, North or South, according to season. Human seasons were more obscure, and Esther's only direction seemed to be out: out of the Church; out of the house; out of her marriage. Out of her mind?

To be exact, Windy Hill, the boarding house, where she had, a few days ago, rented a large, single room, for herself and the boys, was about a mile Southeast of the Rectory. The far end of Blackwood gave on to Catskill Road, named for its view, and Windy Hill was only a quarter of a mile from the back entrance to Blackwood.

What was now the boarding house had once been the main house of another estate, like Blackwood, but on a smaller scale. The stable and carriage house had turned into a bar and grill, a local hangout. These conversions had been made by the Pisacanos, a family descended from the Italian stone masons who had come to White Hart before the turn of the last century to build the mansions, gate houses, and terraces of the large estates. Alan, in one of a series of fits he had thrown when he found out that she had rented a room there, insisted that everyone knew that Windy Hill Bar and Grill was a front for illegal activities. Like Marvin's poker game in the back room, Esther considered, wisely saying nothing.

It was clean, she had argued, and cheap, the only housing she could afford, on her salary, in the White Hart School District. The room faced West and had a breath-taking view of the Catskills. Of course, she didn't expect the view to impress Alan, but she herself found it tremendously heartening. High on Windy Hill, overlooking Blackwood and the mountains beyond, she felt like a nesting eagle, strong, adventurous and clear-sighted. But the indisputable advantage of the room was that it was available immediately.

Because it was so large, as big as a small apartment would have been, the room was kept empty during the Winter to save on heating costs. In the Fall it was rented to hunters, and in the Summer visiting family sometimes used it. Until the end of June, it was Esther's. La Padrona, as everyone called the matriarch of the family, seeing a mother with two children, had told Esther to move in at once. No need to wait for the first of the month.

They had been at Windy Hill only a few days, but Esther was finding the arrangement workable. The children had two beds on one side. The room came furnished, complete with an antique Chinese screen, easily moved, so that it could double as a bedroom wall for the boys at night or provide privacy for anyone using the sink and toilet that stood in one corner of the room. There were several full bathrooms and showers shared by the tenants, another thing Alan found objectionable.

"Single old men!" Alan had ranted.

Retired laborers and one former merchant sailor, Esther had tried to soothe Alan, and all very respectful of each other's privacy. Most of them had known or worked with Fergus at one time or another, and she felt at ease with them. She'd never had to wait for use of a bath or shower, and her fellow residents appeared to be extremely fastidious in their personal habits. Cooking in the room was allowed, though it required some planning and ingenuity, as she had only an old two-burner electric plate and a half-sized refrigerator with no freezer. The only phone was in the bar.

"No phone!" Alan had stormed. "What if one of the children gets sick?"

Esther tensed, dropping a stitch in her knitting, as she pictured Alan on the phone with a barrage of hotshot lawyers. Would he, could he argue in Court that custody of the children be given to him, because she could not provide a fit place for the them to live? No, said the lawyer she had consulted, a woman recommended by her co-workers at the Women's Shelter. "If he wants his children better accommodated, he can pay for it."

Esther picked up the stitch again, feeling momentarily reassured. At least the sock would not unravel. Her relationship with Marvin was a more serious matter than her low income, if Alan was looking for some means to undermine her, prove her unfit as a mother. She'd better tell the lawyer about it. Despite her efforts to be honorable, her arrangement with Marvin had proved to be the proverbial last straw that collapsed the marriage—or, more accurately, the last ton of bricks.

Esther had arrived home from work on Friday to find not Marvin but Alan waiting for her, clearly waiting, out in the driveway. Both kids had been riding tricycles up and down the Church sidewalk—though lately on sunny days Marvin had been helping David learn to ride the new two-wheeler he'd gotten for his birthday. As soon as the boys had seen her, they had abandoned their vehicles and rushed to her, flinging their arms around her legs and her waist as she had emerged from her car.

"David. Jonathan," Alan had said, his voice about an octave lower than usual. "Go inside now. I want to talk to your mother."

Your mother!

To Esther's surprise and distress, they had obeyed wordlessly, slinking away like rebuked puppies, fearful and shamed but unable to comprehend what they'd done. Esther had almost burst into tears right then, but something had warned her to keep a grip on herself.

"What is the meaning of this!"

That's what grownups always do, Esther had thought, still intensely identifying with her sons. They made vague, ominous accusations and expected you to cough up your guilt, yes, to feel guilty, not for one specific act, but for everything, for existing. Well, Esther had resolved on the spot, she wasn't a child, and she wasn't going to be bullied—or allow her children to be either.

"The meaning of what?"

The blood vessels on Alan's face, particularly around his nose, appeared to be in danger of popping. Esther was unmoved.

"You know very well what I'm referring to."

"No, Alan, I don't. You'll have to be more specific."

"Marvin Greene."

"Yes?"

"What was he doing here with the children?"

"Taking care of them till I got home, like he has been for the past four weeks, which you would know, if you were ever home."

She had stolen the march on him! For a moment Alan looked nonplused, confused to have his own game turned on him, to be, however fleetingly, the one at fault. Then he rallied.

"You actually hired him!" It was an accusation.

Come to think of it, she didn't pay Marvin. It hadn't occurred to either of them that it was other than a favor. But there was no need to go into the matter too closely with Alan.

"You told me to make my own arrangements, so I did."

"Without informing me."

"You never asked," she pointed out.

"Well, naturally I assumed you had found someone appropriate. A woman, another mother—"

"That's an incredibly sexist remark, Alan," she cut him off. "Men are perfectly capable of looking after children. If you don't like Marvin taking care of the kids for an hour a day—and you haven't given me any reason why he shouldn't—then you take care of them! I'm perfectly satisfied with the arrangements I've made. Now I'm going in to see the children. I don't know what kind of a scene you made with Marvin—or why—but it's clear to me that the children are upset."

Esther turned towards the house, but Alan grabbed her arm, gripping it with the force of pent up fury about to be released. She'd have a black and blue mark there. He yanked her towards him, and a prickle of fear went up her spine.

"What's going on with you two!" he demanded.

Esther debated saying "with me and who?" but decided that would be pushing him too far. He still had hold of her arm.

"You're having an affair with him, aren't you?"

Alan's phrasing gave her a little more confidence. If he had said "you're in love with him" she would have been lost.

"No."

"Admit it!"

"I will not lie to satisfy you."

"Oh. Little Miss Virtue and Integrity! Well, tell the truth then: you want to, don't you?"

Did she? Esther considered. Did she want to have an affair with Marvin in the sense that Alan meant? No, in fact, she did not. If she had wanted to, she could have long since.

"Why do you assume that?" she asked.

Let him answer some questions for a change. This wasn't a court of law. She wasn't on the stand.

"Esther, could it be that you're even more naive than I thought? Marvin Greene is a womanizer. In fact, Marvin Greene is a gigolo. Do you know what the word means? It means a man who seduces rich women for their money. He's a snake in the grass, Esther. He's even gotten to Spencer Crowe!"

"And just how is that so different from what you do, Alan! Trotting over to Spencer Crowe's every chance you get with home Communion. Power luncheons every week with Alisha Adams."

Alan's hold on her arm suddenly loosened. Before she knew what was happening, he smacked her full across her left cheek, so hard that she lost her balance and reeled to the right. When she found her feet again, she took a step towards Alan and planted herself in front of him.

Slowly, deliberately, Esther turned the other cheek.

Alan gaped, gasped, tried and failed to speak, then he turned tail and ran.

She had scared the bejeezus out of him.

A moment later, she heard his car door slam, and he tore out of the driveway.

Esther remained standing for a time, letting the tears stream on her burning cheek. Then she went into the house, gathered both boys to her, and they all wept together.

Esther felt her tears rising again as she sat in Spencer's room with the absurd, uneven sock. Her vision blurred, and the colors ran together in a wild, unruly rainbow. She had not allowed herself the release of tears since the day she left. There had been too much to do: finding the room, as she had that very afternoon, negotiating preliminary agreements with Alan about visitation, going to work each day, seeing the lawyer, responding to the boys' anxiety and bewilderment. Above all, she felt an obligation to be calm for their sake, to be the still eye in the storm she herself had generated.

"But will Daddy still be our Daddy?" Jonathan had asked the first night she tucked them into bed in their aerie at Windy Hill. Her hatchlings, her fledglings with their round eyes and their soft, ruffled feathers.

"Yes. Daddy will always be your Daddy. Always. And I will always be your mother. Fathers and mothers don't always stay husband and wife. But they are always the mother and father of their children. Always."

"Why?" persisted Jonathan.

"Because, Jonathan," sighed David with the exasperated patience and superior wisdom of a newly-six-year-old. "They have to be. They're born that way."

"Yes, David, that's a good way to put it. When their children are born, a man and a woman turn into a father and a mother, and they can't turn back again, any more than you can be unborn again."

"Oh," said Jonathan, satisfied for the moment.

And she had explained to them again that they would have lunch with Daddy after school every day—or, as had happened twice already, with Nancy Jones—and they would spend Thursday afternoons with him and Saturday nights and go to Church as usual on Sunday morning.

"What it means," said David after some thought, "is we'll see Daddy more."

"Yeah," agreed Jonathan.

"Yes," said Esther, swallowing the bitterness that rose in her mouth.

So much for staying together for the sake of the children! Working at the Women's Shelter, Esther had observed that men could be extremely aggressive about claiming their rights of visitation—the grotesque irony being that often the father's previous neglect of his family was one of the factors straining the marriage to the breaking point. Just thinking about the stupidity, the waste in so many marriages, in her own marriage, made Esther want to scream and tear her hair, which was exactly what she must not do in a rooming house while trying to calm and reassure her children.

What she had not reckoned on in all her careful explanations of the cosmic parental split was that her sons would miss Marvin! Alan had told her, when she'd picked up the boys yesterday, that David did not want to work (Alan's word) on learning to ride his two-wheeler.

"Just forget about it for now," she'd advised Alan. "He's going through enough. He doesn't need another challenge at this point."

She had not mentioned the matter to David. He had brought it up himself last night.

"When's Marvin going to help me with my bike?" David had asked as they ate spaghetti, an easy two-burner dinner, at the card table in their room.

"Daddy can help you after school, just the way Marvin used to," she suggested.

"I want Marvin."

"Me, too!" added Jonathan.

"You're not learning to ride a bike, Jonathan," said David.

"But I want Marvin. Why isn't he there after school anymore? I want to ride in the Mustang. I want to go to Maria's house. Maria gives us cake!"

"I want Marvin to help me with my bike," persisted David. "He doesn't yell at me when it's hard."

"I want Marvin. I want Maria. I want the Mustang. I want cake!" chanted Jonathan.

"But you have Daddy after school now."

"Or Nancy," put in David.

All three of them were silent for a time.

"Well, you'll see Marvin again," she reassured them uncertainly.

"When?" Both boys wanted to know.

When?

Esther didn't know. She hadn't seen him herself since everything blew up. She still didn't know what Alan had said to him that day or if that was the reason for his sudden absence in her life.

Today she had walked from Windy Hill through Blackwood to visit Spencer. She and the boys would walk back the same way. It was not too far, even for Jonathan. It was a lovely day for walking, she had told herself; the fresh air would do them all good. But really, she knew she had been hoping to find Marvin working in Blackwood. She had no idea what she would do when (if?) she saw him. Sometimes she was sure she would fling herself blindly into his arms; other times she feared she would suddenly see—or he would see—that none of it was real, that it was all a fantasy, a mirage that would vanish in the vast desert of separation and divorce.

"Silly goose."

Esther started at the sound of Spencer's voice. She must be talking in her sleep.

"Of course it's real, whatever real may be."

Esther stopped knitting and studied Spencer, whose eyes were still closed. The geese had ceased their calling; Esther had an image of them splash-landing on Blackwood pond, ripples spreading out in every direction, crisscrossing, where one set of ripples met another, into webs. Oddly, it occurred to her to wonder: had Spencer sent her mind that picture? Was the old woman here or with the geese? Waking or dreaming? Answering her own thoughts or Esther's?

"Don't you see?" With effort, Spencer opened her eyes and gazed into Esther's.

Esther looked, and in Spencer's eyes she saw the Spring, everything soft and blue, baby birds just hatching.

"There isn't such a difference as people think," Spencer added.

Between waking and dreaming? Between one person's mind and another's?

"One stirs inside another, till it breaks the other open. And so many, many people just see the bits of broken shell. They miss the bird. She flies away before they see."

Someone had said that to her before. Of course, Fergus.

"Fly away! Fly away, fly away, fly away home!"

Spencer was delirious, Esther thought. But then, why not?

"So you see, I know about you and the Martian."

Did she mean Marvin? How could she know? Spencer had never seen them together.

"Oh, yes, I have." Spencer contradicted Esther's thoughts. "I saw you, the two of you. You made Spring come in the middle of Winter. It confused me. I smelled the apple blossoms. And so I knew it was time. Time for me to go to the Ring of Trees to meet him. And it was, long since time."

Spencer closed her eyes again. Esther had very little idea of what Spencer was talking about, but she gathered that somehow Spencer knew about herself and Marvin, not only knew but was unruffled by the knowledge, perhaps even pleased.

Was it the nearness of death that made all the boundaries permeable, like the thinning of the membranes just before birth?

"I know you are leaving your husband." Spencer opened her eyes again, suddenly alert. "I can't quite remember who he is. Not that it matters. I had a husband once, I believe. I don't remember him either. Nothing came of it. Nothing. And then it seemed too late. Too late. Until I found I could wind it back again. Very clever of me to bring the skein and leave a trail of silver thread, don't you think? Now I can find my way back."

"Yes," agreed Esther, her eyes brimming with tears again. "Very clever."

Spencer reached out her hand towards Esther's cheek. Esther leaned forward and let Spencer touch her tears.

"Yes," said Spencer. "The moon does that. Now there was something I had to tell you about the moon. But I expect you know."

"Tell me," said Esther, pressing her cheek against Spencer's hand, covering Spencer's hand with her own. "Tell me about the moon. Tell me how you know what you know."

Spencer was silent for a time. Her breathing seemed shallow, little wavelets of breath, lapping over smooth, shiny pebbles.

"I know," she spoke at length, "I know, because I am an old woman. I am a young girl, sixteen years old, if you must know. And I am your mother. You took such a long time to hatch, didn't you, little bird, little star."

Spencer closed her eyes again and withdrew her hand.

"My boat is waiting for me. Shoo, little one. Fly away! Fly away home!"

Her breathing eased, following a deeper channel. Her mouth fell open slightly. Esther laid the sock back on the bed, then rose and closed the window. It was time for her to leave.

APRIL FOOLS 37

ESTHER lay on her single bed at Windy Hill, gazing out the open window while late afternoon light and Spring air poured in. The mountains were in one of their undecided moods. Since she woke to see them every morning and watched the sun set behind them every evening, she had developed a personal, if rather fanciful, relationship with them. Today the mountains lacked solidity; they were merely making an appearance, playing with appearance. Imagine we are a tidal wave, they seemed to invite; or a veil of smoke; or perhaps a world of substantial cloud, accessible only by beanstalk, where giants live. She liked the hocus-pocus of the mountains: that on some days they were so clear you could count the trees on their slopes and on others they vanished without a trace. Their color today was evasive, especially in contrast to the almost garish green of the new grass.

It was enough to break your heart, a day like this one, everything so tender. Light seemed to come, not just from the sun, but from within every single thing, those blades of grass, those red buds, the purple and yellow crocuses. Her heart was broken anyway, but not because her marriage was over, not because of Marvin either—she was almost certain of that. It was because she was alive, and, at this moment, had no defense against life.

Earlier that day Esther had dropped off the children for their first overnight with Alan at the rectory. It had been painful, watching them walk to their own front door with their knapsacks on their backs. After doing a load of laundry and a little grocery shopping, she had returned to Windy Hill and an afternoon and night before her with nothing that she had to do. No meals to prepare, no housework, no children to watch. Nothing. It was different from the odd hour or two when Alan used to take the children off on a Saturday afternoon. Then, even if she managed to relax, it was always within the context of her marriage. Her surroundings, her possessions would remind her of who she was, her role, her place.

Here, alone in a furnished room, all of that was gone. If solitude in her previous life had been an oasis, now it was a rolling ocean. She didn't know whether she liked it or not, only that she was awash in it. The sensible approach, she supposed, was to float, just bob up and down on the swells.

After putting away the laundry and supplies, she had gone for a long walk, exploring back roads, cutting across fields of horse and beef cattle farms, getting her shoes and jeans muddy. All her senses had seemed unusually acute, as if layers of herself had been peeled away or shed as a snake sheds skin. She felt so new, so exposed, that she could scarcely distinguish pleasure and pain. Maybe this was what it was like to be a newborn: so much sensation and no way to organize it. No wonder some babies cried so much.

Of course, she had chosen not to be organized, refusing Gale's offer to come and spend Saturday night with her. She had wanted to take the plunge, test the waters of her new life. If she started to panic, she had assured Gale, several of her co-workers from the shelter were prepared to throw her a lifeline. But so far she had not panicked. At the heart of her broken heart was a core of. calm that she traced somehow to Spencer. "I am your mother," Spencer had said. In her newbornness, Esther felt anchored; the rocking sea was a rocking chair.

As she lay on her bed, the sun sank nearer the mountains and the breeze became a degree cooler. In a little while, she would get up and make herself eggs and toast for dinner. When she felt like it. Just now, the sun, partly obscured by cloud, was doing something rather theatrical, spreading its filtered rays over the mountains, turning them rosy. A flashy red car was turning in at the gate, between the stone pillars that marked the entrance to Windy Hill. A stray beam hit the chrome of the car, and it gleamed just before the car left the range of her vision.

All at once, Esther came to and organized her sensations: Marvin. Marvin in the Mustang. Coming to see her. He must be. And she had not been waiting for him; it hadn't been necessary. Ripeness is all, said Shakespeare, said Fergus. She could feel the weight of the fruit in her hand; her tongue anticipated the sweetness. Ripeness is all.

Marvin. Marvin.

Esther pulled on the muddy jeans she'd discarded. Barefoot, she bounded down the stairs and out the door to meet him.

*　　　*　　　*　　　*　　　*

Maybe it was the light behind her—or the view, which he'd never really noticed before: all that green rolling away into blue—but Marvin was stunned by the sight of Esther. All he could do, after stepping out of his car, was to look at her, standing there in front of him. He hadn't guessed it would be like this; after all, he'd known the woman for a while now, seen her in all kinds of moods and situations. Over time he'd watched her turn beautiful, but still he wasn't prepared, seeing her now.

Esther, with her bare feet planted in the dirt, her old jeans, her nipples standing up beneath a loose white T-shirt, her white-girl afro with its Christmas tree lights, standing there, heating the air, staring at him with those green jungle eyes. All there. Solid. The Star woman come into her Strength. Sure enough. Strength. If any woman could run her hand through a lion's mane or ride on its back, it was this woman.

"Come in, Marvin. I'll show you where I live." She turned and led the way.

Her room was so flooded with light, it felt as though they were still out-side—or still inside the Strength card with the hot gold of the lion.

"The boys sleep over here," she was saying, wandering around the room, not facing him. "The bathroom," she laughed, gesturing towards a screen. "The kitchen." A table with a hot plate. "All the conveniences."

She turned towards him again, her hands holding on to each other to keep from trembling; he knew, because his hands were trembling, too. She might be strong, but she was nervous. They both were. Then she closed her eyes and took a deep breath. As she breathed out again, all the jump-iness and agitation eased out, too. She opened her eyes again and walked past him across the room. He turned to watch her.

"This is my bed, Marvin." She sat down on it and looked up at him. "I paid the rent today with my own money. For the whole month of April, this bed is mine. Free and clear."

Marvin felt his bones turning into some other substance. The whole room was swaying, shimmering, as if he were seeing it under water.

"Esther."

"This is my bed, Marvin," she repeated. "We don't have to wait any more."

"Oh, baby."

What was happening to him? It was like one of those dreams where you need to run, and you can't move your legs. Or like what quicksand must be. Somebody, save him!

"We do got to wait."

What was he saying? Was he crazy? The look on Esther's face told him she thought so.

"Marvin, is this an April Fool's joke, or is this for real?"

If he took even one step towards her, the gravity field of that bed would decide everything.

"Maybe we need to talk," Esther suggested. "I don't know what Alan said to you last Friday, but I can tell you what he said to me. He thinks we're having an affair, you and me—or at least he thinks I want to. He considers it possible that you turned me down, because I'm not rich enough." She glanced around her room and laughed.

"I have to admit that if Alan decides to get nasty about custody—and I don't know that he will—he might try to use you against me, although I don't see, exactly, what he could prove. But unless we just...just give each other up completely, people are going to find out; he's going to find out. Everyone's going to say I left him for you." She hesitated a moment, head bent. "And maybe there's some truth in it." She looked up again. "I don't mean that you're responsible. I left Alan for myself, but part of who I am is wanting you. You want to know something funny? It was Gale who told me not to get hung up on the purity of my motives, to face the fact that my feelings for you were going to affect my decision."

"I thank the lady kindly," Marvin managed to say, still standing immobilized in a shaft of sunlight.

"The kids have been asking about you. They miss you. I don't know...." She turned her face away and looked out the window. "I'm trying to see it from where you are. Is it just too much? Too heavy? Hey, I don't want to second guess you. Tell me. Just tell me."

"Esther," he said. "Esther, can you come here? Can you just please come here to me?"

Esther looked at Marvin again. She didn't know what was going on, but she could see—just as plainly as she had seen on the stairs in the Rectory the day of her miscarriage—she could see that he loved her. He'd never said it, but his eyes said it for him. They opened all the way, letting her inside to all his tender, unguarded places. He was trusting her with this glimpse of himself. She would have to trust him—even if he was going to say no, that he'd changed his mind, that he was leaving. She was afraid—and yet, in this moment, it didn't matter. She saw what she saw, and she knew what she knew. It was enough.

Esther rose and walked towards him, stepping into the beam of light that made him look like a dark archangel come down to annunciate. She stood close to him, and all the moving particles that gave the illusion of solid, separate flesh began to dance, rocking and rolling in great waves of energy. She raised her eyes to his—he was only a little taller than she was. Then, at last, sight yielded to other senses: smell, touch, taste, the sigh and suck of shared breath.

"Esther," he murmured into her hair, as the light withdrew and the room grew dusky. "I want you. I want you so bad. You got to know that. I didn't stay away all week 'cause of anything the P.I.C. say."

Esther recognized the code for Alan, though she still didn't know what the initials stood for. Someday she'd ask Marvin, but not now. Who cared about anything to do with Alan now?

"He ain't say much to me anyway. So I figure, I just play it cool, keep a low profile for a while. If I'd known he was gonna accuse you, I would have stayed around."

"It was really much better that you didn't. Leaving the marriage was something I had to do myself. On my own."

"That's why I done wait as long I could stand it before I come to find you. And I ain't made no big scene down at the Church. Just done my job every day, same as always. But I don't care about it. I'm ready to quit. Just say the word."

"To tell you the truth, Marvin, I don't want to make decisions for you, any more than I want you to make them for me."

"All right. I hear you."

"There's just one more thing I need to say. If we're going to be together in whatever way, for however long, the boys are going to be involved. You're going to have to deal with them, too."

"That's fine by me."

He kissed her; she kissed him. One kiss melted into another. Oh, she was hungry; so was he. The heat was rising; they were cooking. It must be about time to eat. They held each other, swaying, falling. The bed was calling. Clothes must give way to skin; out must give way to in.

"Esther, no! Wait! I got to tell you something!"

"Marvin!" Her breath was jagged. They teetered together on a precipice over the bed. "What on earth are you talking about!"

"This gonna sound bugs." He was gasping, too. "A vision. I had me a vision."

"Let's sit down at least. My legs are getting tired."

They perched at the edge of the bed.

Marvin's cock was so hard, he felt like it might burst. He was definitely crazy to do this to himself and her—but he had promised himself, and something other than himself that he couldn't quite name, that he'd give it a try. Of course, he might fail. And right this minute, he sincerely hoped he would.

"You and me, Esther, we done build up a lot of energy, a lot of power between us. Power like that? Well, you can do things with it."

"Yes, like make love."

Tell it, sister, Marvin urged silently, but he felt bound to go on with his insane proposition.

"We gonna make love, believe me. We just got to hold out—let me see now—another twenty-nine days."

"Are you out of your mind?"

"Yes," he said without hesitation. "Go ahead, Esther. Talk me out of this foolishness. Please."

Esther didn't say anything for a minute, but he was sitting close enough to her that he could feel her shoulders shaking. Damn. She was crying; he'd made her cry. The hell with visions, he needed to make love to this woman. Then it burst out of her: laughter, belly laughter. She laughed and laughed. She held her sides and doubled over laughing. Then fell back on the bed laughing and kicking her feet in the air. Her laughter caught hold of him, and some of the tension in his cock found release in his own laughter.

"What's so funny!" he demanded.

"Everything." The tears were rolling down her cheeks now. "This whole scene. Everything."

"You worse than Gabrielle," he said, which for some reason brought a fresh burst of laughter from both of them.

"Marvin," she said, trying to get her breath, "I mean, just look at us. Who would believe it? An ex-pimp, ex-con—a womanizer, Alan called you—and a would-be adulteress, runaway minister's wife alone in a rented room trying to wait, like two virgins, for their wedding night. And you! After all this time I've been saying no to you, you saying no to me!"

"I'm glad you taking it like this. I think," he added.

Marvin suddenly felt dazed and exhausted. He lay back on the bed, too, recovering.

"All right now," said Esther after a moment. "What is the significance of the twenty-nine days? This better be good," she warned.

Esther watched Marvin in the half-light as he rolled over onto his side and raised himself on his elbow so that he could look at her.

"You ever hear of the Great Rite?"

"Oh," said Esther. "I get it. Twenty-nine days. That's May Eve." Fergus had explained to Esther about the eight Pagan feasts called the Wheel of the Year, most of which had been taken over by the Church in one form or another. "You mean the Marriage of the Goddess and the God?"

"That's the one," he nodded. "You and me could do that."

Esther gazed at him. He was dead serious.

"You mean be the priest and priestess? Act it out? Do you think we really could? Would we know how?"

"I believe we could figure it out. Main thing is to open up and let the powers come through. You ever seen Haitian dancers? That's what they do. You and me, we already so open to each other, well, we just open up all the way and let it happen."

"Was that your vision?"

"I seen you and me in that Ring of Trees. It was apple blossom time. I seen the blossoms first."

Spencer had just said something like that to Esther: I smelled the apple blossoms and so I knew it was time, time for me to go to the Ring of Trees to meet him.

"Then I seen you, with the new moon in your hair, like the High Priestess in the Tarot. You wasn't wearing nothing else."

Esther could hear the smile in his voice.

"And what were you wearing?"

"I only seen a little glimpse of myself in your eyes. It's more what I was feeling."

"Which was?" Esther prompted suggestively.

"You go ask Old Man Fergus to explain to you what a Maypole really mean."

"Fergus?"

"Yeah, he be part of this mess we in. Him and his visions. His mother, too. He ever tell you about his mother? What the two of them seen one Hallowe'en a long time ago when Fergus wasn't nothing but a kid?"

"He told me they had a vision of Blackwood as a sacred grove, and that it was in danger."

"He ain't tell you what got to happen there?"

"No."

"Man to man talk, I guess. His mother say somebody got to do it, the Great Rite, right there in that Ring of Trees. Or else Blackwood and all the power stored up in it be lost to the world."

"Oh!" The pieces began to come together in Esther's mind. "So Fergus and Spencer must have....You know, she just told me the other day that when she saw us together, you and me, we made Spring come in the middle of Winter. That's why she went to the Ring of Trees that night in January. And I remember you told me you saw them that same night, saw them as they must have been when they were young. Spencer was trying to go back and do it over. Something must have gone wrong between them all that time ago."

"The timing was off is the way I see it. Time wasn't ripe."

Ripeness is all.

"Look to me like we the ones, Esther. You and me. We been set up,"

Marvin laughed, "set up by the Goddess. We ain't got no choice, except whether or not we want to go with it, get with the program."

"So it is as if we're virgins," said Esther slowly. "Virgin sacrifices."

Sacrifice, to make sacred.

"Marvin," she marveled. "You care about Blackwood, too, don't you?"

"I seen some powerful things go down there. I don't mind doing my part to keep them trees standing, that is, if you willing to do it with me."

They lay quietly for a while, just looking at each other, the current between them strong and sure. It would take them where they needed to go. All the way, all the way to the great mother sea.

"So, Esther, what you think?"

She reached for him with both arms and drew him down on her.

"I'm willing, Marvin," she spoke into his ear. "I just have two questions. One, what if it rains?"

"It ain't gonna rain," Marvin murmured, kissing her. "Besides, if it do, we get wet is all. You sweet, but you ain't gonna melt."

"Question...number...two." She spoke between kisses. "How...are we going to get through...Mmm...this evening. Stop! Let alone twenty-nine...more days!"

They both started laughing and surfaced for air.

"Now I admit, that's a tough one." Marvin sat up, considering. "But I tell you what we gon' do. Next best thing to making love. We going dancing."

"Yes!" Esther clapped her hands. "But don't you have a poker game on Saturday?"

"Game don't get hot till round about midnight. I bring you home, Cinderella, give you a little goodnight kiss—"

"Speaking of Cinderella, I haven't been out dancing in about ten years. You may be Prince Charming, but what I need right now is a Fairy Godmother. I don't have anything to wear, and you, you look so gorgeous!"

He did; she took in the clothes. White pants, practically glowing in the dim light, a silky red shirt, open at the throat to reveal chest hair and a gold chain hung with a sun medallion.

"You got that leotard with you, the one you was wearing when I find you dancing that day in the Parish House?"

"Yes."

"Wear that, with anything that flow. Listen, I be lying down over there on one of the kids' beds. I got to hide my virgin eyes, or I might just lose control."

Marvin stretched out on what he guessed must be Jonathan's bed, because of Ellie, the pink elephant. He hugged the elephant to his chest. Damn the P.I.C. and his threats! When it came to mothers, Esther was the best. If that son of a bitch tried to pull anything with custody...well, Marvin might just be forced to show his hand—to the Bishop. He thought with satisfaction of the material evidence against the P.I.C. stored among the apples in the apple barn, where Alisha, even if she suspected the existence of the videotape, would never think to look for it.

Marvin rolled on his side and looked at the view. A fingernail moon was setting in the Western sky—that meant it would be new again in twenty-nine days, just like in his vision. The sky was turning that shade of purple that suited Esther so well. He could hear Esther across the room, opening and closing drawers, then unzipping her jeans and letting them fall to the floor.

Sweet Jesus, he loved that woman! He didn't need to look at her to see her nakedness. He could feel the silkiness of her secret places, taste the nectar. He closed his eyes, not just his sex, but his whole self swelling, throbbing. He hadn't known it could be like this, life, so good it hurt. It made him want to live forever, and, at the same time, if he died this second, that would be all right, too.

He heard a rustling and breathed her grassy scent. Rolling over onto his back, he opened his eyes. There she was bending over him like the sky in her purple leotards, with a flowing skirt, dark green or black, like the earth. Something silver gleamed against her hair. Crescent moon earrings. Oh, moon, lady moon.

Wordlessly, Marvin drank her in. Then he reached out his hand and cupped one breast. Her nipple rose to his touch. A star, like touching a star.

"We best be going now," he whispered, hardly able to speak.

*   *   *   *   *

Outside in the driveway, they leaned against each other, the warmth of their bodies delicious in contrast to the cool night air.

"I'm hungry," said Esther, after more kissing. "Let's go somewhere to eat first. I've got some money."

"I got a roll, too. What you want? Mexican? Chinese? Italian?"

"I don't care, as long as it's hot and spicy."

"All right! A woman after my own heart."

"Your heart is what I'm after, not to mention other parts of your anatomy."

"Hush now!" Marvin laughed. "Behave yourself! Whose car we gon' take?"

Their cars were parked side by side.

"Well," considered Esther, "if we're going to River City, my car is less apt to get broken into, but on the other hand"—she peered anxiously at the primordial chaos inside her car—"I can't guarantee that those dazzling trousers of yours would be the same color when you get out as when you got in."

"Tell you what," said Marvin after a moment's thought. "We'll take our chances and go in my car. And you can drive."

"Me?" gaped Esther. "Drive the Mustang!"

"Why not? I owe you one."

They looked at each other and smiled, remembering the wild ride to Gilead. And then the kissing started all over again to make up for the kissing they hadn't done that day.

"Come on, Lady," Marvin said at last, reaching into his pocket and encountering more than his keys. "Take me for a ride."

He pressed the keys into her hand and went around and got into the passenger's side.

"Fasten your seatbelt," Esther ordered, as she settled into the driver's seat and buckled her own belt.

"Marvin," she said, putting the key in the ignition. "Are you sure you want me to do this?"

"Would I be sitting here if I didn't?"

"What if I wreck the car? Will you still love me?"

"I do believe so," he considered. "That is, if I survive the crash."

"We both better survive. Twenty-nine days at least."

"Yeah," interjected Marvin. "Just think on them trees."

"Not to mention, I'll be absolutely furious if I die before we make love."

"Girl, we been making love forever."

"I know." She sought his eyes for more. "But at the risk of sounding crude, Marvin, I do want to go all the way."

"All the way," he repeated. "Come on then. Let's go."

Esther started the car, found the headlights, effortlessly put the car into reverse. Then, with consummate skill and grace, she shifted into first, eased into second around the curve in the drive, and drove the Mustang out the gates of Windy Hill into the heavenly night.

APRIL SHOWERS 38

FERGUS woke one night from the dark of dreamlessness to the dark of lying awake on a starless night. There was not much difference between the two states; he might as well be waking and dreaming in the womb. Darkness undid all daytime edges and made everything round and close. Outside, a warm wet wind circled and rocked the apple barn. Sightless and second sightless as he was in the dark, he could almost taste that rain, that warm Spring rain, sweet, salty, drawn from the melting earth and received back into the earth. April was a prankster, blowing hot and cold, but this wind—Fergus could feel it—was balmy. It sang to the Earth:

> Open to me, my sister, my love, my dove, my undefiled, for my
> head is filled with dew, my locks with the drops of the night.

Everything was opening. The rain softened the earth to receive the seed. Yes, he could taste it, salty, sweet. The rain had found its way inside—not some little leak, but the full tender force of the rain streaming down his face. He opened his lips and drank.

Spencer, straining for breath, shifted from dream to delirium without noticing the difference. Something was blocking the air, so that only tiny trickles seeped into her lungs. Someone had dammed the river. Why were they doing that? Didn't they know that stopping the river's flow would cause a flood? Everything would drown, all the little animals in their dens, the foxes and the rabbits, the fieldmice. Her boat was drifting, eddying, rising with the water level—

Fergus! Fergus!

Fergus sat up. She was calling to him. Even in darkness, in blindness, Fergus knew. He threw back the covers of his bed.

Spencer struggled with the sheets. Who had tied her down? Who was trying to hold her under? Drown her in her own river? She won free to a sitting position, gasping with effort, drenched in sweat. There, that was better. She could think now, think what she needed to do. Quieting herself, she listened to the wind, the strong wet wind.

*Awake thou North wind and come thou South, blow upon my
garden that the spices thereof may flow out.*

Fergus, cloak and boots pulled on over long underwear, made his way
down the stairs, through the sweet smell of apples, and out into the night.

When Spencer closed her eyes, she could see the swirling pattern of
clouds, feel the rain on her face, so cool, so fresh, while she was so hot,
trapped in this place. What was this place? Who had put her here? It was
so hard, so very hard to breathe. If only she could find her way to the
wind, surely the wind would fill her lungs, fill her sails. Why, she would
fly! The wind would lift her boat right over that foolish dam. She just had
to find a way to get to the wind, to let it in.

Fergus! Where are you? Fergus!

In the rainy dark, Fergus crossed the orchard. It was coming back to
him, not sight exactly, but sense. He could feel the tight-fisted buds on the trees
quivering with the impact of the raindrops. The ground responded to the fall
of his feet as the beloved to the touch of her lover. He had no fear of stumbling.
The way opened for him, guided him.

Fergus was coming, with the rain, with the wind. She had to let him in.
Yes, that's what she must do. Open the window. Silly Sabine with her fear of
drafts! No wonder Spencer couldn't breathe; there was no air in here. It was
all dammed up. They tried to trick you with the glass panes, making
them invisible. But she was no fool. She knew. She would just get up,
while no one was looking, and open the window.

Now the floor was usually down, but it was so dark, and the darkness
was so round, how could she find the ground? There. What was that
under her feet? The ceiling? Never mind. It seemed solid, it would do. It
must be a big storm, the deck was rolling so. She must find her sea legs.
Never stand up in a canoe, her father had told her. Well, just this once,
she would disobey. She had to open that window or they'd all drown—
the moles, the woodchucks, the porcupines. Her father wouldn't want that.

Fergus! Fergus!

Past the pond Fergus strode, its thousands on thousands of unseen ripples expanding out and out. Then he went deeper into Blackwood, among
the trees that swayed and moaned and drank the rain. Fergus could feel
the heads of birds tucked under wings, and the warm bodies of small
furry creatures, secure among the roots. The ground sloped down and
down. The forces of earth took his hands and tugged him along. Hurry!
Hurry! She's waiting for you.

There, that was the chair where Sabine allowed her to sit for an hour in
the morning while the birds came to the feeders. The window would be

in front of it. Yes. Spencer gripped the sill to steady herself and summoned her last strength for the effort of lifting. Ah, the window eased open without resistance. Darling Esther had left it unlatched. She was such a good child. Spencer lifted and lifted, opening the window as wide as it would go. All the way.

Fergus! Come in!

Fergus climbed the steps to the carriage road. Wait! I'm coming. Wait!

Spent, she collapsed into the chair, which rocked with the sudden impact of her slight weight. The wild, wet wind poured in through the window, flooded the room. She could feel the drops of rain on her face; she could feel the wind lift her hair so it streamed out behind her. But still she could scarcely breathe. Why couldn't she breathe?

I know, it came to her, I must take off my skin.

In the creeping gray of almost dawn, Fergus lifted the loose plank on the porch of the gatehouse. Still there, since his mother's time. The same key.

My Beloved put his hand in the hole of the door and my bowels were moved for him.

Spencer couldn't manage the buttons on her nightdress. So fussy. Frustrated, she yanked, and heard the spray of buttons as they scattered on the floor. The rain beat in on her bare breasts.

Fergus mounted the twisted stair and opened the door to her bower. He saw her for an instant. O my Beloved. Her beautiful breasts, her mermaid hair, her eyes, a flash of blue among the clouds. And then everything dissolved in the warm rain.

Fergus. My life, my breath.

He did not need the sight of his eyes to go to her, gather her. There was no weight to her; she was lightness, light. She was burning up, the flame turning her to air, to ash, to rain.

My Beloved is mine, and I am his: he feedeth among the lilies.

Hold me. Be my breath.

He was here. She was surrounded by him. He was her boat. He cradled her, and the waters rocked them. The river flowed again, slowly, so slowly. Why had she been so worried about the dam? There was no dam. Only the river opening, opening, opening into the sea.

Fergus took her last breath into his own body. When he released it, he was alone.

BOOK NINE

HOLY WEEK

THY WILL BE DONE 39

I am the resurrection and the life, saith the Lord;
he that believeth in me, though he were dead, yet shall he live;
and whosoever liveth and believeth in me shall never die.

AFTER all, thought Esther, standing pressed against Sabine in the crowded church, it was the cadences that mattered, the solemn rolling sound of the words, as if a river spoke, or stone, bedrock.

I know that my Redeemer liveth,
and that he shall stand at the latter day upon the earth;
and though this body be destroyed, yet shall I see God;
whom I shall see for myself and mine eyes shall behold,
and not as a stranger.

Spencer felt that way, too, Esther guessed, for she had left specific instructions that Rite One, lengthier and rich with ornate, archaic language, be used.

For none of us liveth to himself,
and no man dieth to himself.

Spencer had died in Fergus' arms. Sabine had found him in the morning, cradling her body. The image drew fresh tears from a well of tears that seemed to have its depths in the center of Esther's being.

For if we live, we live unto the Lord;
and if we die, we die unto the Lord.
Whether we live, therefore, or die, we are the Lord's.

Blessed are the dead who die in the Lord;
even so saith the Spirit, for they rest from their labors.

But it was hard to imagine Spencer resting. Even though Esther had only known Spencer as an old lady, bedridden most of the time, Spencer had always struck Esther as restless: gossiping, playing poker, entertaining children, and when even those activities became too much for her, she'd let her mind fly with the geese. For Spencer "the blessed rest of everlasting

peace in the glorious company of the Saints in light" sounded like enforced naptime for a wakeful child.

"The Lord be with you," said Alan.

"And with thy spirit," Esther responded with the rest.

"Let us pray."

As Alan read the Collect, Esther stood on tiptoe and took a look around
the church. It was Monday of Holy Week. Word of Spencer's death in the
small hours of Thursday morning had spread swiftly, and for her funeral
the congregation of St. Paul's had swelled to Christmas-Easter proportions
and beyond. Everyone, of whatever denomination, from the whole of
White Hart was here. Raina Washington was up from the City, sitting between Maria and Marvin a few pews ahead. As the church had filled during the prelude, Esther and Marvin had exchanged one lingering look.
Esther knew she could not sit with Marvin; between grief and longing she
would be undone.

Besides, Sabine needed some support. Esther could feel the tension in
Sabine's shoulder. In addition to her own sorrow, Sabine had had to cope
with Geoffrey and Jessica Landsend, who had arrived in White Hart
promptly, taking over a wing of the White Hart Inn with the dozen or so
lawyers, investors, realtors, architects, and planners they had brought with
them. Esther could see their crew on the other side of the church, taking
up the first three pews.

Under all those noses poking around Blackwood, Sabine, in accordance
with Madame's instructions, had tended to the cremation and taken sole
charge of the ashes. Madame, Sabine had confided, had feared that if either the rector of St. Paul's or her nephew-by-marriage got hold of her remains, they would be interred in her late husband's family vault
somewhere in Westchester. There was, apparently, a drawer there with her
name on it. "A fate worse than death!" Madame had declared, or, as she
alternately described it: insult added to injury.

As the congregation sat for the Old Testament Lesson, Esther saw Elsa
Endsley totter up the aisle, too elderly and plump for her spindly high
heels, yet elegant, rather like a bird whose grace is lost in walking. Turning to face the congregation, Elsa read:

> The spirit of the Lord is upon me, because the Lord hath
> anointed me to preach good tidings unto the meek; he hath sent
> me to bind up the brokenhearted, to proclaim liberty to the cap-
> tives, and the opening of the prison to them that are bound:
>
> To proclaim the acceptable year of the Lord, and the day of
> vengeance of our God; to comfort all that mourn:
>
> To appoint unto them that mourn in Zion, to give unto them

the beauty for ashes, the oil of joy for mourning, garment of praise for the spirit of heaviness; that they might be called the trees of righteousness....

The trees of righteousness! Had Spencer chosen this reading or was it just a fluke? The trees of righteousness. Esther closed her eyes and saw the Ring of Trees as she had seen them yesterday at daybreak of Palm Sunday. Sabine had chosen that hour for the burial, because all the bothersome "guests" were sure to be asleep two miles away at the White Hart Inn—unlike the birds, who were awake and singing as Fergus, Sabine, and Esther entered the circle.

Like as the hart desireth the water-brooks, so longeth my soul after thee, O God.

Esther opened her eyes and read the responsive verse of Psalm 42 with the rest of the congregation, still seeing Blackwood and imagining the white hart of White Hart—and the children, Fergus and Spencer, sneaking out on summer nights, to catch a glimpse of moving moonlight among the shadows of the trees.

Why art thou so full of heaviness, O my soul? and why art thou so disquieted within me?

Why? Because Blackwood was in mortal danger, and the magic she and Marvin had pledged themselves to make seemed frail compared to the forces massing against them. Geoffrey Landsend's supreme confidence in himself as sole and rightful heir was awful to behold.

There he was now, going forward to read the New Testament Lesson.

But now Christ is risen from the dead, and become the first fruits of them that slept.

She knew what was coming: Paul was going to explain the technicalities of resurrection, bodily and spiritual, and in Geoffrey Landsend's carefully modulated chief-mourner-and-beneficiary-voice. Could she bear it?

She closed her eyes again to shut out the sight at least and took herself back to the circle with Fergus and Sabine. They had performed their own ritual yesterday, calling the directions and the elements, calling the Goddess, Mary Spencer Blackwood Crowe. They had planted her there at the circle's core, carefully replacing the moss and the grass. And she became the earth beneath their feet, and the dew clinging to the fine threads of spider's webs, and the wind in the branches, but where was the spark, where? She didn't know anymore; she just didn't know.

"Thou fool," said Saint Paul in the mouth of Geoffrey Landsend.

...that which thou sowest is not quickened, except it die.
And that which thou sowest, thou sowest not that body may
be, but bare grain, it may chance of wheat or some other grain:
But God giveth it a body as it hath pleased him and to every
seed his own body.

And what sort of seed was Spencer? What fruit would she bear? What body? All at once, in all its vividness and intensity, Esther's vision of the tender blue fruit returned and with it the knowledge—no, not mere knowledge but a knowing experienced in the wholeness of her being—that everything was connected: cycling, circling, dying, rising. Spencer, Spencer. Tree of life, trees of righteousness. Whatever else Spencer might be, she was Blackwood, its very soil. And what else was the ground of life but thousands and millions of deaths: animals, birds, trees, peoples?

For this corruptible must put on incorruption, and this mortal
must put on immortality.
So that when this corruptible shall have put on incorruption,
and this mortal shall have put on immortality, then shall be
brought to pass the saying that is written, Death is swallowed
up in victory.

But we do die, Esther spoke silently to Paul, and the earth swallows us. We feed, and we are food. But we've told ourselves it isn't real, what we see with our own eyes. Surely the Heavenly Father will come to snatch us away from our rotten, rotting Mother, take us to Heaven, our true home in the sky, where one day he will give our bodies back, raised incorruptible, better bodies, with no sex, no aging, no excrement, no death. Bodies fit for resting with the Saints in Light.

The Lord is my shepherd; I shall not want.

The congregation recited the twenty-third psalm, more or less in unison, given the outbreak of emotion that words so rooted in childhood evoked.

...for thou art with me; thy rod and staff, they comfort me.

Esther thought of Fergus, leaning heavily on his carved staff as they walked back to the apple barn for breakfast yesterday morning. Who would protect him now from the likes of Geoffrey Landsend and Arthur Billings? Well, she would. She would.

Thou preparest a table for me in the presence of mine enemies...

In fact, it was Spencer's enemies who were preparing the table—or anyway hiring the caterers for the funeral reception.

"The Holy Gospel of our Lord Jesus Christ, according to John," announced Alan. The congregation rose.

> *Let not your heart be troubled: ye believe in God, believe also in me.*
> *In my father's house are many mansions; if it were not so I would not have told you.*

In Blackwood there was one mansion. Geoffrey and Jessica Landsend had hired an industrial cleaning company to attack it over the weekend. At this moment, the caterers were setting up tables and chairs, laying out platters of hors d'oeuvres and luncheon dainties, arranging trays full of goblets with wine and sherry, setting up an open bar. Following the funeral, the front gates would open and a slow parade of cars would drive cautiously to Blackwood's mansion over the narrow, pot-holed carriage road, which the Landsends had not had time to re-surface—yet.

> *Thomas saith unto him, Lord we know not whither thou goest; and how can we know the way?*

Beginning at the pond, attendants would be stationed to direct parking and escort guests to the door.

> *Jesus saith unto him, I am the way, the truth, and the life: no man cometh unto the Father but by me.*

Oh, bother your father, said an irritable and irreverent voice, which Esther recognized, with some alarm, as her own.

Then, unmistakably, she heard Spencer laugh.

* * * * *

After the funeral, the throng of people began to swirl and eddy toward the door amidst a torrent of Bach. Esther felt someone pressing up against her, as if it was rush hour on the subway. She didn't need to look to know it was Marvin.

"You going on to the party?" His mouth was close to her ear.

"Yes, but I don't know if party is the word for it."

"Well, let's you and me try to make it one. Forget about the turkey vultures." She had told him Gale's epithet for the Landsends. "You know Old Lady Crowe love to party. You want to ride with us?"

"Sabine and I are going to walk. Maybe stop by the Ring of Trees."

"All right. Give the Lady my regards. I see you there."

Marvin receded, and Sabine and Esther pressed on, squeezing past the bottleneck at the door where people waited to shake hands with Alan and offer condolences—or congratulations in the guise of condolences—to the Landsends. Sabine and Esther walked as swiftly as they could, in high heeled shoes neither was accustomed to, down the driveway and through the break in the wall and into Blackwood.

"Do you think anyone saw that we do not go through the—what is your expression?—the line of reception?" Sabine inquired.

"The receiving line? Personally, Sabine, I'm past caring whether anyone noticed or not. There's too much else to worry about."

"Ah, *oui.*"

They walked past the cars already inching their way up the carriage road. The Mustang was not in sight. Esther guessed that Marvin would have driven to Catskill road and entered Blackwood the back way. Esther and Sabine, wordlessly in accord, turned off the carriage road onto the steps that led to the bridge and deeper into the trees. They continued in silence, climbing the steep slope on the other side of the stream. Then Sabine stopped to rest.

Unfortunately, Esther noted, fortune seemed to be smiling on the Landsends' schemes. It was the loveliest of April days, mild, sunny, the maples, birches, and beeches soft and fleecy as they flowered, sky the color of Spencer's eyes. Blackwood showed to its best advantage. The "guests" would be able to take their drinks and plates of hors d'oeuvres and wander out onto the artfully overgrown terraced gardens to admire the prospects.

"Your husband," said Sabine.

"Soon-to-be-ex," murmured Esther.

"He was very upset not to have the ash."

"Oh? What did he say?"

"Highly irregular, he call it. Arrangements for Christian burial are supposed to be made with the priest. *Bien sûr,* I know that. But Madame always would have her own way. And your husband—"

"Please don't call him that."

"He practically accuse me of stealing the ash."

"Oh, Sabine! How dreadful for you! What did you do then?"

"I show him Madame's writing, her instructions: Sabine Weaver alone is to dispose of my remains. Well, he is not happy. But what can he do?"

"Nothing. There's nothing he can do about it. And you know Sabine, the real reason he was upset was that he didn't get to do the committal or the burial. What you really stole were half his lines. But it's a shame you had to deal with Alan as well as the Landsends. I wish I could have helped, but I probably would have made matters worse."

Sabine gave one of her eloquent French shrugs. "*Eh bien,*" she sighed.

"Shall we stop and speak to Madame? Tell her all the trouble she is causing? She will be very pleased with herself."

They turned toward the Ring of Trees.

"Do you know, Sabine, at one point during the service, I could swear I heard her laughing."

"Madame will have the last laugh," Sabine predicted. "Of that be sure."

"I wish I could be," said Esther. "The Landsends give me the creeps. You can see the dollar signs and blueprints in their eyes. Don't they frighten you, Sabine? What will you do if they take over?"

"I expect Madame has made some provision. But if I must, I can stay with one of my children for a time, until I can find a small place. Maybe I take a room at Windy Hill, *hein*?"

"Oh, Sabine, that would be fun. We've got an extra bed in our room, you know."

They fell silent as they entered the circle, wordlessly greeting the trees. For a time they just stood, watching the play of light and shadow. Remembering.

"*Alors*, Madame, I hope you are amused."

A sudden gust stirred the trees.

"You always were such a child, with your games and your secrets. You have Esther here all worried about your wicked nephew. Yes, I know, nephew-by-marriage. But I tell La Petite all will be well. We must trust to the Lady's will."

The Lady's will, Esther smiled at the expression. Our Mother in the Earth, thy—kingdom?—come, thy will be done in Blackwood, if nowhere else, at least in Blackwood.

The two women turned and left the circle, heading for the pond.

"Sabine." A new fear rose in Esther. "You did warn Fergus about this reception?"

"I did." Sabine sounded concerned, too. "But you saw, after we bury Madame, how confused he is. Outside Blackwood, for years, he has been a little, well, uncertain. But now that she is gone, I think he is lost even here. He does not always know she is dead. *Eh bien*, perhaps for him, she is not."

"We'd better stop by the apple barn on the way, don't you think? Maybe one of us should stay with him."

"*D'accord*."

But when they reached the apple barn, Fergus was nowhere to be seen.

"He must have gone to see what is happening," said Sabine. "He is the caretaker. *Mon Dieu*, he may be trying to chase them off the property!"

"Let's hurry!"

Esther couldn't bear the thought of Fergus standing bewildered in the midst of that crowd, as he must have stood in the church the day that Arthur Billings and Karl Lyle had "ushered" him out. Well, if anyone dared lay a hand on him, she hoped he would lift his staff and raise the wrath of the whole wood. But no, she couldn't hope that. If he threatened anyone today, Geoffrey Landsend might have him ushered out permanently.

By the time she and Sabine arrived, Esther was so apprehensive that she paid little attention to the mansion, which under other circumstances might have interested her. She had an impression of high ceilings, hung with chandeliers. Though the crowd was not fully assembled, the uncarpeted rooms were loud with talk and the clink of glasses. As she strode from room to room, Sabine trailing her, she was vaguely aware of arousing some interest and perplexity. She supposed it was difficult for people to know what to do with an estranged rector's wife, how one ought to address her—or if.

She was beginning to panic about finding Fergus when she caught sight of him through some long French doors that opened onto a terrace. He was sitting with Marvin on a moss-grown wall at the edge of the first terrace. They were both puffing away on their pipes and downing something that resembled sherry in color but which Esther suspected of being stronger. Fergus was dressed in his usual tatters, and Marvin was wearing his white suit.

"There he is." Esther took hold of Sabine's arm as she caught up, and she pointed.

"Ah, *bon*! He is with Marvin."

At a more dignified pace, Esther and Sabine stepped out onto the terrace. An uneasiness at the edge of her vision caused Esther to look to her left where she saw none other than Alan, Geoffrey Landsend, and Arthur Billings. Mine enemies, thought Esther. She could not tell if they were admiring the view of the terraced gardens or if their focus was the rather striking pair in the foreground. Without acknowledging the triumvirate, Esther, with Sabine, walked straight towards Fergus and Marvin. Let Geoffrey Landsend understand: Fergus Hanrahan had friends—for whatever their protection was worth. Esther bent and greeted Fergus with a kiss. Whisky, that's what they were drinking.

Marvin she would kiss later.

"Let me see if I can locate some chairs for you ladies," said Marvin, standing up.

"Just get one for Sabine. If you can sit on the wall, I certainly can," Esther laughed, resisting the urge to brush off the seat of Marvin's pants.

"Hello, Fergus." She sat down next to the old man; Sabine stood on his other side.

"I can't see," he murmured. "I can't see."

"It's the light," Sabine soothed. "It's very strong today, and you're looking straight into the sun. There." Sabine moved to block the light with her body. "That is better. Now just look at Esther. She's right next to you."

Fergus turned to Esther, blinking; then he lifted his hand and touched her face.

"Astarte."

"Fergus, are you all right? Can you see me now?"

"I can see you." He let his hand drop. "I can see you."

Then, soundlessly, he began to weep. Esther reached for his hand and held onto it tightly.

"Who are all these people?" he asked. "I don't know them, but I felt them coming. Trampling her. Why are they doing that? I've got to stop them. She'll be bruised. She'll be broken."

"Fergus," Sabine spoke. "Remember. I told you people would come after Madame's funeral, come to eat and drink. It is the custom. You know she is dead. You buried her ashes yourself. No one can hurt her. She is safe now, safe in the Ring of Trees."

"I came to look for her," Fergus went on as if he had not heard Sabine. "I never went to any of her parties; I never belonged. But this time I had to come. I have to stop them. They're killing her. I have to—"

"Come, Fergus." Sabine spoke with that gentle authority she had used with Spencer. "I am taking you back to the apple barn. I make you something to eat. Then you will rest. You will sleep."

Sabine raised the old man to his feet and began to lead him.

"Astarte!" he resisted Sabine, reaching in Esther's direction. "You stay. Don't let them hurt her."

"I'll stay, Fergus." Esther struggled to keep her voice from breaking. "I'll protect her."

Alone, Esther gripped the wall with both hands, holding on for dear life as the world washed away. The defiance that had gotten her through the funeral, given her the strength to sass Jesus and St. Paul, shattered as cold waves hit her belly.

Spencer, Spencer.

"Esther? Baby, what's wrong?"

She couldn't see; she couldn't speak, but Marvin heard her. He sat down next to her, and encircled her with his arms. She leaned into his warmth. His mouth in her hair. The sun, the strong, Spring sun.

"Esther Peters."

Startled, Esther looked up through tears, rubbing her eyes, and found herself confronted with Raina Washington, who was dressed in a dark tailored suit that contrasted dramatically with her bright African jewelry. Raina had her back to the light, and her face in shadow looked severe. Esther fought the feeling of having been caught in the wrong, found out.

"Yes?"

"I believe we have met at St. Paul's, Mrs. Peters. I am Raina Washington, the Deceased's attorney. I would like to have a brief meeting with you inside, if that is convenient."

"Certainly." Esther got to her feet, shaken by Raina Washington's manner. She felt as though she were being called into the principal's office.

"What's going down, Raina?" asked Marvin, still sitting. Could he have failed to notice that Raina was intent on ignoring him out of existence?

Esther watched Raina's face; the change in expression was barely perceptible, but Esther could sense her fury. A hairline crack appeared in her control. She turned on him.

"Marvin Greene, I will thank you to mind your own business! This way, please," she directed Esther, and she turned at once, leaving Esther to fall into line behind her.

Raina led Esther through the congested rooms, snaking a path through clusters of guests, as she headed for the staircase. At the foot of the stairs, Raina unfastened a velvet rope barrier—the kind used in museums and banks—and stood aside, waiting for Esther to pass before refastening the end she held. As she stood, waiting uncertainly for Raina to resume the lead, it occurred to Esther that she probably would have stepped over the rope or squeezed around it. Yes. Like a child. In contrast, Raina's every gesture communicated authority, adult authority.

On the landing, halfway up the stairs, Esther wished she could look out the full length window to see if Marvin was still on the terrace, but she didn't dare slacken her pace. On the second floor, Raina turned right and proceeded down a hallway to a sunny room with windows facing West to the pond and the mountains and South, overlooking what may have been a kitchen garden. A door in the East wall connected this room to another. The room was empty except for a semicircle of metal chairs, no doubt arranged by Raina for her own purposes.

"Please sit down, Mrs. Peters. I'll return as soon as possible."

Esther sat in the chair closest to the South windows, relieved to be alone, if only for a few minutes. The sunlight reached in, touching her, just as Marvin did, without invading her. She relaxed and looked around the room. The warm light, the ivory trim, the pink wallpaper depicting climbing roses, all combined to give Esther the impression of a seashell and of herself safe within it. The roar and rush all around her, here dropped to a whisper, a lullaby.

She was sitting in Spencer's girlhood room. No question.

All too soon, Raina returned with Geoffrey and Jessica Landsend and a few of their retinue in her wake. Esther felt as though she could hardly breathe. The room got smaller, the wood, the world, as the Landsends and their like took up more and more space.

Raina motioned for everyone to sit, as if this were obedience school and she had charge of a class of dogs. Raina alone remained standing as she set her briefcase on an empty chair between Esther and Jessica Landsend, who was dressed in what Esther supposed must be designer chic. Her dress, if you could call it that, was black with a short tight skirt and sleeves that started at the hip and narrowed just below the elbow. She looked like nothing so much as a gigantic bat. On the other side of Jessica, Geoffrey was visibly squirming, as Raina opened her briefcase and took out some papers. At a signal from Geoffrey, one of the henchmen, armed with a briefcase, got to his feet.

"May I ask just what you think you're—"

"There will be time for questions when I'm through," Raina cut him off, making the sitting gesture again with that air of command no one seemed able to resist. The man sat, fumbling with the clasps of his briefcase. "I do not intend to keep you long. That would be a waste of your time and mine. As the deceased's attorney—"

"I beg your pardon, young woman!" The man was on his feet again; he had forgotten, however, that he'd opened his briefcase. Its contents spilled onto the floor, scattering to the directions. "My firm has been with the family...." His words came out in grunts as he bent to retrieve his papers. "...fifteen years. The late Mrs. Gerald Crowe...complete confidence in our...utmost satisfaction with...."

"Absolutely!" Geoffrey was on his feet now, too. "Now look here, Miss.... I don't know what this is all about. I think you'd better just—"

"Here is your copy of Mrs. Crowe's last will and testament, Mr. Landsend, Mrs. Landsend." Raina handed them around. "Mrs. Peters."

Esther looked at Raina questioningly, but Raina would not meet her eyes.

"Now wait just a minute.... See here...." Geoffrey and his lawyer were still fulminating.

Jessica, in contrast, remained seated. Instead of blustering, she seemed bent on sizing up Raina Washington. Her scrutiny struck Esther as careful and hostile.

"Sit down, Geoffrey, Bates." Jessica ordered. They did, rather heavily.

"Now," resumed Raina. "I have been unable to locate Mr. Fergus Hanrahan and Mrs. Sabine Weaver. Do any of you know how I might reach them?"

"I can tell them how to reach you," Esther offered, her hope beginning to rise. Of course Spencer would make sure they were all right, whatever happened. How could she have doubted that?

"Thank you. I'll give you my card." Raina closed her briefcase, set it on the floor and, holding her own copy of the will, sat down to address them. "Today I am merely going to summarize the contents of this will. It is an extremely complex document, and you may wish to study it further. I consider it part of my obligation to my client to meet with any of you at a time mutually convenient, if you find you need further explanation or help in carrying out instructions. I am the deceased's executrix—"

"Now wait just a minute," interrupted Geoffrey. "This is the first I've heard of any will. My Aunt's attorney and I have been in constant touch with her and—"

"Mr. Landsend, if you have objections to this Will you are, of course, at liberty to take whatever measures you feel are appropriate, but I believe that as you examine this document, you will find that everything is in good order. Now if I may proceed:

"Mrs. Crowe leaves to you, Mr. Landsend, her nephew-by-marriage, first and foremost her deep appreciation for your care of her Estate. Thanks to your careful financial planning, there is sufficient income to support her real property for generations to come. As a token of her esteem, she is leaving to you and to your wife, Jessica Landsend, the sum of five thousand dollars apiece, earmarked for your favorite charity. She felt you deserved a tax write-off."

"But this is preposterous—" Esther watched the spittle from Geoffrey's pronunciation of preposterous glint in the shaft of sunlight. "Preposterous!" Geoffrey sprayed again, getting to his feet.

His lawyer, on the other hand, seemed, all at once, to have received the Gift of Tongues. That was the only sense Esther could make of the strangled sound issuing from his mouth.

"If I may continue," Raina raised her voice.

Jessica yanked Geoffrey down. "We have to know what she's done," Esther heard Jessica hiss. "Then we'll deal with it."

"The rest of the Estate," Raina resumed, "all properties, all financial assets, has been left to the Blackwood Foundation in trust. Esther Peters has been named Trustee. She is to manage the Foundation, for which she will receive a salary, to increase with the cost of living, for her lifetime. She has the power to appoint her own successor.

"There are, however, certain stipulations. Existing structures may be used for any purpose Mrs. Peters chooses. They may be freely renovated. No new structures are to be added to the property, no trees cut, except for the health of the whole property. Gardens may be restored.

"In addition, Sabine Weaver and Fergus Hanrahan are to be allowed to remain in their current domiciles and to draw an income from the estate for the remainder of their lives, in addition to specific bequests, which they will receive outright. There are also some instructions regarding the settling of some gambling debts, the specifics of which need not concern us here."

"Gambling debts? Aunt?"

"Non compos mentis!" bellowed the lawyer, Bates.

"My Aunt was not in her right mind," Geoffrey appealed to Raina, translating, as if Raina did not understand Latin. "I can prove it. I—"

"Prove it to a judge." Raina waved him away. "I have one further remark to make on behalf of my late client. She wished me to make clear that her desire was to leave her Estate to Esther Peters outright. But she was determined that Esther Peters alone should have control. Since Mrs. Peters is a married woman, my client created Blackwood Foundation instead."

Esther sat deep, deep within the glowing seashell. In the distance, surf roared. Blackwood was safe. She, Esther Peters—Astarte—held it in trust. Blackwood was safe.

It was the Lady's will.

After a time, Esther became aware that everyone, even Raina, was looking at her, waiting for some response. Slowly, Esther rose to her feet, tucking the will into her shoulder bag.

"Ms. Washington," she began, "I need some time to absorb what's happened. I'll be in touch with you. I have no home phone. If you need to reach me, you can call me at work. The Sojourner Truth House in River City."

Esther noticed a flicker of interest in Raina's eyes, as she handed Esther her business card.

"Wait! Mrs. Peters!" Geoffrey stood up, blocking her way to the door.

Jessica remained seated, but she had transferred her focus from Raina to Esther. Her look was speculative.

"I don't believe we've met officially." Geoffrey extended his hand, but Esther did not take it. "You're the Rector's wife, aren't you?"

Still Esther did not respond.

"Look, I'm sure this thing is as much of a shock to you as it is to me. I know you understand that my Aunt was not well. There's been a misunderstanding, a mistake—"

"Mrs. Peters." The lawyer stood, too, shoulder to shoulder with Geoffrey. "Now I'm not accusing you of anything, but I want you to understand that there are steps, legal steps that can be taken in a case such as this one."

Esther glanced at Raina, but her face and mouth were closed. They were waiting—all of them: Raina, Black, impassive, female; the two white men, hot under their white collars; and Batwoman—waiting to see what they were up against—or whom. Esther was curious, too.

You are the Lady of Blackwood, Esther told herself. But no, that was not quite it. Really, she was more like the servant of Blackwood. Lady, servant. Was there a word that expressed both? Suddenly, Esther knew.

Priestess. She was Priestess of Blackwood. High Priestess. Deep Priestess. Now was the moment to assume her role.

"Mr. Landsend, Mrs. Landsend, Sir." She included them all in a nod. "I suggest that the first legal step you take be off this property."

Then Esther heard it again: Spencer's laughter, a Mother Goose cackle. Wicked old woman, Esther thought fondly. Sabine had been right. Spencer had set them all up. She was having the last word, the last laugh. Right this second.

"Good day to you." Esther said.

Then, placing a hand each on their arms, Esther parted Geoffrey and his lawyer, like the waters of the Red Sea, and passed between them, heading for the wilderness.

Blackwood was free.

PASSING THE CUP 40

MARVIN pulled up in front of the Church door, then got out and went around to help Maria up from the passenger's seat. She was having the Last Supper with Jesus, while Marvin waited around to drive her home afterwards. The whole thing would be over in about half an hour, Maria had told him. The Last Supper wasn't much of a spread. No offense to Jesus, but Marvin figured he'd give it a miss. It was too much like a scene from Death Row. Matter of fact, it was exactly like that for Jesus, only the courts weren't so backed up in those days. Arrested one day, executed the next, which was how some people wished the system still worked.

After he'd seen Maria to the door of the Church, Marvin parked the Mustang by the Parish House and got out. Reaching for his pipe, he sat down on the steps to have a smoke. Then he changed his mind. The evening air was so sweet, it seemed only right just to breathe for awhile. Pocketing his pipe, Marvin stood and stretched. Maybe he'd take a little stroll into Blackwood while he waited.

He stepped over the gap in the wall, through the trees and onto the carriage road. Uneven ground didn't throw him anymore. He'd found that if he didn't concern himself, the ground and his feet communicated just fine. He walked as far as the steps leading down to the bridge and decided to sit there, listening to the stream and the shrill of the peepers, breathing the scent of skunk cabbages. Some people didn't like the smell, but it was part of Spring, life bubbling up, from way down deep. He didn't have time to go visit the Old Man before church was over. And he didn't feel drawn just now to the Ring of Trees. It was enough to be where he was right now, a free man, on free ground.

Blackwood belonged to itself. He liked how Raina had worked that out for Old Lady Crowe. Esther wasn't weighted down with ownership, though she was still reeling with the sudden change in her life, spinning like a top, now leaning this way, now that way, now wobbling and about to collapse. Where she'd land when the spinning stopped was anyone's guess. They all had to stand back—Sabine, Fergus, Raina, even himself—and let her go through her changes.

Of course, he was going through some changes, too—ten thousand dollars worth of change. That's what Old Lady Crowe had decided she'd owed him in gambling debts. Contrary to popular opinion, he hadn't kept track, hadn't expected anything. In the religion of Poker, there were times when the winnings were beside the point. A player was a priest, a ritual master. You could play for millions or matchsticks; the stakes just gave material form to the mystery.

On the other hand, he felt no shame about accepting the money, deserved or not, though Maria had done her best to shame him. Since he refused to be ashamed, she resigned herself to being ashamed for him. She had gone so far as to pray to Jesus to let her die of shame, so that she didn't have to endure another minute of this sinful life. Jesus hadn't obliged, and Marvin had plans to further compromise Maria's soul by using his "wages of sin" to get her an apartment in a new complex near the center of White Hart that was being built specifically for senior citizens. He and Raina were in agreement about the move—though not about much else. The house by the stream, that had been just shy of sliding down the bank for a decade or two, had finally been condemned by the Board of Health. So the extra cash had come at just the right moment, which, in Marvin's understanding of the Universe, made perfect sense.

The cards, both decks, had taught him that everything was part of the great go round, the flow of energy that cycled and circled, taking different forms—money merely one of them. When you were attuned to the flow, then you knew your part in it: when to receive, and when to give away. It is more blessed to give than it is to receive. His grandmother, like everybody else's, had tried to teach him that. But it wasn't so; the only thing that mattered was not blocking the flow.

When you understood the great round, then you could change things, even after they happened, because every chance came around again, if you recognized it. Helping to ease Old Lady Crowe's dying, setting up Maria in comfort, was a way of giving back what he'd received from his grandmother. At the time of her need, his energy had been locked and blocked in prison. That's what a prison was: an attempt to stop the flow of energy, instead of redirecting it.

Of course, you didn't necessarily need the State to do it for you; concrete walls only made it visible. Poverty could do it, and politics. The rich had ways of doing it to themselves. Old Lady Crowe had sat on her pile most of her life, looking for a way to break down the dam and let that river run free. With her Will, she had done it. Her wealth was beginning to flow in trickles and streams. Some of it was coming his way. And why not? It had to move; it had to go the great round. You can't hold a river in your hand, and you can't push rain back into a cloud. He would be a channel for it; flowing through him, the energy would be free to change form.

The Last Supper must be about over, Marvin figured. He rose and made his way back to the church yard. He stopped the Mustang by the door, just as Maria emerged. In the floodlight, he could see tears streaking her face. She was grieving, grieving for her God, which was maybe a way of grieving for herself, too, Marvin considered. Because who hasn't been betrayed—or betrayed someone? Either way, it was a lonely place to be.

Marvin took Maria home, settled her with her feet up in front of the TV and made her what he called his Bedtime Special, hot milk mixed with what Marvin called a "secret ingredient" so that Maria never had to admit to herself that she was drinking demon rum.

"You going to see her," Maria said, as he headed for the door.

Marvin could hear both accusation and resignation in her voice, along with the pain of plain confusion. Maria had always liked Esther much better than she liked the P.I.C., but she also hated sin. Marvin didn't suppose it would help to tell Maria that he and Esther weren't screwing, that they were waiting, so to speak, for their wedding night.

"Yes, ma'am," was all he said.

Go and do what you have to do quickly, Jesus had said to Judas.

To Maria, what he was doing was a betrayal.

*　　*　　*　　*　　*

"Marvin." Esther's voice answered his knock; it was not a question. She knew. "Come in."

He opened the door to her room and found her washing supper dishes in the tiny sink, stacking them in a rack on the multi-purpose card table. He could hear the even breathing of the kids, the hushed quality it gave to the room. Setting a plate in the rack, she dried her hands on a dish-towel and came to him. They held each other for a while, and though she was silent, he could feel her tears soaking through his shirt. It was that sort of a night. Tears of his own took him by surprise. Well, it was all part of the flow. Let them fall.

"Marvin, I'm glad you came." She lifted her head from his shoulder and looked at him. "This might sound blasphemous, but could you watch with me one hour?"

"You got it," he said, not sure what she thought was blasphemous about the request. Must have something to do with Jesus and the Last Supper. "Let's go sit on the porch."

"Leave the upper room for the Garden of Gethsemane?" said Esther, apparently by way of agreement.

Esther was really into this Biblical shit.

They sat down on the porch steps, as they had many evenings during the past couple of weeks. Because of the open West windows above the porch, Esther could hear if either of the boys cried out.

"What's up?" Marvin asked. They sat close together but not entwined.

"I'm scared," she said.

"Tell me."

"I'm not sure how to explain it. It seems so ungrateful."

"You don't need no license for how you be feeling. What it is, is what it is."

They were both silent for a moment; he could feel her relax a little.

"I'm glad, more than glad, that Blackwood is safe—as safe as it can be, anyway—from the Landsends. I always wanted it to be, but despite Fergus and his visions, you and your visions for that matter, I never really believed Blackwood surviving or not surviving had anything to do with what I wanted. Now it has everything to do with me. It scares me, that much responsibility. My role scares me. It came to me right there in that room, Spencer's old room, where Raina told us about the will, that I'm being called to be Priestess of Blackwood. But I don't understand what it means. I don't feel equal to it."

"You feel like running?" Marvin asked without judgement.

"Almost. More like: If it be thy will let this cup pass from me, but not my will but thy will be done. Then I say to myself: What is your problem? No one is threatening to crucify you. You have a hell of a nerve comparing yourself to Jesus Christ."

"Hold up," Marvin interrupted. "I hear you talking yourself down. You ain't got to be nailed up to be like Jesus. What the man did was to give it up, go with his fate."

"Fate! What do you mean by fate?"

"Reason you here on this Earth."

"You mean, whether or not I think I'm up to it, I'm somehow fated to be Priestess of Blackwood?"

"Yeah. Something like that. And just 'cause it's good, something you want, don't make it easy. You still got to let go, lose control."

"But that's so confusing, Marvin, because at the same time, I have to take control. If I don't, plenty of people will be happy to do it for me—which I guess has been the story of my life until recently. Would you believe it? Alan is suddenly talking about trying again, going to see a marriage counselor with me. How transparent can you get? He wants to help me 'fulfill my potential,' which I think means running a Diocesan Retreat Center in Blackwood.

"I've had the School Board approach me about creating new athletic fields. The Town Board is sure that I want to make it into a recreational center with picnic tables and portable toilets, playgrounds and electric hook-ups for camping vehicles. Geoffrey Landsend calls me every day at work to try to 'help me to understand his position.' His lawyer calls to threaten me with charges of 'undue influence.' I mean maybe Christ on the Cross as an image isn't so far off base. Marvin, Goddamnit, it's not funny!"

"I know it ain't, but it is!"

"Thanks a lot. Okay. Now it's your turn. You tell me what you know I should do."

"Is that what you want?"

"Yes. No." She raised her arms and tugged at her hair; then she started laughing, too. "The thing is," she resumed after a time, "if it was just preservation, border patrol, I could manage that. But I have a feeling it's something more that's being asked of me, a new vision. But I'm not a visionary. You and Fergus, you're the seers. You have visions. By the way, has Fergus told you that he wants you to be his successor when he dies?"

"I got the feeling he ain't planning on hanging around for too long."

Neither spoke for a time, thinking on more changes to come.

"You haven't decided yet how you'd feel about that, inheriting Fergus' life."

Esther was picking up on his feeling of what...doubt? Why not admit it? Fear. Fear of his own fate closing in on him. It gave him a keener sense of what she was going through.

"No," he acknowledged. "Tell you the truth, I ain't seen too much further than May Eve. Or anyway looked."

"Me, either. Maybe that's enough for now. Enough for us."

Her voice was low, soft, and desire for her rose in him. It didn't seem possible at this moment to live until then—or beyond.

"Marvin, you know, what we're going to do there in the Ring of Trees, whatever happens to us afterwards, it's not just for us. Or even just for Blackwood. It's making the ground fertile, sowing the seeds, opening the way for a new birth, a new life that will grow in Blackwood. I sense it, but I can't see it. I'm just an ordinary woman. Don't take this wrong, Marvin, but even without a house or a husband, I still feel like a fucking housewife."

"Relax. Come May Eve, you be a fucking priestess."

"But Marvin, what if there's been a big cosmic mistake? What if Spencer, Fergus—hell, the Goddess herself—just made a mistake, and I simply don't have what it takes. That's what your cousin Raina thinks, I know."

"Yeah? Who say so?"

"I just know it. Around her, I feel not only ordinary but silly, a light-weight. She despises me."

"If she do, which I ain't saying, what's that got to do with anything?"

"Oh, nothing. She's just Spencer's executrix, not to mention Maria's daughter and your cousin."

"Listen up, Esther. You know what you doing right now? You hiding. Yes. You can't run, so you hiding behind this I'm-just-ordinary shit. So, who ain't? Even Jesus got himself born and died. You think he was always so sure of hisself? If he was, how come he be all the time asking: Who do you say I am? He ain't know. He have to take it on trust, same as the rest of us. Hell, the man was a carpenter. His mother wasn't married to his father, which mine wasn't either, come to that. We all got our problems.

"Far as Raina concern, if she hate you, she hate you on principle. You making a big mistake to take it personal. I know for a fact she don't despise you. She respect how you handled yourself, telling the turkey vultures to clear off the property."

"I still can't believe I did that. That I actually had the nerve, that it was me who did it."

"It was you, Esther, the real you. Trouble with you, girl, you don't see yourself. That's your blind spot. Telling me you ain't never had no visions. Who made that playdough figure I done find in the icehouse? That time in the Parish House, when you was dancing? Can't tell me you wasn't seeing things then. And if you wasn't, I was!"

"Oh, Marvin, I just remembered a vision I had! The first time I saw you, sitting behind me in the church? You had horns! I was so ashamed of myself; I thought I was seeing you as the Devil, and that seemed terribly racist. But now I understand it, and it's true!"

"What you mean true!" Marvin felt his skull, and they both laughed.

"The horned god, Marvin! I thought Fergus explained it all to you. Whose part do you think you're playing on May Eve?"

"You mean I got to wear horns!" Marvin protested. "Seem to me like I'm horny enough as it is."

They laughed some more, leaning against each other for support.

"You're right, Marvin," Esther said when they'd calmed down again. "I do see things. Since that day when the Goddess just appeared in my hand, I've seen a lot of things."

She didn't elaborate, but he could almost feel her thinking, remembering. She drew herself a little apart from him. Not blocking him out, not withdrawing, just being separate, allowing him to be. They sat that way for a while, listening to the night, looking into the darkness. Alone. Together.

"I guess I have been hiding." She spoke again. "Most of my life, mostly from myself. But you," she turned to him, "you keep blowing my cover! You keep showing me to myself."

"Why not? You something to see."

"I'm still scared."

"Ain't no shame in that. I'm scared, too. I'm just more used to it is all. You blew my cover a long time ago."

"When?"

"That day on the back steps, when you said you was in love with me. I couldn't hide from myself no more. I done have to admit I'm in love with you, too."

"You are?" she said. "Well, then...pass me that cup."

Marvin met Esther's lips with his own.

GOOD FRIDAY 41

WOULDN'T you know," said Theresa, sweeping into the office of Sojourner Truth House, a gust of wet wind, "whenever the kids have a day off from school, it rains."

"'And the veil of the Temple was rent in twain,' " quipped Esther; Theresa was a Roman Catholic and would get the reference. "It's about time for the thunder and lightning."

"Please!" Theresa hung up her coat. "You must have had some morning, kid. Sounds like a full house."

Theresa gestured towards the dining room where lunch was in progress.

"Esther, here." Sally, one of the residents, came in. "You've got to try some of my soup, homemade minestrone." She placed a bowl and a spoon in front to Esther. "Oh, hi, Theresa. I'll bring you some, too."

"No thanks, Sal. I'm fasting."

"Theresa, get real! Last week, Esther, when we were trying to watch the Pope on TV? The poor man couldn't get a word in edgewise with Mother Theresa here wisecracking and cursing. Honest to God!"

"Well, you know me," Theresa shrugged. "Always at the extremes. Love, hate. Feast, famine."

"Right." Sally turned to go.

"Great soup, Sally," said Esther. "Are my kids doing okay? Not giving you any trouble?"

"They're doing fine. I wish mine would eat like that. Really, take your time."

"So your kids are here, too."

Theresa was standing by the file cabinet, glancing at a list of the residents. Ninety days was the maximum stay, but the mix changed continually. It was not unusual to arrive at work and find that one or two families had left and two or three others had just arrived.

"Yes," said Esther. "That's one of the perks of the job for me, that I can bring my kids when I have to."

"Then you really had your hands full. I apologize for being late."

"It's all right. I'm only just writing shift change. And obviously I don't have to pick up my kids today. Did you go to twelve o'clock Mass?"

Esther, for the first time in her life, was not attending a Good Friday Service. The Service at St. Paul's would be over by the time she got back to White Hart, but she didn't want to go there in any event. Maybe she should stop in at a Catholic Church on the way home, and light a candle.

"Actually, it wasn't a Mass," Theresa was explaining, "it was the Stations of the Cross. And get this, Esther." Theresa turned towards her. "There's fourteen Stations of the Cross, so the thirteenth, right?—the only chance a woman gets to speak, so it would have to be thirteen—"

"Thirteen is a lucky number, Theresa. It's the basis of the lunar calendar."

"Well, trust you to know that. So it makes sense. Anyway," Theresa resumed, "I had forgotten it or never noticed it before, but the Blessed Virgin Mary gets a chance to say something in her life besides: Be it unto me according to thy will. It really blew me away. It goes something like this:

"Don't call me Naomi, which means pleasant. But call me Miriam, which means bitterness. I will weep, and I will not be comforted, for the Lord God hath dealt bitterly with me."

She would light a candle to Mary, Esther decided.

"I mean, wow!" Theresa went on. "Mary, meek and mild and obedient, the model of womanhood, rammed down our throats all those years. Telling it like it is. It made my day." Theresa turned back to the list. "Oh! I was afraid this would happen. Ann Harris. *The* Ann."

"Yes," confirmed Esther. "She got here last night."

"Well, I didn't think it would work out, going back. That guy's a psycho of the first order. You know, the kind that can convince everybody he's the very standard of normality? I saw him do his thing in court."

The first week of Esther's job at Sojourner Truth had been the last week of Ann's previous stay. All the women who passed through the Shelter Esther found memorable in some way. Each had an effect on the communal life of the House. Weeks could go by when, despite everyone's best efforts, the residents remained a collection of disparate and understandably depressed individuals living in enforced community. Then someone like Ann came along with some sort of vital spark and people caught fire. The TV would get turned off, and women would talk. Cooperative childcare arrangements abounded, cooking projects took off, support groups fulfilled their purpose, and individuals began to take pride in a collective identity and purpose. A woman like Ann acted like yeast in a bread; the whole body would rise. No staff member, however gifted, could do for the

House what one such resident could do, igniting a powerful chain reaction: She can make it; I can make it; we can make it.

Ann's efforts to make it had been disciplined and systematic. Since finding housing was a major problem for a woman with four children, she had tried first to get the Family Court judge to order her husband to vacate their apartment. Her husband had refused to consider divorce or legal separation. The judge's unspoken attitude was: I don't see the black eye or the arm in a sling; but I see a woman with four kids, looking for public assistance; let's save the taxpayers some money.

"I like to keep the family together," he pronounced. "Reconcile with the man." Ann had quoted the judge's favorite refrain.

Finally, with strenuous advocacy from the shelter, Ann had hacked her way through jungles of red tape in order to qualify for Section Eight subsidized housing. She had found a possible apartment, when Social Services announced that Section Eight funding had been exhausted for that calendar year. Ann's husband, meanwhile, kept entreating her to come back, swearing that this time things would be different, that he had changed. At the end of ninety days, with no place to go, almost no possibility of finding work, because she could not afford to pay for childcare, Ann had opted to believe him.

"How is she?" asked Theresa.

"Pretty down," said Esther. "I would say she hasn't had much sleep lately. I talked her into lying down for an hour. The kids did fine. They settled in right away, even though they didn't know any of the other kids who are here now. When she got up, she helped me with the Easter Egg dyeing. She even whipped up a new batch of playdough—those cans in the playroom are all moldy. She saw that some of the kids were having a hard time taking turns with the dyes. They were all overexcited. Nothing calms kids down like having their hands in their own lump of dough that nobody is threatening to take away."

"Ain't it the truth."

"When we finished the eggs, Ann and I talked some. I guess things were better for a few weeks, long enough so she could build up her hopes and have them dashed. Pretty soon it all started again. For the last couple of weeks, he's been locking her and the kids in the apartment; he ripped out the phones. When the truant officer came to investigate, he went into his Mr. Reasonable act, and she managed to get out the door with the kids. She was afraid to say anything to the officer directly, for fear her husband would make counter-accusations and the kids would end up in foster care.

"You know, Theresa, in some ways that's just as scary or scarier to me, how easily the courts can become abusive, too. We're not just dealing with individual nutcases. Maybe I'm getting paranoid, but it almost seems like the abuse is systematic."

"You're catching on fast, kid. Well, at least we've got another chance to get it right this time."

"Ann says she will never allow herself to be within four walls with him again. She actually said: 'Summer's coming. We'd be better off on the street.' "

"And did you know, Esther, that statistically speaking, she's right? I kid you not, a woman has more chance of being killed in her own home than of being violently assaulted on the Street. But when men in high places talk about 'getting tough on crime,' you and I both know they don't mean domestic violence."

"Well," Theresa sighed, hanging up her raincoat, and Esther understood that Theresa was also setting aside the enormity of the big picture in order to have the energy to respond to the particular needs of the day. "The Blessed Mother said a mouthful. So, is everything all set for our visit on Sunday to—what is your estate called again?"

"Blackwood. And I keep telling you, Theresa, it's not my estate. I'm the Trustee. Yes, it's all set. I've even made several copies of directions, complete with map. I'm taking some of those eggs we dyed for an Easter egg hunt."

"You're planning on good weather?" Theresa rolled her eyes towards the heavens. "You got connections up there?"

"Haven't I told you I'm a witch? Oh, ye of little faith. Anyway, if it rains, there's still the whole huge house."

"So, Esther, when are you giving notice? You're on salary for life, right? What are you hanging around this madhouse for?"

"My salary hasn't started yet. It's going to take a while for everything to be in place. If Geoffrey Landsend has his way, it'll be a long time. Besides, I don't want to quit my job here, not until I'm more sure of what I want to do...."

"Do? What you want to do! It's not enough for you, estate manager?"

"I don't know, Theresa. Maybe it's too much. Too amorphous. I can't see the shape of it yet. Well, I better go take my kids off Sally's hands." Esther stood up. "Have you got enough cars and drivers?"

"As of this moment," said Theresa, sitting down and glancing at Esther's notes, preparatory to filing them.

"Well, I'd say give me a call if you need me to make a trip, but I still don't have a phone."

"You know, Esther, for an heiress, your lifestyle leaves a lot to be desired. I know, I know," Theresa said, before Esther could protest. "You're not an heiress."

Esther put on her raincoat and gathered up the boys'.

"Hey, Esther, what's this?"

Theresa picked up an object from the desk, which had been obscured from sight before by the open manilla folder, and cradled it carefully in her palms.

"It's playdough, actually," Esther explained, looking at the figure that had taken shape in her hands while she and Ann had talked earlier.

Esther started to laugh. Theresa eyed her with concern.

"I'm missing something. Clearly. Or maybe you are," she suggested. "Like marbles?" Theresa turned her attention back to the playdough figure. "You made this?"

"Well, sort of."

"What is this 'sort of'? Either you did or you didn't. You've been holding out on me. You never told me you were an artist."

"I'm not," Esther began reflexively, then stopped to reflect. "Well, maybe I am, not intentionally or professionally, but the way we all are artists."

"Not all of us," argued Theresa.

"Yes, all. Look at children. Is there one who won't use crayons or play with dough or make up songs and poems? You know what I mean. Most of us stop doing it. But maybe that's the point. Of our being here."

"What? Playing with dough?"

"Something like that."

"So, tell me about her. It is a her, I believe."

Esther walked back to the desk and studied her handiwork in Theresa's hand, curious herself. The ample figure was reclining luxuriantly on her side, her head supported by one hand so that she could survey the abundant landscape of her body.

"Yes, it's a her, all right. It's Her—or do I mean She."

"She," Theresa repeated; Esther didn't know whether Theresa were making a grammatical decision or affirming Esther's identification.

Esther continued to contemplate the vision that had flowed through her fingers into this nourishing form. Yes, nourishing. She was literally edible. You could take her, add a few more ingredients, and turn her into bread. She was edible also in that every curve of her body expressed abundance.

As Esther gazed, her vision quickened. The heavy breasts became ripe clusters of grapes, her thighs loaves. Take, eat. This is my body. Atop the swell of her hips, curled into her belly, sheltered by her breasts, scampering over and about her legs and feet were smaller figures: women, mothers with babies, children; there was other forms, too: rabbits, deer, birds, honeybees. Her hair was a river alive with snakes and fish. Then, Esther saw quite clearly, circling her navel: a ring of trees.

"It's also," Esther said slowly. "She's also, well, that's Blackwood."

"Blackwood?"

"You know, the estate that's been entrusted to me."

My Kingdom is of this world.

"Sure," said Theresa after a moment. "I get it. The underlying meaning."

Except it wasn't hers, and it wasn't a kingdom; there was no king. Blackwood belonged to Blackwood.

"Fertility or something, right?"

Blackwood is of the world. Blackwood is of the earth. On earth.

"With a body like that, you could grow anything. Talk about a green thumb!"

On earth as it is in heaven. Here, where our roots are deep and our branches brush the stars.

Today shalt thou be with me in Paradise.

"I'd better be going, Theresa."

"You're going to leave me holding the Lady? What do you want to do with this? It's beautiful. Maybe that's not the right word. Powerful."

"I don't know. Roll it back into a ball. That's what's so nice about play-dough. It's not meant to produce immortal works of art. It's just flour and water and salt."

Like bread, like life.

"You do it, then. Not me. I'm no Protestant. I have a healthy respect for idols and graven images."

Esther laughed and took the figure. "Oh, could you hand me the soup bowl, too, Theresa? I better take it back to the kitchen."

"I'll take it in a few minutes. You've got enough on your hands."

"That's for sure," agreed Esther. "See you on Easter, Theresa."

"Until the Resurrection, Esther."

Holding the reclining Goddess, Esther crossed the hall into the dining room where the table was littered with lunch in various stages for some seven women and ten or so children. The surface looked like a traveling carnival had just pulled up stakes. Ann was still at the table feeding her baby daughter in the highchair. Becky sat with Sally's two-year-old in her lap. Mary, a woman in her seventies, who'd been beaten by her son, was beginning to clear the table while Darla, a seventeen-year-old, fleeing her step-father, romped with some half-dozen kids in the next room.

"David, Jonathan." Esther paused in the doorway to the living room. "Time to go."

Cries of protest. "We're having fun!"

Esther turned to the other mothers. All of them sighed, shook their heads, and exchanged looks of perfect understanding.

"I'm going to get the eggs," she shouted into the pandemonium. "Your raincoats are right here. You better have them on by the time I'm ready."

Esther turned to cross the dining room to the kitchen, then paused, looking at Ann's profile as she spooned soup into her daughter's mouth. Her face was gaunt, and though she was quite dark, Esther could see that the side of her jaw was darker with bruises. Her hair, cut very short, revealed the beautiful shape of head and neck. Even when she was sitting, you could tell that she was graceful. Esther had a fleeting image of Ann as matriarch arrayed in gold and flowing robes, surrounded by children, herds of cattle, heaps of grain, all tangible symbols of abundance and well-being.

"This is for you, Ann." Esther placed the figure on the table. "I made it from the new batch of playdough while you and I were talking. You don't have to keep it. You can put it back with the rest of the dough. I just wanted to give it to you."

"What is it?" Becky was asking as Ann picked up the figure.

Esther hurried into the kitchen. Exchanging a few words with Mary and Sally, she put two dozen dyed eggs back into cartons.

When she re-entered the dining room, Ann, still holding the figure, looked up and flashed her a smile.

"Esther, this sure is one powerful mama."

"It's you, Ann," said Esther, suddenly realizing that it was. "And you, Becky." She smiled at Becky, holding Sally's now sleeping son. "She's us, you know, all of us. Well, see you all on Easter."

"On Easter, Esther," said Ann.

Holding the Lady in one hand, Ann raised her in a liberation salute.

EASTER 42

ESTHER, I have to tell you something that I don't think I've ever told anyone else," said Gabrielle, giggling in anticipation, "or ever will."

It was Easter morning, cloudless, the sky a perfect Easter egg blue. Esther and Gabrielle, each carrying a basket of eggs, were on their way from Windy Hill to Blackwood, where they would hide the eggs. Then they would walk on to meet David and Jonathan at St. Pauls's for the Easter service. Before they'd left, Marvin had arrived in the Mustang to collect Gale and take her back to Maria's kitchen where the two of them would prepare a moveable feast for the Moveable Feast of Easter.

"Do tell," Esther encouraged.

"Well," began Gabrielle, "hiding these eggs is like the fulfillment of a life-long fantasy. You see," Gabrielle lowered her voice and linked arms with Esther, "I've always wanted to be able to lay eggs, and I'm not talking ovulation. That just doesn't do it for me. I mean the kind of eggs you could wake the barnyard over."

"I love it!" cried Esther, relishing the image of plump mother-hen Gabrielle clucking over a clutch of eggs.

"BRA-bra-bra-bra-BROCK-brock!" Gabrielle gave a perfect rendition.

They leaned against each other, laughing as they walked.

"You know, I used to do that?" Gabrielle, of necessity, had learned to talk and laugh at the same time. "Like, if some guy referred to me as a chick, I'd cackle at him? Or if somebody called me a bitch, I'd bark."

"Pussy?"

"Hiss-s-s-s." Gabrielle became a cat. "You know, I scratched a guy once and drew blood. That was in the days when I still had long red finger-nails. At least they were good for something. And think of what we have to look forward to, Esther. Old bat, sow, cow...."

Squeaking and oinking and mooing, they turned in at the back gate to Blackwood.

"You know that reminds me of one of my fantasies," said Esther. "I used to imagine that when I had a baby, I wouldn't just nurse, I'd milk myself and keep milking myself. I figured, if cows can keep on giving milk, why not me? My plan was to start a line of mother's milk products: bottle it, bake with it, make milk shakes, ice cream, open up a little roadside stand. An authentic Dairy Queen, you know?"

"Well, did you?" Gabrielle was intrigued. "I mean milk yourself when you had David and Jonathan?"

"No," said Esther. "I don't think I even remembered the fantasy then."

"Have another baby," said Gabrielle, casually, as if she were offering another bagel. "With Marvin, why don't you?"

"Oh, Gabrielle."

Esther felt for a moment as if she had the sun, a glowing Easter egg, in her womb, heat radiating from that center to her furthest extremity.

"Wow!" said Gabrielle. "I can feel you blushing! You're hot to the touch."

Esther laughed, but Gabrielle must have sensed her tension. Gabrielle knew Esther and Marvin were still waiting to be lovers, though she didn't know why.

"You know it's going to be all right, don't you?" Gabrielle added. "If you have a baby, or if you don't have a baby. It's going to be fine."

"Yes," said Esther. "I think I do know that. I'm also beginning to understand that there are a lot of things you can make when you make love. Passion is the Tree of Life; it bears all kinds of fruit."

"Ooo, I like that, Esther. That's how I feel about Gale and me. Like, we may not be having an actual baby together, but we're fertile. You know? We do things together, make things happen."

"Absolutely! Lay those eggs, Gabrielle."

They had arrived at the mansion.

"So," said Gabrielle, "what are we doing? Do we want all the eggs outside or some inside?"

"Outside, I think," said Esther. "There's nothing much to hide them behind, or in, or under, in the house. But we also don't want kids wandering off, getting lost, falling into the pond or the poison ivy. Let's stick to the terraces. I'll do one side of the steps; you do the other."

Esther and Gabrielle wended their way slowly down the terraces. Among daffodils and periwinkle, Easter lilies and tame roses gone wild, they laid their eggs.

*   *   *   *   *

Fergus leaned against the Crone Tree and gazed at the pond. Overhead, the apple blossoms swelled, just barely restraining themselves from bursting. It wasn't quite time yet, not quite the moment for her to bloom; to be the Bride again, the shining Maiden. It was her mystery: the old woman growing young, following the moon-spun thread back to the heart.

This time, she was taking him with her. All need for separateness, for striving, was coming to an end. She fed him on morning air. She showed him her face in the still water. Even as his flesh fell away, and bone burned through, she made him a bed in the grass, soft. The sun's light touched his face now. He closed his eyes and let the warmth lick him, like some great mother animal.

Ah, he could smell her now. It was as if the earth came closer to him, the fragrance of grass, soil. Her breath stirred him, just feathering the surface of the water. He swam up from the deep to her hand. His hand. She was pressing something into his hand, something smooth and curved. Her footsteps faded into the leaves; her laughter flew up into the branches. When his eyes drifted open again, he saw the curve of the sky resting in the palm of his hand.

*   *   *   *   *

Gale could have been a five star general, Marvin considered. Everything around her seemed to respond to her natural sense of command. If she needed a utensil, it found itself, came to attention, and jumped into her hand. She didn't just chop vegetables; she karate chopped. It was a martial art. She organized those hampers of food as if they were an army preparing to march.

Of course, he had his own ways with food, his own specialties: mixing, seasoning; timing, too, anything that rose or fell or that had to be whipped to a certain consistency. Gale respected his area of expertise and kept out of his territory. They did all right together.

"Marvin!" Gale had just emerged from the depths of Maria's refrigerator; they had about twenty more minutes before take-off time, and she looked like she was about to come unglued. "I just found two dozen hard-boiled eggs!"

"Hmm." Marvin stuck a finger into his whipped cream. "Easter bunny been working overtime."

"No, no! You don't understand. These eggs were not laid by any rabbit! We were supposed to make deviled eggs! How could we have overlooked that? You can't have a picnic without deviled eggs. Especially on Easter!"

"Well, let's get cracking, girl."

"Mar-vin! This is no time for puns. Honestly, you and Gabrielle!"

"You know how to devil eggs without cracking them first? This I got to see."

He had to duck to avoid the wet sponge Gale threw at him. "All right,

all right. I'm being serious now. We both peel them. You dissect them, I'll
do the deviling, then you can stuff them again."

"Deal."

*　　　*　　　*　　　*　　　*

Esther and Sabine sat together on the upper terrace watching the joyous
chaos of the Easter egg hunt fanning out around them. Sabine had brought
sons and daughters and several sets of grandchildren to the celebration.
Some of the older ones, along with Raina's daughter, Tana, were half su-
pervising, half participating in the hunt. The adults were strolling or sun-
ning or helping to unveil the feast.

Fergus sat on some steps below Esther and Sabine. It was not clear that
he understood the events of the day, but he appeared to be at peace, possibly even at play. He puffed steadily on his pipe, sending smoke rings
out across the gardens. Sometimes, it seemed, he chose a child to wreathe
with rings or a child would chase after a ring. Once, a ring that held its
shape for an unnaturally long time wafted to a certain chink in a wall
where she'd hidden an egg. One of Ann's sons, following the ring, found
the egg and yelled with excitement, running to show it to his mother.

"You know, Madame would be very happy to see this," said Sabine. "All
these children! And she loved parties. She loved games. If she were here
today, she would be right in the middle of it all, on her hands and knees,
if she could manage it. Well, you know she broke her hip playing base-
ball.

"She wanted children of her own so badly. She did not speak of it much,
but you could see it. She made friends always with all the children, the
servants' children, the children at St. Paul's, the whole village. It is sad she
never adopted. She did take in refugees after the Second War for a time,
but her husband did not like it. I think, though she never admitted it, that
she feared him. I think, too, there is a superstition among his people—
maybe because they come from the English—about the blood."

"Blood will out?"

"Yes, that is the saying. So they did not adopt. A pity for Madame."

"So children in Blackwood would please her, you think?"

"Oh, yes. Very much."

"Sabine, I've been doing some thinking—just thinking at this point—
about Blackwood. I'd like to call a meeting with a few people after lunch.
Of course I want you there. I need you."

"Bien sûr. I am eager to hear."

"I'd like Fergus there, too," she lowered her voice, "unless you think he would just be confused and upset."

"No, I don't think he would be," considered Sabine. "Now that he knows Blackwood is in your hands, he is no longer afraid. He is letting go. He does not have to try to make sense any more. It is a relief to him. Let him be there. If it is too much for him, he will just take a little sleep, the way Madame did so much in her last days."

"Good," said Esther through the tears gathering in her throat. "I won't trouble him now. Maybe you could just gather him up when the time comes."

"Time to eat!" Gale's voice rang out across Blackwood.

"Therefore let us keep the Feast!" someone answered, probably Theresa.

"Hallelujah!" Unmistakably Maria.

*   *   *   *   *

After helping to corral the children and then handing them plates of food, which they stared at for a moment before running off again to play Easter egg roll, Easter egg catch, and Easter egg touch football, Esther heaped her own plate and ate while moving from cluster to cluster. Marvin, she noted, had taken a plate to Fergus and was sitting next to him on the steps. Maria and Sabine had settled down with some of Sabine's grown children. Gabrielle was sitting with Mary, the older woman from the shelter, laughing appreciatively at one of the ribald tales Mary liked to tell. Gale was engaged in animated conversation with Ann and some of the other younger women. Theresa and Raina had found one another and were probably exchanging DSS horror stories. Esther decided to approach those two, even though she was still intimidated by Raina. As she neared them, Theresa stood up and, catching sight of Esther, called to her:

"Esther, the powder room, please!"

"Anywhere you like." Esther gestured expansively.

"No plumbing!"

"Once and future only."

"You didn't warn me about this, dear!" Theresa called a reproach over her shoulder as she turned and headed down the terraces.

"Sorry!" Esther couldn't help laughing.

Then the sight of Raina's back as she sat alone on the steps sobered Esther. She girded up her loins like a woman.

"Hello, Raina, I mean Ms. Washington." Esther stood, feeling foolish, hesitating; finally she decided to risk sitting down next to Raina. "I'd like to talk with you for a moment."

"Yes?" Raina was hardly encouraging.

"I want to have a meeting after lunch, say in about fifteen minutes, with you and a few other people."

"About?"

"Well, about Blackwood. Some possible future plans."

Raina regarded her silently for a time. Esther called on reserves of strength to keep from squirming or blithering.

"You know, Mrs. Peters," Raina spoke at last, "my obligation to my client does not extend indefinitely into the future. My role in regard to Blackwood is purely transitional. Do you understand what I'm saying? I am the late Mrs. Crowe's attorney. Not yours."

"I understand," said Esther. "I guess I didn't make my request very clearly. I thought that as the executrix you would have to review any plans for Blackwood to see if they're in keeping with the terms of the will. Also, if you're interested, I might like to engage your services on my own behalf—or rather Blackwood's."

"Don't do me any favors. Don't ask me any."

Esther checked the impulse to defend herself, to justify herself, but she could not, for the moment, come up with any alternative.

"I am sick to death," Raina went on.

Raina was about to lose it; Esther could feel it coming. Well, let her. Let her get it out; then at least Esther would know the worst.

"Sick to death," Raina repeated, "of white women from White Hart doing me favors, asking me favors. It's over. Do you hear me? All debts have been paid. It's over."

"Yes," said Esther.

They looked at each other. It was that ancient struggle. Who was going to look away first? Raina did, abruptly. Esther turned her gaze in the same direction. There was Theresa emerging from some shrubbery.

"I should have warned her about the poison ivy." Esther spoke her thoughts aloud. "I hope she knows what it looks like."

Raina remained as stone. Her silence was impossible to ignore.

"Marvin says you hate me on principle," Esther ventured.

"Marvin's got a big mouth."

"You're angry about us. Marvin and me."

No response.

"Well," said Esther, standing up. "How you feel is your business. And it's up to you whether or not you want any further involvement with Blackwood or with me. I'm going to go tell other people about the meeting. It'll be in Spencer's old room where you handed out the Will. If you decide to come, I'd be interested in your response to the ideas."

Esther walked down the steps to meet Theresa.

*   *   *   *   *

Calling the circle. It dawned on Esther, as she unfolded the metal chairs and arranged them, that she was doing just that. Calling the circle, casting it: a great net for fish, for stars. A web. Of course she needed a circle: the crown of Resurrection, the rolling back of the stone. How else would anything be born?

As the others arrived, Esther sat down in the circle to do the work of rooting, reaching, recognizing the sanctity of circled ground. Esther closed her eyes for a moment, silently calling the directions and their elements. She was sitting in the East, and she sensed that someone in each quarter was conscious of the sacred circle. It felt strong, strong enough to enclose, strong enough to stretch.

When she opened her eyes, Esther saw that everyone she'd asked to come was present. Her intuition had been accurate: each of the four directions was grounded by someone who knew the Lady. Marvin was in the South with the sun; Sabine in the West, the embodiment of earth's abundance. Fergus had migrated North to the air, awaiting his turn for flight. At various points in the circle sat the others: Gale to Esther's left and Gabrielle next to Gale on Marvin's right. On Marvin's other side sat Maria, then Sabine. Ann, holding her sleeping daughter, sat between Sabine and Theresa. To Theresa's left was Fergus and between Fergus and Esther sat Raina.

Ten, Esther counted, ten adults, and the baby made the total number eleven. Eleven was the number of the Strength card in the Tarot deck. And ten? Oh, yes, among the Greater Trumps, ten belonged to Lady Luck, the Wheel of Fortune. Among the lesser trumps, Marvin had told her, ten signaled transformation. Well, it was up to Esther to begin, to give that Wheel the first spin.

"I asked you all to meet with me," Esther began, the trembling in her hands apparent also in her voice, "because the vision of Blackwood that's come to me isn't just mine—or anyway, I can't bring it to life alone.

"I loved Spencer very much, and I am overwhelmed and moved that for some reason, in some way, she made me her daughter. I am not her heir in any conventional sense. Also, I'm not cut out to play Lady of the manor. For Spencer that role was real, who she was. For me it would be a hopeless trap.

"So the first thing I'm asking of you all," she paused and included each of them in a glance, "is will you hear some ideas and consider working with me? I don't know what the legal entity of such a group would be. Maybe I should just tell you, first of all, what I see.

"As I understand the terms of the will, I am, as Trustee, free to renovate all existing structures. The building we are sitting in is enormous. There are also old carriage houses and stables and other out-buildings, whose sound condition, after all this time, is nothing short of miraculous."

She looked in Fergus' direction with a smile, but his head was already nodding. Theresa had removed the pipe from his hand and was holding it cradled in her own.

"What I would like to do," Esther continued, "is apply for government loans and grants in order to renovate the buildings as low-income housing for battered women."

Slowly the wheel began to turn as the members of the circle took in her statement.

"Esther! You sly old thing!" exclaimed Theresa.

Ann bent her head, hiding her face as she hugged her daughter. Gale and Gabrielle whispered to each other, and Sabine and Maria held each other's hands. Catching her eye, Marvin sent Esther a look that quickened that glowing, golden egg within her. Fergus dreamed on. Esther did not turn to look at Raina, but she sensed that Raina's silence was now attentive.

"If we can get the money for renovating from outside sources as well as some salaries for administering the project, there would be money from the Estate for other salaries."

"Excuse me." Raina's tone was not hostile but skeptical. "I'd like to point something out. There is no denying that country living has its good points, but what about goods and services, agencies where women would have to go, jobs and whatnot being mostly in River City?"

"That's a consideration," said Theresa reluctantly.

"It is," agreed Esther. "I've thought about that. Blackwood is within walking distance of trains and buses. It might also be that some people will have cars and can pool rides. Another part of my vision is a daycare center and nursery school, not just for residents but for the general public. Some people, like Ann, I'm hoping, would work right here. Other people would be able to get to jobs and agencies more easily if they had affordable childcare. I know it's going to be complicated; it may take several years to get it all going.

"Another thing I'd like to do—and maybe this is all just a dream—is to have at least one building available for small conferences, workshops, retreats. A small conference facility would also provide jobs for residents.

See, I'd like there to be a flow in and out of Blackwood of all kinds of people: healers, activists, artists, ecologists, whatever...."

People were silent, maybe taking it in, maybe concluding that she was crazy.

"I know right now it is just a vision," Esther said. "Maybe an impossible one, and you haven't even heard all of it yet. There's expanded vegetable and herb gardens in the vision, too. Maybe even cows and chickens." She exchanged a look with Gabrielle. "What I want to know now is this: is it just my idea? Do you have dreams and ideas? Do you want to work with me in some way? I've said enough. I need a reality check."

"Honey," Maria spoke first, "I do believe you planning a trip across the Jordan. That river be wide and deep and it's sure enough cold, but there's milk and honey on the other side. Milk and honey, that's what I hear you talking. What with my arthritis, I don't know if I be much use on the boat, but if you want my company, you got it."

"Esther," said Sabine. "Chérie, you know I am with you."

"You've got your work cut out for you, Esther," said Gale. "Our work. It's not going to be easy. I do know grantswomanship, though, and I can teach it, too. The gentle art of getting blood out of a stone."

"Most of us here have had close encounters with granite," put in Theresa. "Right, Ann? I think we should go for it, starting with staff meeting at Sojourners tomorrow. You know we've all been praying for a way into second stage housing. I even said a Novena a couple of months ago. Thanks, Mare." Theresa made the O.K sign in the direction of the ceiling.

"Esther, all I can say is I want to help you in any way I can," said Ann. "Help us all," she added.

"I second that emotion," sang Gabrielle, and everyone laughed.

Esther turned to Raina. "I know working full-time in the Bronx, you can't—"

"Esther," Raina cut her off, addressing her by her first name for the first time, "I am perfectly capable of saying no by myself. I don't need you to do it for me. You asked me to hear you and say what I think. Well, I'm intrigued."

As she released her breath, Esther realized she'd been holding it.

"I won't deny that," Raina went on. "It's not that often that an estate as well endowed as this one and a dream like yours come together. Sure, it's a dream at this point, but it's a good dream. Unlike most dreams, it's got some solid ground under it. Literally.

"I'll be straight with you," Raina added. "I don't know whether I see a role for myself or how much time and energy I'd want to commit. You're going to need legal counsel. No question. One thing you haven't thought of, as far as I can tell, is how the Town is going to react to your plans. I'm afraid you'll find out: when people hear 'low-income housing,' they hear Black; they hear welfare mothers; they hear drugs; they hear crime; they hear lowered property values. If they're white, which the majority of people in White Hart are, they tend to get hysterical, and believe me, that is not a pretty sight.

"But even supposing attitude was not a problem, you have to find out about zoning and about building permits. In other words, you've got to start at the local level with local politics, and, regardless of my involvement, you're going to need a local attorney, preferably someone plugged into the good ol' boy network, the kind of person people owe favors to. You want to know how this town works? I mean really works, behind the scenes, the dirt, don't ask me, ask Maria. You made a smart move getting her in here."

"Now, Raina!" Maria protested; then she seized her opportunity. "Honey, you know I ain't never been one to tell you what to do. But don't you see? This here's your chance. The Good Lord be calling you back to tend your own vineyard. You come on home now. Get my granddaughter out of that nasty city. Just come home. I'll leave you alone. You ain't even got to know me on the street."

"Oh, Mama!" Raina laughed, and Esther wondered how long it had been since Raina had called Maria that. "You know you can't deliver on that promise. Let's leave the Good Lord out of it. If he has something to say to me, he'll have to learn to speak more clearly. Esther, all I can tell you today is you have my respect and my best wishes. Your plans are very much in keeping with the terms of the will. I believe my late client would be pleased."

"Thank you, Raina," said Esther. "That means a lot to me."

Esther took a deep breath and closed her eyes again, just for a moment. When she opened them, she found herself looking directly into Fergus' eyes. He had come out of his doze, and his gaze was clear and intent.

"Easter," he said quite distinctly. Was he calling her Easter or naming the day? "Easter," he repeated. "The bees are awake."

At least she thought he'd said bees, but it might have been trees. The trees are awake. In her mind she saw them, the trees of Blackwood, alert, humming with life, humming with bees.

"The bees?" she questioned, but it was too late. The moment of clarity had gone; the clouds rolled in again.

"Well," Esther concluded, "maybe that's enough for today. Thank you all for hearing me. Let's go back to the feasting."

"Wait a minute," said Raina. "I have one more question."

"By all means," said Esther.

But Raina directed her gaze Southward.

"Marvin, my dear cousin, I haven't heard a word out of you. Just what is your role in this endeavor?"

All eyes turned towards him.

Marvin didn't answer for a moment, appearing to be deep in thought. Then a slow, sweet smile spread over his face.

"Me?"

He glanced at Raina, acknowledging her question; then he let his eyes linger for a moment on Fergus who looked back at him. Finally, he turned the full intensity of his gaze on Esther.

"I'm the Sexton."

Gabrielle started the laughter; then everyone joined in, those who knew the origin of the joke, those who didn't, even Raina. Raucous laughter rocked the room.

When it subsided, Esther sought Marvin's eyes again. Everyone else, for a moment, faded from her vision, and she spoke to him alone.

"No, Marvin, you're the Priest."

BOOK TEN

MAY EVE

SOMETHING was about to happen. The bees knew, winging drunkenly through the dusk, gilded with pollen, heavy with the nectar of apple blossom. The old orchard knew, pelting Fergus with its soft storm, whitening his path. Moonlight you could touch, moonlight you could taste. The moon knew, too, ripening Maiden. She was a boat tonight, a little coracle, lingering in the Western sky, waiting for what was about to happen. The pond knew, but reflected only the mystery of sky, not purple, not blue: the birthing place of stars. The stars knew, and all the trees of Blackwood knew, too.

The Ring of Trees had witnessed preparations that Fergus had missed while he dozed away the afternoon in the orchard, knowing only the hum of bees. Now Fergus stepped into the Circle and saw that someone had dug a shallow pit and laid wood for a fire. Nearby stood a newly erected Maypole; the impatient breeze played with the ribbons. There was just enough light to discern the colors: gold, scarlet, white, rose, blue, green, purple, black. A lush patch of moss had been strewn with white petals.

Something was about to happen. Not a moment too soon, not a moment too late. Fergus receded from the circle and joined the trees in waiting.

* * * * *

Esther sat in one of the old claw-footed bath tubs at Windy Hill, her hair weighted with water and hanging in ringlets just past her shoulders— it had grown quite long. As she gazed out the open window, a whole flock of starlings lighted in the spreading branches of the maple tree on the lawn. Their sound wafted through the screen with the first of the evening chill. Esther's breasts tingled in response. She tried for a moment to find a word to name the color of the sky. Then she gave up and rose from the tub, taking with her the glimpse of sky and the crazy joy of the singing tree.

In another bathroom down the hall, Marvin stepped out of the shower and stood naked before the mirror. There were no windows in this bathroom, and the whir of his electric clippers covered other sounds. He closed his eyes, feeling the menacing caress of the blades as he guided the clippers over the contours of his head, his cheeks, his chin, leaving his hair and beard a mere shadow on his skin. Opening his eyes to mirrored perfection, he unstopped a bottle of musk and splashed it on his neck and arms, then, smiling, on his thighs. Satisfied, he knotted a towel around his hips, collected his gear, and padded barefoot down the hall to Esther's room.

She was there already, naked in the dusk, gleaming like that slip of moon outside, brushing her hair dry. A tidal wave of desire swept through him, and he held on tight to the doorknob, because his knees sure weren't any use.

"Oh!" she said, turning towards him. "You're not supposed to see me yet."

"Says who?"

The knot in his towel, strained by his erection, gave way, and the towel dropped to the floor.

They both had to laugh.

A little while later, dressed in ordinary shirts and jeans, they set out, arm in arm, for Blackwood. They were stopping at the mansion first where they would change into their ceremonial robes. The evening was cool, but not so cold as to make their intended rite ridiculous or uncomfortable. Every moment more stars appeared, and the slender new moon skimmed the trees of Blackwood.

"Now you can say: I told you so," said Esther.

"All right." Marvin was agreeable. "I told you so. Now what I tell you?"

"You said it wouldn't rain."

" 'Course it ain't raining. It knows better."

That was true, Esther reflected, as they turned from the road into the deeper dusk of Blackwood. Whatever *it* was—and *it* seemed an inadequate pronoun for, well, the creation—*it* had a stake in what she and Marvin were about to do together. Like any other marriage, the one they enacted tonight was not a purely private matter. They might be the only two of their species present, but there would be witnesses: the trees; the moss beneath their dancing feet that would also receive the full length of their bodies; the birds, heads tucked under wings, dreaming in the branches above; the deer bedded down in the thickets; all the nocturnal creatures: bats and owls and mice. The very life, seen and unseen, of Blackwood.

"Marvin," Esther pressed closer to him as they approached the dark, empty mansion. "Aren't you scared?"

"Of ghosts? Naw, not really. Fergus say his mother in charge of haunting. If she anywhere around tonight, she ain't gonna get in our way. You and me? We a dream come true for her. Same with Old Lady Crowe, the way I see it. I done me some thinking about how we gon' be doing our thing, right where her ashes be buried? Well, I don't believe she mind at all. Matter of fact, I think she be glad to be part of it."

"Yes. She'll have a supporting role. Literally," mused Esther.

Sabine must have agreed that Madame would be pleased. She was supporting them, too, by taking care of David and Jonathan for the night at the Gatehouse, feeding them pizza a la Niçoise for supper and tucking them into Spencer's old three-quarter bed in the round room. Somehow this image was comforting.

"I hadn't even thought of ghosts," Esther said; the ghost of Fergus' mother did add an unnerving dimension. "I meant us, finally making love in this cosmic way. Do you think we're up to it?"

"That's up to us, ain't it?"

Just before the front door of the mansion, Marvin paused and turned Esther towards him, kissing her. Esther held onto her lover dizzily, suddenly aware of the whole spinning universe.

"But aren't you nervous?" she whispered between kisses.

"Sure I am," he said simply. "Come on now. Let's get ready. It's time."

Hand in hand, like children, Esther thought, they tiptoed through the hall and up the stairs to Spencer's room. Marvin found his matches and lit the candle Esther had brought there earlier. Watching each other wordlessly, they undressed. When their clothes lay pooled at their feet, they stood for a moment, drinking each other in.

You are beautiful, so beautiful. Their eyes spoke plainly.

Then Marvin turned, walked to one of the metal chairs and got Esther's robe: pale green satin, moss green, moon green, trimmed with purple velvet. They had gone shopping together a few days ago, choosing, in effect, glorified bathrobes. They did not want to fumble in the Circle. They wanted garments that would slip off at the right moment, melt away into the night.

Esther held out her arms while Marvin put on her robe. Making each motion a caress, he wrapped her in the watery smoothness of satin, then knelt to tie the sash at her waist. Lightly, she touched his head. She loved the hardness of it, the polished roughness of his close cut hair. She gasped as he parted her robe and kissed her belly, just above her pubic bone, where her stretch marks were, her womb.

Then he stood before her again, and she robed him in gold satin and red velvet. The sensual solemnity of robing made Esther feel that the ritual had already begun. Still, it was hard not to laugh while trying to fasten the robe over Marvin's buoyant sex. Finally, she gave up her attempt to confine it within the folds of the robe and pressed it against her cheek. Marvin groaned, half in pleasure, half in protest. Then Esther kissed the tip of his penis, attempted once more to throw the robe over it, and stood up.

"I have a surprise for you," Esther announced. "I'm not sure you'll like it, but at least I want to show it to you."

Esther went to the closet where the surprise was hidden and returned to Marvin with her hands behind her back.

"Your horns, Sir."

She presented them: molded onto a black hair-band, two curved golden horns.

Marvin burst out laughing. "Girl, you something else!"

"Come on," she urged. "Try them. They're very light. I made them at the shelter out of paper-mache."

"All right. You put them on me."

Marvin bent his head, and Esther arranged the headband so that the horns reared from his head where they should have grown.

"Magnificent!" She clapped her hands.

"Guess I got to take your word for it," he said dubiously. "But you know what? You should be wearing these. You the High Priestess. That's how I seen you, with the horned moon in your hair."

"Oh, but they match your robe."

"Well, I got something to match yours," he said. "Be right back."

Marvin disappeared into the connecting room and returned bearing a wreath of periwinkle, still dripping from the water he'd preserved it in. Star-shaped flowers the color of dusk, twinkling from amidst their own dark-green leaves.

"Oh, Marvin, how perfect!" Her eyes suddenly filled with tears.

"The color make me think of you," he said, crowning her tenderly.

"Marvin, oh, Marvin. I can hardly believe this is happening, that you're willing to do all this—"

"What you mean!" He was indignant. "If I remember right, this was my idea. You the one had to be talked into it."

"True," Esther conceded. "But most men wouldn't—"

"Lady." He cupped her face in his hands and brought his mouth almost close enough to kiss hers. "If you don't know by now that I ain't 'most men,' well, you about to find out."

"Mmm." She kissed him. "Mmmm."

Somehow Marvin's ingenious penis had parted both his own robe and hers.

Honeyed thighs, the phrase went through Esther's mind. What had Fergus said? The bees are awake.

"Come on, Esther."

Marvin stepped back, turned to one of the chairs and handed Esther the bear-shaped tambourine they'd borrowed from Jonathan. His own instrument was a long-necked dried gourd from Maria's sideboard.

"Let's go give it up."

Esther blew out the candle. In the dark, they found each other, then found their way to the Ring of Trees.

*   *   *   *   *

Full night. Fergus drifted in and out of sleep as the moon drifted down through the trees. Waiting, waiting. Then, at last, she was there.

He saw her, the Green Maiden, with the horned moon in her hair. Her lover rose with sudden flames, horns flashing, robed in the fierce gold of the sun. They had come, springing from earth, flying from heaven: Venus and Mars. They faced each other across the circle, across the fire.

Then she raised her arms and loosed her voice. Fergus did not need to know her words; he could hear the waters answer, the joyous rush of surf, the soft insistent fall of rain. Then her lover raised his arms, and sparks leaped from the fire to greet the stars, whistling, singing. Now she crouched low over the earth, crooning, and all the green life quivered in response. Grass grew in the dark, and sticky leaves unfolded all the way, tasting the air, floating on the wind that answered his call.

Slowly, they began their dance, the Green Maiden and the Horned One, first just swaying like the trees, listening, answering each other's rhythm, the undulating hiss of the rattle, the pounding shiver of the tambourine. Heart beat, breath. Fergus did not need to see to know they began to move their feet. He could feel each footfall in his palms that cupped the earth, in his spine that rested against a silver birch. They circled, trailing green and gold. They circled the fire; they circled each other, with each turn drawing nearer the Maypole until, at last, they took up the ribbons and began the weave. Green, gold, scarlet, purple, changing seamlessly to white, black, rose, blue. The ribbons rose and fell, rose and fell, sea swells, sea birds. The dancers vanished into the dance, and Fergus dreamed again.

A sudden stillness called him back to full wakefulness. Opening his eyes, he saw them clearly, standing close together on the far side of the flames. The green and gold had burned away to naked black and white; the stars and night loomed behind them, a curling wave with a foamy crest. Suddenly their soul lights blazed, fanning out from their bodies, meeting in a double arc. Hand in hand, they leaped the fire.

Fergus felt the moss receive their warm weight. Then he felt only the warmth, the moist heat of all beginnings. Sun penetrating fathoms of sea. The hardness of stone parting veils of water. And the ripples, wave on wave, circle on circle....

When Fergus came to himself again, he knew it was time to go. Grasping his staff with one hand and the trunk of the birch with the other, he coaxed his stiff limbs to stand. Then he leaned against the tree for a moment and gazed into the Circle. The moon had set, the fire burned to coals. The colors of the streamers were lost to the night. In the afterglow from the fire, he could just see them: Astarte and the Marvel—he knew them now—resting in each other's arms. Soon they would begin again, and he would be gone.

Without rattling a leaf or breaking a twig, Fergus walked to the edge of the Ring of Trees. There he crouched and, summoning the last of his powers, released his carved stick. With a swift, snaking motion it glided away, then came to rest, a stick once more, beside the Marvel.

Fergus rose and went his way unaided. When he emerged from the thick of the wood, he saw the pond, teeming with stars. And then he beheld her, across the pond, waiting for him. She wore her bridal gown at last. It shimmered in the dark. Trembling with joy, Fergus walked around the pond to the ancient tree grown young. He paused for a moment and stood before her face to face.

Mother. Sister. Lover. Death.

Then he lay down, curled in her lap, and gave himself back.

ACKNOWLEDGMENTS

I would like to thank the following groups and people for guidance, support, and inspiration in the writing of *The Return of the Goddess: A Divine Comedy*: members of the Quaker Worship Group at Green Haven Prison, especially Larry Gross and Booker T. Briggs; members of Wild Vine; residents and staff of Grace Smith House, a Shelter for Battered Women and their Children; Starhawk; Margot Adler; my husband, Douglas C. Smyth; and my friend, Deborah Stone, who read critically and responsively at every stage of the writing.

I would also like to acknowledge my use of the following sources: *The Book of Common Prayer: and Administration of the Sacraments and Other Rites and Ceremonies of the Church, Together with the Psalms and Psalters of David, According to the use of the Episcopal Church* (Seabury Press, New York: 1977), copyright 1977 by Charles Mortimer Guilbert. I have quoted the Nicene Creed and brief portions of "Communion under Special Circumstances" and "Proper Liturgy for Special Days: Ash Wednesday." Biblical quotations are all from the *Authorized*, or *King James Version*. Also quoted are the first six lines of "She walks in Beauty" by George Gordon, Lord Byron from Volume 2 of *The Norton Anthology of English Literature*, Third Edition (W.W. Norton & Company, Inc., New York: 1974), copyright 1974 by W.W. Norton & Company, Inc. The epigraph from *The Divine Comedy* by Dante Alighieri, uses the John Ciardi translation (W.W. Norton & Company, Inc., New York 1977), copyright 1977 by John Ciardi. I have also briefly quoted Tertullian from "On the Apparel of Women," in *The Ante-Nicene Fathers*, volume 4 (Grand Rapids, Michigan: Erdmans, 1956). For the chapter, "Who is she?" I did onsite research in an Episcopal church with permission from the Rector.